Red Thunder

David Matheson

Media Weavers, *L.L.C.*

First Edition

FIC
M4277re

Copyright © 2002 by David J. Matheson

Published by
Media Weavers, L.L.C.
P.O. Box 86190
Portland, OR 97286-0190

Designed by Donnelleigh S. Mounce, Graphic Design Studio, LLC

Printed in the United States of America

Library of congress Cataloging in Publication Data
Matheson, David
    Red Thunder / by David Matheson
        p. cm.
    ISBN 0-9647212-5-2
    1. Title   2.Native American Fiction
2001092796

This book is dedicated to all the elders,
past and present,
of the Coeur d'Alene Tribe.

Introduction

We are the Schi'tsu'umsh people, now called the Coeur d'Alene Tribe, French words which mean "heart of the awl." At first contact, our people were very shrewd traders and difficult to get along with, which partially explains the French description: "sharp hearted" or "pierced heart." Our native language is a Salish dialect and unique to us, but with some differences, common to other northern plateau tribes of our area including the Spokane, the Flathead, the Okanogan and the Kalispel. Other neighbors adjacent to us included the Nez Perce to our South and the Palouse to our West.

I have spent a lifetime learning and living the teachings herein depicted, talking to many of our elders and practicing our culture and traditions in everyday life. Hunting, root digging and berry picking/camping are a major part of my wife's and my regular routine, as are traditions and ceremonial dances and events.

RED THUNDER is a story of harmony: man's harmony with the natural world; peace and unity of purpose with a Higher Power; and understanding all of life and oneself in it. It is a story much of the world is ready for, even yearning for . . . because, it is a story of faith, courage and togetherness. The deep and sincere feelings with which our ancestors conducted their lives, tradition and culture is the story within me crying to be written. The functional aspects of our native ceremonial life can only be truly understood through appreciation of the great degree of kindness, humility and faith with which our ancestors lived their everyday life.

The setting is sometime around the early 1700's prior to any European contact. The law was our tribal law and the laws of nature. The geographical setting is our originally claimed territory including North Idaho and extending into Eastern Washington and Western Montana. The backdrop to the story is part of our genuine oral history regarding the life and times of our great prophet chief, Circling Raven. The miracles that are depicted here in this story are actual accounts told by all our grandparents of most every family band in the tribe about Chief Circling Raven.

This book is not the culmination of journalistic research and inquiry. It is the reflection of true life among our native people as handed down from generation to generation. Several generations of Schi'tsu'umsh family are followed through time to capture the full picture of native life. This is a story that has never been told before. Those who really knew kept it to themselves; and most all who knew are gone now from this earth. Much of our tradition has been a guarded secret for many reasons, partly from fear and partly from a deep feeling to protect what we have left.

At one time, we were prohibited from talking our language or practicing our traditional ceremonies and customs. This instilled a deep fear in our grandparents, who as little, defenseless children, bore the brunt of ignorant acts to assimilate them by stomping out our culture. No ordinary author could ever use typical research methods and interviews to access and acquire the native teachings, stories and traditions that are in this book. They would never have been told the full, guarded story. There have been writings and mechanical analyses of certain aspects of native life, but always with a perspective tilted toward some personal experience or dominant views. This causes misperception and even a hidden, coded judgment reflected in their writings. Often times, even many native authors focus only on the modern social state of being in Indian Country or society today while magnifying prejudice and racism.

Life has a beginning and an end, no matter who you are, or whom you think you may be. The Kolunsuten, Creator, promised no one a tomorrow or an easy time. The "first prayer" is for your own life, always thankful for it first and foremost. Therefore life begins with each new day and a sincere thanksgiving for the extension of the very special and sacred privilege of life itself. This is a foundation of our culture and of the story you are about to read.

Dear Reader,

I was born on the Coeur d'Alene Indian Reservation in 1951 at the home of my grandparents, Nick and Margaret Campbell. My mother is Pauline Campbell (Matheson). My grandfather's mother's name was Poo'li. My mother was named after her, Poo'li to "Pauline." The family name Campbell was given by the local church and government officials.

My father is Don Matheson and my grandparents are Charles and Mattie Matheson of the Puyallup Tribe in Western Washington. I was enrolled at birth in the Coeur d'Alene Tribe (Schi'tsu'umsh). I have worked most all of my adult career and lived most all of my adult life on the reservation, except to seek employment elsewhere for brief periods of time.

We have our own problems, like any and all communities. But, all in all, we are individually and collectively the descendants of the great people of generations past who laid down the foundation for our very existence in the world today and the future.

I have a deep love for my people. I dearly love to see my elders, the ladies with the long Indian dresses, long braids and bandannas; and the gray men, some with long braids. Some of them carried the stories of the old days, of the songs, of the tragedies and of the triumphs. I love to see them and greet them, or perhaps better said, it is always my honor to shake their hands and tell them something kind and friendly.

I hope the Kolunsuten (Creator) guides these teachings to those who will be benefited by them the most and those who will take care of them the best. Perhaps you are one of these people so guided.

Dave Matheson

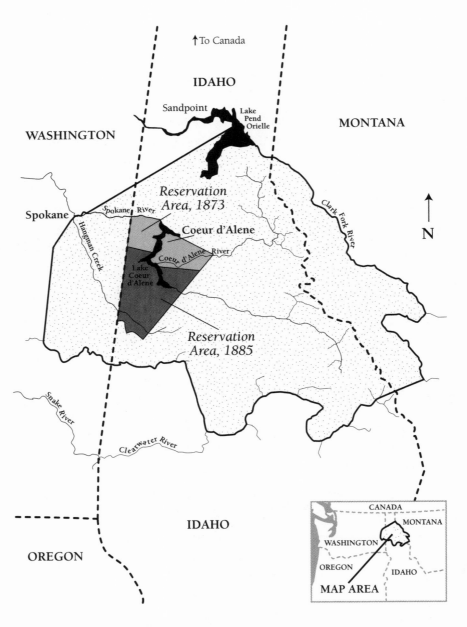

*The Coeur d'Alene Tribe's Aboriginal Territory spans almost
5 million acres of today's Washington, Idaho and Montana.*

Reservation Area, 1873: 590,000 Acres

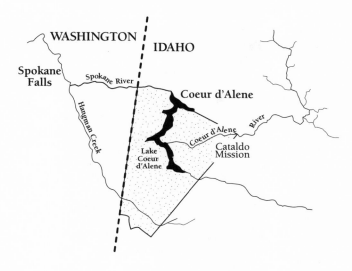

Reservation Area, 1885: 345,000 Acres

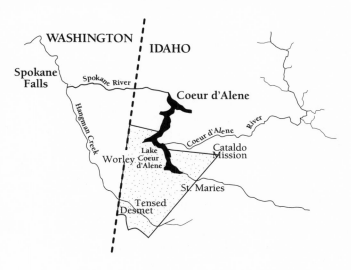

Original Territory
Schi'tsu'umsh (Coeur d'Alene) Tribe
4,000,000 Acres

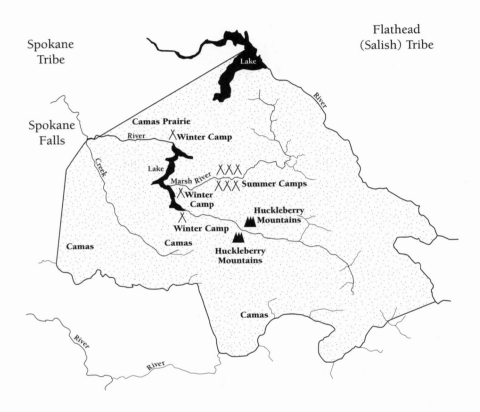

Spokane
Tribe

Flathead
(Salish) Tribe

Lake

River

Spokane
Falls

Camas Prairie
X Winter Camp

River

Creek

Lake

Marsh River   X X X
              X X X Summer Camps
X Winter
  Camp

Huckleberry
Mountains

X
Winter Camp

Camas

Camas

Huckleberry
Mountains

River

River

Camas

Nez Perce Tribe

Camas & roots are located in all meadows.
Herbal medicines throughout country depending on type.
Other family bands used different camps all around the lake
and rivers, as well as different berry picking mountains.

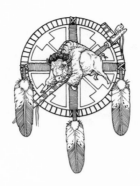

GLOSSARY
Salish Vocabulary

Word	Meaning
Peepa	Father
Noona	Mother
Sila	Grandfather (Maternal)
Checheya	Grandmother (Maternal)
Kolunsuten	Creator
Amotken	Creator, One seated at the top
Camas	Roots for food, a staple
Camas Cakes	Way of preparing camas in underground oven
Sweat Lodge	A small circular structure made of willow used for cleansing by pouring water on hot rocks.
Schi'tsu'umsh	(pronounced schee-sú-umsh) The discovered people, the ones who were found here; traditional name for Coeur d' Alene Tribe prior to European contact.

red thunder \ `red `thəndər\ *n.* A phenomena rarely seen in nature. It is a red flash in the sky at night, evening, or early morning before it is fully light.

In our native language, the word "thunder" also may apply to the accompanying and expected lightning. Further, the four thunders are known ancient and holy beings of nature possessing great powers and certain qualities and attributes, lightning being one of them.

Therefore, this red flash is termed for the power or being actually behind it, the Red Thunder, *kwel* (red) *stalonem* (thunder) in our language.

The Thunders may be called upon in certain ways and their presence may be interpreted depending upon the situation and whatever ceremonial prayer requests had been offered.

It is a sacred sign.

CHAPTER 1

Huckleberry Mountains
Circa 1700 A.D.

How fast could a young boy run in new moccasins? I wondered. I ran like the wind. My mind and my senses were one and the same. My pounding heart was a drumbeat with which I kept perfect time as I ran harder and harder. An easy grace was mine. The power of being alive exhilarated my spirit and the wind as it blew by my face. I bolted up the small knoll and yelled my war whoop, not in challenge or defiance, but in the sheer wonder of innocent joy and happiness.

My mother just finished my new moccasins. She said I am growing faster than a young colt. I loved new moccasins. The soft deerskin tops and sides with the buffalo sole smelled like gentle smoke and felt like soft furs.

Mother, Noona, I called her, always cut three fringe on each side and etched a design across the top that looked like a deer hoof print inside an arrowhead. She said it was her wish that I be swift and strong like the deer and a good hunter someday. I never wondered to question it. I just knew she already made it to be that way for me. I got my first deer when I was seven, an elk when I was eight. Soon I would ride with the men on my first buffalo hunt.

My father, Peepa, guided me to be a warrior. I never questioned it because I knew it, too, was a road already made for me.

Not long after my birth, Peepa and my Grandfather, Sila, took me and sang songs holding me up to be recognized by the Mother Earth and all of nature. They dipped me in the cold running creek waters and asked the great waters to recognize me, cleanse me and protect me while on the road of life. They thanked the Great Creator, Kolunsuten, for my life, putting my first footprints in the sand alongside the water so that I'd be known and taken care of on this road of life.

My Grandfather, Sila, rubbed the ground heart of a special hawk mixed with the powder of white clay and some herbal medicines on my chest right above my heart. He called upon the Kolunsuten to pity him and sanction this ceremony at my birth and to allow him to call upon the great warrior bird, the hawk. By sacred words and incantations known only to a few of the elders, Sila invoked the great bird to impart a piece of his great warrior strength and bravery to me.

Then, in the teepee with the hawk feathers, he fanned me with the incense of blue spruce needles and cedar. As the soft power of the feathers extended the magic of the incense to me, he announced my childhood name would be Sun Boy, because the sun came out from behind clouds as Sila meditated for my name. Someday, when I was a young man, I would get another name, my manhood name.

But today, all I cared about was the exhilarating feeling of freedom and strength vibrating through these huckleberry mountains, our late summer/early autumn home. We called them Grandmother and Grandfather Mountain and Grizzly Bear Mountain. But all the mountains in this same area were our huckleberry gathering camps. To me, it was a paradise, heaven on earth.

These huckleberry mountains were at the center of our country: big mountains, some of them bald at the top, covered with flat jagged rocks.

The higher you went up the mountain the smaller the trees became and the taller the grasses grew.

Where I stood, above the tree line, I studied the large shale rocks scattered and stacked about the side of the mountain. And behind me, I admired the detail of the bear grass growing in big clumps, wiry and tough.

From here, I could look out far off to the east and see the Bitterroot Mountains. In the north, I could see the jagged mountains up by the big lake. Some of our people had their huckleberry camps there.

To the west well beyond our beloved lake was the flat and open country where the sagebrush grew. Well to the south, we had our neighbors, the Ni-mee-poo (Nez Perce) people.

It was a vast country. In late summer, the grasses were a rich golden color with green trees of various leaf and needle varieties. Many wild flowers blossomed this time of year.

The colors of the land, the grasses, trees and plants, combined with the many lakes and rivers, made for a magnificent view. I breathed in the warm summer air like it was a great medicine. My parents and grandparents always said it was a great medicine. With it, I could smell the high country aromas of bear grass, mountain spruce and wild flowers.

The air even felt different in the huckleberry mountains. Although it was warm out it had a light crispness to it. Maybe it was the high mountain rocks that gave it its unique smell, there were so many large, flat rocks scattered about.

The short, sparsely spaced evergreen trees gave the land a special color and feel that contrasted with the light buckskin colored grasses of summer.

Mountain woodpeckers were plentiful as were many other birds. Looking out over the cliff, I could see a lone red tail hawk soaring below me hunting for food in the canyon.

This time of the year, it would be hot down below. But it was comfortable high up on the mountain, especially in the shade.

The sun was bright yellow, almost white, at times. The sky was huge, never-ending. How could any blue be that bright and colorful?

The mountaintops were connected by saddles and valleys of mixed evergreen trees, meadows and large jagged rocky areas. It seemed ancient to me, as though it had seen the beginning of life.

The sky was mostly clear, but held a few high, round clouds. When I stared at them long enough, I got a strange floating sensation. It was magical.

The mountains and hills rolled out from my view, seeming to go on forever. In the distance, there was a gentle haze hovering mysteriously, yet harmless and peaceful.

My Sila and other elders often talked of sacred sites where miraculous things occurred as all of Creation prepared for the coming of mankind. Maybe something happened here, too.

As I ran across the saddle between mountain peaks, I slowed to peer down the ledge. Below was a big huckleberry patch and my mother, Noona, was there with my sisters, aunts and grandmother. The big flat jagged rocks hid me from their view and I decided to sneak up on them. I knew I would try to get up as close as I could, then jump out and scare them. My heart filled with excitement at the idea of innocent mischief. Noona said my eyes always twinkled with my smile when I was up to practical jokes, so she could tell when to watch me.

But this time I was hidden and I would be as silent and invisible as the greatest of our warriors and hunters. Well, at least I would imagine it this way.

Uncle always said, "Go still first, and silent, like the deer. Pull in all your energy, all your sound. Make no sudden movements with any part of your body, not even your eyes. Don't bob up and down. See the ground without looking at it and never step on anything you didn't intend to."

I tried my best this time and made no mistakes.

Gradually, quietly I moved down the steep mountainside. Even my breath went slow and smooth. I tried to calm my feeling and my thinking. It was all falling into place. I felt invisible and a part of the land. I was totally concealed and I knew it. Near the bottom of the rocky cliff there was an open area with only scattered brush. I would have to time my movement through the opening with Noona's berry picking motion.

As she reached to pick, I made my move, a smooth trot while hunched over, and hid behind the first bush. As though I was part of the bush and always had been, I slowly moved my head to look out between the limbs. So far so good.

The other bushes were close. I knew I had it made now. My heart pounded, my mind raced with excitement. "This time I will do it."

Closer and closer I moved until I was one bush away. Now I will jump out and surprise her, I thought. Just as I set myself to lunge forward, without even turning and looking, Noona said "Hello, Sun Boy. How's my son today? Are you doing what your father told you to do?"

"Oh, Noona, how did you know I was here? I never let myself be seen at all," I asked her with disappointment in my voice. All my excitement and anticipation fizzled.

"I just knew," she said, "and I felt comfortable with the presence, so I said to myself 'It's my son.' Keep practicing, but talk to the land and the forest, and the animals that have the power to camouflage and conceal. They must authorize you to use a part of them to conceal yourself."

That's exactly what my father, Peepa, my Grandfather, Sila and my uncles said to me all the time. When will I ever get it right, I complained in my own mind. But I would never say it. I already knew to watch what you say because life might become the way you talked.

Noona saw my mild disappointment and quickly added, "You almost have it though, Son. I barely noticed you at all."

Right away I felt tall and proud. She could always do that for me, even just with her approving smile.

"Your sisters, cousins and younger brother are playing right down there. Let me see if you can sneak up on them," she challenged.

"The most powerful of our people don't think weak, lazy thoughts or how to get away with something by doing less," was his explanation.

Finally, I reached the top. The impressive beauty quieted me while my heart and mind tried to absorb the honor and privilege that was mine at that moment. Just to behold the great miracle of the Creator: Mother Earth and all of the holy Creation was overwhelming.

I could see all our country, and beyond it. Looking down, the lake reflected the brilliance of the blue sky. The shadowy river meandering into the lake was more winding and crooked than I had ever realized.

Standing on a granite ledge, I could peer straight down the cliff into the canyons and valleys below.

The air smelled different up here on the very top. It was crisp, and absent of the smell of our evergreen trees. Maybe it was the smell of the giant rocks in the warm sun, but it was just different.

I didn't know how to speak my thoughts or my feelings. I wondered how many of our elders from past generations had stood here and been recognized by this ancient place — the altar of the Amotken, my Sila called it. Often, when our people prayed, they faced the tallest mountain in view and called the Creator, Amotken, "the spirit seated at the top." Otherwise, we called Him the Kolunsuten.

The wind blew gently into my face, my long hair flowing and bouncing with it. I could smell the wild flowers and the huckleberries from below. It was a fragrance that almost whispered its sweetness to me.

I could really sense something from the plant life and trees. They were happy. They had feelings and they let me know their life was sacred, precious and powerful too. It was like a dream, but real.

The sacred bird, the eagle, flew by and checked on me to see who was here on the mountaintop. "Ahh! Great and holy one," I called to him. Thunder rolled across a distant mountaintop.

Peepa and Sila told us to always sing at these times, but make the feelings that are beyond words a part of your song. I tried, but I didn't really know how. So, I just gazed and daydreamed, then sang a little again.

I felt moved to climb near the ledge again. The view looking straight down made me feel like a bird, a great eagle.

I sang my song with more intensity, but this time I put out my arms and flapped them like great wings. I was the great bird for a few moments. Maybe I would just take off and fly away.

As I gazed at the sun, it became a reddish orange in the western sky. Fire colors is what they were called: the yellow, orange, red purple and black. All these colors were in the sunset and it was grand to behold.

CHAPTER 2

Good Food and Strong Family: Powerful Medicine

Suddenly, I noticed the sun was getting low in the sky. Down the hill I ran. Noona would worry. Parents always warned that the tree limbs may become arms after dark that grab children. Also, there are other beings, part spirit, part human and part monster that take children if they're alone. I think maybe the grown-ups tried to frighten the little children into never, ever wandering off where something might happen to them. Still, way down deep, I wondered about it, although I would never admit it to any older kids. I was older now — eleven winters, almost a man. Maybe I had nothing to worry about anymore.

Just as the sun was fading into a brilliant golden orange and purple sunset, I arrived at camp. The yellow flame somehow made a soft reddish glow throughout the camp. The teepee looked mystical in the sunset, a shadow, but highlighted with the red, orange and yellow light flickering from the outside campfire.

The light colored deerskin hides covering it looked like darkened charcoal near the top where the smoke escaped. And there were long spiraling poles fanning out above it somehow connecting it to the sky. The door was flung open as if to say, "come in and be welcome!"

Noona and Checheya (Grandma) were just finishing the trout. I could smell it. Oh boy! My mouth watered! She filleted it, stretched it over sticks and cooked it over the fire.

Camas cakes had been baking under the ground all day and Checheya was gathering them together. All my favorite foods! I couldn't wait, my anticipation, and my hunger soared and roared.

"Hey! My son!" my Peepa cried out with his happy-to-see-me tone. "I think you grew even bigger today. Yes! No doubt about it. Yesterday, you came up to about here on me," he motioned to a level along the top of his chest. "Now you're almost to my neck!"

To me my Peepa was a great man. He was a great hunter and a powerful warrior, but always a kind and loving father first and foremost. In the big winter camp the people and children would stand when he walked by because he was an honored warrior and a veteran.

"Is it time to eat?" I asked first.

"Almost," he answered. "Go wash up in the spring. Your grandma and grandpa, Sila and Checheya, are going to tell stories after we eat. Did you find arrow tip rocks?"

"Yes, six rocks," I proudly answered, walking back to give them to him.

"You are a special boy," he offered, putting one hand on my head.

My older sister, Berry Woman, was on her way back from the spring with all the little kids. We all play wrestled as we passed just to show we were all glad to see each other. I barely washed up, only splashing water on myself. I was hungry like only a young boy can be.

With a quick pace, I walked back to camp. Noona had all the food in carved wooden bowls and woven baskets on top of a blanket made of elk hide.

Her weaving was immaculate. The baskets could hold water without leaking. She used the rattlesnake design of diamonds and the mountain emblems to decorate them. They were beautiful. The elk skin blanket had no hair on it and was older now, but my Noona kept it very clean.

The setting had an order to it. First, there was the water that brought the vegetation. So the water was set at the head. Then, the roots, and the berries were set, followed by the game. This was a history of Creation, and Creation was moving to take care of humankind again that we could continue to live.

What a feast: Hot trout right off the fire, camas cakes, fresh huckleberries and smoked deer meat! No one could cook trout or camas cakes like Noona and Checheya.

My uncles and aunts were arriving from their camps nearby. They cooked and brought over some wild carrots, bitterroot and baked moss. It was incredible. All the most delicious foods of the world! I quickly sat by the setting of food and rubbed my hands together.

Peepa announced, "Come and sit by the fire my relatives, the foods are waiting on us." As everyone settled in, he continued, as everyone knew he would:

> "As always, we will pray to express our thanks for the food, and for life. We are a rich people because we have each other, and because we still have our elders among us to guide us and teach us. They are the ones who know life because they lived it, and they have the wisdom reserved by the Creator only for those who have walked through the doorway of old age. Therefore, we will depend upon my father-in-law, my children's Sila, to offer a prayer for the food."

My Sila rose to his feet more slowly and deliberately than usual. "Drum" is what other people called him, although it seemed like he was related to everyone. It was an ancient practice to call people by the term of your relationship, not by their given name. To call relatives by their name would be uncaring.

> *"Kolunsuten, Grandfather,"* he opened, holding a fan made of hawk feathers, *"pity us and recognize us."* His voice was rather

old and slow, but still strong. *"We are your people, the children of the Mother Earth. You made our bodies from the red earth, poured the sacred life-giving water into us, put a spark from the fire within our hearts and blew your great breath of life air into us upon setting us on this road of life. All your holy elements of nature make up our very existence, and we turn to these divine Creations again, the great foods of the earth, to find the power that will continue our lives. From the earth, these foods have come because our Mother Earth and Creator take care of us and provide for us, like children.*

My parents and grandparents of generations past called these foods holy people. These holy people have life, and the power to sustain life. Only in my old age do I begin to understand deeply what this means.

Each of these holy people, the foods, have their own song, their own name, a traditional name. That's why our women medicine leaders sing these songs before we first gather them, and then we talk to them, pray for them. We treat them with respect and kindness, never to gather them without reverence.

You provided these great foods that we can live on again another day. Bless us by these holy people foods, that we will have courage and strength into a new day.

Let it be so," he concluded.

Everyone remained still as my Sila and Checheya took a little food from the bowls and baskets. They were our elders. They sacrificed so very much for all of us. If it weren't for them, we wouldn't even be here. It seems as though their children and grandchildren are their whole lives and I can't think of a time they were not a part of my life, teaching, helping, supporting, caring and comforting.

It was time. The adults dished up food, all smiling and joking with one another, teasing their brother-in-law or sister-in-law. I tried to look and act like I was totally patient and mindful to pay my respects, but inside now I could taste the trout and the camas cakes.

Finally, the children started to dish up, all helping themselves to this great setting of food. I took a bite off a whole, big fat trout. Noona cooked it just right, moist natural oils, flavor like nothing else in the world.

I followed it up with a bite of camas cake. Mmmmmm! Checheya spent days preparing it and baking it under ground.

Camas is one of our primary foods. It is a root, a bulb. The plant has an identifying flower on the top. When cleaned and skinned, it looks like a little white ball. Mashed up and baked under ground mmm, mmm, mmm!

Delicious!

I thought I would just keep eating all night.

I topped it off with a bowl of fresh huckleberries. Such delicacy, such blessing was ours! As everyone got full, the attention gradually turned to more visiting and laughing. The foods and the goodness of life made us happy.

My Peepa announced, "Let us go into the big teepee, for nightfall is upon us." Everyone gradually got up and went toward my Sila's teepee, entered and took their seats. I loved this teepee. The poles were extra long and they spiraled at the top. The hides all matched and were of the same color and consistency. They seemed spiritually alive. If I stared at a spot long enough, I could see images and designs, like looking at the clouds.

The fire always seemed to burn brighter in his teepee, and the charcoals would get a red with a bluish glow flickering off them. The fire was alive and ancient like a caring friend or relative of my Sila.

I took my usual seat, as did everyone else.

Gradually, everyone settled down and it became quiet.

Right next to me, Rock sat down rough and ungraceful, but in a playful way.

"A rock must move like the buffalo bull on the long grasses of the prairie," he said grunting and throwing his elbows around like a great bull trying to get comfortable.

"Hey! Brother-friend, watch out! I like to throw rocks into the lake. I might throw you in by mistake!" I told him teasingly, grabbing him by the neck and playfully shaking him.

Rock was my good friend, and he was the funniest kid in the whole tribe. Many, many adults would warn him about being too silly. It didn't do any good.

He was so quick to smile and laugh. He was a little chubby, and sometimes unkempt, but had a friendly expression that made you want to like him or even laugh.

"I want to hear some stories about the Chop Faces," Rock said with his usual tone, rubbing his hands together like waiting for something good to eat.

"Chop Faces" means enemy in our language. Most every little boy dreams about gloriously defeating them in a great historical battle.

"When I meet the Chop Faces in battle, I'm gonna beat them up and cut off their tail!" Rock exclaimed.

"Cut off their tails?" I asked, giving him a look of disbelief and wonder.

"Yeah! That way they can never, ever come back to bother us or any-body!" Rock explained.

No one else ever mentioned a tail before.

"Rock, uh, I don't think they have tails. They're people just like we are, only different."

"Sh, sh, ssshhh . . . I think I'm the only one who knows," Rock said softly, looking around like he had to be careful no one else was listening.

"You fool!" I challenged, pushing him, calling his bluff.

Sila was wearing his buckskin leggings, shirt and breechcloth. He had a skin draped over his shoulder and grizzly bear claws around his neck from a bear he killed himself. These were the only people who could wear the claws, who had the right to. You had to kill it yourself the old way. His slim build made him look sleek and agile. His long graying braids looked like horsehair ropes.

"It is in this teepee of your elders, in the huckleberry mountains that you will learn your language and your traditions," Sila explained. "Many teachings and lessons of life will be imparted to you. With these, you will know how to be, who to be, where to go and what to do. You can simplify life, and bring order to it."

All the older children leaned forward to listen even more intently. Many of my cousin brothers and cousin sisters were here, too. The small children were being quieted down by my aunts. "Yem, yem," they urged the little ones, "Grandpa's going to talk."

"Way back in time, there were the ancient ones, the First People. They are the ones who had many of the ways used by our people today, including the sweat lodge, the use of the holy sage plant as a cleansing medicine, and more. They had many stories and legends to record what happened at the beginning of the world — when everything was alive and moved around, even the mountains.

"A few of the ancient ones became a part of our people. We have some of these stories to tell, teach and learn from." He began the story, talking in his animated voice to bring the story to life.

> One winter, many people were suffering. The snow was deep and the air was cold. But even when it warmed, the game was nowhere to be found. The animals seemed to disappear. The band was puzzled. They prayed and sang about it, but no change.
>
> Finally the family band leader, Yellow Root said, "Someone go to see my son-in-law, Raven. He always has meat. He is married to my daughter, I'm sure he will help us.
>
> So, some of Yellow Root's sons and sons-in-law went to see Raven, including Coyote. Coyote was kind of a show-off and a braggart, but everyone knew it and just tried to ignore him. "I don't know why father-in-law wants to go see Raven," said Coyote. "Just give

me one more day and I would've had all the meat we would ever need," he boasted.

Finally, they arrived at Raven's camp. "Ahhh! Hello my brothers," Raven greeted. "Come in and warm yourself at my fire. Good food, good company and strong friendships will make great medicine for us."

They all went inside his lodge and ate of his food. He had deer meat hanging from the lodge poles in numerous bunches of two. He even had two bunches hanging from his belt. He always had meat.

The sons of Yellow Root explained their dilemma and the need for food. Raven said, "Sure. Let's go. I know right where to go," and they all left.

It was already late in the day, so they didn't get far when the sun started to go down. Raven said, "We should make camp here." He walked up to a dead, dry tree, jumped and struck it with his foot and made sparks come out that everyone quickly built into a fire.

"Everyone knows that trick," said Coyote trying to diminish what Raven had done. He walked over to the tree, jumped and kicked at it but only fell down in a very funny manner. Everyone laughed and laughed at Coyote. "We already have fire," he said. "Maybe I'll do this trick for tomorrow's fire," Coyote bragged.

The next day, they went hunting. Raven was on the trail of deer. He told everyone: "We will only kill two deer. This is part of my pact with the deer and part of my Sumesh power. We will kill only two."

With careful precision and stone silence, he moved in on the deer. The deer started to walk away in a line of about six animals. He shot the deer at the end of the line first. Down it went. Then he shot the next deer in line. The four deer in front, he let go.

But Coyote was excited about it. "We need enough meat to feed everyone," he said "and the Holy Nature is giving us all six deer. We must shoot them all now," Coyote justified as he charged forward.

The deer began to run and dodge with their white tails bouncing high in the air. Raven yelled "No! Let them go! Do not shoot anymore!" But Coyote let go an arrow. He missed. Quickly and without a good shot or careful aim, he let go another one. He missed again. Then he carelessly let go a third arrow. Somehow the arrow struck one of the deer, but only wounded it. "I got one! I got one!" he cried.

"Oh no," exclaimed Raven. "What have we done? He raced over to where the deer lay.

Raven doctored the wounded deer with herbs from one of the bundles he kept on his belt. Almost immediately, the deer jumped up and ran away. "I'm sorry, my brother," Raven called to the deer.

They all went on to continue the hunt elsewhere, taking no more than two deer at a time, as Raven had instructed. When they had enough, they returned home to the family band and everyone had enough to eat."

Sila concluded the story the way that all stories ended, "That's the end of the trail," he said. "So my children and grandchildren," he explained, "never take more than you need, never be wasteful and never be boastful. Remember what happened to Coyote."

"Have respect for our brother, the deer, for they are a great and holy brother indeed. For how many brothers would willingly give their lives so their people could eat for a while and live another day? Raven knew this and he found something out about it, more than most people would understand. The deer have a Sumesh of their own and it can be used to help you as it did Raven or hinder you as it did Coyote.

"Take the deer only in the respectful manner, pray thankfully for him. Talk to the deer spirit about why you have taken his life. In this way, the deer will be happy for the good purpose for which he has lived and died, and you will be blessed. Otherwise, you could become a troubled or confused person.

"And, what is the final lesson in the story?" Sila asked.

"Always take care of your relatives!" everyone answered together, followed by laughter and giggles.

"That's right," rewarded Sila. "Just like Yellow Root and his sons, son-in-law and family, we must always take care of one another."

Really satisfied and fulfilled, everyone agreed, "hey, hey, hey." Gradually, the talk turned to visiting and joking. I looked to the front, and my Checheya was holding baby sister Rainbow Girl. She was slowly rocking her while humming a traditional lullaby song. Every now and then, she'd add her own words into the song.

"My baby girl is all right now, because Grandma is holding her," she sang, and then hummed the melody, repeating the song all over again until baby sister fell fast asleep.

Every one of the kids in the teepee knows that song. Checheya and it are some of my earliest memories. I wondered, if maybe all the adults here remember it the same way I do, their earliest of memories too.

I felt myself starting to fade into sleep. I think I'll sleep at Checheya's too, I thought, as I did so many times over the years.

CHAPTER 3
Yellow Horse

I slept soundly that night and dreamed about the beautiful land. In my dream, it moved slightly and gently as I walked by it and over it. I could hear a faint song coming from the trees. I awoke to the song of the birds and the early dawn light. I looked around. Sila and Checheya were already gone. I put on my moccasins and went outside. They were both facing the sunrise, praying and crying.

"Thank you for the new day, Kolunsuten," Checheya said. "All I am is a mother and grandmother in the world. But to me, grandmothering is a great and wonderful gift. So bless my children and grandchildren with this holy dawn."

Sila added, "You promised no one a tomorrow. When the new day comes, we are to be thankful for it. It is a new time — not used by anybody. Therefore, we are to use it for good or even great purposes. Thank you Kolunsuten. We will take care of our lives together and the time given us in this new day."

They cried as they spoke words of prayer. I always wondered why so many elders cried when they prayed. Maybe you just had to be older to understand.

By now, the sun was starting to peak over the horizon.

It was a brilliant light coming up in the eastern sky making colors of red, yellow and purple. Mixed with the blue sky above and the black sky all around, it was a spectacular sunrise.

Eventually, you could see the direct sunlight hit the highest peaks and move downward on them.

My grandparents put their hands out to it and motioned their hands back over their heads just as the first rays of direct sunlight hit their heads. They continued to motion their hands toward the sun as they followed the direct sunlight down their bodies. It seemed as though they glowed with the light when it touched upon them. They continued all the way to their moccasins, reaching toward the sun and motioning the light to them with their hands. The day just burst alive with sunlight everywhere.

My grandparents are amazingly kind, good and loving people, and the land, the sun, the sky and Kolunsuten Creator knew it.

"Grandson, Sun Boy," Sila called to me. "Come here. Put your hands out to the sacred sunrise and receive its blessing." As I did this they drank water from a carved dipper made of hardwood, poured a little on their hands and put it on their heads.

"Use the water, too, Grandson," Checheya instructed. I drank and poured a little on my hands, then rubbed it on my head, arms, chest and my thighs, then I washed my face with it.

"Hey Sun Boy! Are you ready to be a young man yet?" my Peepa quizzed me in a challenging way. Excitement moved within me. I wondered what great adventure do I get to share in with the men? Maybe hunting, fishing or wild horses? Maybe the Chop Faces, our enemy, were coming and I could ride with the warriors.

I could tell my Peepa just came back from running the mountain.

He was wearing no shirt and only his breechcloth and his hunting moccasins.

Often I would run with him. We would pray before we ascended, again at the top, as the sun would rise. Then, we would drink water at the saddle with my Noona, and wash up.

He was muscular and strong looking, but he was also kind and good.

"Yes, Peepa, very much so," I answered in confidence. "I'm ready."

"Well, then, after you eat a little, go and gather the horses," he instructed me.

"We have a special guest among us. My friend, Buffalo Horn, is visiting his sister, your aunt by marriage. He is a great warrior. Bravery is his great power. He fears nothing. He will join us today, too," he added.

My Noona was by his side. Every morning they went together to the mountain. She stayed down at the bottom with the water. She always prayed as my Peepa ran. All the while Peepa ran, he prayed, and then prayed and sang on the mountaintop to greet the new day.

Noona said that when they prayed together perhaps it was more powerful. A man was made by the Kolunsuten to take care of a wife and children, and a woman was made to take care of a husband and children. If they both did this with full commitment and devotion, a blessing of strength and happiness would be theirs and their children's. I never wondered to question it. Obviously, it was the simple truth.

"I'll get you some roots and berries," my Noona offered as she hurried toward our teepee.

I couldn't eat very much. I was anticipating the great adventure in which my Peepa was including me.

The horses were usually predictable about where they would be. The leaders were very tame and part of the family. The followers stayed around the boss horses. The horses were all colors: bay, black, red, buckskin, white, gray, paint, pinto and Appaloosa. There were many wild herds to pick horses from. Some were stolen from our enemies.

Horses are great and holy beings, all the people say. I really believe it to be true.

Sila and Peepa tell many stories of the many wonderful things horses have done. I thought about these things as I walked to gather them.

Take care of the horses and they will take care of you. They are our brothers who came through the animal kingdom to be with us. These sacred brothers carry us to find food for our families and they help us to protect our loved ones from enemies, and the best horses never fail in these duties.

The really great horses get a traditional name at the name giving ceremony. The traditional feather, placed in the hair of a person when they receive their name, is placed in the forelock hair of the horse at the top and front of his head. His name is announced and he is called by his name like a person. The eagle feather is his, as is the honor and privilege.

The horse is painted up according to his deeds, the nature of his character and the understanding of the people who ride him. Such a horse is a great prize, the kind about which our horse songs are composed and sung.

These great war horses or buffalo hunting horses earned their honor and praise by their deeds of bravery. Perhaps, they charged into impossible odds right into the enemy lines screaming their own battle cry while fighting the enemy horses; perhaps they were wounded but never quit, never gave up; or perhaps they always ran just to the right angle and rate of speed to give the rider a clear, smooth shot into the buffalo's heart, even though the bull might be lunging to hook and gore the horse with its horns.

"Treat your horse like you would want to be treated," Sila always told us, over and over again. "He is a great brother to come among the human kingdom to enable and further our living. How many brothers do you know who would come and do that for you, even die for you? Not many," he explained. "But the good horse does that for you."

I thought about all these things as I walked to gather the horses.

Maybe we will go after some horses in the valley, I wondered. Peepa keeps some there with herds belonging to others.

I imagined riding into battle on a fierce and brave horse with all the power and confidence of our greatest of warriors, dressed and painted in the brilliant style reserved for such men. I made fighting noises and moved my arms with my imaginary war club and shield.

Suddenly, a bird flew out from the grass just where I was going to step and made me jump. I looked around a little startled. Quickly, I calmed myself.

Mostly, I kept it to myself, but this was my biggest problem: fear. In spite of all that had been done for me and all the training I do to strengthen myself, my first reaction is too often fear. Some of it I have overcome.

I used to be afraid of barking dogs. Everyone would laugh at me, so I dug some measure of strength from way down deep and beat it. Maybe I can do the same in all other areas too, I hoped.

Peepa and Sila knew this about me and always talked to me about bravery and courage, but they would usually explain too that fear is an extension of the basic will to live that all living creatures have. At first, being brave isn't about feeling no fear. It is about doing what you have to do even though you are afraid, they would explain.

I pondered these things as I walked wondering if I would ever be like the greatest warriors who seemed to never even fear death.

Then, just as I suspected, the horses appeared in the second meadow, peacefully eating grass. I paused, and like Peepa and Sila always told me, I thanked the meadow for caring for and feeding our horses. I put a handful of kinicknick tobacco down as I prayed for continued blessing for our horses, including protection.

I called to my horse: "Good Horse, come here now. It is time to be useful to the people again. This is according to the pact between my people and yours, governed by the Creator. We will be good to you in return. We will feed and water you in the bad weather. We will treat you with kindness, respect and honor."

All their ears were up and pointing at me. Peepa said they can understand what you tell them if you really mean it; so never speak harshly to them. They know if they are cared for properly and respectfully so they can meet you halfway to do their part. Otherwise, something might go wrong or you might get hurt. Again, I knew this was all the simple truth that anyone could understand.

Good Horse took a step toward me. So I turned away from him. I kept my eyes averted, my arms down and my hands still with my finger turned inward like I was always taught. This way the horse would remain calm and wouldn't run off.

"Great brothers, it is a good day to do something worthwhile," I repeated quietly as I approached. "Easy now, Hmmmmm hmmmmm," I calmly told them.

Gradually, I reached and held the neck of my horse, wrapped a braided rope around his neck and led him off. He always had a kind but knowing look in his eye. I dearly loved horses, their nature, and their presence, even their special smell. I could spend all day with them, and often did, just keeping them company and watching them.

Peepa said if you have a young horse you really care about and you want it to turn out special, spend time with it first. Stay in the corral near it at night. Then, the horse will bond to you as though you were his best friend horse in the herd, even like his mother. He will trust you and believe you. So, if you don't do anything to violate that trust, he will eventually go all out for you only because you need him to. These horses are amazing and great creatures.

Some of our people are able to attain the great horse medicine way and communicate directly one on one with them through the horse language and spoken words known only to these horse people. But it is rare and very difficult because a whole way of life goes along with it.

You have to be a loner, living outside, mostly with the horses. You have to regularly and often fast and pray. And, you could only eat certain foods that were bland. This way, the horse would trust you as "one of his."

All the young men want the horsepower, but only a few actually get it.

I put the bridal on the boss horse and mounted Good Horse when my Peepa rode up on one of his horses he kept in the corral. "Sun Boy," he called, "I thought I should check on you. Brother-in-law, your uncle, lost a horse last night in the lower meadow. It was a grizzly bear."

Nothing struck fear in the hearts of people quite like a grizzly. Generally, they stayed their distance. We respected them and prayed for protection. I wondered if they were evil, but Checheya said to never think badly towards anything in nature for it all is sacred and has its place according to Kolunsuten.

But every now and then, bears struck without warning and without provocation. Sila said that all things lead us to the good, that life is sacred and precious and must never be taken for granted. Besides, how could a man be really brave if he were never tested in life?

The day just got more interesting: horses to gather and ride, and now a grizzly too! My heart and mind soared. All the stories I heard the men tell of bravery and great deeds. Maybe I could witness some of the action and greatness myself.

"How did you know to go look for the other horses?" I quizzed my Peepa.

"Your Sila said the magpies were acting strangely so I better check on everything and everybody," he explained. "Magpies have a power to find meat, but maybe they were behaving strangely because what they found was one of our horses.

"We will not change our plans," Peepa announced as we rode into camp. "We will break and train some horses to be ready for the fall buffalo hunt."

"Hey, hey, hey!" everyone from my uncles and older cousin brothers said in agreement.

As we began riding down the hill, one of the boys asked one of my uncles if we could sing. He told him it would be all right because we are in the mountains of our own country and we have scouts ahead who told us everything is all right. We're not hunting or moving swiftly and quietly.

Uncle Center Feather went ahead to scout. He had the great horse-power and he was a tracker like none other. Everyone could track, and everyone could train and ride horses. But Center Feather was a legend in the family. He is the one who held all the knowledge of the horses and the great secrets reserved to those like him.

Center Feather could disappear into nature in an instant, simply covering himself with it, he explained. He had the power of the deer to help him and like the deer; he could use it to go invisible in the forest. The deer was mystical and magical. He was only seen when he allowed himself to be seen. So it was with Uncle. He was so quiet, he rarely even talked. When he did, it was incomplete. Usually, he only used sign language.

The boys started to sing a traveling song, but every now and then Rock would add in a new word to make it comical and everybody would laugh.

> *Yo wanna yo, hey ya hey*
> Hey yoy, hey you
> Yo wanna yo, hey ya hey
> *Hey yoy hey you!*
> *We're following the stars home,*
> Because I want to see my people!

Rock would take the song by singing louder than everyone else, and change the words.

> . . . We're following the stars home,
> Because my butt hurts riding this horse!

Even the men would laugh, look at each other, and then shake their heads in disbelief at this funny boy.

As we continued, the men were visiting and talking up ahead. My Peepa and uncles really enjoyed visiting. It was their primary form of entertainment. They were talkative, even excited to have Buffalo Horn among us. I could tell by their tone, the types of stories they were exchanging, and even the way they rode their horses, straight and tall, and proud and alert.

The day was beautiful. It was mountain majesty at its finest. It seemed wherever we rode the plant life, the rocks, the hillside and the meadows all knew us. They glowed with a bright color and seemed to subtly move as we passed by them. Just like my dream the night before. The earth was truly our Mother and cared for us like her real children. This made our lives fulfilled and wonderful. This was a happy time, a great time.

At the lower meadow, there was a small band of horses and they were alerted to our presence. They turned to look at us with their ears up, some snorted and raised their tails in preparation for flight, to run away from any possible threat or danger whether the danger was genuine or not.

Peepa said, "The yellow horse there in the front is the one I traded buffalo hides to the Palouse for. She has never been ridden. Today, I will ride her and get her ready for the trip to buffalo country."

"Hey, hey, hey," everybody agreed. This is where we would begin the day, gathering and training horses.

These horses had been handled before or they would have been long gone already, but we didn't want to get them running either if we could help it.

Peepa got off his horse and slowly began to move towards the horses. He kept his lariat of braided buckskin behind him. He quietly hummed the horse song, adding some words to it from time to time.

"Come here my good brothers. Together we will do something great. You will be honored by my people and yours . . . ."

"Hey-ya, hay-hay-yah, ah, ah! Hey, yo-ay!"

He put some tobacco down on the ground with some words, and approached the horses. The yellow horse held still and waited for him. He walked all the way up to him and wrapped the lariat rope around its neck, then fashioned a halter around the horse's nose. "Good brother," he said as he patted him on the neck and rubbed his withers. The horse took a deep breath and sighed, communicating that he had relaxed again and had trust in us.

Peepa told him, "We will never hurt you, we will always care for you. You are a great and holy brother — the Kolunsuten is our father the Creator, the earth is our mother, as they are to you. So we are truly brothers in spirit." Peepa took a root out of his mouth that he had been chewing and put it in the horse's mouth. This way, the horse would know what Peepa was trying to communicate and he would understand what was expected of him.

Nearby was a small corral Sila said they had used when he was a small boy. He didn't know how long it was there before that. Every year we would replace some of the limbs, brush or rocks to make sure it was sturdy enough to contain and hold the horses. We led the horses into it and they were content.

Center Feather appeared out of nowhere next to the corral. "Ahhh, Uncle. It's good to see you," I told him. "Are you going to help us train horses?" I asked.

He shook his head no. "You ride better than me," he said in sign language. We all laughed knowing his awesome abilities.

Uncle Center Feather wore simple clothes and a plain hairstyle, for he stayed outside with the horses and nature full-time, day and night. This is the way of life for those with the horse power. Yet, he too was a decorated warrior, proven in battle to be brave and successful. He had once walked right through an enemy camp while they slept, and stole their weapons without ever being detected. That would be hard to do because of enemy scouts and because of the keen awareness that some of the enemy warriors had that was almost equal to Center Feather.

"Go ahead, Brother," he called to my Peepa, "ride her," he motioned with his hands. They called each other brother in an Indian way, meaning they were closer than friends, like brothers. So, to me, he was my uncle.

Peepa led the yellow horse out to the open area knowing he would run. But to the downhill side were rocks and trees providing a natural barricade. To the east were thick forested areas and to the west, a scattered rocky and bushy area before a cliff that dropped down to the river. The only way to go was up or across. This way, a horse would run himself out. Anytime a horse begins to run away or buck, turn him uphill. When he accepts you, pet and calm him, talk to him. He will understand.

Peepa went around and around the horse, getting him used to being touched and handled. Every now and then, Peepa would jump up alongside the horse but not get on. Finally, he jumped up and with one fluid, yet swift motion was sitting on the horse's back. The yellow horse took off, not sure what was happening. So the horse responded the only way her nature told him to — he ran.

Back and forth they went, up the grassy hill and across. Finally, the horse quit running and Peepa steered her gradually across the hill or slightly downward. When she started to run, Peepa turned uphill again. Suddenly, she realized she was all right and that if she didn't run, it was a lot easier.

"Now she's starting to think," Center Feather explained. "Good, he motioned with his hand.

Every time Peepa pulled a rein and he gave her head to the pressure, he let go and petted her. The yellow horse readily accepted his training. In no time, Peepa began directing her back to where we were alongside the corral.

"I think she's going to be a good one, maybe a great one," Peepa said as they came riding up. "She has a willing attitude, yet she has his own mind in a tough kind of a way. This is what the brave, work-all-day sort of horses are made of," he surmised.

"Yellow Horse, you are fulfilling the pact between my people and yours, so I shall fulfill my part of the pact. You are another blessing to my home and family, and a protection just by your presence. Thank you for this, and thank you for carrying me for all good purposes. One day, you will help defend my loved ones from danger or threat. I cannot tell you that I will never ask you to do something that may bring harm to you. But I will ask you only what is necessary."

"Hmmmmm, my good relative," Peepa soothed the horse.

Suddenly, the ears went up and the horses were all alerted. Center Feather said they are reacting to smell, not sound or movement. Fear moved into the horses and they started to run around. But Peepa was riding an unbroken horse so he had no control in this kind of situation.

Away bolted his horse and the faster she ran the more worked up she became. I rode after Peepa. His horse was heading for the brushy area right before the cliff. Just as he approached a patch of tall brush, the grizzly lunged out. It was a monster, much taller than a big man, with a massive brown body.

They were different than other bears. They knew the animal kingdom was their domain, not man's. And they would fight ferociously anything in it.

The bear growled and swiped at the air with his paws, and giant, hook-like claws. His voice shook the land about us and reverberated through my body. A deep and ancient instinct told me to fear and run away, too. He opened his mouth wide and his bottom lip shook back and forth. All his body, claws, mouth and eyes said just one thing: powerful rage to kill.

If only one among us had the bear power, then it would be different. People with this Sumesh, spirit helper power, could talk to the bear like scolding a dog and the great bear would listen. But we were on our own this day.

Peepa's horse turned down the hill along the cliff and the grizzly followed. The men started to yell at the bear, "Hey yah, hey yah!" trying to get his attention, but he stayed right after Peepa. I was still on my horse because I never dismounted. But my uncles were trying to catch their horses and having little luck because of the bear. The smell of fear was thick in the air.

Some grabbed their bows and arrows and began running towards the direction of the bear and my Peepa. I followed behind them but stayed back, I was stiff with fear but I wanted to see that my Peepa was all right. "This is what I've been telling you about Good Horse," I told my mount. "It's time to go, my great relative." I kicked him and he accepted the direction and ran toward the action like a brave warrior, but I felt fear through my whole body. My mouth was dry, my legs ached, my arms quivered, my stomach tossed and turned and my mind said run away from this terror, now!

Down over the next hill, Peepa was turning the horse in a large half circle, and the grizzly was trying to cut off the horse with a sharper angle inside the circle. Suddenly, the bear cut across the inside of the circle causing the horse to break to the right — but there was nowhere to go except right over the cliff. The horse tried to stop but its momentum carried it and my Peepa right over. Down they went splashing into the water. Luckily, they ran downhill enough so that it wasn't quite so high for them to fall, and they came back up to the surface.

That grizzly was in such a ferocious rage he ran to the ledge growling and lunging. The rocks gave way under his feet and down he went splashing into the water.

I dismounted, ran to the ledge and could see my Peepa swimming for his life with the bear after him. But a man was no match for a grizzly at swimming. The men showed up on foot and some started to shoot arrows at the bear, some were sticking out of his back.

Buffalo Horn stood on the rocky ledge right where my Peepa fell from and yelled his war cry.

"The Kolunsuten promised no one a tomorrow!" he shouted. "When that day, the last day, is here for you, it is a time to be brave and strong! Hey-yah! Hey-yah!"

I thought he was shouting at my Peepa. Oh, no! I was horrified. The bear was right upon my Peepa! I could not watch him be ripped and torn to pieces. My stomach knotted and turned.

Peepa turned and swam with a powerful determination, but with a fear upon his face, I had not seen before. The grizzly had his nose out and forward, like an arrow he made a bee line for his prey.

Suddenly, Buffalo Horn leapt from the ledge, his knife in his hand. "Wow! Owww!" he yelled. He looked like a guardian spirit flying through the air, long black hair flowing in the wind with buckskin fringe shaking back and forth. His muscular body and arms looked like he could stop and kill anything.

Surely, he would save my Peepa. My hopes were lifted for the first time. Boom! Splash! He hit the grizzly right at the middle of his back. They both went down.

Suddenly, and almost effortlessly, the bear spun around in the water and jerked. Buffalo Horn Fell off.

Right as he came to the surface, the grizzly lunged out and onto him, raking him across the side of the head with his claws. He was thrown several body lengths across the water and lay there motionless. The water turned red around him.

The great bear swam over, grabbed him by the back of the neck with his powerful teeth, and shook him back and forth. Surely, he was dead.

All hope was dashed. Several of my uncles standing near me fell to their knees. Some of my cousins started to cry.

"Get away, Peepa!" I shouted, in a voice of muffled hysteria.

My Peepa was swimming furiously again with the grizzly after him. One of our great warriors and good friends was killed almost effortlessly. No one could stand against this monster, it seemed.

I felt like crying, some tears began to flow down my cheeks. I tried to talk, but my voice only crackled.

I thought about many of the times my Peepa had taken care of my siblings and me, nurtured and loved, guided and directed, and provided and protected. Mostly, I could feel the gentle strength of his approving presence, when he would put his hand upon my head or shoulder happy to see me.

"Poor orphan boy . . . ." I could hear a voice in the wind.

I ran in the downstream direction, where Peepa was heading. One of my uncles was just getting there carrying a long spear he had just fashioned with one of the stones I had gathered the day before. "Quickly, Uncle, give me your spear," I said to him.

With a puzzled look he handed it to me. A boy ordering his uncle around was unheard of. But all I could think of was my Peepa and what he meant to me, how he cared for me and all our times together.

I ran towards the far rock and leapt as far as I possibly could. I was coming down straight toward the grizzly which was now upon my Peepa, and Peepa had turned toward the bear holding his knife out. "What have I done?" I wondered too late.

No time to think. I just held out the spear below me as tightly as I possibly could. Down, down I fell. It seemed an eternity. Boom, splash. I hit the water. The spear pierced the grizzly at the back of the neck. He was bleeding badly and stunned. "Son," Peepa called, "swim away quickly."

Suddenly the bear lashed out blindly and viciously like only a wounded animal can. He turned toward me. I knew I was no match for this bear in the water. Some men, even boys, have killed black bears in the water, but never a grizzly.

My Peepa rose up out of the water with his knife and stabbed the bear in the back. The bear roared in pain and anger and turned swiping with his claws, ripping my Peepa across the shoulder and knocking him across the water.

We both tried to swim as fast as we could but bears are great swimmers. He was gaining on us, then right upon us!

The yellow horse was swimming around the cliff wall where she had no way out of the water, afraid to swim around the grizzly.

Then, without explanation or reason, the Yellow Horse mysteriously swam near my Peepa. The grizzly turned on the horse, jumping on her back and biting her on the neck. The horse screamed and went under water.

Peepa dove under and caught the horses' reins. As quick as anything I had ever seen, he wrapped it around the bear's neck while the bear had a hold of the horse. The bear pulled back to get away and lost his grip on the horse, but the reins began to pull the bear. The horse was already dead and slowly sinking in the water. The bear struggled against it.

I dove under the water and swam beneath the bear. I grabbed his hind foot and pulled him back and downward so he couldn't get his head up for an occasional breath of air. Peepa found his knife in the bears back and began stabbing repeatedly.

Slowly, the grizzly ceased motion. When I was sure, I let go and came up for air.

We killed the giant grizzly with our bare hands! We killed the grizzly with our bare hands!!

My Peepa came up for air. "Son, are you all right," he asked. I couldn't talk. I was in a daze, a stupor. I couldn't stop shaking.

"Oww, Yowww, Yowww!" all my uncles and cousin brothers yelled their war cry. As we pulled ourselves out of the water, they raised their right hands towards us and yelled their war cry again to pay us honor. Some of them danced on the ledge, others began to sing.

We made our way to some rocks along the shore. He offered a short prayer:

"Thank you Kolunsuten for my life and most of all, for my son's life. But most of all, remember my brother, Buffalo Horn. Bless him in spirit. We are told you have great rewards and wonderful blessings for our warriors who give their lives for the people." He paused in deep emotion. He motioned his hand like he was trying to get a rhythm to continue talking.

"And thank you for my great brother, the yellow horse. We barely knew her and already she brought her protection to my son and me. Already, she has done something great to be honored by my people and hers. Bless her in spirit for she has fulfilled a great purpose." He panted to catch his breath between words.

He put his hand upon my shoulder and I felt his love, concern and relief. His prayers were never just words that sounded good. His word was his law and he lived his prayers totally and truly each and every day. I just wanted to be with him, and be just like him in every way.

I felt like a little boy again. I just wanted my Peepa to take care of me. I quivered uncontrollably, folding my arms trying to warm myself. I felt so cold.

A slow realization moved through me about what I had done. I looked at the high cliff and the distance to the water. I gazed at the sunken remains of the grizzly with the spear and arrows sticking out. I remembered how unconquerable the bear looked and how afraid I was. I began to feel faint and dizzy.

I looked at the body of our great warrior, Buffalo Horn, floating in the eddy. His head and neck were torn to pieces. He was dead. I had never witnessed violent death before, nor seen the results upon the human body.

I felt a deep nausea. I started to fade.

"It's all right son," Peepa offered. "It's all over now. We're safe and we've done a great deed."

We took our time going back up the cliff. A few of my uncles and cousins stayed behind to help us and they were still excited about what happened. They were war whooping and dancing around still.

Very slowly, we walked our horses back to camp. Most everyone else had ridden ahead and told the camp about what happened. Riders went to other camps to tell them the news.

I was slumped over my horse, not knowing what to do. I felt like I could talk if I wanted, but I didn't want to. So, I gave my Peepa a pleading look, like "help me, Peepa."

He was wounded and bleeding. Somehow, when we are just children, it doesn't seem like our Peepas could feel pain and fear like we do.

"Thank you, Son," he said to me. "That was a brave deed you did for me. Of all the men there, some of them proven warriors, you were the only brave one."

"I'm not brave, Peepa . . . ." I said, my voice starting to crack like I would cry. I tried to choke it back. "I was afraid. I'm still afraid. I can't quit shaking."

"The brave warrior way is a hard and difficult way to follow, Son," he consoled.

"And . . . Buffalo Horn . . . " I started to talk but I choked again pretending I was clearing my throat. The picture of him, so alive, and strong, then floating — dead and gored in the water stayed in my mind. I could not shake it. I couldn't say it.

"Death, losing life, and fighting for life are sacred things," Peepa explained. "The warrior way is not about glory and celebration. It is about doing the terrible things you must do, that no one else of the people can do, in order to protect your loved ones from danger, suffering or death.

"My brother-friend, Buffalo Horn, he understood this. He wanted to live. He chose life. But he dedicated his life to protecting others. He accepted that one day he might lose his own life in the protecting of and fighting for others. That day would be the appointed day reserved for him by the Kolunsuten."

"Is it always like this, Peepa?" I said in more of a little boy voice. "Is it always fear and horror? Is it always death and loss?" I sniffled and pulled back tears.

Peepa paused and thought about it a good while.

"Yes, Son. Yes, it is," he answered me.

I felt like crying all the way home. I mourned Buffalo Horn. I felt a trauma deep in my mind and my soul.

Peepa was leaning over his horse by now, the wounds on his shoulder and arm were making him weak. He had a makeshift wrapping on it, but he needed Sila and Checheya to doctor him with herbs and other medicines.

As we rode into camp everyone was there and waiting for us, dressed in their finest clothes, hair neatly combed and braided. Even Rainbow Girl, my baby sister, was wearing her fancy buckskin dress with elk teeth. My Noona looked beautiful. She was smiling and crying at the same time, her hair combed down straight, shiny black and long.

All the people started to sing a welcome song while some yelled their war cry. My cousins were running alongside the horses all excited, calling my name. We stopped right in the middle of camp. It was a hero's welcome like I had seen only several times in my life, but it was for me this time!

As I dismounted, all the boys wanted to take care of my horse for me, but my little brother was standing there, too, looking so proud and excited. He wanted the reins.

"Sun Boy, Sun Boy, let me put Good Horse away for you," he begged.

"Little brother, Snow on the Mountain, take my horse," I told him giving him the reins. He led the horse toward the corral, hopping and jumping, half squeaking a little boy's war cry. Other little boys followed along with him. "My big brother flew off the mountain and stabbed the grizzly," he said. "Hey, hey, hey" they all chimed.

I saw my Noona and went and stood by her. "I am so happy and proud of you, Son!" she told me, putting a hand on my shoulder and pulling me closer to her. "I am very thankful to the Kolunsuten and the Mother Earth that they granted you protection today," she said in her soothing yet emotional voice.

My Sila and Checheya walked over to me wearing their finest clothes and adornments. Buckskin, fringe and seashells traded to us from tribes to the west decorated Checheya's dress. Her hair was gray, but her eyes were clear and bright. Like most of the old ladies, she was still a mountain climber in the huckleberry hills. She was still strong and steady.

Checheya couldn't even talk, she just moaned emotionally, "Ohhh, ohhh, ohhh," and gave me a big hug from way down deep. Sila put his hand upon my head. "All right, it's okay. It is good, now," he said.

I melted into the arms of my grandparents. Their nurturing was going somewhere into me, right where I needed it most.

All the people were still loud and excited as Peepa rode up to the center of camp. He sat tall and proud in the saddle. You would never know he was hurt. He turned his horse around several times and war whooped to the people. They yelled back to him and raised their right hands or a weapon to him. Some people blew their eagle whistles. It was the most colorful and glorious day I had ever seen. But, I felt a deep confusion and dissatisfaction.

Peepa ran his horse through the camp, periodically stopping quickly and whirling the horse around the other direction like he was pivoting for position in battle. He took out his bow and dramatically shot imaginary arrows here and there. "Owww, Yoww," he yelled. "My son flew through the air to kill the great grizzly! Great joy! Great day! Owww, Yowww," he hollered. He was a warrior and a veteran. He had the right to do this display.

He slowed his horse to a walk and then stopped in the center of camp. With obvious difficulty, he got off his horse and began to stagger.

"Oh my!" Noona gasped, "My husband is hurt!" She ran to him to help him. Uncle Center Feather caught him and Noona propped him from the other side to help him walk. She was worried and deeply upset, but she didn't cry because that would be bad luck, like mourning. Maybe things would get worse and crying inappropriately would be the sign by which things turned.

Rainbow Girl started to cry, but it was okay because she was a small child. Checheya picked her up and started to comfort her.

Keep your faith, say your prayers and then know everything would be all right, Sila always said. So Noona and Center Feather calmed themselves and tried to turn their attention to helping Peepa.

"My son, my son," Checheya said following over to help. She had to call him son to address him directly and to touch him. Mother-in-laws to son-in-laws and father-in-law to daughter-in-law rarely talked and never touched each other. So she called him son in order to help him.

"Drum," she called to my Sila, "get your herbs and things and some soft deerskin."

"I am fine. I'll be all right. Tomorrow we will finish the horses," Peepa assured everyone. All the people hollered back to him, "Hey, hey! Oww, Yowww!"

"Remember our great warrior, Buffalo Horn!" he shouted like a war cry. Everyone war cried back to him.

Buffalo Horn's sister and brother-in-law, and a few others had already left to take his body back to his home village and family.

What a sad day, I thought. Then, I looked at all the people in joyful celebration. I didn't understand. I felt like we all needed to be quiet and still. Clearly, it was a glorious day too, somehow.

My aunts helped to dress me in some new clothes and they fixed my hair in the style of a young man, not like a boy's. "There will be singing and dancing tonight, a feast, too," she said. "It is in your and your Peepa's honor. You must look your best."

By evening time all the food was nearly done and final preparations were underway, but some different hides were out upon the ground. Then my Peepa came out of the teepee with Center Feather and Noona by his side. He walked to the buffalo robe and sat upon it, and he motioned to me to come join him. I sat by him, on my knees like a strong young man.

Sila came out of his teepee carrying ceremonial bags with the long fringe, special markings and designs on them. In front of the buffalo hide where we sat was a deer hide, including the ears and tail with all the hair still on it. He put the deer hide on with the ears coming right over the top of his head. He placed some deer antlers upon his head that were laced with sage in two places. He took out his horn rattles and started to shake them.

"Kolunsuten, help me and sanction what I do here in your name for something good using your holy nature."

"Hey-ya, Hey-ya, ho-mowie ho . . . ." He sang the deer song three times. Then he called to the deer: "Great brother, you came to me as a young man. In a spiritual and mysterious way, you allowed me to know a small part of your good nature. You are kind and gentle. You are favored by the Kolunsuten and the Mother Earth, and you are powerful."

"Our son here was touched, struck by one of the great beasts of the animal kingdom of your world. Before he can be doctored physically, we must address what happened and the impact of it. The bear has a powerful nature and when the vicious part of it has turned on us, we will be hurt. Maybe a part of that vicious nature moved with the swing of his claws. We want and pray that this affect will be spiritually removed from my son-in-law so that he can get well."

Sila sang the deer song again three times.

"Great and holy spirits of nature," Sila called out in ceremonial prayer, "you came to me on the hilltop. You allowed me to call upon that great spark of life to use it to help my people. I call upon you now in deep need." Sila cried as he prayed. He was bearing his soul to the Creator and to the Great Beings of nature for his son-in-law.

"Help me now, I beg of you." He called out some words none of us could understand. Maybe it was the true names of the great Holy Beings of nature. A gentle thunder rolled around a nearby mountain peak.

It was getting dark, but you could see the mountain peaks like purple and charcoal shadows or ghosts.

The crackling fire popped to break the temporary silence. Even the smoke seemed to rise ever so slowly and mysteriously.

Sila put his hands out toward the thunder and then grabbed towards it very quickly and hard.

He went to Peepa and motioned his hands around him like he was pulling something off of him. Then he would motion to the fire like he was disposing of it. He repeated this three times, and he covered my Peepa's body from head to toe.

"Now, we can doctor the wound," he announced. "Our brother the deer and the holy nature took away the vicious spirit that touched upon my son-in-law." He called him son-in-law now because Checheya was all through cleaning and dressing the wound, and you could not doctor spiritually your own children.

"All these herbs and medicines have their own identity, their own spirit and their own Indian name. They have a song and a ceremony that goes along with them. You can't just pick them and use them," he explained.

He quietly sang a song and prayed as he applied a white powder derived from the white clay located at a special place. He said this was for the bleeding and it would stop now.

He had some other green and brown herbs, he sang their songs and called to them. He made three jagged marks on the ground, took three steps toward the east very quickly, and said some words of which we had no knowledge. He rubbed the herbs into Peepa's wounds and said these are to promote healing and fight infection.

"It will get well really fast," he said. "You will be amazed how fast."

We all knew to believe it that way. All the people agreed, "Hey, hey! Hmmmm," they all concurred.

"My grandson," he said to me, "use this incense from the blue spruce and the sweetgrass. Be thankful for your life. We are very proud of you," he said dropping it on the charcoals of the fire.

I used the smoke, motioned my hands toward it, and covered my body with it. Then, he took out a grizzly bear necklace and placed it around my neck. "Today, you are a man among the people." I felt so proud and humble at the same time. I couldn't help but think of Buffalo Horn, too.

To be a man, a boy in the rites of passage had to go to the mountain top three or four days to fast, pray and confirm his spirit helper. But, Sila announced that this day I was a man because nature had already tested me through the great bear.

"Many of us men know what you are feeling right now, Grandson," he counseled me. The horrors of war and battle are never made up for in honor or recognition.

"Some men cannot do it. None of us want to, except the crazy ones. Battle and fighting for life by itself is not glorious. But, the causes and purposes for which we fight are glorious and pure in intent: our people, our loved ones, and in this case, your very own Peepa."

I put my head down and cried.

"We find our comfort and strength again in finding what we have fought for has been preserved.

"May the Kolunsuten bless you, Grandson, Sun Boy, and your Peepa, my son-in-law."

I thought about my Peepa, the feelings I had before I jumped into the water. I looked at him enjoying the company of my Noona and younger brother and sister. "The greatest man in the world . . . ." I thought to myself.

"Gather around everyone," Sila ordered. "Take your seats."

"Before we eat, we must be thankful. Thankful for this food, this day, and our lives. We must be thankful for the lives of our relatives who fought with the great grizzly and killed it."

"Now, first and foremost, we must remember our good relative, Buffalo Horn — a truly mighty warrior. It seemed like nothing, no one, no enemy, no beast could ever defeat him. Yet, today he is gone.

"There are people of ours who are now in mourning, only just hearing about the loss of their son, their nephew, their brother, their father or their uncle. They are shedding tears tonight.

"Tomorrow, some of us will go to their village camps to pray and be with them as they return our great relative to nature and the Mother Earth.

"I will ask for silence and your good thoughts in memory of Buffalo Horn as I put the incense upon the charcoals."

He quietly said some words toward the Kolunsuten and burned the cedar and sweetgrasses. He paused as we all silently remembered Buffalo Horn.

I pictured him at his best, laughing and joking with Peepa. "Thank you, Uncle," I said in my mind.

I couldn't help but see him in the water, lifeless and gored. It startled me and I opened my eyes like waking from a bad dream. I looked around, but no one noticed my dilemma.

"Kolunsuten, bless our relatives in mourning . . . ," Sila continued as he dropped more incenses upon the charcoals of the fire. He paused again.

"Hey, Hey, Hey!" everyone agreed.

"But, also, we must remember our great brother, the yellow horse. Barely did we solidify the pact with him and he moved the only way he could to help save our people and protect us. First, away from the young boys, then over the cliff, and finally in the water to accept death that the people could live."

Sila had a deep wisdom, a ceremonial sense that always made him see things differently than the younger people. It seemed he always knew the whole of what was going on, even beneath the surface.

"The horse is a great brother to us. We must never forget it. Tomorrow, I will go to the place where he lost his life and in prayer and ceremony, leave tobacco for him. In spirit, he will be happy and fulfilled and we will continue a blessing because of him.

"And, we must be thankful for the great grizzly," he announced.

I didn't understand. Some of us looked at each other puzzled, but all the older people nodded their heads in agreement.

"The grizzly has made us stronger and more worthy to walk upon the road of life," he explained. "He has made my grandson to be a man this day. And, with the bear's ferocious touch doctored away, now the good medicine power of the grizzly is among us and we are at peace.

"We are reminded that this life, the land and all of nature do not belong to us. They belong to the Kolunsuten. We only get to use them for however long we are here, while taking great care to be mindful and harmonious with all of it."

"So we say these words of thanks and recognition today for all these things, and the lives of my son-in-law and grandson. Bless them, make them strong, protect them. Be a healing power to my son-in-law. With this food, we pray. Let it be so," he concluded.

Everyone ate according to the tradition. Toward the end of dinner, I got to tell the story of what happened, what I was thinking, how I dove off the cliff and stabbed the bear. Everyone cheered and celebrated each part, even though I didn't tell it well because I was shy, like most boys my age, and because I felt awkward, unworthy and confused.

Peepa talked, dramatically describing in detail everything about the bear, the horse and what we did. Some of the little children became afraid because he told it so well. Everyone was entertained and so excited. It was a spectacular evening, the first time I ever told a story and deed before all the people.

Relatives started to sing and dance and the celebration went on into the night.

I was sitting outside by a fire as festivities dwindled down to socializing and some singing. Most all the boys were gathered with me. Some of the little boys followed me around.

"Did you notice, Sun Boy?" Rock asked me in his silly voice. "The bear almost has no tail, just a little nub."

"Yeah . . . ." I told him, waiting for his point.

"Well, someone probably cut it off a long time ago. That's why they leave the people alone for the most part."

"Uncle says Coyote cut it off long ago, before there were even people," I explained to him.

"See!" Rock said confidently. "That's how you deal with these kind. You cut their tails off! Then, they leave you alone!"

All the boys laughed.

"Rock," I tried to interject.

"Yeah, yeah!" he interrupted. "That's how I'm going to deal with all enemies of the people. I'm going to cut their tails off!"

Rock made a motion like he had a knife and he was cutting something dramatically. He made a sound like he was cutting something juicy.

Just his goofy look and demeanor made everyone laugh.

It was a great night, a great day. I went to bed seeing it all again in my mind.

CHAPTER 4
Rites of Passage

Ordinarily, I may have waited several more years before going to the hilltop in the sacred mountains. But, because I participated in the killing of the great grizzly, I had the right to wear the claws around my neck. However, only a man could do this, not a boy!

Sila and Peepa said I must already be a man, for only a man could take the great bear; but, the formal ceremony had to be conducted anyway to pass into manhood.

What will a person really do when they are severely tested? When it is life and death at stake for you and your loved ones, will you call your bravery?

I felt different because of the experience with the bear, more settled and mature. I felt a new confidence. But, a brush with death makes a person not want to act foolishly either and take unnecessary chances with the one life you have.

Every day, my parents got me up early before daylight. I had to run and they talked to me and prayed with me along the way. Uncle Center Feather took the time to talk to me even though he said just a little. He was so quiet. Every word was measured and precisely accurate. He didn't waste talk at all.

"You must run, Nephew," he counseled as he ran alongside me. "Open your heart and your mind as you do it. Don't just run as a physical motion. Picture the bright spirituality of the early dawn, breathe it in and take it into your mind and body."

"Talk to the morning star, greet the new day, Nephew," he continued. By running, you will be made stronger. By thinking right, you will be made powerful."

We slowed to a walk and headed toward the sweat lodge made of willow saplings and covered with mats and hides. Four willows were stuck into the ground at each of the four directions to form a perfect circle. A pit was dug at the side of the door to put the hot lava rocks into.

"The rocks are nice and red," Peepa said almost as though describing a delectable meal after working hard all day. "We're going to have a good one!" he predicted with confidence.

My Sila was already inside the sweat lodge getting his things ready, cedars, tobaccos, sweetgrass, some deer hooves, a buffalo horn and other herbs.

"Come in, Grandson!" he called out to me.

I stripped down and entered, sitting right in the center facing the door and the east. The pit for the hot lava rocks was just inside the door and to the side.

Peepa sat beside me as Uncle Center Feather brought in the hot rocks using deer antlers as a shovel.

After the last of the twelve rocks was brought in, Uncle fixed the fire and entered the lodge, pulling the door closed behind him. Sila started to dip and pour the water back into the wooden bucket as he talked to it.

"Holy water, you are a powerful element of nature. You can make life itself come out of the land and for each and every one of us. You can give life, and you can take it. You have the power to cleanse, to cook foods and to make medicine. You are all these things, and in spirit, you are a medicine in your own right.

"The great spirits of the water are upon and within our great lake and streams. There are nations of beings who live among you, our brothers the fish and others."

"Be with us now," Sila offered and requested.

When you make medicine, you have to know the songs of the specific plant you are gathering and the ceremony that goes along with it. As you prepare it, you must talk to it about the purposes for which you will use it. If it is prepared with water, you stir it and dip it as Sila was doing with the plain water. He was making a medicine, a spiritual medicine.

"Grandson, the sweat lodge is a sacred place to us. It is a gift directly from the great Kolunsuten Creator himself. He put a holy spirit of his in it. Therefore, it is a holy being too, like the eagle or the morning star. It has the power to purify and set right a person's mind and life.

"The sweat lodge has his own songs that are to be sung here. First, I will sing one of these songs and pray for you as I meditate."

My Sila was elderly, but he was totally prayerful and ceremonial. He knew all the old stories and teachings. Sometimes, I thought maybe he even knew what people were thinking and why everything happened the way it did.

Even the grizzly bear attack, he understood it in a sense I never would have. He interpreted the magpies acting strangely and sent my Peepa to look for me that morning.

What else does he know? I'd better behave myself and think right, I concluded. My Sila might even know what I'm thinking.

He sang beautifully even in his old voice. My Peepa and Uncle joined in, singing with deep feeling and energy.

"Kolunsuten, by this holy lodge and ceremony, pity us and bless us.

"My grandson is preparing to go to the mountaintop to search for his spirit helper as he embarks on his journey into young manhood. This is something great and important to us, your Schi'tsu'umsh people.

To be a man, you must be a successful hunter and provider, a warrior, or a healer and teacher. In order to do any of these things, you need a spirit helper.

"Without one, a person may be relegated to a life of poverty and hardship. To gain this help, a boy must be disciplined and deemed worthy. My grandson is making these preparations to present himself to you and to your divine natures."

All the while he sang, he periodically poured water from the buffalo horn dipper on to the hot rocks. The water made a mysterious mild roaring sound as it instantly converted to steam.

"The great fire, the holy water, the divine air and the land, represented by the rocks, combine to make this holy medicine, the steam," Sila continued. "Bless my grandson with it. Make him strong, clear minded, cleansed in body and spirit. As he would breath it in with your divine air, help him."

He went on to address other aspects of nature and call upon it to help me. Much of this he said was so sacred, it had to remain secret, and so I have kept it to myself.

The sweat went on through its procedures, continuing three rounds. Three times, we entered and exited. After each round, we bathed in the river, asking the great water for its blessings and help in bringing me a spirit helper and to make me strong.

CHAPTER 5
Thunder Arrow

As we finished up and walked back toward camp, I noticed a pack of little girls being herded around by my Noona. Just like the boys, they got up early in the morning and ran. Then, they prayed by the river before they swam.

Noona was talking sternly to them. "You do these things so you will be strong, never lazy. Laziness is your worst enemy. It will make you suffer, maybe even starve!"

All the young girls were lined up, listening intently. Baby sister, Rainbow Girl, walked toward the girls, at first like she just woke up, then more alert and excited. She stood by her older sister, wanting to be a part of what was going on. People of the camp were noticing and pointing with big smiles at this scene of intense sweetness.

"You all need a Sumesh, a spirit helper, too. It will help you to gain things you need to live by. You will get this Sumesh by working hard, running, praying, swimming in the cold water every day!"

"Be strong, girls. The women are the foundation of the people. The home belongs to us. All the food of the home, even the meat the men bring, it belongs to us. We can dry it, store it or trade it as we see fit to take care of our homes."

"A woman can even live on her own with no husband if she has the power to gather, prepare and trade. Some single mothers are even wealthy because of their power to find foods and prepare them with ease, then trade for meat, hides and other goods."

Rainbow Girl studied our Noona while she talked. Baby Rainbow was so precious, with chubby little cheeks, shiny black eyes and her trusting, yet inquisitive look.

Noona made eye contact with her briefly and gave her a very subtle smile with her eyes. Rainbow got it though and smiled really big and grabbed hold of her big sister's leg.

"All right, girls," Noona said, concluding her lessons, "we will gather roots and some medicines today before you do anything else. Go get ready."

Everybody went off in groups of two or three to eat breakfast and get ready.

Rainbow and older sister, Berry Woman, saw me and headed in my direction. As usual, I twirled my baby sister around and growled.

"Let's go hunt grizzly bears!" I told her. "You can be my bait. Growl, growl." I teased.

"No, no," she squealed playfully knowing it was only a teasing game.

"Look what I have for you," I said, putting her down.

I handed her a little toy bow and arrow. She took it and right away knew what to do. She set the arrow on the string and pulled it back, closing the wrong eye.

She got a really determined look and expression and let go the string and the arrow. It went off in another direction where she wasn't even looking.

"Look out grizzly bears!" I said with a hint of amazement and approval. "Rainbow Girl has a bow and she's not afraid to use it!"

Berry Woman said they had to go. She was being prepared for her rights of passage as well. She was undergoing strict training, too, just like me.

She had to get up and run, pray, sweat and swim in the river. Then, she joined the other girls for their ritualistic training.

It was difficult, but we understood enough that we must obey our parents and elders in every way. Life could be harsh for us, but even more so for the weak and unprepared.

Older sister, Berry Woman, took Rainbow to our parents' teepee, ate a very little amount of food, and drank a small swallow of water. She sat and waited for whatever her next assignment or task might be.

Our Noona entered the teepee. "Quickly, daughter," she ordered, "Go to your Sila and Checheya. They have the next steps you must take, the things you must do to become a strong woman."

As she sat in our grandparents' teepee, waiting, they were very methodical with their movements gathering up bags and parfleches of folded hides with their precious belongings inside.

Checheya gave Berry Woman some root to chew on while she waited.

Finally, our Sila laid out some bundles in front of where he sat. He unfolded one in particular. Inside was an old arrow. He took it out and held it delicately, studying it and then moving it strongly about himself.

"This is a sacred medicine arrow, Granddaughter," he explained. "You will take this arrow over the big hill to a special place, the marsh where the great Grandmother Loon lives."

The arrow was definitely a spiritual instrument of some kind. It was painted red and black with yellow stripes spaced evenly about the tail end of the shaft.

"These are the colors of the Thunder Beings, and the arrow is their instrument," Sila explained. "For many, many years, I have kept this. As a young boy, the Thunders came to visit me on the hilltop. I heard a voice speak to me. I turned and looked, and it was the loon. She is called our grandmother.

"The spirit loon is related to the great Thunderbird. These feathers on the shaft are from this sacred bird, and the small piece of leather tied around the arrowhead also contains an offering of tobacco to this grandmother, and to the Thunderbird."

"We are told to use this arrow only for a purpose of great need, maybe just once or twice in a lifetime! In my life, I have never used it, except to pray, and renew it at the winter dances.

"I want you to take it to the marsh, the swampy part of the lake where it will be returned to nature. It is my prayer that maybe one of my granddaughters will pick it up again one day, in spirit, and it will help and protect them."

He handed it to Berry Woman very gently, like he was handling a sacred pipe or bundle.

"You must go now, Granddaughter," he urged her. "Do not leave it undone. Do not stop and play in the woods or at the water. You must do exactly as I have told you, or else you and my other granddaughters will miss this great spirit helper."

Berry Woman accepted her charge and walked off over the hill toward the trail that led to the marsh.

Sila continued to talk, and no one noticed that little Rainbow Girl followed after her big sister. She stayed just a little way behind. Big sister was so intent on holding the arrow and fulfilling her mission, she didn't think to observe around her and notice Rainbow Girl. She was so dainty, carrying her little bow and arrow, occasionally running to keep up.

Away she walked, further and further down the trail, over small hills and across meadows. Rainbow Girl was afraid, but didn't cry. She struggled to keep up.

Over and over, grown-ups warned about wandering off. Still, sooner or later, they were searching for a lost child. She should not have followed her sister.

As Berry Woman approached the marshy area, she scanned for a place to put the arrow. Straight ahead, there was an open place in the shallow water, and then some reeds and grasses growing up. She would wade out and leave the arrow there.

At the waters edge she offered a few words.

"Um . . . um . . . my Sila already prayed about this. He told me to leave the sacred arrow here for Grandmother Loon, the bird that lives here. So, this I do, as I am told," she concluded, walking into the shallow water.

Very gently, she slipped the arrow into the reeds and let it slide out of her hand. She watched it float between the grasses. Slowly, she turned and walked back toward the shore.

Rainbow Girl stood on the trail, holding her toy bow and arrow, smiling as big as the lake at her sister. Suddenly, an enemy charged out of the bushes and grabbed Berry Woman, holding her up over his shoulder hollering and laughing. Another enemy stood up. It was the Chop Faces.

Big sister was terrified! She was a captive. They might steal her and take her to their homeland, or they might kill her!

Poor Baby Rainbow Girl! She'd only heard about the enemy in stories. She started to cry.

They carried Berry Woman away from the shore out of Rainbow Girl's view, but she had nowhere to go. She was lost without her big sister.

She followed the trail down by the water over to the small knoll where the enemy carried Berry Woman. She peered over the top, still holding her little bow.

They were tormenting her big sister pushing her back and forth between them and laughing loudly. Her instincts were to hide. She scurried back down the little mound.

Perhaps they would both be captured and killed. It was a dangerous, life-threatening situation. Still, when a young boy or girl is sent to seek spirit helpers, they must go alone.

As Rainbow sat and cried, she looked at the water where Berry Woman put the sacred arrow.

Suddenly, a loon with a jet-black coat and brilliant ring around its neck swam out from the reeds. As it swam away, in its wake floated the great arrow.

Rainbow, just a tiny little girl, looked at the arrow, then at her little bow, then again at the arrow. She got up, walked to the waters edge.

A woman's voice said to her, "Get the arrow little girl. You know what to do."

Rainbow looked around, and she saw the loon skimming across the top of the lake as it swam swiftly around.

She took baby steps into the water, and the arrow somehow floated toward her. Slowly, she grabbed it.

The enemy toyed with Berry Woman in a bully game. She was just a young girl herself, only preparing for womanhood.

As one enemy held her down with his foot, the other talked about what they would do.

One of them had painted his face all black and wore raven feathers. He looked evil. The other was a little chubby and wore black and white lines on his face.

"Maybe we should keep her and bring her home," the evil one speculated.

"We came after horses and maybe a scalp or two," the other countered. "She will only get in our way," the other countered.

"Well, then, if we can't keep her, let's rape her!" the evil one said boldly. "Then, we will kill her."

The other one laughed and shook his head.

Berry Woman cried and pleaded, helplessly.

At the camp, Noona was calling for Rainbow Girl.

"Rainbow Girl! Rainbow Girl!" she shouted. "Has anyone seen my baby girl?" she asked everyone.

"She must have followed her sister," she surmised.

"Husband, our baby girl followed her sister toward the marsh. Please find her!"

My Peepa took off running and I followed with some of the other men. They took different routes just in case she was lost and wandering.

I ran my fastest, but I could not keep up with my Peepa yet.

Rainbow looked at the sacred arrow, then back at her bow and tiny arrow again. An idea started to take shape. She walked down to the waters edge and slowly grabbed the thunder arrow then climbed back up the knoll.

She put down the sacred arrow and grabbed her toy arrow that didn't even have an arrowhead. Like a little girl, she clumsily bound the arrow on the bow and string. With a scared and desperate look, she pulled back the string. She raised herself up to shoot over the knoll and let go the arrow.

"Twang!" It went off straight to the side and down.

The evil one pinned down Berry Woman and peered into her face. He tore at her dress. He put a knife to her throat.

"Help me, help me, Peepa." her scream was now high pitched, frantic and crazy scared. Then, it went to a moan.

Berry Woman couldn't help but think of her Peepa and Noona. Whatever had happened in the past, they were always there to help and protect her. Whether she just fell down and got hurt, sick or lost in the woods, they were there.

Surely, they would come to save her. But where were they?

"Peepa! Noona! Help me! Help me!" she shouted in desperate crying.

Then she went quiet again and moaned, "Where are you Peepa? Why won't you come?"

Peepa was running as fast as he could, but he was still a good distance away!

Rainbow looked at the sacred arrow and picked it up. She looked out to the water and the loon still swam around, looking at her.

She loaded the arrow, rose up over the knoll and fired it with her little toy bow. The arrow sailed upward, slowly, almost floating.

It was a clear nice day earlier, but some clouds had rolled in as the arrow was placed in the water.

Rainbow Girl followed the arrow in flight, moving up into the blue sky and the rolling clouds.

As it reached its peak, a strong thunder clapped and exploded, then rolled across the sky.

The enemies looked around, then upward. The arrow struck the ground and stood upright right near them.

They moved away from Berry Woman. She quickly ran away.

"Where are they? Where are they?" the evil one repeated with fear in his voice.

"Let's leave this place," the other pleaded.

They nervously scurried across the meadow to where they had horses, and they rode away.

As they disappeared, Peepa showed up.

"Rainbow, Berry Woman," he called.

"Peepa," Berry Woman answered, "Peepa, you saved me."

"What has happened? What is it," Peepa quizzed.

"The enemy came and captured me, but your arrow saved me."

"What arrow? What enemy?"

Rainbow Girl made her way toward us now. "Peepa, Peepa." she shouted in her baby, little girl voice, like she does when he's been gone a long time and she is glad to see him.

He picked her up. "Baby girl, we were looking for you."

"Peepa, Peepa," she said all excitedly, "the men came and hurt Berry Woman, so I shot them with the bird arrow!"

"What bird, what arrow, shot who?" he asked.

Uncle Center Feather arrived on the scene. "There were two enemies here, brother," he explained. "They struggled here and ran off that way, where they probably had their horses."

"They stole me, Peepa," Berry Woman explained. "Then the thunder cracked and rolled, and an arrow hit the ground by us, then the enemy ran off."

Uncle Center Feather reached toward the arrow, but stopped short of grabbing it. "Here it is, brother. But it is not for me to touch."

"I shot it at the bad men, Peepa," Rainbow explained in her little girl voice.

Peepa looked at her in disbelief. But there was no other explanation.

"Shall we go after the enemy?" Uncle Center Feather asked my Peepa.

Peepa seemed dazed. After a long pause he said, "No, we will take the children home. We will get the enemy some other time."

Peepa had Berry Woman get the arrow, because she was the one who brought it to this place, and she's the one who was saved by it. She would bring it back to our Sila. He's the one who had the thunder power. He would explain what to do, and what had happened.

Another dinner was prepared. Offerings of prayer, tobacco and food were made. Then, Sila began to talk to us.

"A long time ago, the people were saved by the thunder beings. A man who had this power kept two arrows painted this same way. Red and black with some yellow on it. He kept them high up on a teepee pole in his lodge. Rarely and almost never did he take them down.

"One day when the enemy surrounded the camp in overwhelming numbers, taunting and bragging that they would kill everyone, he took out the arrows.

"He shot one up into the sky toward the enemy. The thunder rolled. He said it was the Thunder Beings coming to see what he wanted.

"He talked to the Thunders about the situation as he fired the second arrow. As it flew toward the enemy, thunder cracked and lightning struck some of the enemy. The others all rode off."

Sila paused to let the story sink into our minds.

"So, children and grandchildren, this sacred arrow was shot into the air in a time of great need, and the Thunders responded.

"We put it back in nature with an offering to the grandmother loon, that maybe one day it would return to one of my granddaughters as a protection and a spirit helper.

"It has come to granddaughter Rainbow Girl. Someday, it will be her power to use as she is able. The loon brought it to her."

Rainbow Girl looked so proud of herself. Never did I see her sitting so still and listening so intently. She knew exactly what was going on, and that everything Sila said was true.

"The bird gave me the arrow, Noona," she explained again.

"Hm-mm, yeah," Noona answered in that high pitched voice used for talking to babies and very little children. She patted her on the top of her head.

Sila continued, "Granddaughter, Rainbow Girl, this arrow belongs to you. I will put it away and keep it for you until you are older. Then, you must keep it in your lodge alongside a teepee pole."

Older people always said you should talk to babies and small children like they were adults too. They could understand.

Rainbow stepped forward toward Sila and put her hand out for the arrow. Everyone looked at her and Sila. He paused and handed it to her.

"Hold it gently, little Rainbow," he cautioned her.

She smiled and held it proudly, knowing she had the most precious gift in all the world. She looked down the shaft of the arrow. She motioned as if she was holding a bow, loading an arrow and pulling it back. She closed one eye and motioned like the arrow was launched upward into the sky. She made a gurgly, deep noise, and moved her hands and fingers up like rain was falling.

Then, she simply said, "Go on, bad men, Chop Faces." She briefly held a scowly look as she said it.

Everybody laughed and said "Good, good. Hey, hey."

She had told the story of what had happened which was our tradition. She didn't even have to be told. She knew already.

"From time to time we will take the arrow out and pray for my granddaughter. One day, she will be in charge of it herself, and she will pray with it," Sila concluded.

Everyone ate and visited until dark.

As I got quieter and more thoughtful, I wondered, where is the enemy? Will I run into him again? Will Rainbow Girl and Berry Woman be affected by him in the future?

Oh, well. It was a good day, as it turned out. The Kolunsuten's plan was fulfilled, and it doesn't always just come easy or for free. It comes with a sacrifice.

I heard some of the adults say they would do ceremonial prayers for the girls so they would never be affected negatively by their trauma.

"I hope no one is ever mean to my girls ever again," Noona said holding and rocking them.

Rock came over and sat by me in his usual rough but likeable way. He moved around me back and forth like he was trying to make himself comfortable.

Rock looked at me like I knew what he would say and was waiting for an answer.

"I asked my Peepa," I said. "The enemy do not have tails."

"Shhh." Rock cautioned. "Some day, I'm going to show you. Then they will never be back to bother us in our lifetimes."

"Okay, brother-friend," I gave in to him. "Whatever you say."

My Sila got up to do more storytelling.

"Attention everyone, listen to your Sila," my Noona ordered.

"In the time of the ancient ones, the people who were here first, before they were changed into the animals and other things of nature, sacred and powerful things happened," my Sila began in his old, but animated story-telling voice. You could tell he was beginning a serious legend of our history.

> *In the ancient times, when the animals were people, like us, but they had great, great powers, some of the women were gathering roots on the prairie. Thunder was known in those times to sometimes kill people. He came and killed some of those women.*
>
> *Their five brothers were deeply angered and they vowed to fight Thunder and kill him. They went to this place on the prairie he would often be and they fought him, one brother at a time. When one brother was nearly overcome or fatigued, the next would take over and fight.*
>
> *The battle went on for days.*
>
> *Finally, Thunder pulled back totally fatigued and said, "All right, let's not fight anymore. There are human beings coming and all the world will change. If you let me live, I will change you into human beings and you will become a part of the Schi'tsu'umsh people.*
>
> *I will take care of you. When you go into battle, tell me. Sing the thunder song and I will protect you. No harm will come to you.*
>
> *These ancient ones agreed and became human beings, and part of our tribe."*
>
> *"That's the end of the trail."*

"Hey! Hey!" everyone said in agreement.

"Different ones of the ancients became part of the Schi'tsu'umsh. They brought with them the knowledge of the ancient times. They had our names in addition to their type of being. Some of those names are still carried on and used today by our people.

"That is why, we say we too are brother to the animals, and we are one with nature.

"That is why we make offering and talk to the four thunders. There is a certain way to do this known only to the descendants of these ancient ones.

"And, this is why we have and use a thunder arrow. Some of us here, all my children and grandchildren and all my descendants forever, we are related, too, to the people of thunder, and therefore to the thunder itself!

"Know this, Grandchildren. Someday, the thunder will move again to help and protect you when you need it most."

He sat down.

"Hey, hey, hmmm," everyone reverently agreed.

CHAPTER 6

Four Seasons of Nature, Four Stages of Life

Like a big circle, our country extended many miles to the east across the mountains[1] over to the Salish country; to the north, all the way to the big lake[2]; to the west all the way to the great falls[3] which is the border to the country of our brothers, the Spokanes; and from there to the south all the way down to our Ni-mee-poo (Nez Perce) brothers[4].

It is a big country. We called it ours but sometimes the elders or chiefs would correct us. It was not ours to own, but ours to care for. It felt right. It all felt like home.

Within this big circle that was our country, the nature was different. We had plenty of forest, natural open meadow, free flowing waters

[1] The Bitterroot mountains just across the Idaho border into Montana

[2] Lake Pend Oreille, North Idaho near the Canadian Border

[3] At what is now Spokane Falls at Spokane, Washington

[4] At Marsh Hill near what is now Moscow, Idaho

and lakes, both big and small. Mountainous areas were snow covered until summer.

Some areas were rocky, big rocks, like an ancient giant scattered them about here and there. Some meadows were smooth with grassy fields. Timbered evergreen forests were only a short distance away.

Pockets of hardwood trees like cottonwood and ash grew around the low, wetter areas.

It was truly stunning. Our homelands evoked deep and inspiring feelings in me, and in all of us.

And, there was the lake at the mouth of the river where we built some of our winter camps. The sun was lower in the sky toward late autumn. Occasionally, it peaked out of the sky from behind fast moving clouds. It made beams of light, like a fan, appear in the sky, and then disappear.

My Peepa noticed me gazing at the wonder of the natural day. "It is good, Son," he sighed standing next to me looking out in the same direction across the lake. "It is home, but so very much more, too."

"We feel its life, and it knows us," he continued. "It has been reserved, and it has reserved itself, for us and all else the Creator, Kolunsuten, has made within it. The spirit of the forest, it is a face that moves across the woodlands and the meadows. No one else can really know it like those of us who live with it and by it day after day.

"The mountains and the lakes, they are a part of us. Of all the tribes around us, we are the only lake people. The rest are all river people. But we know the origins of the great water and the power of the holy water spirits. It is the mountain snows that feed the lakes that flow into all the rivers to our west. These eventually feed into the big salt water, the ocean."

"Yes," I heard my Sila join in the conversation in his elderly voice as he walked up to us. "It feels like us, like we do. The country is alive. It knows us. It is related to us. It is our Noona, our mother. It is our family. It is our belonging."

"Father-in-law," Peepa called to him. "Tell your grandson about some of the invaders who came to our land."

"Over the years," Sila began. "Many, many, generations ago, different kinds of people tried to come to our land and take it. One such group came from the north. They were first sighted camped by the big lake in the north, on our land! There were hundreds of them. Men, women, children, elderly, a large tribe.

"Immediately, riders and warriors were dispatched. Our scouts examined and evaluated the situation. They were dug in and prepared for war. We attacked.

"A furious battle ensued and continued for days. Eventually, they picked-up camp in a break of the fighting and departed to the east. Our riders rode up to them to chase them out. In sign language, they said they were leaving. They looked pitiful and poor, like they were wandering with nowhere to go. No more were killed. They were followed across the mountains where they turned south again."

"Did we turn away every intruder that ever came here?" I asked.

"Yes!" Peepa and Sila said at the same time, and then chuckled.

"Every one of them." Peepa said with confidence and commitment. "And no one, no one will ever come here and take our lands. We will run them out," he said loudly.

"Ayyy! Ayyy! Oww! Oww!" My Sila war-cried like a young warrior.

"Hey-yah! Hey-yah!" I said joining in, as everyone chuckled. Peepa grabbed my shoulder and gently pressed.

Even in my young years, I began to understand bits and pieces of our life and what it really meant to be Schi'tsu'umsh.

It really was our land, and we were its children. It did not belong to us. Rather, we belonged to it, as did all our brothers of the forest, the animal kingdom. We were all one and connected.

When we went to visit neighboring tribes, the country changed and the feeling was different.

Whenever we returned to our homeland, we could feel the land aware of us and become one with us.

I looked down toward the water of the lake. Sunbeams came out between the clouds and brightly reflected off the water. The wind blew ripples across the top of the water making the sun's reflecting glare dance. I thought I could hear drums and a distant song in the wind. Maybe the ancient ones are dancing in the sunbeams across the water, I wondered.

The great rocks of granite and the natural beach looked like too much fun to pass up. I ran to jump and climb. I could smell the sweet, fresh scent of fir trees and spruce permeating the air.

As I ran I scooped up a straight long stick that was like a spear, then ran and jumped up on a big rock and hopped over to the other side, and down to the beach. I ran one direction, then the other, holding my spear up ready to throw it.

Up a ways from the shore, the grasses were long, golden brown and dried. I could feel my hand brush by the tops like a gentle scratching. I darted around the evergreen trees and gazed up at them. Pine needles in bunches swayed in the wind with dried brown ones falling to the ground with every gust.

As I ran back toward the water I could hear the drum again from the water and I could see the sun's reflection dancing across the water.

"It's running with me," I thought. I looked toward it as I ran along the edge, holding my spear up to it. The sun and the moon followed me, moving whenever I did. These beams actually seemed to follow me.

"Cha, cha, cha," I heard the great eagle scream above me. I stopped and looked. It was a golden eagle. It dived, then turned up again using the wind to ascend. At the bottom of its dive, it yelled, "Cha, cha, cha."

It hovered in the wind as if to acknowledge me, then dipped its wing, banking to the left and glided off.

I watched the water and the sunbeams for a while, but clouds covered the sun again and then they were gone.

From this cliff, I looked all around at the majestic beauty that was mine, at least mine to behold and be a part of. The sky was a bright and pure blue with the snow white clouds running across it.

The mountains to the east already had snow on them. They stood there, like a guard watching over all the land surrounding them. It is where the Thunder dwelled. My Sila said to always turn toward the nearest high mountain when you pray. This is where the Kolunsuten will be. They are sacred places. When we prayed toward the mountains or the sun, we addressed the Creator as Amotken, the one seated at the top.

I looked at the snow-covered peak. I said nothing, but I had a deep feeling that I didn't know how to express, so I just raised my hand towards the mountain. How do you say in words what are the deepest feeling of the heart? Sing your songs, that's what we're told.

The clouds seemed to gather around the top. Sila said the trees call for the rain. The Thunderbird hears them and sends his children, Cloud and Rain.

Suddenly, I remembered Peepa. I was supposed to be helping him with the winter lodge. I ran back toward camp.

"Anchor the mat below it first," Peepa shouted out orders. "They must overlap to keep us warm and dry all winter," he explained.

We were putting the finishing touches on our winter lodge, a big teepee-like structure but with a pole at the top horizontally connecting two teepees together, and holding additional poles framing a wall on each side between the two semicircles.

It was big enough that as many as seven or eight could live there comfortably so my Checheya and Sila would live with us during the winter. Also, from time to time, some of my cousins would stay all night.

The brisk wind blew the tule reed mat around as we tried to tie it to the poles with leather strings. "The nature is lively today!" Peepa exclaimed, smiling as he wrestled the mat back down.

The wind definitely had a new cold to it. We were moving to our winter camps right on time.

My Noona was gathering wood with my sisters and Checheya. They would build a woodpile that would be used only in the very extreme weather when it was impossible to go out for it, because the snow was too deep or when the cold was overpowering. However, that weather was still perhaps one or two moons away. Otherwise, they would go out every day, early in the morning and get wood for that day.

"Are your arrows ready, Son? And what about your new bow? You're going to do some of the shooting this year," my Peepa reminded me.

"Yes, Peepa. I'm ready. Let's go now!" I said with joking urgency.

"In the morning, Son . . . first thing in the morning," he said like it was almost time.

This time of year, we had the last big hunt. This hunt was for our brother, the deer. We hunted off and on all year for fresh game to supplement dried meat, but this was the big hunt we did once a year in late fall.

We used our dogs to run big herds of deer down the draws into confined but open areas. Where there might be spaces where the deer would be able to turn and run off into a different direction and get away, we lined them with old clothes and moccasins that were strong with the scent of man. This would turn the deer the way we wanted them to go.

The deer were plentiful, running in herds numbering in the hundreds. Sometimes, in the winter, we would come across herds of more than a thousand.

We only wanted several dozen to add to our meat supplies and get hides for our clothing, teepee covers and bags.

The next day we went out and had everything ready. The dogs were anxious. They knew what to do, and they knew what was happening next.

I patted my favorite dog on the head. "You're a good dog," I told him. It gave him a happy and proud look. Like horses, they could understand you.

"Friend dog, you are good help to the family. You always watch our door for us and let us know if anyone is approaching, human or non-human. Now, you're going to help us some more."

He barked a happy bark and darted around like he was saying, "Let's go, let's go."

He wasn't very big, but he had a big heart. He was fearless, even though he didn't look it with his bushy, light brown coat on his scrawny frame.

I played with him for a short while. I thought about the stories how the dog came to be with the people.

Way back as the Creator, Kolunsuten, was making everything ready for the coming of man, He had a meeting with all the animals. Everyone agreed they would accept helping man in some way, except the owl, but that's another story.

Some would give their flesh that man could live. Some of the birds said they would lend their feathers and their great spiritual strength to use when man really needed it. Others said they would let man use their powers to doctor, heal or protect.

However, when Dog's turn came to commit, he said, "I will stay with man and help him. I will watch his door and protect him. I will be loyal and helpful to him always. I will never turn against him."

"No," the Kolunsuten said, "It cannot be. The animal domain and the realm of man are separated. It will not work."

"It's all right," said Dog. "Whatever it takes, I will do it. I will be the one to do this for man."

The Kolunsuten thought about it. "There is only one way this can be done," He said. "For you to be able to live with man, you may be called to give up your own life for him. If some threat or danger were coming to befall him, you must take it. Many times, when death, sickness or injury is coming for a member of the home you are a part of, you must take it and you will die for that family member."

Dog pondered this a few moments. "Yes," he decided. "I will do it."

"Then, it is done," the Creator decreed.

That is why dogs are always glad to be among us.

As Sila walked by all the excitement of final preparations, I asked him, "Why did Dog decide to be among people when he could run free like the wolf and coyote?"

"Not many people know the answer to that," Sila said seriously. "But, I'll tell you."

"Maybe the dog knew that the Kolunsuten loved man just a little bit more than the animals," he explained. "He is the only one of all the animals who knows this. By helping man in this way, Dog may receive blessings unknown to the other four-legged animals.

"But it is a sacred pact the dog has made, that is why we must never beat him or even just kick him out of the way.

"People who are mean to dogs have bad luck," Sila explained.

Sila always said to let the little children keep a pet puppy to raise and be close to. In this way, people will understand that animals, all animals, have feelings, just like we do. Where there is a heart, there is a spirit, where there is a spirit, there are deep feelings.

It was another simple truth to me.

CHAPTER 7
The Kolunsuten's Blessing

We were all in position. Uncles and Sila would let the dogs go down three different draws that all led to one bushy meadow. In the brush and on small trees were some of our clothing to turn the deer down the narrow passage that ended at a granite wall on one side. On the other side, we would be camouflaged in the brush and the grass. We would stand just as they approached and turn them toward the rocky wall where they had no way to escape, the dogs blocking the way they had come from, the hunters blocking another, and nothing but a curved rock wall in front of them.

I could hear the dogs on the run, barking loudly. They were coming. The deer would be a good distance ahead of the dogs. I went still. My heart pounded with excitement.

I could hear the sound of bushes rattling and snapping. Something big was coming. And plenty of them.

The first bunch rounded the corner. Some of my cousins hiding farther back stood up. The herd turned toward the rock wall; another bunch followed, then another. They ran about nervously, maybe forty of them.

It looked a good mix of bucks and does. A few really big bucks were included in the herd.

Peepa rose up on one knee from a clump of bushes. "Do not shoot the big buck," he said. "This is his herd he has brought to us," he explained while drawing back his arrow.

That was our sign to go ahead and fire away.

"Wssht, wssht," the sound of the arrows letting go filled the air.

I dropped one, and then another. Peepa got several more.

One mid-sized buck was looking right at me. Just as I fired the arrow, he jumped and moved. I missed. I looked at him in disbelief.

Some of the other hunters shot at him. The same result.

I heard my Peepa laugh. "You boys better let that one go," he said. "It's not his time. Someday, he will be the leader of this herd."

We let the rest escape. We had about 30 deer for our big family band.

I was so excited. My heart was pounding. I wanted to yell out, but I knew we had to be reverent and respectful to the deer. I felt strong and proud because for a boy to run free with nature and hunt our food for the winter was pure happiness. No one would ever take this strength and pride from our people or me. I knew it.

I looked around at my relatives. The younger boys were starting to show up, running excitedly. Some of the women were right behind, including my Noona.

Noticing my Noona, I couldn't help but look at my moccasins and the design of the deer hoof inside an arrowhead. I had been prepared for these times since birth.

The women were walking fast and talking excitedly. "Sun Boy, you did good," my Noona greeted me. "The Kolunsuten has blessed us again. Thank you Kolunsuten," she said looking upwards.

"And thank you for our hunters," she added, smiling at me with that approving smile that made me feel like I could do anything.

As usual, my Peepa said a prayer to give thanks for our brother the deer. Then, we began skinning and quartering.

There is a certain way, a specific order to skin and quarter a deer. If you broke from this order, you might have bad luck hunting or elsewhere in your life. This was one of the respects we had to follow that was passed down to us from generations gone by.

After the deer was skinned, it was cut into seven different pieces, in order: the quarters, front left first, then the hindquarter, left first, followed by the right quarters. Then, the two rib sections and back, and finally the neck. The women gathered up the guts, the heart, the liver, the tongues and some of the brains to be used for tanning hides. Nothing was wasted. The head was not just thrown carelessly on the ground for the dogs. It was put in a tree, but the eyes were removed and buried so that birds could not just peck them out.

Some of the boys, my cousins showed up with horses. We would pack most of the quartered deer back on horses.

After the deer were gutted and bled, some of the boys carried them the old way by cutting through the skin between the hamstring tendon and the muscle on the hindquarters and running the front legs each through this hole. Then they picked up the deer and put it on like a backpack with the head hanging down. They would cut it up into seven pieces back at the camp.

Back at the camp, fires were already burning. This meat would be smoke dried. The smoke helped cure and preserve the meat, compared to sun drying. Smoking the meat had a better rate of preservation through the long winters.

That night, we had a feast. It was the last feast for the foods. It was a thanksgiving. The last of our native roots had just been gathered, the water potato. It grows in the shallow waters around our lake and has a leaf that looks like an arrowhead. That's how we know where they are. The last of the meat was harvested, dried and put away for the winter. Firewood was gathered. Shelter was prepared.

The Old Man in the North waits for no one, my Sila always said. You must be prepared or perish.

So, we prayed our thanksgiving, and we danced our food and water dance while men sang the prayer and thanksgiving song to the beat of a drum. It was a happy and fulfilling feeling to know we were ready for winter.

CHAPTER 8
Nature's Blanket

The days got shorter and shorter, and colder and colder. The snows had come and covered the earth.

"The Mother Earth has been covered in a white blanket while parts of nature will rest. But she is preparing even now to greet us in the spring with new life and our native foods again," Sila always said.

"You must always try to make it to the spring time," Sila said, too. "No matter what burdens befall you, no matter your trials and tribulation, make it to that next spring and everything will get better."

I thought about these things as the men of my family prepared to jump into the cold water. My Peepa and Sila were praying by the bank of the creek.

We were preparing for our winter medicine dances, the most important of all our ceremonies. They were all important and everything we did ceremonially was sacred. But this was something in which everybody participated.

Also, it was a time to take care of your Sumesh, your spirit medicine power. By dancing and singing, you expressed your thanksgiving and respect. By giving away material things or feeding people by a feast, you made an offering to the Sumesh spirit. Very, very sacred it is . . . and deeply ceremonial. It gets to the root of our very identity, our traditional beginnings and our relation to the nature around us. It is about being a Schi'tsu'umsh person.

We stood on the bank of a nearby creek preparing to seek our cleansing and purification in preparation of our medicine dances.

"As we enter the sacred water, we pray to you first, our great Creator, Kolunsuten," my Peepa prayed. "Before we use any part of your great nature, we always pray to you about it that you would sanction what we do.

"Bless us as we prepare our hearts and minds for our winter medicine dances. We sweat and we cleanse, sometimes we fast without food or water, and we enter your sacred running water looking for your purification and cleansing. Bless us and make it this way for us."

He put tobacco upon the bank, and extended his hand dropping some right into the water. He dropped his robe. We all did the same, and walked into the stream about waist deep and knelt down.

The weather was cold. A light snow fell, but not much. Peepa said it was too cold to snow hard. There was ice on the edges of the creek.

I didn't mind. It was something I had done now hundreds of times. It's just a state of mind. It is cold, but it does not hurt you in any way. It isn't suffering. Actually, the water was warmer than the air.

All the men continued to pray out loud even in the water. Some prayed silently or meditated.

My Sila prayed about his intentions in the winter dances. It was all about Rainbow Girl and the Thunder Arrow. He wanted to acknowledge it, respect and pass it on to her spiritually, even though it had already been given to her physically.

Others prayed about the coming year, hunting, protection in battle, or their loved ones.

I sat in the water and closed my eyes, leaning my head back. The pine trees were snow and ice covered with parts of the green showing. The clouds were a light gray color, and the ground was completely covered in white snow.

The country around the lake was magnificent. As beautiful as it was all the other times of the year when I was sure there was nothing prettier in the entire world, every winter I felt, now it was the most beautiful.

Each winter, hundreds, perhaps thousands of eagles came to the lake to feed. From the creek, I could see six eagles in the sky soaring about.

I closed my eyes. I felt like the nature moved or shook. I opened my eyes.

The nature, the winter season, the spirit of the forest, it all seemed alive. The evergreen trees looked like people holding their arms out and down. Snow covered their shoulders.

A low flying eagle passed overhead looking intently back and forth through the forest. He was the guardian of the land, the protector against evil. Should he ever disappear or cease to exist, the land and all upon it would perish.

The water cleansed me. Whatever I thought, I could envision it. My mind was clear.

Some of the boys were getting out of the water. I made my way to the bank.

Now, it was cold! I wiped off with a soft deer hide someone passed to me and wrapped an elk skin hide around me, and put on my winter moccasins.

In the winter, all the people gathered at the various winter camps. It was easy to call big groups together for the religious dances.

However, the primary reason they were conducted in the winter was because that's when they were supposed to be done. Some ceremonies were meant to be done in the daytime, some at night, some in the summer, and some in the winter. This particular kind had to be done in the winter — when the blue jay frequented the camp areas. And, it was an all night ceremony. It was always finished with three morning songs as everyone faced the east and the holy dawn.

My Sila wanted to call everyone together to give his thanks to the Thunder Beings for the miracle of the thunder arrow and Rainbow Girl, and for the great grizzly my Peepa and I fought and killed.

At the camp, the ceremonial lodge was erected and visitors were beginning to arrive. My Noona and others had food ready and offered them a meal as they finished their greetings.

After dark, everyone was ready. The medicine man arrived. Stone Man was his name. Many powers did he possess and many wonders did he work among the people. Sick, even dying people were made well by his prayers and ceremonial understandings.

At these dances, he used the power of the blue jay to see pieces of the future so we would know were to go, how to find game and how to avoid the enemy as much as possible.

The dances continued on for several days. My Noona and others were tireless in their cooking and accommodating guests. She did this with a good feeling for people and a belief that the foods and the spirit of hospitality would bless her home, her husband and her children.

It would make her husband and her sons good hunters; her root and berry gathering could be good and plentiful. The dried foods would preserve without going bad. Her loved ones would never go without food and water.

As usual, the medicine dances were done with the greatest degrees of respect, sincerity and reverence. Goodness and kindness were the ways of the spirit, and the guiding force to get to them.

The medicine dances were attended by both men and women equally. We expressed our deepest feelings through song and dance. The various spirit helpers were called upon, recognized and addressed. Honesty and humility were essential ingredients. Anything else might cause a person to be hurt or killed.

It was cold outside, bitter cold. But we went from one season to the next without question, without complaint.

Winter was supposed to act like winter. Summer was supposed to act like summer. When they didn't, there was a basic disharmony between man and nature, and it needed to be addressed ceremonially.

So, the winter was a blessing, a great blessing, and it was beautiful. It brought us the winter dances that reinvigorated and renewed the people. It blanketed and covered our Mother Earth.

In late winter, we begin to get tired of staying inside. Everyone stays busy, working full-time cutting, tanning, sewing, making and shaping arrowheads.

From time to time, I could go out and hunt to supplement the dried meat. But we were unable to go far. The weather had been warmer and the snow was melting in all the lower valleys. It gave me hope.

When I first saw the open ground again, I felt excited and happy.

Certain stories are only told in the wintertime. Sila announced he would tell his last winter story this night.

After dinner he began:

> *"My children and grandchildren, long ago . . . long, long ago . . . there used to be only forested land, plentiful in water and game to our west. Now it is arid and only sagebrush grows there.*
>
> *"Another tribe over there, they did a ceremony to call on the rain to come there because they had been without rain for some time. Thunderbird heard them, so he sent his children, Cloud and Rain to help the people.*
>
> *"After they got there to help them, the people did a ceremony to try and keep Cloud and Rain so they could use them whenever they wanted to."*

Sila stood up.

"After a while, Thunderbird wondered what happened to his children so he went looking for them. As he flew, the flapping of his wings sounded like thunder. Wherever he would look, lightning would bolt downward."

As Sila would tell the story, he hunched over, moved his arms like slow, giant wings, and looked about side-to-side stopping his head abruptly. Peepa rapidly beat on a hand drum. It sounded like thunder.

"Thunderbird looked and looked. Finally, he found them and saw what the people there had done. With a furious storm, he rushed in and freed his children, Cloud and Rain. He knocked down all the people's lodges.

"When he returned to his home somewhere out in the great waters of the west, he flew back and scooped up a mountain of dirt and created a whole mountain range between him and the people who tried to take his children, so that they could never do it again. Now, that country is dry and arid. Where he scooped the dirt, it made a deep bay from the ocean inland."

"That's the end of the trail," Sila said concluding the story.

"Now, then, why did those tribes do this, try to capture Cloud and Rain?" he asked everyone.

"So they could have rain whenever they wanted it," all the kids said in unison.

"But you cannot do something for good purposes in a wrong way," Sila explained.

"Why did Thunderbird go after Cloud and Rain?" he asked quickly and more loudly.

"Because they are his children," all chimed in.

"And . . . ." Sila said like a question.

"Because families take care of one another!" everyone said in loud unison. Then everyone laughed and cheered. Peepa beat on the drum.

Even in his old age, my Sila sang the Thunderbird song. He danced around flapping his arms, turning his head quickly, and jerking as he sang the song. His voice was old and crackly, but it was a special treat to see Sila animated and excited.

Everyone cheered and reveled in the moment. We all began to sing along with Sila.

Peepa beat on the drum even harder.

At the end of the song, everyone cheered again.

"Hey-yah! Hey-yah!" Sila said, breathing hard.

"All right," he said sitting down. Winter is over. We fed the several horses we had to keep near in the harsh weather. We gathered sticks for firewood in the snow.

"We helped our neighbors in need whose dried food went bad that we would not be hoarders while we had people of ours who were suffering.

"Now, it is time . . . it is time to greet the new season."

Everyone cheered once more.

Peepa started a happy song.

We went to bed happy.

CHAPTER 9
First Fruits Ceremony

The snows melted quickly, sometimes flooding the streams. However, they never flooded us out of our home. We communicated with them; we were in harmony with them; and we were a caretaker and steward for them.

Gradually new life started to appear. First shoots on the brush and small trees then small blossoms followed.

All the grasses were like a green elk skin robe, a deep and brilliant green. The cottonwood trees had buds ready to burst into leaves.

The birds were returning and they announced each new day with a chorus of songs. Sparrows, meadowlarks, flickers and finally the great osprey, the guardians of our lake decorated the sky.

As I rode to check on the horses, I took it all in. When there was no wind, the sun already felt warm. I turned my horse into the sun and held my hands up to it. The warmth went into my hands first, then my face and head, then my shoulders and body, and finally, even my feet felt warm.

My horse went calm and quiet.

As we rode into the valley where the horses would be, new life was everywhere. Some wild flowers were beginning to show up and decorate the meadows and hillsides.

Even in my youth, I felt a deep realization: "You must make it until the next spring time. There is a blessing of new life waiting for you." The teachings were real.

I could feel it. I could feel it strongly and powerfully. The beauty of nature was more than something good to look at, more than something to get food or shelter from. These were sacred purposes.

Nature has medicinal power just to be in it, by opening your heart and your mind to it. As you turn your mind to it, the soul is refreshed. When the soul is renewed, the heart and mind are joyous, and the body is healed.

It makes you turn to the Higher Power in thankfulness. Moreover, in your spiritual thanksgiving, the soul rejoices. The healing power of the natural world was truly incredible.

As we walk through the forests and foothills, ride our horses through the mountain passes, and paddle our canoes across the lakes and down the rivers, we breathe this great spirit air. We absorb the warmth and the light of the sun. We walk humble and true steps upon the land.

And, in it all, by it all, we live a great blessing.

As I made my way back to camp, I noticed my Peepa down by the water. He was preparing a canoe.

"Let us go to the big village and down the river, past the first falls and to the splashing water falls where our brothers, the Spokanes have their winter camps," he told me. "Your Noona says her sister and brother-in-law there have lots of dried salmon. We will trade."

Without lengthy planning or scheduling, we left, Peepa, Uncle Center Feather, and me.

As we paddled across the lake, trout were jumping everywhere. They were hungry in the springtime.

Occasionally, an osprey would swoop by, crash into the water, and catch a fish. We stopped paddling to watch. Further off, there were eagles fishing.

The canoe was nearly silent, gliding across the water, except for the slight dunking sound the paddles made.

We had a big bundle of dried meat and camas we brought to trade for salmon. Noona wanted a change of diet.

As we approached the big village at the headwaters on the other side of the lake where it drained into the river that led to the Spokane brothers, residents there ran out to greet us. We visited briefly. Peepa knew people everywhere and he joked with everyone.

We headed down the river. Now, we could just ride the current. I put my hand down in the water and its cool freshness massaged my fingers. It made a quiet trickling sound.

I breathed in the fresh spring air and took in the sunlight. The giant spruce and the fir had a sweet, lingering smell. Time seemed to stop.

On the bank, otters scurried into the water. The colors were like a checkered pattern on a woven basket in the shallow, rocky water.

In the distance, we could hear the first falls. It sounded like running water at first, then like thundering hooves in a buffalo stampede. We walked around it. It was spectacular.

White water splashing everywhere made a mist. In the mist you could see several sunbows, little rainbows. These are the children of Thunderbird and Rainbow, legends tell us.

Giant granite rocks, how did they get there?

We continued down the river to our brother neighbors and the big falls.

We traded, visited, and stayed the night. The next day we headed back. We borrowed horses to help us get back upstream and then paddled across the lake to our home camp.

"I'm so glad," my Noona said with a big smile, so happy to get the salmon.

"Your sister says she will come to see you in one moon," Peepa told her.

"In one moon, we will gather bitterroots and camas again," Noona said. "After the first fruits ceremony, of course."

We could not gather or partake of any of the native foods until we did the first fruits ceremony each year. Certain prayers had to be made, songs had to be sung, and women were chosen to go and get the first native foods.

The foods were brought back and a ceremonial dinner was prepared. More prayers and songs were conducted. The food was served in a specific order based on the stories of Creation and what came first. Then we ate.

After that, everyone could go out and gather all the foods and berries for the rest of the year.

"And then, after that, it's berry season," Noona said with a far away, deeply satisfied look. "And, the huckleberry mountains," she said smiling and clapping her hands together.

CHAPTER 10

The Animals are Our Sacred Brothers:
10 YEARS LATER

The day was warm and a soft breeze soothed the land as we rode down through the foothills returning from the annual trek to our beloved huckleberry mountains. I took it all in as a blessing of goodness.

I touched the great grizzly claws I wore around my neck and thought of that day ten years ago, when my Peepa and I fought the great bear. My Peepa and I were already close, but that experience made us almost inseparable. We hunted together, rode together, prayed in the sweat lodge and ran together every morning.

Some mornings in the winter, he would wake me with large chunks of ice and tell me to get up and run holding the ice in each hand. "You cannot pick the day and time the enemy may come and attack. You must always be prepared on a moments notice to do whatever you must to defend yourself, children and the people," he instructed. So I ran.

Sometimes it was large rocks or a log he had me carry. I believed him, whatever he told me. He never told me anything wrong or harmful.

In ten years, I had grown into a man. All the disciplines and training instilled in boys and the young men were mine. The teachings of the elders and the religious ceremonial practices placed limits of direction to guide the great strengths I had developed.

In gaining my manhood, I had lived an upbringing of physical development including strength, stamina, stealth, concealment, tracking, hunting and sacrifice. I provided meats for other families, elders and orphans that were in need.

Several times a year, my Peepa would send me out in the wilderness all alone, with nothing but my stone knife. I had to acquire food, shelter and fire on my own.

Today, I felt as though it was all worthwhile. I felt a warm and peaceful strength in my heart and mind that spilled over into all my body.

"Sun Boy, my son — oh, I mean Sun Bear," I heard my Noona call to me. Sun Bear was my second name, my adult name. After I fasted on the great mountain when I was thirteen, I was named Sun Bear. Sila conducted the naming and the dinner, but Peepa announced my name. Sila said Peepa was the one who had the right to give me that name because he had half of the claws and the mark of the grizzly across his shoulders and arm.

Sila said the sun broke from behind the clouds as he meditated about a name for me. Since my childhood name had the sun in it too, my adult name should be "Sun Bear." They had a big dinner and give-a-way for my name. Everyone shook my hand, repeating my name to me.

However, my Noona, she said I would always be her boy, so she slipped, often, and said my childhood name.

"We're almost home," she said. "I'm always glad to go to the mountains and I'm always glad to come back to our valley camps too," she explained.

I had to agree as I looked out at the tall brown grasses, the green brush and the evergreen trees standing as a backdrop. Along the rivers and creeks stood the massive cottonwood and ash trees, their leaves rustling in the gentle wind. The sun glistened, reflecting off the water of our home river. It was home, and I felt like maybe somehow it was glad to see us again too.

In the distance, I could see the great lake along which so many of our people made their homes.

The water was still and smooth, like blue ice, only deeper and alive. Osprey were actively fishing, diving right into the water and coming out with a fish in one claw. Others were perched in trees watching and waiting for their chance to grab a meal out of the water.

The sun had moved to the western sky and reflected brilliantly off the water. Seated on my horse, I looked down and I thought about my youthful days playing on the shore, running and dancing with the ancient ones as they sang and drummed with the wind, the water and the sunbeam. I looked at a straight stick on the ground and thought about picking it up.

Across the lake, I could see that at every bay there were family bands camped: teepees erected, looking like mystical cones with dark smoke stains at the top. There were some canoes carrying people, probably fishing. Children were playing and swimming at the shore. I could hear their unrestrained laughter in the gentle breeze.

Many people were already back from gathering huckleberries. Huckleberries were one of our sacred foods, and they were our favorite. Noona called them the "sweetness of life." These little purple and near black berries grew on a little bush only at the higher elevations, the huckleberry mountains.

Noona, and all the women, were always excited to go gathering and picking. Noona said she always dreamed about our berry campsites, the mountaintops, the berries and the bushes.

She said it was always reassuring to her when every summer she would see it again and it was just as she remembered it, just as she pictured it in her mind.

Several canoes were going downstream and some boys on horseback rode up along the bank. Up over the hill from the bank were some teepees.

"Oh, good," I thought. "My brother-friends are back already."

Our neighbors downstream were related to us but one of my cousins there, I called my brother-friend. With him, his younger brother and my younger brother, we made many adventure seeking trips, and will make more in the future, I am sure.

I galloped my horse up and over the top of the next hill. I looked back at my home valley and teepee sites.

"Thank you, my home place, for welcoming us back," I said to it. "You are a sacred place, like a mother you care for us, shield and shelter us."

"Greetings great waters in the river and creeks, my brothers, the fish. We are returned to you and have never forgotten you."

"The great meadows, thank you for accepting us and our lodges, and for feeding our ponies to make them strong and fast."

"The hills all around us, you watch over us and provide the game for us to eat, the wood for our fires and many of the medicines we use to take care of our people in need. Thank you. We are returned to you."

"All of you are my home. In our home lodges, we will speak gently and always take the best care of you. We will be happy because we are in harmony with you," I said talking to our homeland directly. Sila always said to do this, as though it was a person just like me. Again, it seemed to be the simple truth.

Today, I understood why the adults and older people wouldn't let the children race down the last hill into camp. For the first time, I knew I had communicated with the land and nature that it heard me and answered back so softly, "Welcome home my children, I missed you. It was lonely here without you." It gently whispered back to me.

I walked my horse down the hill reverently with my hands turned out to the land, the hills and the trees. I felt emotional, yet satisfied. I got off my horse at the river and strolled to the water where I drank. Even my horse was content and peaceful.

"You're beginning to understand it, aren't you Son?" my Peepa said, surprising me with his presence.

"It's all wonderful and sacred, this life we have been given," I answered.

"The Kolunsuten didn't give us this life. He only loaned it to us, Son," Peepa corrected. "Someday we will have to give it back. That's why we must be so careful to take proper care of it, each other and the holy nature," he explained.

"Yes Peepa, yes. I'm beginning to understand," I answered him.

The land, the water, all of nature, it belongs to the Kolunsuten. We are only permitted to use it for however long we are here on this road of life. Obviously, this is but another universal truth any good person with a good heart would understand and appreciate.

I got on my knees. "Thank you Kolunsuten," I prayed. "Thank you for this wonderful life and the many and great blessings I find in it." I picked up a small bit of dirt and rubbed my hands with it, then touched my hands upon my head, chest, arms, stomach and then legs to put its blessing upon me.

I looked across the small, grass meadow and Sila was praying and putting down tobacco, making an offering to nature and no doubt talking to the home place. The kinicknick plant is what we called it. It was a tiny bush, growing low to the ground. Its little green leaves were our tobacco for smoking or offering. Noona and others were already starting to put up teepees while others took care of horses, supplies and the huckleberries.

I had now seen twenty-one winters in my lifetime. I was a mature man, a proven warrior and a successful hunter. Therefore, I wore the hairstyle and feathers depicting my status. My dark, almost black hair hung down, straight and long. My eagle feathers, three of them, one for my name and two for bravery, I wore down along the right side of my head. My feathers were from the golden eagle, white with black at the tips.

I had my Peepa's powerful arms and upper body, but also, I had Noona's lanky legs, which I used to run. I could outrun everyone in the river camps in our footraces during celebrations.

My Peepa and Noona were aging gracefully with all their physical abilities intact, but a touch of gray beginning to show in their hair. Peepa was still one of the bravest, fiercest and most feared of warriors. He was always one of the first to charge into the enemy and engage them. All the young men admired him.

But my Sila and Checheya were starting to age noticeably. I was glad to see them hiking the huckleberry mountains in good spirits. Sila was much older than Checheya when they married, and Checheya gave birth to my Noona at an older age, so they were older than most grandparents of people my age. I worried about them now.

My younger brother now was a man too. He was strong and quick, but he was rather quiet. That was fine. The people respected those who were quiet, strong, thoughtful and dependable.

My older sister Berry Woman was married with two children of her own now. Her husband, my brother-in-law, had become a good help to the family, and a good friend to me. His name was Mountainside. My parents arranged the marriage when they were both children. They said their natures matched so they would be a good couple and be very happy. Sometimes, though, she didn't look happy. Other times, she was bruised on her face and my parents worried for her.

Rainbow Girl, my baby sister, was a young woman now. She had numerous young men trying to talk to her and coming over to see her. Some mature men even came around and tried to negotiate a wedding, but Noona said no — she and Rainbow Girl would pick her husband, subject to Peepa's approval, of course.

"Hey, big brother," I heard her voice just as I thought about her. "Are you going to see our relatives downstream? I want you to take me to see my cousin friends and aunties, too," Rainbow Girl called to me. She had on her elk skin dress with quillwork in small colored designs with trade shells. Her moccasins matched her dress. Her hair was straight, long and black, and her eyes still twinkled with a deep joy and inner laughter. She was beautiful, kind, good and precious to the family and me. Checheya still babied her sometimes.

When her horse fell off the cliff and was killed, Rainbow cried and cried. Finally, Checheya held her and rocked her, singing her lullaby, comforting her till she was calm and able to be talked to about life and death. She had such tender feelings. She and Checheya were so close. She took care of Checheya more than anybody now.

"All right," I answered her. "Let's get some different horses so these can rest," I advised her.

"Oh, wonderful day," Rainbow Girl said. "Now I can see them and hear what they did all month in their huckleberry mountains to the north. Besides, there are some roots and medicines along the way that Checheya needs. I'll get some and bring it back to them."

Maybe some of the girls found someone to marry, maybe some of the older girls that were already married were pregnant. She couldn't wait to find out.

As we rode into their home camp, children started to run excitedly. "Sun Bear is here, and Rainbow Girl," they announced to everyone.

Uncle and Auntie came out of a teepee. "Quickly, get some food for our people," they ordered.

It was our way to feed visitors, no matter what. It was always said that it was an honor and a privilege to receive and care for visitors. Greet them with friendship and hospitality. Give them food and water. In turn, you too will be blessed and the spirit of hospitality will stay with you and bless your home. It was part of the great circle of life.

"Brother, many moons have passed since I have seen you," I heard my brother-friend, Rock, say.

"Hey yah! Hey, yah!" I hollered out in joy. I jumped off the horse and we greeted each other by grabbing each other's shoulder.

Rainbow Girl was already off visiting, laughing and giggling, I saw her give Auntie a big hug.

"So, what have you girls been doing all summer?" she quizzed them. "Did you get your dresses ready for the gathering and celebration? And, where is Rain Clouds, my best friend?"

Just then, Rain Clouds walked from around the teepee. She was talking to a young man who came to see her, and you could tell they liked each other.

"You must be the famous Rainbow Girl," a voice called to her from the side, it was another young man. They were from the lake camp to the north, and apparently, they had met my brother-friend's family along the huckleberry trails.

Rainbow Girl was shy to people she hadn't met before and she said nothing. This was the proper response.

"You're the one everyone is afraid to talk to and court because of your father and brother," he said. "My name is Deer Hooves, and I'm not afraid." She looked at him, finally, puzzled about him talking so boldly toward her Peepa and brother. "Because I'll just run away as fast as I can," he said chuckling. His disarming humor made her laugh, but still, she said nothing to him.

She looked at her cousin friend, pleadingly, to introduce her.

"Deer Hooves, this is Rainbow Girl, daughter of Black Hawk and Basket Weaver, granddaughter of Drum and Shawl Woman and Yellow Shirt and Red Bird. She lives upstream along the river."

"My parents are Badger Skin and Rabbit; my grandparents are Turtle Shell and Soft Rain," Deer Hooves offered in identifying himself. "I live in the north lake camp, home of our great Chief Circling Raven."

"So, tell me about your summer," he said to Rainbow Girl, trying to get her to talk. "Did you gather enough huckleberries?"

"You must talk to my Peepa before I can talk to you," she told him, avoiding eye contact.

"Friend, Sun Bear, I have heard of you, let me shake your hand." He introduced himself to me.

"Ahh. Good," I told him.

"When the father is not present, the older brother has the responsibility and authority for the younger sister. I am asking your permission to talk to Rainbow Girl."

She looked at me, knowing I had rarely acted for Peepa. I could tell by the look and glint in her eye she wanted me to say yes.

"All right, go ahead," I decided, "but only if she wants to talk to you and only to tell about yourselves and only in my presence briefly. If you want to talk further, you must get permission from our Peepa."

"Again, I am Deer Hooves," he repeated.

"You already said that," Rainbow jokingly corrected.

"So, tell me," he said kind of slyly, "do you have a favorite suitor?"

Rainbow just looked at him.

"You know," he said, "a serious suitor that you are waiting for and putting all your hope in."

Rainbow looked shocked over his boldness, and looked to me. I said nothing.

"I am not going to talk to you about that," she countered. "Maybe I won't want to even know you as a friend, let alone as anything else."

He laughed easily. "I apologize. Tell me about your family, about your summer and what you will do next. Tell me about what you like to do, what makes you the most happy."

"You're strange," she said with a teasing tone, and they both laughed.

Rock strolled up beside me. "Uh-oh," he cautioned. "Love is in the air. Watch out."

Rainbow and Deer Hooves looked at him a little embarrassed-like, then laughed it off. They talked as I listened. He said he would be over to see our Peepa tomorrow and talk to Rainbow some more.

She was unusually quiet on the way home. "What's wrong baby sister?" I inquired of her.

"So, what did you think of him?" she asked back. "Who?" I quizzed.

"Oh, you know, Deer Hooves," she specified with a definite grin.

"Didn't you notice his hair and eyes were just so dark and shining, his leggings and moccasins matched perfectly, and he walked strong and smooth, like Peepa," she chimed. "He seemed strong, yet kind, even humorous, just like Peepa, even though he doesn't look anything like Peepa."

"If you say so, Baby Sister," I humored her.

CHAPTER 11
Circling Raven

The next day, some riders came into camp. "Be ready, gather at the big camp at the headwaters west of the lake," they instructed. "Circling Raven will talk to us about the buffalo hunt."

It put some excitement in all of us. But usually we waited about a half of a moon after returning home from gathering huckleberries to start getting ready for the hunt to rest the horses. Everyone had other horses though. On top of that, the huckleberries were early this year. We were almost a full month early in our hunt. I wondered why.

Rainbow Girl was staying close to camp, looking out toward the trail every now and then. I knew she was watching for Deer Hooves, and I had told Peepa what I had decided for him. He said it was all right. That's what older brothers were for.

Just as we were mounted and ready to ride, Deer Hooves and his brother rode toward our home camp. "That's the man I told you about, Peepa," I told him as I pointed out toward the riders.

Deer Hooves rode up to Peepa and dismounted, introduced himself by identifying his parents, grandparents and home camp again.

He said, "It is a great honor to meet you. I have seen you around the camps and the gatherings."

"Ah. Good," that's all Peepa said to him, putting him in the spot to state his intentions.

"I met your daughter last evening downstream and I would like to talk to her further with your permission," Deer Hooves said nervously.

"What is it that you are, or have ever done that makes you stand out or more worthy to talk to my daughter than other men, some of them great hunters and warriors?" Peepa challenged him harshly.

With obvious fidgeting, yet a steady voice, Deer Hooves offered, "I am but an honest person, and I bring my sincerity and kindness. I will always be truthful and good." Deer Hooves looked worriedly at Peepa, hoping and praying this was an acceptable answer to him.

I knew Peepa would like the answer because he always said that truth and goodness were more important than anything. You could not be a great warrior or hunter without those qualities; or a good father, or a good help to the people.

"We are just riding to the big village at the headwaters. You can ride along with us. Once there you should camp with your own family," he ordered.

I thought Deer Hooves would war whoop and dance right then and there. "Yes of course," he answered, trying to contain his excitement, turning himself in definite movements and shaking his fist.

On the trail Rainbow and Deer Hooves talked and talked.

I couldn't wait to get to the big village. Circling Raven was perhaps the most powerful, prophetic and spiritual of chiefs our people ever had. His power was the raven. It would circle and tell him things about what would happen, the future and how to prepare. Sila says that the Kolunsuten himself had spoken to Circling Raven.

There were so many stories about him, the great things he had done, and the miracles that were performed. The way he talked, it was mystical yet practical. He always said things no one had heard before. He didn't just repeat things others had said before him.

We settled into camp and went toward his teepee. Already people were gathered in fairly large numbers, mingling, waiting for Circling Raven. Noona was telling the children to all go down to the chief's teepee. He is a great man. He has enormous knowledge and wisdom. "Children go and learn. Pay attention."

Finally, he emerged from his teepee and walked to a spot prepared for him to stand and talk.

"My people, my relatives and friends," he began. "We must prepare for an early hunt. I have been told the huckleberries were early because there will be an early winter. The old man in the north will blanket our Mother in white while some of her children sleep and rest beneath this blanket. However, she made the huckleberries early so we could be prepared.

"So, we will travel to our brothers over the mountains, the Salish. We will visit them and then hunt buffalo. Prepare your horses. Double the soles on your moccasins. Fix your arrows and lances. In four days, we will depart.

"Every dawn and every sunset, we will sweat and pray to tell our great brother the buffalo we are coming and why. We must purify ourselves and ask the Kolunsuten and nature to allow us to take the mighty buffalo again in a good way and with good luck.

"Remember, it is our sacred brother that feeds us in the winter and shelters us from the cold. He does this by giving his life up for us. Know him as a loving and sacred relative for this. Pray for him, give thanks for him. Have respect for him."

"Go now and be ready," Circling Raven concluded.

We knew the Kolunsuten himself guided Chief Circling Raven, so it never occurred to us to question or doubt his instructions. He was a grand and powerful man.

He wore upon his head a full eagle headdress and carried the flag of our people, a long lance with twelve eagle feathers to make this announcement about the buffalo. But sometimes he wore a deer antler headdress, depending on the occasion, the ceremony or the announcement. He wore a deerskin shirt all white with red colored quillwork around the shoulders and arms with matching leggings and moccasins. He wore a blue colored elk skin robe around one shoulder and a grizzly claw necklace.

Afterwards, people were talking and shaking hands with Circling Raven. I hung around hoping I might get a chance. He walked right toward me, looking at my grizzly bear claw necklace. "You must be Sun Bear, son of Black Hawk and Basket Weaver," he inquired. "It's good to see you, Grandson," he told me. Sila and he must be distantly related as cousins, that's why he called me grandson, because a cousin is like a brother, a brother's children like your own, so his grandchildren are your grandchildren.

"I have heard of you," he explained further. "I want you to ride with me over to the buffalo country."

"Nephew," he called to my Peepa, "with your permission I will ride with and talk to your son."

"It is a great honor. Thank you, my Chief," Peepa told Circling Raven. Peepa was really proud, I could tell. All of our hard work, teaching and diligence were paying off. I knew he hoped I would gain some knowledge or wisdom that would help me in life.

I could hear the familiar rustling footsteps coming up behind me. It was Rock. A young man now, he was big but still a little chubby.

"Let's go eat somewhere," he said. "If we go visiting, some of our aunties will give us meat and berries."

"Didn't you eat today?" I asked, knowing he'd never miss a meal.

"Hey, a growing boy can never get too much to eat," he jovially explained putting his hand to his stomach, then his fingers to his mouth and then laughing.

Rock hadn't really changed since he was a boy. He always saw humor in everything first. He did all the harsh training required of all of us, without complaint and he knew how and when to be serious.

Still, without warning, and even in improbable situations, he would inject comedy.

Everyone liked him, although the elders of the tribe still scolded him from time to time for being too silly. At those times, he would just put his head down, but it never stopped him for long. Besides, many times, even the most serious of our elders would get a good belly laugh over Rock's comedy.

Some said he was a fool, or a little "off." I knew that wasn't true.

"Well, then, brother-friend," Rock said, "lets get ready for a great adventure. I'll help you make arrows and train the horses."

For several days, preparations were made and finalized. Every morning at dawn, and every evening, we went in the sweat lodge and prayed. Some went to the mountaintops and made their offerings.

The mountains for fasting and praying were the great peaks above our huckleberry mountains. We could go there only reverently and prayerfully. These places were above the tree line.

After you had completed your fast, you were supposed to build a pile of rocks to represent what you had done. At these places, there were hundreds, even thousands of rock piles put there by our people since the beginning of time.

Some villages and camps hosted the buffalo dance. This dance was done to tell our brother, the buffalo, we were coming for him, and why; and to ask the Kolunsuten for his permission and blessing.

All this was done to purify ourselves and tell our brother the buffalo we needed him again. We had to ask nature for him. We had to be prepared and worthy by being physically able, we were thankful and respectful to the buffalo, and our horses were ready and willing.

The days were filled with the final horse training, arrow and spear building, and moccasin making. The arrowheads were shaped by chipping, as were the spearheads. The men were experts at this. Most would do about six in an evening, including tying with sinew.

The designs on the arrows were unique either to a family or to one person. You had to have the right to use the design you painted either because your power gave it to you, or you inherited it from your family. Otherwise, you might have bad luck.

CHAPTER 12
Mountains of Hope

With all the preparations completed, we were finally breaking camp. Sila and Checheya almost stayed behind because of their age. But, Checheya said she had to go one more time because something was calling her. She had to go.

Rainbow Girl was almost frantic. "I'll stay with you, Checheya," she offered. "Or, I'll help you through the mountains." They were always together. Rainbow Girl was what we call a "Grandma's girl," always caring for or being with a grandparent. Sometimes, I knew it was the other way around. By taking care of our elders with kindness, there was a special blessing passed on to her, a caring they could give maybe only in spirit, manifested in a strength to the caretaker.

"We're going with you," Sila directed. "Get your Checheya's things and put them on the packhorse."

Finally we were ready.

Off we went, some ahead of us, some behind us on the trail. Every now and then Rainbow Girl and Deer Hooves would talk and laugh. I could tell she really liked him.

It is a beautiful ride across the mountains into the buffalo country of our Salish brothers. But we were going much slower than usual to accommodate Sila and Checheya.

"Why do you like horses so much?" Rainbow Girl asked Deer Hooves.

"Because they are so special and so powerful," he replied. "We wouldn't really be able to hunt the buffalo effectively without them. The buffalo can run just as fast as the horse and they are just as quick. All the horse has is the confidence and trust of his rider and that's more than enough for him."

"I had a favorite horse, but she fell and got killed. She saved me. Sila said the horse took some hardship or maybe even a death that was coming for our family, or me. I really loved that horse and I remember her, sometimes in my prayers."

"I care for my horses so much that I don't want anything to ever happen to them, not even for my sake," he claimed.

"Don't say that," she corrected. "You know better. They are your protection too. That's what makes them so admirable and sacred."

"I know, I know, but I do care for them," he explained. They talked on and off all day. I heard her tell her friends all about him and how much she liked him.

We camped at the base of the giant, imposing mountain leading up to the pass. These were the headwaters of the rivers that flowed into our great lake. The terrain was rough and rugged, steep and rocky, the brush thick. Prayers and offerings were said to seek our permission to pass.

The next day we went up and over the mountain. It was a long and difficult journey for my grandparents. However, we all made it.

Finally, we could see the Salish camp. Riders came out to greet us. "Ayyy, Ayyy," they yelled. "My brothers are back among us," they shouted. They rode off back toward their camp. Some of our boys got excited and took off after them, dipping from side to side on their horses as they rode. My younger brother, Snow on the Mountain, turned around and rode backwards.

We entered camp to be greeted by many warm and happy faces. A feast was prepared and everyone was dressed in their finest clothes. There would be singing and dancing later.

What a feast, there was. All the usual foods, the roots and the berries, but also fresh buffalo. We had smelled it cooking as we rode in.

Visiting and laughter, joking and storytelling, it was a happy, joyful time.

After dinner there was social dancing and singing. People were dressed in their most beautiful clothing with their hair fixed and styled perfectly. Our tribes were a beautiful people. I was proud and felt somehow stronger just to be among them.

From the oldest to the youngest, they were happy and healthful. Even the elderly were strong and physically fit, except for the very eldest. They had to be cared for, even have their food chewed for them. However, everyone was celebrating tonight.

"Deer Hooves is the most interesting and easy to know young man I have ever talked to," I overheard my sister tell a group of girls. "We talked and talked all the way here. I feel like I've known him forever. His hair and eyes are so dark they match each other. And, his clothes, with the way he walks, it fits and matches him just right. He laughs so easy and he makes me laugh all the time."

All the girls sighed together, then all laughed at each other. I walked off around the teepee and across the village. Over by the first horse corral was Deer Hooves.

"Anybody know how to play this thing?" he asked the handful of young men around him. They all laughed teasingly at him. He was holding a flute. Some men played love songs on the flute. It was widely known that girls possessed a deep affinity for music, and that when love songs were played with feeling, the melody and tempo were heard by their hearts and minds. It helped them understand how a person felt toward them.

"Deer Hooves must be in love," Rock said teasingly. All the boys joked and teased him, then pushed him gently, slapping him on the shoulders.

"I met a girl, Rainbow Girl. She makes me feel as though I can now begin to understand what our parents and grandparents teach us about love, devotion and commitment. I believe I would do anything for her," he replied.

"What if she doesn't want you?" his friend asked him. "All the young men, and some older warriors, wanted her and she would commit to no one. You must find out, tonight." The other boys all agreed and encouraged him to find out in the old way.

First, he had to find out what teepee she was sleeping in. Usually, the young girls of marrying age would stay in a teepee with other girls of the family, and maybe one older auntie. The teepee would be placed right between other teepees of the parents, uncles and brothers for protection.

Then, a young man could, with permission, enter this teepee after the girls had gone to bed, go over to the bedding of the girl in whom he was interested, and stand on the edge of her blankets. If she told him to get off her blankets, that meant she would not marry him and did not want him to pursue it any further. If she said nothing, that meant she was interested in possibly marrying him and he should pursue it further.

Therefore, with great nervousness, Deer Hooves set it all up. Of course, Rainbow Girl knew he was coming. All the girls were excited, even though Noona and Peepa would still have to approve.

As the night was winding down, Deer Hooves made his move.

His stomach turned and churned. His mind raced.

"What if she says get off my blankets?" he wondered. Still, he had to know. His heart was lovesick.

He walked weakly to the teepee. Fumbling at the entrance, he collected himself and remembered his manners. He knocked by scratching at the hide door cover. "Cheets Hui, come in," a voice answered.

As he entered he tried to talk to Auntie, but nothing would come out of his mouth. His voice didn't work. Auntie was sewing some repairs on a buckskin shirt and didn't even look at him. With her chin and lips, she motioned and pointed toward Rainbow Girl. Feeling faint, dizzy and his heart pounding, he walked toward her bed. He hesitated as if to run away.

Ever so cautiously, he stepped on her elk skin blanket, first one foot, and then the other. Then, he stood and waited . . . and waited. The sweat beaded up on him and he felt like he couldn't get a full breath of air.

"What's taking so long? I can't wait," he thought. Time stopped, but the night went on. He wasn't sure if hours passed or minutes.

Finally, it dawned on him. She was not going to say anything. She didn't tell him to get off her blankets. She was serious about him too.

He turned to Auntie for reassurance, but she just kept on sewing, and then motioned toward the door for him to go.

He swiftly walked to the door and ran, leaping out of the teepee. He skipped and jumped then turned around. "Ayy, ayy!" he yelled. His friends were waiting a short distance away. They hollered back at him.

"Quiet you fools," my Checheya scolded through her teepee. "Only a fool would be out hollering like a coyote after all the people have gone to bed."

Deer Hooves and all the boys obediently tried to restrain themselves and walked toward their own camping area. He told them all about it as they walked.

In the teepee, Rainbow Girl was squealing and talking so fast, telling everybody all about it. "I can hardly believe it," she repeated over and over. "Tell me Auntie, what did he look like to you? Wasn't he strong and handsome looking?"

"He looked like a sick baby elk, stumbling, trying to get up," Auntie answered. Seeing her concern, Auntie quickly added, "But they only look like that when they are so in love they cannot control their movements any more."

"Oh, do you think he loves me, Auntie?" she moaned pleadingly.

"Yes, of course, my child," Auntie assured her. "But don't forget about your father. He must approve, and your young man must be worthy and ready to make a home and family. He can't just come around and say the right things, you know."

"I know, Auntie, but Peepa will know to make me happy. I just have a feeling that everything will be all right."

Rainbow Girl laid down again as the teepee settled into its night time routine again. Nevertheless, she couldn't sleep. She thought about her life, growing up, all the great people in her family, about Checheya and about all the suitors who came to court her. None of them seemed like the one she could commit to for a lifetime. Either they were overly arrogant expressing their worthiness, or they were deficient in personality.

Checheya always told her, "Just take your time. Wait for the right man. He'll be along, and you'll know he's the one. Keep in mind what it is that makes a man loveable over the course of a whole lifetime."

"To a young girl, it could seem the cute one, or the loudest one should be the best. But it's not true and any older woman could tell you so."

"It is the kind man whose strength is quiet, who is prayerful and ceremonial in his everyday life, who is good to animals and helpful to children and the elderly. Such a man can hold a woman's love for an entire life and you can grow old together, and you will see your children grow and bring you grandchildren."

"So, take your time granddaughter," Checheya would tell her.

It was all starting to make sense to Rainbow Girl.

As Deer Hooves laid down for the night, he pondered with deep satisfaction and happiness his victory at the teepee.

Then anxiety overcame him.

"Oh, no, her father still must approve," he shouted in his own mind. What if he says no? What if I really am unworthy? What have I ever done to prove myself? I'm a good hunter and I provide for many elders and widows," he justified. "But everyone does that much," he argued again.

"You have to be worthy by proven deeds and how you live your life," he repeated the teaching to himself.

Then there was the matter of a dowry. He knew that her Peepa turned down great warriors and powerful hunters who came with massive dowries. What was he going to do to match that?

Now the worrying set in. However, he resolved that he would do whatever it took to prove himself and collect the appropriate gifts necessary to prove his worthiness.

CHAPTER 13
Foods of Life Must be Earned

The tribal bands rested a few days after the long trip, and made final preparations for the hunt. Buffalo hunting horses were especially trained. These were some of the most valued possessions a person could own. They could enable you to feed your family while keeping you safe and protected. At the same time, they had to be very brave and courageous, powerfully strong and energetic, yet easily trained and willing.

It didn't matter what color they were. Sila and Uncle Center Feather always said it was what's underneath the color that mattered. But Peepa believed that the sorrel horse, the red one, would usually be the strongest. That's what he always rode for buffalo hunting and for war, so I did, too. Many of our people followed this teaching.

Targets were set up for practice spear throwing and shooting arrows, all from horseback.

We perfected our aim by shooting tipless arrows into small circles of bent willow that were set up next to steep hillsides of dirt or sand. But, now right before a hunt, we had to shoot arrows with stone tips. They flew differently with the tip on and we had to be sure and accurate. The sandy dirt would preserve the arrows for use again.

The bravest and most powerful of hunters would ride bareback and use a spear. You had to have a very powerful arm to penetrate the buffalo's hide with a spear and kill it. A hunter's young sons or nephews would ride along carrying extra spears for him.

The horse had to be extremely well trained, willing and brave. After you picked and focused on a target buffalo, the horse took over the steering and all control. He had to rate the speed of the buffalo, move in close, but stay just a little behind and to the right side. This way you could shoot an arrow just above the flank avoiding the ribs and penetrating the lungs and maybe the heart.

It took a lot of skill and expertise. Sometimes the buffalo would hook at the horse with his horns, maybe even knock you right over in a herd of stampeding buffalo and horses. It was very dangerous, but everyone knew how to prepare and purify themselves. Sweat lodge, fasting, offerings to the spirit of the buffalo, the Mother Earth and nature were required to be made.

My mother, my Noona, came to see me as we were making initial preparations to depart. "Here my Sun Boy, I mean Sun Bear," she said as she handed me a new pair of moccasins.

"All these years I have made you moccasins with the arrowhead and deer print design," she explained, "hoping you would grow up to be strong, fast and a successful hunter. My prayers have been answered and my wishes have come true. I want you to be protected and safe. So, I stayed up all night holding these moccasins as I prayed for you. May a mother's love and prayers be worthy enough before the Kolunsuten to grant you safety and protection," she concluded handing me the moccasins. She had a warm smile for me, but also, a hint of tear in her eyes.

I quickly put them on and thanked her. For these many years, my parents and grandparents lent me some part of their strength and protection and, combined with my own prayers and preparations, it had never let me down.

As I moved around and proudly examined my new moccasins, I still could feel that old urge inside of me to run as fast as I could and war whoop. I felt protected and blessed. I knew I wore the love of my mother upon me, like a cloak of protection.

I looked at her with a pleased feeling, and she gave me that look all children, all people know: the approving smile of a mother, the one that makes you confident enough to go out and do whatever you have decided to do.

She said I would always be her boy, and today I knew it was true. For me, too, I would always just be her boy for her, respect her and try to bring her peace and happiness.

"Checheya and Sila are coming, too," she added. "Checheya says a movement within her, a spiritual feeling, is telling her to go one more time on the buffalo hunt."

As we talked, the rest of the camp was struck. All the hide coverings were removed from the poles, and the poles were taken down. Just that rapidly, the entire camp started to move out. It was an impressive sight, all the people, hundreds of them on beautiful horses, moving out together to the east.

All the men wore buckskin leggings with a breechcloth covering front and back, with a buckskin shirt. Various decorations of painted designs and quillwork colored them.

The women wore buckskin dresses similarly decorated, some with shells and elk teeth. Little girls were dressed like little women, but the boys might only have breechcloth and moccasins, or leggings but no shirt.

Everybody had combed or braided hair, some with feathers or plumes. And, all the horses . . . . I could smell the horses mixing with the perfumed air of spruce, fir and pine trees. But, even more, I could smell the excitement.

People moved with a bounce in their step and a gleam in their eye. Even the horses pranced and whinnied from time to time, and threw their heads around in anticipation.

Scouts and riders were already out ahead. Uncle Center Feather was with them. They would find the buffalo and warn us of any danger from the Chop Faces.

The Blackfeet were the enemy. Their homelands were farther to the east and north. Sometimes, we had to fight the Crow, but most of the time we would stop and trade with them.

Sila said they had come across the Sioux and Cheyenne many times before and made friends. We would trade them dentalium shells, and other items from tribes to our west for various goods they possessed. Our people very much liked their style of war bonnets and would trade great amounts of our goods to get one.

Sila also told us we had even traded with the Blackfeet once when he was young. It looked like there would be a fight; both sides stood in a line ready to charge, but held back. Finally, a parlay was held and we traded goods.

Then, that very same night, they came and tried to steal all the horses we had just acquired from them in trade.

The elders said the enemies were murderers and had no sense of value or goodness. They even took pride in being evil murderers. They were belligerent, obnoxious and war-like. We were not afraid of them, but we were told to never be like them, either. Never kill for glory or simply the sake of killing, we were told.

Our best and most powerful warriors were out front. They could almost turn invisible in nature. They were silent and deadly if need be. The elite hunters scouting ahead all had the special buffalo, deer or elk power. They understood hunting and the spiritual side of it. Offerings had been made and ceremonies were conducted to call upon our mighty brother for the great sacrifice he makes for us.

Periodically, you could hear different people sing the buffalo song, or they would stop, pray and leave offerings on the ground trying to communicate with the buffalo.

"Our brother knows we are coming for him," a voice right behind me said. I turned to see. It was my Peepa.

"The buffalo knows we are coming for him and nature will let us harvest him only if we are worthy, only if we are not wasteful and only if we never forget to be thankful. I feel good about this hunt," he said confidently.

"Still, though," he added, "your Checheya has me a little worried. Why is she being called to participate?"

Maybe because of my young age, I hadn't wondered about it. But Peepa was right. Why was that?

On the way over the mountains, I was to ride with Circling Raven, our greatest chief, ever. I could see his family band up ahead so I rode up to join him as Peepa rode back to join our little family band.

He told me and some of the other men a lot of things about life and nature. "The birds are acting strangely," Circling Raven said. "Something is going on, or going to happen. We must pay attention and be alert."

We traveled a long way, and camped for the night. The camp was active with visiting and laughter. The people were confident, happy and feeling under the protection of the Kolunsuten. Rainbow Girl was taking care of Checheya, who was taking care of many little children. Deer Hooves was near and I saw them looking at each other, but he kept a little distance. I assumed he didn't want to push a conversation with my Peepa until he was ready.

Everyone was milling around in their little groups when a crier made an announcement:

"Everyone, listen to me. Be quiet. Our High Chief, Circling Raven will say some words to us. Gather around. Be quiet."

As everyone settled down, Circling Raven began to speak:

"My relatives, my friends, my people, again we travel long distances together across this land and along the great road of life. The

Creator, Kolunsuten, has provided for our needs, even ahead of our being in this world.

"He thought ahead for our provision of food, water, medicine, shelter and family nurturing and belonging. He made us to be near and in harmony with nature, that we would be a ceremonious and prayerful people with it. He is the one who put the ways of prayer, and the great virtues of faith, love, hope and brotherhood upon the land for his people to use and understand. And, he gave us these things to use in prayer and communication with him.

"He did these things to make complete all his provision for us, that nothing and no one would be forgotten or left out. And, he did these things so that we come to him with a sincere and humble heart for a good and virtuous purpose. He will hear us and he will answer our prayers.

"We seek today a part of his great provision for us: the food our great brother, the buffalo, brings to us. So, we must pray and make ourselves ready."

He sang a beautiful prayer song with a beautiful, powerful voice. The night came alive, but also grew still. A gentle wind picked up and then went still. I looked up. Even the stars seemed to listen to the music. They brightened and appeared as though they moved closer to us. He began to pray again:

"Kolunsuten, hear us, your children. From our Mother Earth we pray to you. We are the children of the land, your people. Recognize us and know us.

"Together we travel and hunt. Together we live life, and together we unite in prayer to you. Pity us and bless us O Creator, Kolunsuten. We seek our great brother, the buffalo that he would bring us food and shelter again. We know he gives up his own life that the people will live. He has a spirit and a powerful will to live. He has feelings and knowledge.

"Maybe other peoples treat the animals like they don't know anything, like they are ignorant. We know the animals do what they do because it is what you told them, and they never forget it, they never disobey, and they never change.

"Man has been told by you to choose right over wrong. We have been given knowledge and teaching. But sometimes we do not abide by it and find ourselves lacking or even suffering in some way.

"For these reasons, we know the animals possess knowledge, they are sacred and they are powerful. They have a special relationship with you, and they are creatures of the Mother Earth. We have a special relationship with you, and we are children of the land also. So, the animals are our true brothers.

"What a sacred brother we have who would give his life that our people would have food to eat. This is what our brother the buffalo does. Bless him, Kolunsuten, strengthen him, and let him multiply. Give him good grasses to eat and good water to drink. We are told the animals need and are benefited by prayer just like we are. Bless our brother.

"Kolunsuten, help us to find him. We ask nature by our offering for a successful hunt. We never take without asking, and we never take more than we need.

"By this prayer and offering of tobacco, I address my brother the buffalo. Thank you Brother, for by your flesh we will have food, and we will have shelter by your hides. In spirit, we are brothers and you are one of us.

"Kolunsuten, hear my prayer that we will find the buffalo herds. We will take them only respectfully in the old way and pray our thanksgiving whenever we partake of him.

"Make it so. That is all."

He wiped tears from his eyes, regained composure and lit the carved red, pipestone peace pipe. It had a long carved stem and red quillwork wrapped around it. He smoked it. "My relatives," he went on. "I will sing the buffalo song. You may dance and pray for our hunt and our protection."

Circling Raven sang his buffalo song. It was so beautiful that even animals came out to see what was that wonderful sound. Coyotes, rabbits, deer, night hawk, all mysteriously appeared at our perimeter. Some people started to dance, some knelt and prayed. Some offered tobacco to the four winds and put it on the ground. Others joined in the song. It was a sacred and wondrous moment that seemed to make time stop.

Some of the men imitated the buffalo, dipping down low and grunting. I knew then the buffalo spirit was among us. They really did know we were coming. They were going to take care of us, but only if we were worthy and prepared.

The dancing and praying went on for some time. Eventually, the great chief excused everyone. The people went to bed anxiously anticipating the coming hunt.

The next early morning dawn, I awoke and went outside to greet the new day. Others were already outside praying so I added my prayers to everyone else's so our collective offering would be acceptable to the Kolunsuten.

I planned to run, to make myself more ready but Peepa saw me and waved at me to stop. I realized he was right. We were here and ready to do what we had already prepared for. We must save our strength to use it for the people.

I looked around. Rainbow Girl was helping Checheya and Sila with their water at the conclusion of their prayer. Deer Hooves was only a short distance away.

The camp came alive with activity. Early morning foods of dried pemmican, huckleberry and deer meat mix, were prepared and hastily eaten.

Soon after, the camp was struck and we moved out again. We traveled long into the afternoon when riders showed up, sprinting their horses over a big grassy hill.

"The enemy is coming. Many of the enemy are riding upon us now," they shouted over and over again. "They are about two fingers movement of the sun away."

People rode up to Circling Raven's band to hear what to do. The men got out their weapons of war and started to shout, yell and war whoop. They rode their horses back and forth imploring each other to be brave and fight hard.

Circling Raven walked into the open and prayed tearfully for the people. "We have many brave men who are among the best of warriors in all of Creation, but they are sons, they are fathers, they are husbands and brothers. I do not want good family people to die unnecessarily," he offered. "Help us great Kolunsuten, have pity on your good people."

Just then, a raven flew overhead and made strange sounds unlike his species. Circling Raven uttered strange words that were not of our language. The bird flew away. It was sacred, for sure, but mysterious too. Why else would a bird, especially a raven, act this way? It was not their nature. They usually avoided people. This one sought us out and communicated something.

"The raven has carried the message of the Kolunsuten. We are to fight only until seven of the Chop Faces have fallen. After their seventh has been killed, we must fall back and kill no more of them. If we do this, none of our people will be killed or injured. There will be no funerals, no mourning songs and no orphans or widows," he explained.

The men acknowledged the instructions and rode ahead to form two protective lines between the approaching enemy and the people, others rushed to get weapons and prepare.

Soon, the Chop Faces rode along the ridge of the hill to show themselves. They began shouting and taunting. We know all their tactics and methods. They want to show off first, and then demonstrate bravery and total disregard for death. They were different than us, warlike and cruel, hateful and mean, belligerent and conceited. But they were dressed magnificently in war regalia with braided hair and feathers. Their horses made a stunning and dramatic picture.

Suddenly, one warrior rode out of the pack alone straight toward our warriors. He was going to count coup or maybe strike with his war club and try to get a quick kill. He was yelling and war whooping, coming in at top speed. His horse was a beautiful black Appaloosa with a white blanket and spots. He wore a porcupine hair roach with feathers atop it and hanging down the side. His face was painted black from the top of his forehead to just below his nose. He was a formidable enemy without fear.

Just as suddenly, a warrior from behind our second line rode out on a beautiful and snorting red horse. It was my Peepa and he was painted up in the style that was his: red paint from his eyes up, then a yellow line on the border and the mark of the grizzly across the right side of his face. He wore eagle feathers, seven of them, fanned out behind his head and the grizzly claws around his neck. He carried a shield in one arm, and a war club in the other. His horse was painted with a circle around one eye to give him good vision and senses, lightning bolts down his front legs to make him swift and quick. My Peepa's handprint was on his shoulder to represent the bond and pact between the horse and the man who rides him. A sun and blue and white lines were painted over his hind quarters representing the sky from which he came and the number of times he had counted coup. Seven handprints on the sides of his rump represented the number of enemies he has killed. The horse also had a feather in his forelock representing his Indian name and the acceptance of him as one of the people, one of the family.

Peepa let the horse go and he ran toward the enemy with fierce determination. He yelled his war cry.

The enemy ran toward Peepa and both sides held their lines to let their two best warriors fight. Both sides hollered their exaltation to their champion. I prayed for my Peepa with all my heart and put all my strength behind him. I knew my Noona and the rest of the family was doing the same.

They ran right at each other, closer and closer, neither one letting up at all, not one little bit. If anything, they were riding with more intensity. The gap between them closed and they clashed smashing each other with their war clubs, but each absorbed it with their shield.

They turned quickly and circled toward each other slashing again, turning into a smaller circle. They were side by side smashing at each other. Peepa's horse was biting and striking at the enemy's horse. This made the enemy work at controlling his horse.

Peepa dipped behind him and quickly dodged back to his original side. The enemy turned to meet him on the opposite side and before he could turn back again, Peepa struck him in the back. He fell off his horse and didn't move.

Peepa's war club was a large rock tied on to a thick wooden handle with raw sinew. As the sinew dried, it shrank and held the rock tightly. The enemy probably died of a broken back.

Peepa got off his horse and picked up the enemy coup stick and counted coup on him. All our people shouted and hollered their approval and excitement. Then he mocked the enemies with the coup stick like he was counting coup on all of them while he did a scalp dance.

All the enemy could see that one of our warriors killed one of their best warriors with ease. Still, we knew them. They would attack. They must.

With one war whoop, they all rode down on us. Our first line advanced, leaving a second line of defense with the women, children and elderly.

Circling Raven rode to the perimeter of the battle. He looked majestic in his full-length eagle headdress and trappings.

The battlefield was horrifying, yet awe inspiring. The men were so brave, so powerful, they seemed unbeatable. The horses were screaming, the dust was flying and the yells were blood curdling. They were all fighting for life.

Gradually, one enemy fell, and then another.

I rode into the hysteria. I thought I heard my Noona call me.

Some of the horses understood battle and knew how to get around in it. My horse was skittish and all over the place. An enemy rode by me and swung a war club at me. I ducked as it whooshed over me. My brother-in-law, Mountainside, yelled, "Sun Bear, look out behind you."

I whirled my horse around just in time to see an arrow being fired at me. I shrunk behind my shield and it ricocheted off. I swiftly grabbed an arrow from my quiver and fired it at the enemy striking him in the chest. He went down.

I whirled my horse around again. I saw my Peepa charge right into two enemies hitting the first one on the side, knocking his horse down. The rider tumbled across the ground. Peepa ran alongside the second enemy, smashing at him with his club, finally diving at him, tackling him from his horse. They struggled over a knife but Peepa out maneuvered him and stabbed him through the throat.

The first enemy pulled one of our warriors from his horse and they struggled in a hand-to-hand fight for life. Other Schi'tsu'umsh warriors jumped off their horses onto the enemy and overwhelmed him. He went down.

Men began to shout, "Circling Raven said to pull back. Pull back now."

We all stopped and moved aside just enough to let the enemy escape. They rode off a short distance and looked puzzled. Some of them ran off over the hill.

I rode over toward the enemy I had shot. "No, Son," I heard my Peepa shout. "Never look at your slain enemy in the face. Just like animals are powerful, so are the humans, and the physical remains of both. It will bother you in your everyday life and in your dreams if you look into his face."

I believed him and turned aside.

We backed off some more, taking with us the horses the enemy left behind. When we were far enough away, they sent riders down at a walk to collect their dead. After the last body was picked up and carted off, a lone enemy rode parallel along our side. My Peepa rode parallel to him.

In sign language, their rider asked, "What kind of people are you, what tribe are you?" He rubbed the skin on the back of his wrists and pointed with his hand and his chin to ask this.

Peepa made the sign of the flat bow and arrow, which is sign language for our tribe because all the men use this bow rather than the curved bow. The flat bow is fired holding it sideways which is the sign for our people. The recurve bow is held upright. The enemy acknowledged. "Forever you people will be our enemies," he vowed to my Peepa.

All the warriors hollered, war whooped and all the people joined in. Little boys were pretending they were fighting and shouting their little boy war cry. Some of the elders were crying and praying. Even the horses were celebrating, running around and showing off.

Now, I deeply understood the value to our people of the great war horse, why they honored him, gave him eagle feathers and an Indian name. A horse that is brave and knows how to fight is a great asset, a spiritual ally, and a sacred brother, indeed.

I patted my horse on the neck and thanked her for carrying me through battle. Maybe she would understand war and battle later, because she did well for her first time. Uncle Center Feather said he had a medicine to give to horses that showed promise to be good war horses. It was given only in a ceremony that helped them to understand what you wanted of them. It was still up to the horse, though, if they would overcome fear and be truly brave.

Peepa told me to ride down the hill with him. We celebrated and the people cheered us as we rode by. I knew he wanted to show Noona that we were all right, no wounds or injuries. As we passed our little band, Noona looed the woman's cry which is given to honor some feat or achievement. Then she raised her hands, palms up, toward the sky and the Kolunsuten in prayer and thanksgiving.

Circling Raven gathered everyone around him. As people settled about him, he spoke:

"My people, we have had a great and complete victory. However, this is true only because we want to do right and be right before the Kolunsuten. We want to live on this sacred road of life and partake of the foods that are life-sustaining, our brother the buffalo.

"So we must first and always thank the Kolunsuten." He went into prayer —

"Thank you Kolunsuten for our great victory today. To be right before you, we know that we can never kill indiscriminately, but only as needed in self-defense. You sent your messenger, my spirit brother, the raven to tell us this and how to conduct a battle in accordance with your ways.

"Thank you for this and that none of our people were hurt or killed. Thank you for our mighty warriors, bless them again, strengthen them, always protect them.

"Bless us all again as we journey on this buffalo hunt road. Bless us with our brother the buffalo again. Make it so."

He went on to instruct the people: "This evening we will camp at the next river by Yellow Point. There we will feast to honor our warriors."

The whole tribal band was in a buzz of excitement as family members greeted and cheered their sons, brothers and husbands, their warriors.

I rode around to take in the excitement and share in the victory.

I noticed Rock riding up toward me. He war whooped a victory cry.

"Let's go cut off their tails!" he told me with a goofy smile and his usual sign language of a cutting action and throwing it upward.

"Are you still carrying on about that?" I asked Rock, shaking my head.

"Owwww! Owwww! Owwww!! Hey-yah!" he yelled out to answer me, riding off like he was chasing the enemy.

I gazed back at the tribe and their victory celebration. Rarely, never in my or my parents memories, did the whole tribe witness a battle. Now, everyone could see what the warriors were called upon to do in order to protect the people.

They were awed.

That evening, Circling Raven had all the warriors come up near him in a line. The ones who killed an enemy were first. He gave them eagle feathers as a representation of their deeds for the people and as a symbol of the Kolunsuten's wing of protection over them. A separate, different ceremony, called the buffalo ceremony, would be done for them later so they would not be bothered or affected by the enemy life they took.

I got another eagle feather. It was my fourth one, counting the one I got at my naming.

"My friends and relatives," he announced, "these men, these warriors are your great brothers, your great fathers, your great husbands, your sons, grandsons, nephews or uncles. They put themselves between you and any danger or threat that befalls the people. When they decide to be a warrior, they decide that their life may be taken at any time for the protection and preservation of their loved ones. This is a great and beautiful sacrifice to make. It is the sacrifice our animal brothers also make for our living. It is sacred.

"The blood our warriors shed, and have left upon the ground over the seasons of time, is the foundation upon which we stand, we walk, we build our homes and we raise our children. Never forget them, never take them for granted.

"Everyone come around this way and form a line, shake their hand, and tell them you appreciate them.

"And relatives, remember in your nightly prayers to talk to nature and our brother the buffalo," he concluded.

We celebrated, but not too late, for we had another mission, the buffalo hunt. As I walked through the camp, people would stand up as I passed, out of respect for me. I wore the new eagle feather proudly. Even young boys would stand and move out of the way. This was the way of my people. I felt like a warrior now, but still I grinned at them sheepishly like a young boy.

I thought about the great warriors and scouts that lived out in the night watching over us, keeping an eye out for danger or threats to us. Uncle Center Feather was out with them. The special brigade of warriors was invisible and silent. They could track anything, even when there was no sign to the average person. They had highly developed senses. They almost seemed to see in the dark. They could smell anything out of the ordinary. They heard movements from miles away. They interpreted signs from nature and the animals. "Bless them Kolunsuten," I thought.

As I settled in for the night I wondered what great thing tomorrow might bring.

CHAPTER 14
The Hunt for Life

We moved early in the morning and traveled until about high noon. When riders rode in we knew they had found buffalo.

"About five hills over to the east, there is a large herd that extends as far as the eye can see," they reported. "Leave your packs here so the buffalo do not hear us. Ride around to the south so we stay down wind," they said pointing the way.

Excitement peaked. I felt the churning of great anticipation. Everyone moved hurriedly. Even the women were walking quickly, smiling as they quieted the children.

We stopped one hill away from our brother buffalo and made final preparations. The horses were groomed and painted. The hunters painted themselves and fixed their hair with eagle feathers. Weapons were gathered and strapped on.

Everyone began mounting their horses, all riding bareback. It was a beautiful sight! We prepared ourselves in feathers and paint because we respected and honored the buffalo. Final prayers were offered. We moved ahead, an impressive sight.

I carried a lone spear, but I strapped my bow and arrows on my back. I had worked toward this all year as I had run up hills carrying rocks and thrown my practice spear over and over. I would take a young buffalo bull the old way this day, by a lone spear.

The proven hunters all lined up in one horizontal line, over one hundred of us. We walked in formation up toward the ridge. On the top we gazed at the thousands of buffalo spread out over miles of prairie and rolling hills.

We walked our horses all in a line, side by side toward the buffalo herd. Some of the buffalo showed anxiety but did not take flight. We crept slowly forward waiting till the last possible moment before they stampeded.

I looked at the line of hunters, mostly quiet and determined in appearance. My own heart raced with excitement, my mind soared with anticipation. The horses threw their heads and snorted. Next to me, my Peepa was praying to the Kolunsuten and talking with the buffalo.

"Help us, our Creator. Bless us with food and shelter through another winter. My sacred brothers, in prayer to our mutual Creator, I address you. You have known of our coming and you let us find you. We approach you now with respect and reverence for the sacrifice you make for us," he said in prayer.

It is well known the buffalo can run as fast as a horse and can even outrun some horses. If they stampede before you are near enough, you lose the opportunity and have to try again later. So the prayer and preparation were essential to the successful hunt, for the buffalo allowed himself to be harvested only if he felt right about it.

We rode on. The nearest buffalo trotted nervously ahead, but the leaders held. The buffalo all turned and watched us. Finally, we were close enough. Still, the herd held its ground. We were so close, almost upon them.

Finally, they had enough. They broke and ran. That was our cue. We charged full speed ahead. The horses were released and they knew what to do. The quickest and swiftest of horses were already on the buffalo toward the back of the heard, but they pressed on into the middle of the pack.

The dust rose up like smoke. The stampeding hooves sounded like the loudest of thunder inside my ears. Some of the buffalo were agitated. They snorted, grunted and raked their horns around defiantly. My horse put her ears down and challenged these buffalo. I felt confident.

Uncle Center Feather always said that to ride like the horse and rider were one, you have to be totally confident about what you're doing. If you are unsure, unsteady or nervous, don't expect the horse to be otherwise. I focused my mind. All doubt left me.

I chose a buffalo bull, probably about a two year old, and guided my horse up to him. My horse knew what to do. She pushed herself up into the correct position, just slightly behind the bull, her neck even with his ribs but to the right, so I could throw the spear right-handed across my body and into his heart and lungs.

My horse judged the speed perfectly and held position. I cocked my arm back, holding the spear tightly. I focused on my target, but the bull jerked back and turned into me raking my horse across her left shoulder with his horn. She adjusted herself and dodged sideways just as the bull raked toward her ribs. She twisted her ribs away while lunging sideways, still at full speed.

I had dropped the reins after choosing the target buffalo; I was holding a spear above my head and had little or no control. I trusted her with my life. I dug in with my right knee to catch up to where she was and pull myself back to the center of her back. She regained her stride and stayed with the bull. She had her ears flat against the top of her head and was making biting motions at the bull's back and side. I didn't hesitate this time. I believed in all my preparations. With confidence, prayer and a feeling of power, I threw the spear. Right on the mark.

The bull slowed and turned to the left. I picked up the reins and my horse knew to leave that bull. I would find him later by the design on my spear.

I looked at the awesome spectacle all around me. Bareback riders steering with faith and body language riding at full speed, harvesting the mighty buffalo with spears, bow and arrows. Brave and courageous hunters, powerful in their own right, free and independent, neither owing nor beholden to another man, making their own way without question, without hesitation and without doubt. It was Kolunsuten's plan and it was wonderful.

I chose another buffalo, this time a young cow. My horse focused on it. I dropped the reins as I pulled my bow over my neck and head. In the same motion I grabbed an arrow from my quiver. Wwwwshht! It hit its mark but did not penetrate enough. I let go another one. Wwwwshht! The same result.

I rode up a little further to chance getting an arrow between the ribs and into the heart. Wwwwwwshht! It hit the mark and penetrated. The buffalo slowed and then fell.

I got two more buffalo before I pulled up. I turned and looked back. We had plenty of meat for the winter and to trade for salmon with our relatives, the Okanogan. We would have many hides to trade with the Nez Perce for some of their finest of horses. People were celebrating and war whooping. Others were praying and putting tobacco down by the first downed buffalo they came to.

Further back, others were already starting to butcher. The families could tell which buffalo were theirs by the family design on the arrow or the spear. If there was ever a dispute about whose it was because the arrow was buried or broken off, it was an honor to be the first to decline it and gift it to the other family. Maybe they were in dire need with limited hunters. The people admired and rewarded generosity. The truly rich people did not own the most, they gave the most.

I rode back to where I got the first bull with the spear. I couldn't see him but I could see Noona, Rainbow Girl and Checheya gathered around something. As I got closer, I could see it was the bull. They were already butchering.

"Good job, Son," my Noona said. "Oh, my, you'd better take your horse over to Sila. She is bleeding badly."

I almost forgot she was raked by this bull. I got off to examine her. The blood was pouring out profusely. I spit in my hand and asked the Mother Earth to help as I picked up a handful of dirt. I rubbed my hands together and prayed, "Kolunsuten, help my horse. She is a great relative of mine. She brings honor to me, my people and herself. Bless her. Stop the bleeding and let her get well quickly."

I rubbed the Mother Earth into her wound. I led her back to Sila.

He had all necessary things ready to help a horse or a rider. He wanted to be ready to help even though he didn't ride anymore.

He took out a white chalky powder and rubbed it into the wound. This is to stop the bleeding," he explained. Slowly, the blood trickled and then stopped.

He chewed a medicine plant that looked like a miniature fern, and then he spit it into the wound. He sang a healing song as he rubbed it in.

The first rule of horses, he always said, was treat them how you would want to be treated, no differently. So we used the same medicines to make them well that we used on ourselves. We prayed for them in the same way we prayed for each other, or ourselves.

Each medicine has its own song; some of them have a special ceremony. Sila said the words and sang the songs.

"She'll be all right, Grandson," he announced. "Let her rest a few days and don't ride her for a moon or two while it heals. Put this plant on her every day so it doesn't get infected," he reassured me, handing me a portion of the medicine plant.

My horse was special to me as a friend, a companion, a helper, and a trusted ally in life. I led her away and consoled her. "There, there, there my girl. You'll be all right," I told her. "You're a great horse and a beautiful person. I am proud of you. You have brought honor to me, my people, and to yourself and your people. The horse nation and the spiritual horse people are proud of you too."

She seemed to take comfort and solace in what I told her. I had spent so much time with her when I first started to train her. I had even slept in her corral near her. She came to trust me and depend on me like she did her own mother and her best herd friend combined.

We knew that horses respond to prayer, even more than people. Some people just turn their horses out when injured and some don't heal right. I would doctor her with affectionate care and sincere prayer.

Some of my nephews, other boys and men that didn't ride, were already erecting a corral for horses. I left her with them and picked up another one of our horses.

I rode back across the fields and hills where the buffalo lay. All my aunties, sisters, cousins and many other women were butchering buffalo.

My Peepa and younger brother rode up to me. "Peepa got six, I shot three," he shouted to me.

With the four I shot, that made thirteen for our little home, plus what my uncles and brothers-in-law harvested. My Noona would have at least thirteen buffalo robes herself to prepare.

That night, a great feast was prepared of fresh buffalo, camas and bitterroot. But before we could eat, we all knew prayer and offering had to be made. Circling Raven got up and moved to the settings of food when everything was ready.

"Kolunsuten, hear us again."

"Thank you for this great bounty of food from the Mother Earth. Thank you for receiving and hearing the prayers we made to you for this day, that we would have this successful hunt, and that our sacred brother would come to feed, clothe and shelter us again.

"Our prayers have been answered. We have been protected from enemies. We have been guided and directed by you, and the great and holy beings of nature. We bring ourselves near to nature to pray to you; and it is through nature your spirit moves to pity us and help us. Thank you, Kolunsuten.

"Bless our foods, for we know it is a sacred being of nature too. It has the power to sustain life. Therefore, it is great, powerful and holy and you recognize it when we put it out before you in prayer.

"Bless our brother the buffalo. He gave his life that we the people could live on into the future. Bless the buffalo who were sacrificed this day on the prairie, that they would be satisfied and happy in spirit, because your plan and purposes have been served and fulfilled.

"In turn, let it be so that we would be blessed and strengthened by their great power. Our elderly would live on in a good way, our children would grow up strong and healthy, and all our people would be protected and strengthened.

"Make it so, Kolunsuten."

He took a small portion of each food and put it in a bowl and instructed one of his nephews to put it out in nature for the spirits and the passed away, our deceased relatives.

Then, he instructed some bowls be prepared for the very elderly, followed by all the elders who gathered and sat at the setting. Finally all the adults, and then children, took seats and all began partaking of the feast.

What great food! We were hungry. A great day, a great trip, a great battle. We had stories to tell.

Visiting and laughter dominated the occasion. The people were happy and content, strengthened and encouraged, blessed and harmonious. Storytelling went on and on in most teepees.

As I sat in our teepee, my mind wandered from the visiting.

I looked at my new moccasins with the same hoof print inside the arrowhead and thought about my Noona and what she did for me making them and staying up all night to pray for me. I had not even a scratch or a minor bruise upon me. My eyes swelled up with tears of joy and deep thanksgiving.

"Always respect your mother" is an ancient teaching of our people. Never talk harshly to her, never get ahead of her and try to talk down to her. In all the world, no one is going to love you so unconditionally and with such absolute dedication.

"Your mother will be the best friend you ever had in the world," elders always said. "Once she is gone, no one — NO ONE — will ever take her place."

I rubbed the fringe and the sides of my new moccasins and studied the pattern she always drew on the top.

I looked at my Noona and Peepa and could tell they were talking about me by the way they were looking at me. They were commenting to each other, agreeing and then looking at me again. Their expressions showed pure pride and joy.

I closed my eyes. I turned my mind to the Kolunsuten. I thought about all that had happened on this buffalo hunt road, all the preparations I had made and the sweet harvest of dedicated prayer and faith through bravery and hard work.

"Thank you my Creator, Kolunsuten," I said silently to myself. "I am beginning to understand how truly wonderful, precious and sacred this life you have made really is. Even though I am a young man with much to learn, I feel the goodness that you have made in nature, in the family band and all of life.

"Bless my mother this day, too. Take care of her always."

I choked back my emotion and looked around the gathering of people.

I noticed my sister, Rainbow Girl. She was laughing and visiting. Of course, Deer Hooves was not far away. I looked to my Sila. He looked old, but not so tired this great night.

The evening was festive, yet thankful. Some of the men started to tell dramatic stories of the hunt and battle. It made for great entertainment, for this is how we enjoyed ourselves: prayer, feast, storytelling and song and dance.

I looked at my Checheya. She looked happy, yet a hint of concern or worry flashed in her eyes.

Why was she called to participate in this hunt? What purpose would she fulfill? Or did she already serve it just by helping in the butchering, cooking and drying?

The unknown is a great mystery. Circling Raven says that which cannot be known by man is the domain of Kolunsuten. Leave it up to Him. Do not try to know too much. Be happy and thankful, and always have hope.

I tried not to worry about it and leave it to the Creator.

By the commotion stirring next to me, I knew Rock was making his entry. As he sat down and looked at me ready to speak, I said, "Don't even say it, brother-friend. They don't have tails. I killed one of them and rode around many of them."

"That's what they want you to think," Rock said justifying his logic. "They're pretty sneaky." He started to make his motion of cutting, but I just looked the other way.

CHAPTER 15
Young Love: The meaning of life?

"What am I going to do?" Deer Hooves shouted in his own mind. He knew not to holler it out loud because it might disrupt the flow of nature about him.

"I only shot two buffalo, and my own mother needs at least that many. What am I going to offer for a dowry? How can I ever approach Rainbow Girl's Peepa with nothing?"

He knew he would need at least several buffalo robes, and maybe at least two horses as well, four would be even better. "I only have two horses. If I give them both away, how can I take care of a wife and a home?"

He was in a major predicament. Maybe he could trade for horses. No, they would want buffalo robes in trade and he had none. He knew he could not honorably ask his Noona or other family, because they already allocated uses for their robes.

It is not that wives are bought and paid for, or traded. But the goods of a dowry represented a worthiness to gain and provide, rather than take a beloved daughter and relegate her to poverty or just poor care.

"Perhaps people will gift us all the things we need if I just give away all that I have," he thought. "No. Her Peepa will ask me where are my horses and weapons I will need to take care of his daughter and I will be unable to speak anything but the truth."

"Maybe all my family members will contribute something for me if I ask. But how can I ever ask without appearing unworthy, without truly being incapable?"

His mind and heart plunged into helplessness. There was no honorable solution that made everything right. He couldn't go out and hunt more buffalo all by himself with enemies about. He couldn't go fight the enemy all by himself. And, he couldn't go and catch more horses until he got back home.

"Hold it." He stopped his mind and saw the answer. "Horses, the enemy has many horses. They probably brought at least two horses each and there were probably seventy-five of them."

He ran back to tell his friends of a glorious plan. He would ride in the direction of the enemy camp, find their herd and steal as many as possible. Then, drive them all back to our camp. A foolproof plan.

Some of his friends were not as enthusiastic. What about what Circling Raven said, "kill seven of them and there will be no death or injury to our people?" his friends queried.

"No one can tell another what to do," he answered. "This is a warrior decision. It is what will make some men great warriors, or not," he challenged.

"My older brother sleeps with the sky in nature as a scout and protector. He told me the enemy is camped only one day's ride to the north. We could be there by dawn if we left now," one of this friends offered.

"Your love blinds you, brother-friend," another cautioned. "Just wait till we get home. We will all help you get the best horses for your woman."

"This is the trip of destiny we are on now. I must propose the wedding to her Peepa while we are still here," Deer Hooves countered.

"Besides, are we warrior hunters, or scared little children?" he challenged.

The challenge, combined with real warrior opportunity was too much. They all joined in and quickly moved to gather their things.

As they left the camp area, they rode toward where the one friend's brother would be standing quiet as an invisible guard. He called to him in the night bird code. Within a few minutes, he was there.

He, too, tried to talk them out of it but to no avail. They were determined. He told them how to find the enemy.

Off they rode, desperate to reach the enemies' camp before daylight. All night they rode hard. The horses kept trying to turn and go back toward camp. This was a little unsettling to them and they grew quiet.

Horses have a sense, an intuition that people do not and they use that sense to protect themselves. Maybe the horses knew something about the mission they did not. Or, perhaps they were only reading the young boys' nervousness.

They were young warriors. They were strong and fast. They could hold their own with most any warriors of the world, and they knew it. Still, they had no guidance of the chiefs or the elders, and no prayer or ceremonial preparation and protection. They had to do it right as they understood it, and their understanding was limited by youth.

They crossed the valleys and streams, they went over rolling hills. All night they rode.

"I wonder what I will really do in battle," Deer Hooves thought. "I always imagined myself among the bravest as I played warrior as a boy. What is this nervousness and fever I feel? I must be strong to build my home upon the foundation of this trip of destiny."

He pushed on with the long night to think and meditate. The excitement of the adventure kept all the young men active and awake. No one felt tired or asked to rest.

Finally, as the sky in the east appeared just a little lighter, and with a brilliant morning star, they could see the enemy camp in the distance.

The enemy may have guards out as well, so they had to be careful and silent.

With a lifetime upbringing in stealth, they made their way toward the enemy camp. There appeared to be a creek down below the campfires. That is where the horses would be, as they would need water.

"Help me Kolunsuten," Deer Hooves prayed. "I only want something good for myself, a wife, a home and children of my own. Bless me and protect me."

Finally, they could see the horses along the creek. They would leave their horses back so they would not alert the enemy horses. If they acknowledged each other, the enemy would know of their presence.

"We came here only to take horses, not to kill. Remember what Circling Raven said. We have already killed seven of them," Deer Hooves instructed.

"The warrior road will dictate what happens here and we must be ready for anything, even death — or we shouldn't be here," his friend corrected, and everyone knew he was right.

They knew what to do. With only sign language, Deer Hooves sent two out to one side as he and his brother went straight for the herd. He would try to get one or two horses from the front to lead the way. From the sides and the rear, the rest of the herd would be pushed to follow the leaders across the creek.

"There must be two hundred horses," Deer Hooves said. "If we can just get back with thirty or forty it will be a great victory to coincide with this trip of destiny that brought me a wife, a home and a future family."

Their guards must be here somewhere.

They quietly crept forward. Deer Hooves gave them all a short time to get in position and catch a willing horse. If they couldn't quietly catch one, they would have to break and run at the sign and try to rope one or even jump on one.

As Deer Hooves approached the herd, he surveyed the situation. They would have to move silently but as naturally as possible. If you appeared to be moving strangely, the herd might interpret that as stalking them and begin to run away.

He walked steadily toward the herd, holding a horsehair lead rope and a leather string bridle.

"My brothers, I have a deep appreciation for you," Deer Hooves whispered to the horses. "You know me as a friend. I will take good care of you, and some of you will take care of me, even bring me a wife. Do not forsake me. Help me."

As he crept forward, a curious horse watched him and waited, but did not move away. He carefully walked right up to it, petted it on the neck and face, and slipped the rope around its neck, then the bridal into its mouth.

"It's all right, good brother. It's all right, now," he told the horse.

The sun was not far from the horizon. It was time, now or never. He called out the early morning birdcall. The others knew this was the sign, not to call back, but to act now.

Deer Hooves mounted just as the commotion started in the back of the herd. War whoops and stampeding horses immediately dominated the pre-dawn air.

Some were riding; others were running on foot looking to rope or do a running mount on a horse. The camp awoke with defiant war cries as enemy warriors ran down the hill. Some were already on horseback. They must have had their best horses right next to them.

Deer Hooves kicked his new mount toward the creek as the others tried to push the herd from the back. It worked. They all started moving toward and across the water. Everyone had a mount. Now it was time to ride with everything you had, all your strength, all your belief, and all your hope.

The herd sprinted across the prairie with all the young warriors yelling and war whooping. They had the herd believing they should sprint their very fastest with them, but they weren't out of danger yet. The enemy would try to catch and turn the herd.

Some of the enemy were running parallel to us on our left. They would try to run into the horses as near the front of the herd as possible and turn most of them away. Other enemy would try to catch their invaders and do battle.

As the enemy made their move and cut into the startled and thundering herd, they successfully turned most of the horses away and back, perhaps as many as one hundred. But, about twenty stayed with the leader, Deer Hooves, and another twenty were held and kept by our riders at the rear of the herd.

They rode for miles and miles. As the horses became winded, they slowed to a trot.

The boys who had stayed back with the horses that they had ridden all night, met them, war whooping their congratulations and approval. They quickly switched horses because even the horses that had been ridden all night were fresher than the ones the young warriors had run so hard.

"We must keep pushing. The enemy will pursue us all the way to the edge of our camp," Deer Hooves told his companions. "Let us go to claim our place in destiny," he hollered and everyone cheered and yelled.

Just then, the enemy appeared atop the next hill over, across a wide meadow, about ten or fifteen of them. But there were only six Schi'tsu'umsh, and none of them were proven warriors, some were only boys. There were surely more enemy warriors coming, too.

"Ride my brothers, ride like the wind," Deer Hooves shouted.

They pushed the horses into a sprint. With less than a half-day's ride to go, they could make it. Deer Hooves was questioning his judgment in pursuing this horse-stealing trail.

"His older brother shouted to him "We must be prepared to fight with all the fury and bravery of our greatest of warriors."

Deer Hooves knew he was right. He hollered back at him, "Ayy! Ayy! Hey-yah! Hey-yah!"

Kolunsuten promised no one a tomorrow. When that new day comes, be thankful for it. Use it for a good purpose. Have courage and be brave. He reminded himself of all the teachings. With this new day, he would have to be brave.

"Rainbow Girl, my own home and family, and a life together, it's worth it. Good does not come without effort and sacrifice," he encouraged himself. He felt strengthened. A surge of courage and bravery jolted through him. He turned and yelled his war cry at the enemy. All his brother-friends responded. His confidence and courage were contagious, spreading to each of them.

Nevertheless, you cannot fight the laws of nature. Working with nature, you could do spectacular, even miraculous deeds. Men could get incredibly amazing stamina from the horses, even run them for days without serious injury. But the Schi'tsu'umsh horses had been ridden hard all night long, and now run at a frantic pace all morning to near noon. The enemy had fresher horses.

Deer Hooves looked back. The enemy had gained ground. Two raced parallel with them up on the ridge. This time though they would not turn into the horses to recapture them. They were after blood.

Through meadows, up and down hills, leaping through small streams, the party pushed on. If they could just make it a while longer, their scouts might hear them and come to their aid.

The enemy on the ridge turned downhill riding directly toward Deer Hooves.

Back at the camp everyone was drying meat for the journey home. Big racks had been erected for smoking and drying. Rainbow Girl noticed that Deer Hooves was not nearby as usual. As the day wore on, she wondered where he could be. Finally, she sought out someone at his family's camp.

"Where is Deer Hooves?" Rainbow Girl asked Aunt.

"He did not camp with us last night, and he was not to be found this morning," his aunt answered. "We are afraid for him. Maybe he went to steal horses. His brothers and friends are all gone, too."

Rainbow was shocked into worry. Her mouth fell open. Her heart sank. Her stomach turned.

"Has anyone gone to check on them?" she asked, looking for reassurance.

"Yes, several scouts and other men rode off in the direction of the enemy camp a while ago. It will be all right," she added, seeing her worry.

Rainbow ran for Checheya and Noona and her friends, telling them all about it. Checheya said they should all pray and they went into the teepee. Checheya and Sila got out their cedars and needles of the blue spruce and started to pray with Rainbow Girl.

All she could think about was Deer Hooves. She tried not to cry, because it would be a bad sign that it might turn out tragically. She fidgeted in worry and made an effort to think toward the Kolunsuten, rocking back and forth.

Sila threw some cedar and blue spruce needles upon the charcoals of the fire asking Kolunsuten and the holy powers of nature to be with and protect Deer Hooves. "Give us a sign," he pleaded.

Just then, the wind, blew open the door to the teepee. A lone bird, a crow, landed at the door, crying "Kaw, kaw, kaw."

Rainbow quickly looked to Sila with a panicked look waiting for an interpretation. "His fate is in his own hands granddaughter," he solemnly explained. "Your young man violated Circling Raven's divinely inspired instructions. He is in danger. But the crow is not the messenger of death. Deer Hooves must ride hard, and he may have to fight hard and be brave."

Rainbow Girl was beside herself with fear. She laid upon the ground, then quickly rose to her knees. "Oh please, please, I beg of you Kolunsuten. Help and protect Deer Hooves. Let no harm come to him. Bring him safely to me." She rocked back and forth and clasped her hands over and over again. She wanted to cry, but it would be a bad sign. Her heart and stomach were overcome with worry. Her mind raced back and forth to the worst outcome and to Kolunsuten in silent prayer.

It is hard to have a focused faith when overcome with fear and worry.

I ran to the teepee, having heard the situation. "Kolunsuten, if anybody in this world deserves something good, and to have her prayer heard, it is my baby sister," I offered in silent prayer. "Hear her, my baby sister, answer her prayers." I pleaded, then looked at Rainbow. She returned my look with an expression of deep desperation and pleading.

We stood vigil with Rainbow Girl. She just kept rocking back and forth, and pleading for the Kolunsuten's pity.

We didn't know what would happen. The turmoil and stress my baby sister faced was tremendous. If only this can have a happy ending, I hoped and hoped, then prayed and prayed.

Deer Hooves whipped his horse, talking to it in his mind, "I have never asked you for every measure of strength you possessed. Now I must, my brother-friend. Run, run like your life, our lives depend on it."

The enemy was swooping down the hill with momentum. Even from a distance it could be seen that their look was of pure hate and anger. Their faces were painted all black, an expression of mourning.

He remembered Circling Raven's instructions to kill only seven and then pull back, that no Schi'tsu'umsh would be killed or injured. Maybe if neither he, nor any one of his party killed any more enemies, he and his brother-friends would be spared. However, stealing enemy horses was not pulling back. He didn't know what to do. Maybe they were on their own, so he ran hard.

His horse responded to his urging because he had a deep love in his heart for Deer Hooves. Deer Hooves outran the enemy just enough to stay ahead. The enemy ran even with the middle of the herd of horses. If Deer Hooves could just stay ahead long enough until their own scouts came, or they were closer to the camp, they could survive this race.

None of these enemy riders had bows and arrows but carried war clubs. He turned and looked again. One of them was the warrior who rode parallel to Rainbow Girl's Peepa at the end of the battle, swearing and vowing the enemy relationship for all time.

The enemies could smell the aroma of revenge. It was within their reach. The ten or twelve behind were only a few hundred yards back now, but they were only five or six hills away from the Schi'tsu'umsh camp. The enemy had to decide either to press harder for a while longer and get the leader Deer Hooves the other Schi'tsu'umsh riders and all the horses back or cut into the herd now and risk letting the leader and some of the horses go.

The enemy in the lead signaled the others and they turned into the herd and slowed them up enough for the enemy riders behind to catch up. The Schi'tsu'umsh boys circled to the outside. The fighting began. Vicious fighting. War cries, blood chilling yells of kill or be killed filled the air. One of our boys was smashed with a war club, his ribs broken on one side. Another got an arrow in his leg, but they fought on. All of them tangled in life and death clashes. Several of our boys had bows, but because they were having trouble maneuvering to stay away from the enemy, they were having difficulty getting shots.

Finally, an enemy fell. An arrow stuck through his throat.

Another enemy fell. A war club smashed the back of his head.

Deer Hooves looked back and saw his brothers and brother-friends fighting for their lives, outnumbered and on tired ponies. He thought, "I have at least twelve horses and I could ride off to be with the love of my life." He thought about it. Something urged him to turn and run off, take a wife, raise a family, enjoy the one life Kolunsuten gave him.

He started to turn and run for the camp, but stopped cold. "How will I ever look in the eyes of my wife, or any of my people, if I leave my brothers and friends to be slaughtered on the prairie by enemies?"

He turned again and rode into the battle. He carried a war club and a shield, but he had a bow behind his back with arrows. He always wondered what he would do and how he would do on the day, he was truly tested for bravery, courage and strength.

"Let us find out," he boldly said. "Ayyy! Ayyy! Ayyy! Hey yah, Hey yah!" he cried. The fear in him was pushed down as a warrior spirit emerged.

He was painted for war already because they went to steal horses. His hair was down, long and straight. He had a single eagle feather tied to the side. He rode with the wind and his horse found a new, second strength again.

A friend went down, wounded with two arrows and smashed numerous times with clubs. Deer Hooves' intensity multiplied and focused as he entered the fracas.

Just as the enemy who killed his friend yelled his victory cry, Deer Hooves let go an arrow, "Wshsht!" Right below the chest, the arrow hit its mark and penetrated deeply. The enemy went down.

Other enemies now brought their attention to Deer Hooves as he pulled another arrow.

He looked to see his brother stalled on his horse fighting off two enemies, a dangerous situation because he could be hit from a blind side, or ridden into. He raced toward his brother and let go a long shot with a prayer to guide the arrow. "Wssht!" Right in the back, it struck the enemy. It must have gone right between the ribs because it penetrated deeply.

He yelled a battle cry while circling fast now to the left. He wasn't a foolish boy now, or an unproven young man. He was a Schi'tsu'umsh warrior, a great and powerful force to be reckoned with.

He rode toward the enemy who was fighting his brother, knocking into his horse throwing the enemy to the ground. He tried to smash the enemy with his club but he ducked and ran off.

Suddenly, the enemy pulled back and started to ride off. Deer Hooves' family and several elite scout warriors were riding toward them, hollering and screaming their battle cries.

It was a miracle. Deer Hooves pulled up his horse, lifted his war club in the air and yelled his victory cry. "Owww! Owww! Owww!" he yelled. All his party yelled and celebrated. "Victory! Home! Family! Marriage! They are mine!" he shouted. "Horses, warriorship, glory...it is mine," his friend shouted.

Wshsht, wshsht! He felt the sting and the numbness in his back. He turned and the enemy he knocked to the ground had shot him in the back.

"No, no, not now," he prayed desperately. Deer Hooves' body shook and went limp.

Wshst! A third arrow struck him in the chest. Down he went.

Several of the riders of the Schi'tsu'umsh crushed that lone enemy then got off and mutilated him. All the others rushed to Deer Hooves.

"Somebody do something to help him please," his brother begged as he turned him over and held his head.

All the others gathered around him. They could see there was nothing to do. His brother continued to plead.

Deer Hooves coughed and tried to speak but could not. He tried again.

"Tell my love I fought for her and I fought for our life together. Tell her my love is true without question or doubt. Therefore, I want her to live her life in happiness and beauty, not in sadness or mourning.

He coughed and strained, and struggled to breathe. He talked ever so weakly. "Tell my Noona, thank you for being a good mother to me . . . ."

He let out his last breath, the same breath the Kolunsuten breathed into him, at his birth. He was gone.

He had fought bravely and saved the lives of his brother and friends. He was a man, a warrior, a hunter...but he was gone.

All the men stood around him in silence. It's always somehow more tragic when a young person dies before their time.

Some of the men rode after the enemy. Others gathered horses. But no one talked. It was a great loss.

Rainbow Girl still rocked back and forth in worried prayer in the teepee with her family. Finally, they could hear riders. It was messengers from the rescue party.

They all ran out to see them talking to Deer Hooves' family. His mother, father, sister and aunties started to wail and cry. She knew what had happened. She could feel it. She started to cry. "Oh, no, please no," she wailed. Her legs went weak and she staggered.

One of the riders rode over to our teepee and only shook his head.

Then, he said, "Two of our boys have been killed fighting the enemy, four have lived. Seven enemy were killed, three of them by Deer Hooves. We have fifteen more of the enemy horses. But Deer Hooves was killed. It took three arrows to stop him."

My Peepa nodded at him, but his worry now was Rainbow Girl. This brash, at times outspoken, but sincere young man had her heart and her love. And she was so extremely sensitive and deep in her feelings. She did not handle death or loss well even when it was distant. If she saw a family crying, she cried too and went to help them.

How would she ever handle this?

Rainbow Girl fell to the ground, clutching the grass and the dirt, tearing at it. She moaned and cried. She screamed her shock and horror. Noona and Peepa tried to help her, but she wanted no one to touch her or help her. They pulled her arm and hand. They tried to hold her but she screamed and struggled against them. Her eyes looked different and lost. She sounded crazy.

The scene was tearing at the hearts and the minds of all who could see. It was pitiful. I didn't know what to do, so I got on my knees next to her and cried. Then Noona and Peepa did the same. Sila and Checheya stood by us and prayed. My brother and older sister knelt and cried with Rainbow Girl, too.

"Kolunsuten," Sila said, "it is for this time we prayed to you for strength and blessing, when we do not know what to do or how to help ourselves or our loved one. Guide us now. Help us now."

Rainbow Girl continued to cry, but more sobbing now then screaming. She wasn't violently tearing at the ground anymore, but her mind was gone.

Peepa told me, "Help me get her into the teepee Son." She wouldn't walk, but only fell limp. So, we picked her up and carried her in the teepee as she moaned and cried.

She cried herself into a stupor. She just lay there, moaning and sobbing. Sila fanned her with his sacred feathers and sweetgrass smoke, then brought some water, but nothing worked.

Checheya came into the teepee walking with a cane. She was very elderly now. Her hair was white, her face was wrinkled and cracked, but she had a look of determination and concern, like a parent rushing to help their infant child when hurt or in danger.

"Move out of the way, my children and grandchildren," she ordered as she made her way around the teepee toward Rainbow. I got up and moved over, as did my Noona, Peepa and Sila. Checheya carried a buffalo bladder bag, around one shoulder, which she used to pack water.

She slowly lowered herself next to Rainbow Girl with the help of my Sila and Noona. Rainbow Girl laid on her side facing the small fire in the teepee, on a buffalo robe. Checheya lifted her head and set it on her lap.

"Kolunsuten, help us now," she said looking up toward the sky, then down at Rainbow. She put her hand on her head and stroked her hair back out of her face. Her voice was old and sincere.

"This is my Granddaughter, my baby girl, and she is suffering. For all that we are as people, for all the powers to do and to make you have given us, there are things that we cannot do, needs for which we cannot provide and some deep problems which we cannot solve on our own. For these things, we can only turn to you, nature and ceremonial prayer."

"I'm just a grandma, a lone woman praying to you. But I have a great love in my heart, and that love has been the guide in my life." She started to cry, sobbing as she prayed.

"This baby girl of mine, like all my children and grandchildren, taught me about the true meaning of life, about the wonderful power of love and about the sacrifices of grandparenthood for your loved ones. I would do anything for her to help or protect her. She is precious. She is a treasure."

Checheya took out the container of water, poured some on her hands and rubbed it on the head and face of Rainbow Girl while she prayed.

"Oh! Kolunsuten, hear this old grandma. Now I know why I was called on this trip, to be with and help my baby girl. If I had great and mysterious powers, I would use them now to make my granddaughter better, but I only have the deep and devoted love of a grandma, and prayer. Let it be enough for you to bring your power, your spirit and your comfort to my baby girl," she pleaded with a desperate, kind tone in her voice.

She continued to rub the water on her, which made Rainbow Girl regain some measure of composure and consciousness as she looked around a little. But she then went back to her crying.

Checheya lifted up her head and set it upon her lap. Gently and softly, she sang her lullaby song, cradling Rainbow Girl and rocking her back and forth. It was the same lullaby she sang to her as a baby and small girl to put her to sleep in the huckleberry mountain camp.

I couldn't help but think of that one night and other times she held Rainbow Girl just like this and sang her to sleep, or comforted her when she fell and hurt herself. Often times, Checheya was the only one who could comfort her. Maybe it was the power of a grandmother.

Just as she did for her as a small child, Checheya put in the words:
"My baby girl is all right now.
Because Grandma is here
She's grandma's girl,
Hey, hey yah, hey yah ah!"

She continued the song as Sila quietly prayed. Peepa held his head down, looking concerned and afraid, because his daughter was hurt.

My Noona had a look of spiritual grace upon her. Tears streamed down her face, but she appeared overwhelmed with the beauty and true righteousness of what had taken place.

Checheya hummed her song now, but still put in the words. Rainbow Girl stopped crying and moaning, then looked around. She gazed at Checheya with a helpless little girl look and just accepted the comforting and encouragement being passed to her.

"Thank you Kolunsuten for this miracle," Sila prayed offering our incenses to the fire. "Your great miracle powers do not come through the boastful or elaborate doings of men, but through the humble sincerity of family people. That is all we are, poor family people. But humility and sincerity are the roads to you, and they are a part of your greatness. Thank you." He threw the incense on the fire.

I sat in amazement. When nothing else would work, it was the love of a grandma for one of her own that brought the Kolunsuten's comfort. It was the basics of our traditional teachings. This is why she was called on this trip. Danger loomed and she may have been needed to help her loved ones.

"Checheya, Checheya," Rainbow Girl said, "what am I going to do?"

"You'll be all right, my baby. Shshshsh, now. Rest and calm yourself. Your Checheya's girl and I have you now," Checheya reassured and comforted her.

Rainbow girl rested, her breathing returned to normal. Still, every once in a while she would wipe tears from her eyes. We stayed with her all day and all night, never leaving her alone.

CHAPTER 16
End of the Trail:
A new beginning

Several days later, we were back at Yellow Point, one of the places we had camped on the way to find buffalo. This was a traditional camp area of the Salish. It was at a bend in the river, along the inside where the water seemed to wrap around it. The land here was flat and sandy, with plenty of grass for the horses. Downstream from the bend was a big, natural eddy where the water was deep and still.

Sometimes, in previous years and over the generations, it was here we met our brothers on our way to hunt the buffalo.

Since Deer Hooves was half Salish on his mother's side, he would be buried here. His relatives on this side had already joined us. Messengers rode to notify them of the news as soon as the tragedy happened. We would camp here and make final preparations for the burial.

The tribe set up camp as usual, but we did so quietly and reverently so as not to upset Rainbow Girl. She was better now, though mournful and hurt. At least the horrible shock that took her mind and shook her spirit had gone from her. Still, she grieved and mourned. Sometimes, I could hear her crying in the night.

Deer Hooves' whole family was hurt and in mourning. We didn't know them well, only by reputation. They were good people, strong and respectful. It always seemed like no one, certainly not the good people of the world, deserved this kind of suffering. I was anxious again to hear how the chiefs and elders would interpret this tragic occurrence within all the great victories and blessings. I knew they would somehow make it come out right, but I had little idea how.

It seemed as though we had everything — all good with blessings of prosperity, then a cloud came over us. However, the cloud did seem rather thin and light today, now that Rainbow Girl was better, and maybe going to be all right. She was hurt way down deep, where the most tender and strongest of feelings were kept in her heart. It would take prayer, talking and time to heal her. We all knew this, even though she probably felt she would never be really all right ever again.

For now, we had to be quiet around her because people in this state are very sensitive. "You must not talk loudly, nor let them hear harsh words," was the teaching.

As night fell, a mournful spirit fell over the camp. The feeling was different. The night animals behaved strangely and sounded sad, even angry. A wolf howled a lonely cry. Farther off in the distance a lone owl hooted, but there was no response.

I looked up in the sky and a shooting star flashed from the south to the north, a bad sign among my people. A star from a different direction would not be ominous. I started to worry, and said a silent prayer.

The traditional wake was about to begin. This was a very important ceremony to my people. We felt compelled to address the living of life as a special and sacred privilege of the Kolunsuten as we returned a loved one back home through nature. Also, it gave family and friends an opportunity to address the deceased one last time before their spirit departed.

Maybe there was unfinished business between them. Maybe there were harsh words exchanged that would otherwise be left as bitterness or a burden of guilt upon the living. Whatever it may be, even just fond remembrance and song and prayers for the surviving family, this was the time for it.

As I approached the special lodge erected for the wake, they were already singing inside. I came in and took a seat along the side. The leader was Turtle Shell, Deer Hooves' grandfather.

Various people were getting up before the gathering and remembering Deer Hooves, his character and friendly nature, things he did or amazing feats he achieved. Some of the older ones talked about his childhood.

An older uncle of his on his mother's side got up and slowly walked to the front. He was graying and looked every bit the respected elder of his family band.

"My nephew was a good boy," he said. "He will be missed."

"I remember when he was still in his mother's womb on the way here. My baby sister was so excited for him. She only ate certain foods. She was never around any negative kind of talking or carrying on so that her future son would have the best of nature about him.

"I remember when he first laughed when he was only a few months old. Some little puppies were playing and wrestling. He thought it was so funny, he just laughed and laughed." The old man paused a few moments to compose himself and choke back tears. Others around the room could not and they cried their sadness.

He started to talk again. "I remember when he took his first steps upon the Mother Earth. And I remember when I first took responsibility for him as the uncle on his mother's side.

"He was the best of us, the best of our family, the best of our tribe. He was kind and good. He was alive with energetic joy and happiness. We will miss him.

He started to cry.

With his voice, cracking and struggling to speak, he said, "Remember us, my relatives, for we are in mourning. Remember his mother for a part of her is gone now. A mother's love for her child is sacred and powerful. One of the most powerful forces in this world.

"She will cry her loneliness and mourning during this one year period. She will miss him, what he used to say, what he used to do, where he slept, what he liked to eat, the songs he sang, everything.

"Pity my baby sister, relatives. Shake her hand, tell her something good."

He concluded his remarks, sang beautiful songs and added powerful prayers for Deer Hooves and the family of mourners.

As the service went on throughout the night, various families got up in the front and talked, prayed and sang. Sometimes, people would get up and reverently dance with the song, or just bob up and down.

Toward early morning before the sun came up, Turtle Shell announced the time would be for the mourners, the immediate family of Deer Hooves.

"My relatives," he said to everyone, "as is our custom, this early morning we will give time to the family to address their final farewells to my grandson, Deer Hooves. Now is the time, whatever your last concerns or issues left unaddressed may be, you should say them now before we put him back to the Mother Earth for his journey, that these things may not be left to burden you."

One by one, different family members got up and talked about their son, nephew, brother or grandson, Deer Hooves. Sometimes they added prayer and song. It was their prerogative and time to use how they wanted to. They all had their faces painted black, not the whole face, just a mark. They would leave that paint on for four days.

Finally, his brother and cousins got up. They kept their heads down, and looked nervous. Their words were hard coming out. They cleared their throats.

"Uh- relatives," his older cousin began, "I want to say something." He spoke very unevenly and he was hard to hear.

"My cousin brother, Deer Hooves, uh . . . uh," he cleared his throat. "He meant everything to me, to us.

"I, uh, none of us, uh, we don't talk in front of people. Uh, I apologize about it. My uncle, he always said actions speak louder than words. So we try to live that teaching.

"Anyway, our brother Deer Hooves . . . ." he broke into tears and choked. "I'm sorry we could not save you. I'm sorry we could not talk you out of this horse stealing trail."

He paused and they all stood there looking hurt and mournful. Their uncle started a song and everyone joined in.

As the boys walked away, I noticed my Peepa was walking toward the front with my Noona and Rainbow Girl. I got up and walked up to stand with them.

Rainbow Girl stood back with her head down. She was already crying desperately.

First we faced the body of Deer Hooves, laying there in his finest of clothes, white buckskin. His hair was combed immaculately and he wore matching beaded jewelry and quillwork. He looked peaceful.

Peepa said a prayer, and then led a song. We all sang with all the feeling of love and hope we had. Everyone joined in. It was beautiful and spiritually powerful.

"My relatives," Peepa began as we turned to face all the people, "this is a tragic and mournful time. But, just as this darkest hour of the night will pass to bring the Kolunsuten's first light of a new day, so will the overpowering hurt pass to bring us new hope and understanding.

"I hope and pray and believe that the good family of this young man, Deer Hooves, comes to this peace as nature will pass from dark to light.

"Also, this is my daughter, Rainbow Girl. Deer Hooves and she had it in their minds to wed. It was this thought that led this young man on his horse stealing quest.

"My daughter is still very young. So I will, as her father, speak for her. It is not only my right, it is my responsibility.

"I say that my daughter has had her heart broken and her mind turned upside down. She wishes that her fiancé would have accepted another way to simply and humbly begin their lives together.

"Still, she remembers him in a good way. She put all her love and hope in him, and it was crushed for her. We all know how we depend upon our spouse. So we can imagine how it feels for my poor daughter."

Peepa started to cry. He choked back tears and spoke to the family, offering prayers and then song.

He said words for what happened to Deer Hooves for Rainbow Girl's sake. This way she would not be burdened as if it were her fault that Deer Hooves was killed. Many times, people let this time pass without addressing things properly and then they are hardened and burdened for the rest of their life with deep regrets. "If only I would have done this . . . . If only I could have told them that," they say over and over.

Peepa did not want Rainbow Girl to be burdened with needless regrets that might consume her.

As people were singing, Turtle Shell painted Rainbow Girl's face black, just like she was a member of the family. Peepa must have arranged it with the leader because this would never be done without permission.

The leader wrapped her in an elk skin blanket. Then he smoked her off with the incense of sweetgrass. She was seated on the south side and told to remain still, to stay wrapped in the blanket.

"At dawn, before the sun comes over the hill, your daughter must wash her face in the creek," the leader told Peepa. "Otherwise, she would have to leave it on for four days," he explained.

As the first light moved across the eastern sky, the sacred morning songs were sung and we concluded. It was a genuinely blessed ceremonial wake. But the hardest part was always putting a loved one in the ground.

Noona took Rainbow Girl to the creek where she washed her face. They went to our teepee to get ready for the burial.

Some of the family stayed with Deer Hooves as was our custom to never leave them alone until they are returned home through the Mother Earth. Others cleaned up and made final preparations.

Rainbow said she felt drained but somehow better and clear minded.

As we settled in, messengers told us the family was ready for the burial. We started to make our way to the burial ground, a small hill overlooking a bend in the river. All our burial grounds were situated just like this.

Rainbow Girl had not seen Deer Hooves since the day before he left to steal horses. Putting a loved one in the ground is the hardest thing in this world to do. We knew it would be unbearably difficult for her. But, she had to go. It was our way to have respect, and show respect. She would know to be brave and strong.

No one considered Deer Hooves' death a problem between the families. It was not our way, not anywhere in our thinking.

It was the Kolunsuten, His way, and His law that took Deer Hooves. I didn't know why or how. I wanted to hear from our elders and chiefs to understand more.

The family had a spiritual leader praying and singing over the body. He went to each of the four directions with his arms out, holding an eagle feather in one hand as he began the top of the song. Toward the end of each verse he walked back toward the body. A helper held a braid of burning sweetgrass, the smoke from which he fanned with his eagle feather toward the body.

As he finished his song, he paused and introduced himself. "I am River Rock of the river band west of the headwaters," he explained. He explained who he was by who his parents and grandparents were, which is our tradition.

Then, he announced for the family and all Creation that we were returning and recommitting our relative, Deer Hooves, to the Mother Earth from which he came.

"When we come into this world upon this road of life, we are announced to and initiated with the divine nature, our holy beings of Creation. We live a lifetime with it and by it. When we leave this road of life, also, we must address nature from which we come.

"Kolunsuten, this life you have made, and we are thankful for it. You have made the Mother Earth, the fire, the water and the air. From them and by them, your great miracle of life is enabled, and our bodies are composed of all of them. When our lives are completed, our bodies must go back to the nature from which they came."

"Mother Earth, thank you for this young man, Deer Hooves, and the strong life and strong body he was given. All of Creation moved to give him a mind and a nature of goodness, kindness and likeability, which was the Creator's plan. We prepare to return his remains to you that in spirit he would go on to the other world, the happy spirit place where all our ancestors dwell."

He paused and fanned him off with a tea made up of rosewood, again to the four directions. The family had already washed the body with this same tea as they sang certain songs to clothe him. Then they used this tea on themselves. As usual, before and after, they were smoked off with the incense of cedar and blue spruce. This was done because the physical body in death is very, very powerful, and those handling and dressing it had to be protected so they wouldn't be unnecessarily affected in their dreams or in their thoughts.

Deer Hooves, like all our deceased, was dressed in white buckskin because this was considered our finest of clothing. Upon the ground, he was placed atop an elk skin burial robe. His hair was combed long and straight. He wore a bone choker around his neck.

As the spiritual leader for the family finished, he announced that Circling Raven himself would speak for the tribe and, especially, the family in mourning. Wise interpretation by our elders and chiefs is what I was waiting for, what we all needed.

"My good relatives and friends," he began. "This is a solemn occasion for which we gather. We all know the hurt of mourning. We all have buried loved ones at some time or another. It is a sad and extremely hurtful thing to do.

"It is not our choice. It is not our way. It is the Creator, Kolunsuten. If it were only up to us, everyone here would have all their folks with them, happy, healthy and together. But, it is not that way. The Kolunsuten is the one who made our world for us, and He is the one who fixed an end to our lives. So many of our loved ones are gone from us.

"Kolunsuten promised no one a tomorrow . . . no one. It doesn't matter who you are. Today, we are here. Tomorrow, perhaps we won't be. When tomorrow comes, a new day is dawning, rejoice and be thankful in prayer, truly rejoiceful. Let the tears of your joy represent the strength of your understanding. Then you will be blessed.

"Our relative here, Deer Hooves, has gone on to the other world, the day for him has come and we stop here to respect him and his life. But, he is in a better place. A home camp had been prepared for him by his relatives, his grandparents, maybe some uncles, aunts or cousins. This home camp is a wonderful, beautiful place.

"In the home camp in the other world there is no pain, no suffering, no fear, no hunger and no thirst. There is no more wondering why about the unknown, why there is suffering in the world, what it is or the meaning of our lives. The Creator's ways are made known to you and you are fulfilled with his understanding, spirit and acceptance."

Everyone was frozen at attention listening to the words of the great chief. Even the mourners looked directly at him, absorbing the healing words like a medicine.

"Why was this young man taken at such a young age with a whole lifetime before him? We do not really know, and we probably will never know. This is the Creator, Kolunsuten's domain.

"Perhaps, he just came here to teach his mother and father about true love and family happiness. Perhaps, he came to teach his brothers and sisters how sacred they are and why they must take care of one another. And, perhaps this powerful young man came to show all of us how sacred and precious this life really is.

"Therefore, we should hold our children and grandchildren dearly this day, and all days. We must honor and respect one another, and be especially mindful of our warriors who willingly put their lives between the people and danger or threats."

"Finally, perhaps Deer Hooves came here into this world to tell a young woman and all people, that love and hope are powerful forces, the principle forces upon which families and homes are built."

Rainbow Girl started to cry.

"Perhaps he gave his life to protect and preserve this for her, and for each and every one of us from some unknown enemy or evil. Maybe he killed the enemy both physically and spiritually who would have brought some disastrous harm or damage to our people. He gave his life that his people would live and be happy.

"For this we owe our dear deceased relative a great and special honoring, an expression of gratitude and family love. From this day forward, may our young homes, young families, our little children and all our people be blessed and prosper from the sacrifice he made."

"Someone might say that he should have listened to the Chief and not gone on this horse stealing quest. But that is not for us to say or to truly know without any doubt. We do not speculate about the Kolunsuten's plan. We only go along with it.

"His last words were that his fiancé should know his love was true, but that her life go on in happiness and beauty. That his mother knows he was thankful and loving to her for being a good Noona."

Rainbow Girl hadn't heard his last words yet. We didn't tell her. She sobbed her grief as more of the hurt festered from her heart and poured out from her.

"To his mother, I say, may the great and good Kolunsuten bless you and keep you, and be with you during those times you are alone remembering your boy, around the time he was born into the world, when something happens in the home and you think what your son would say if he were here, when you look at the empty seat at your family setting of food."

Some of the family wailed their cries of grief. Even the men cried unashamedly.

"This young man lived only nineteen years and he was snatched from this world even before the prime of his life. All the hope, all the love, all the prayer that a parent feels for their little child, these mourners today feel it too today. But their loved one isn't here anymore . . ."

Circling Raven choked up and cried as he felt such strong compassion and sympathy for the family.

"So, may the surviving family members be blessed and comforted. May all the mourners among our people be blessed and comforted this day. Remember them, my people. Go to them. Be kind and merciful to them. Pray with them. Cry with them. This is our way.

"So, my relatives, we will sing the honor song and the burial song, three times each, which is our custom."

He started to sing and all the people joined in one mournful, prayerful voice. Drummers kept the solemn beat. An eagle appeared overhead, soaring by with an easy grace, then turned and circled. Then, three other eagles joined him to make four. My Peepa said they were sent by the four directions for Deer Hooves and to make complete the meaning of his life among the people, just as Circling Raven expressed.

Many people started to cry, shaking their hand back and forth in time with the song, and singing with deeper sincerity. A spiritual healing feeling came over everyone like a soft light as the mourning song was sung, but we cried our grief and sang harder. Circling Raven blew his eagle whistle. In spirit, it would line the pathway for Deer Hooves to the spirit world.

As Circling Raven started the burial song, Deer Hooves was put into the ground. People prayed and sang even more intently. Some got on their knees and put their hands out to the heavens.

It was a heavy burden, but the people picked it up and carried it together for the mourners. The feelings of harmony and unity were complete among us. A spirit of hope entered our hearts. The presence of Deer Hooves was evident now, and he seemed joyous in the glory of the other world. Today, he had become what the Creator made him to be, more than a man, maybe all that he ever hoped he could be and more. It was a beautiful, even glorious thought.

As the song finished, relatives began moving the dirt with flat pieces of wood and carved bowls, covering Deer Hooves. His feet faced the east, toward the down current of the river, that the water will show him the way.

"Our relative is at peace now in the other world. We can feel it. But he lives on also in nature, in the day, the night, the wind, the eagles. Maybe he runs with the deer or the buffalo, or swims with the fish. Maybe he rides the rainbow or sits with the stars. Now he fully understands why we call the earth our mother as he has gone home to her. It is all spiritual and glorious."

"Shake hands with the family. Remember the mourners in your prayers. Bring them food. Talk to them, encourage them and strengthen them with your presence."

With that, the funeral was concluded. Everyone shook hands or hugged the mourning family, and many came over to wish Rainbow Girl well. She made her way up to the front to support the family.

As she shook their hand, they all hugged her even though they didn't know her. Deer Hooves' mother cried and sobbed as she held Rainbow's hand, then hugged her. They cried together.

"It's all right, my girl," his mother told her. "My boy wants us to live on and be happy. One day, you will feel that way, even though we will never forget him."

Rainbow Girl just held on and sobbed. Then she told her, "You poor mother. I'm so sorry for you." They both cried together.

She moved to his father. He just kept looking down, avoiding eye contact, which was the custom of people in mourning. "He was a good boy . . . all good." He said no more.

In the words that were spoken, the prayers that were said and the songs that were sung, grief and mournful hurt was expressed and released. Deer Hooves' life was put into a context of respect, honor and achievement. What we could not know, we left it to the Kolunsuten. Everyone felt somehow better.

We went down to the dinner, which is our custom after a funeral. Prayer, offering of food to the deceased and talking took place as usual. But people visited with a friendly atmosphere, even quiet laughter and joyous conversation could be heard out away from the family.

It really was a great trip. We defeated the enemy. We got all the buffalo we needed. We captured enemy horses, and only two of our people were killed.

Rainbow Girl would not officially or formally be in mourning, but she would quietly mourn. Otherwise, she would have to cut her hair, go through some harsh ceremonies and maybe go off with Deer Hooves' family for a while.

But since they weren't married, she would quietly mourn with us.

Mourners did not go to social gatherings or dances, nor did they hang around people laughing or carrying on to silliness. They stayed in mourning for about one year. Then the family would hold a memorial dinner to remember their passed-away loved one. After that, they would go on again, free to live fully and attend all functions.

People in mourning could not gather our traditional foods, nor could they hunt. They could not re-marry, court or be courted till the mourning period was over. It would be dangerous to take this tradition lightly, someone could be hurt if we did.

When one is in mourning, the spirit of the loved one is still around you. Your feelings are deeply hurt. The presence of a spirit will make you feel differently, dream strangely and act oddly. Foods for the people were too sacred, with a life giving power of their own to be gathered or harvested in a cloud of death and mourning. The spirit of a life now gone was too powerful to be disrespected and ignored at a social gathering.

So, we would take care of Rainbow Girl.

That night, Sila prayed as we concluded our day and prepared to rest.

"Thank you Kolunsuten for another day of life. Thank you for all the blessings in it, our foods, our shelter, our loved ones, our horse brothers."

"Give us another day, too. Let that sun come up for us again to bring us happiness and joy. You promised no one a tomorrow, so we pray you would make it good for us. Let it be so," he concluded throwing incense upon the charcoals of the fire.

Everyone went to bed.

We hung around camp longer than we should have, but the chiefs probably wanted to give the mourners time before we had to travel. We stayed with our Salish brothers for several more days.

It was getting late in the year. The air had a crispness, especially in the morning and at night. The horses started to look a little fuzzy, since they were already growing their winter coats.

It was time to move on home and prepare our winter camps along the higher banks of lakes and rivers in our own country. It would be a somber trip for some of us.

CHAPTER 17
The Harmony of Nature

The trek home and anticipation of arriving was always as welcome as the excitement of beginning a journey. We headed out from the plains and prairies of the buffalo country westward to our homelands.

In my mind, I could already see the rolling timbered hills, the fresh, natural meadows, our rivers as they flowed into the lake, the sun glistening off the water and the grand mountains in the distance.

I felt a deep awakening in my mind and a powerful energy surged in me. I could hardly wait. I wanted to gallop my horse ahead, but I breathed deeply and waited.

Each family had numerous packhorses, filled with buffalo meat and hides. It made for slower going, but it was a good feeling to know we had food for the winter. We would trade with our brothers, the Okanogan, and the Spokane: buffalo meat and hides for dried salmon. The Okanogan would invite us to fish for ourselves, as we did at their falls every year. At the home camp, we already had caches of dried roots, camas, bitterroot, wild carrot and pemmican, the dried meat mixed with dried berries and fat, stored under piles of large rocks, wrapped in hides and bladder bags.

We were traveling easy and content. The slower going made it easier for the elders like Checheya and Sila to keep up.

But Circling Raven was worried, and we knew to respect his knowledge and understandings. We heard he was concerned that we had stayed too long. The delays added about half a moon cycle to our trip. We were no longer ahead of our usual schedule. He warned us in the beginning that we had to depart early because winter was coming early.

The scenery continued to inspire me. The foothills of the great mountains were colored with early fall as we traveled along the river valleys making our way. At night, the boys of most every family had fresh trout or deer to eat with our other foods.

The sun had a golden tint to go with the golden grasses and the red or yellow leaves. The green of the evergreen trees never seemed brighter or more alive. You could smell the crispness in the air, although it warmed every afternoon. The dry grasses of the prairie had its own feel and aroma. With the yellowing and orange colors in the brush and the trees, it looked like the Mother Earth had painted her face, and she would look upon us as we passed.

A family of hawks followed us diving around, playing in the autumn air. "Cha, cha," they screamed at the bottom of their dive, just as they turned upward.

"I'm very proud of you, Son," my Peepa said, surprising me with his presence. "You are very special. You bring your mother and me a great amount of joy and happiness. It is a beautiful world, this country of ours." He looked around contented and sighed.

I knew he was glad that no harm or death had come to me, like it had the others. I always held stubbornly to the teachings of our elders, teachings of life, teachings to live by and prosper; prosper in spirit, not in material gain. "Take your course and your guidance from nature interpreted by the elders who really know," we were advised. So far, everything worked out.

Why is it that things work out well for some people and not for others? I pondered this deeply. My Peepa sensed this and advised me:

"If you listen to all the teachings carefully and apply them to your daily living,

"If you are always disciplined and prepared for anything and everything,

"If you have done right and good in your life and not left things undone,

"And if you are willing to work hard and have faith, things will work out for the best.

"It sounds as though you described my sister Rainbow Girl," I said not arguing, but looking for answers. "And things haven't worked out too well for her . . . ."

"Yes," he continued, "but sometimes other people's lives affect our own life. Decisions and poor judgments of others are sometimes the worst of burdens for us to carry.

"You, Son, have a good nature. Some others may have a flaw right at the core of their basic nature. This can be caused by nature or for other reasons. They may have become overly self-proud or forgotten how to take care of the needy in our tribe. Perhaps, their flaws or misfortune are inherited from their parents or grandparents in some way we do not understand. Or, maybe, they have not spoken right and proper words and this has come back to burden them.

"Peepa," I said questioningly, "Deer Hooves seemed to have all these good qualities and still he is gone, with all those he cared most for left hurt and mourning. How is this?"

"A simple little thing, Son," he answered softly. "Always listen to your elders who really know. Our prophet chief said not to engage the enemy after seven of them had fallen. This divine direction was not heeded.

"You have had a special upbringing, almost like those a medicine man would receive. When you have a good stock of roots and berries, and the Kolunsuten adds his rainwater and sunshine, it grows and prospers. It is just like this in raising children, but the rainfall and sunshine is teaching, it is guidance, it is love, but love enough to discipline.

"It has worked for my children, and all our people for many generations.

"All is good, Peepa," I told him. "Even Rainbow Girl will be all right."

"All these teachings of hard work and faith still apply to my daughter. Everything can and will still work out well for her. It is up to her not to leave these sacred teachings. Do not change. Do not lose faith. Do not bring hardship into your own life," he counseled.

Rainbow helped Checheya with the small children already, but she stayed close to camp never venturing off. Checheya and Sila had great grandchildren now and the little ones' parents wanted them to be around their great grandparents to learn, to gain some strength and understanding.

I could hear the women of the family tell them to behave, do this and do that, "because my Checheya always said . . . ." That is exactly what Checheya herself used to tell us, that her grandparents told her those things and she was passing them on. I could see the full circle of life the elders talked about, right now in the circle of our family.

Rainbow was troubled though. It seemed to come to her in waves. Powerful hurt and a mournful feeling would overcome her, then subside a little. She didn't eat much and became thinner.

"What am I going to do?" she thought to herself. "Nothing makes sense anymore. Things don't really work out for people even if you have all the faith in the world."

Several nights as she slept, she had a dream about a bird alongside a stream. It was a beautiful eagle with black and white tail feathers. She enjoyed its majesty, just to behold it. As she approached the bird, she could see a dead eagle floating in the water. The eagle on the tree limb turned and hollered at her and she would awaken.

She was troubled by this mournful dream but told no one. She kept everything inside.

Each day we rode on. It was getting cold in the mountains. A cold wind blew in the day. At night, there was already frost. This was unusual for the middle of autumn. In the morning, the bushes looked like mystical beings of crystal with heavy frost and ice glistening in the morning sun.

We kept winter-type fires in our teepees at night. Nevertheless, there was no complaint about the weather. That would be like complaining about being alive, and unthinkable. All the people looked to the good and were always deeply thankful. All the nature, and all the weather — we got along with it perfectly.

The sacred nature provided our food, our shelter, our method of travel, our tools, our weapons, our medicines, our religion and our ceremonies. We lived by it, wholly and totally. It was not an inconvenience, ever, not in any way. It was the Creator's way. It was life itself. The road of life is built upon nature. In the beginning, our people were given a sacred compact with the Creator and nature to provide for our survival and good living. Our responsibility was to use it wisely and not to be wasteful.

Harmony with nature and all it is, is not merely a principle or concept. It is a state of being to be attained along the course of a lifetime, earned only by how you live your life. True and living examples of respect, reverent offerings in prayerful, sincere ceremonies and peace with the Creator, this was the only way to achieve this harmony. Our people had it, and we felt its blessing.

It was a spectacular journey. I watched the family of hawks that kept us company. As they dove and played in the wind, I realized, they are one with the wind. They do not try to use the wind or take something from it, nor do they change it or force it. Also, the salmon, and all the fishes, are one with the water.

Likewise, all the people must be one with nature by the way we live each and every day, by the way we think and by the way we believe, pray and communicate with it. There really is no difference between our everyday life and religion; and no difference between religion and ceremony. So we pray to the Kolunsuten to sanction all that we do religiously and ceremonially first, bringing ourselves near to nature that He would move to bless us and fulfill our prayers through nature.

I felt strengthened and encouraged, and deeply fulfilled in my own thinking. The teachings of our elders really do come to life in our living if we try to uphold them by our own conduct.

We moved with nature, the land, the seasons, the animals and the weather. The earth is our Mother, the sun is our Father, the mountains are our grandfathers, as are the four directions; not in symbolism, but in fact of spirit. They all care deeply for us, their children and grandchildren, and we feel a deep and abiding love for them in return just as we would for our physical mother, father or grandparents.

I got off my horse and walked with my Sila awhile. No matter how many times it happened, I was always surprised when he knew what I was thinking and feeling.

"It is sacred, Grandson," he said to me. "It is all part of the Kolunsuten's great mystery."

We slowed our walk to a stop. He talked animated with his hands and gestures.

"The Kolunsuten sent Moon to finish all the final changes in the world and make ready for the coming of Man, humankind. He changed all the ancient people into animals. The nature of their character is manifested in the way they are as animals today. They were like us, but they had great spiritual power.

"He changed some into the salmon, into roots and berries, and deer, elk and buffalo.

"Moon killed monsters that they would not be harmful to man. His brother is Sun. They were the Chiefs of all the ancient ones' world, and all of nature.

"They put one man and one woman by each river and some lakes. They multiplied and became the different tribes living there today.

"All our provisions come from the land as Moon provided. We talk to Sun and Moon and leave offerings of thanksgiving to them. Sometimes, we pray to the Amotken, Creator, while we face them because He is right above them.

"No one will ever come to take our land or way of living from us, or impose their laws over us. If they try, we should ask them if Moon and Sun authorized them to do this. If not, we can kill them and run them out of our country."

"Hey-yah, hey-yah," I agreed.

"Even the mountains used to move around and they were like a man. Moon changed them. They were one of the ancients. Stars, river, echo, everything," he said.

"We even know the real names of Moon and Sun, and even their parents and grandparents. Some of our people are named after them. We are their people, their descendants.

"So, Grandson, take it all in, all the nature, the land, the air, the season, the great Creations. We are related to it as one family."

"Hey, Sila," I said. "Thank you."

I thought about all these things. It was a long trip, but time didn't matter to us. We had the days, the moon cycle and the season to conduct our activities.

But what about Rainbow? And her reoccurring dream of the eagles?

Sila prayed for her often, and fanned her off with feathers and incense. He explained the eagle mates for life. When one is taken, the one left behind does not take another mate. It mourns, and then lives on. Does this mean she will never take another mate? Or does it mean she is out of harmony in her hurt state of mind, and the eagles only show this?

The eagles are a powerful and sacred bird. Their feathers are not to be played around with or used merely for display.

Some of the people are very proficient at trapping the eagle and removing some of the tail feathers. Others were somehow guided to find deceased eagles in nature. Then, they could remove feathers, talons and wings as needed for ceremonial use.

It was unthinkable bad luck to outright kill this holy bird. He was in fact like a deity, protecting and watching over all the land. Without him, evil would consume the world.

So, to dream about this great bird was no doubt meaningful, even sacred. But what did it mean?

All Schi'tsu'umsh people are sensitive to nature as we are a part of it. We cannot be separated from it. Our signs to follow came through it, as did our blessings from the Kolunsuten.

Sila said Rainbow would be all right in time. When we returned to our home camp, he would get someone to do a water healing ceremony for her to bring her mind back fully, and bring her back in harmony.

As we crossed over the mountain pass and into the heart of our country, trail talk and counseling turned more to joyful anticipation and laughter. We could feel it.

The land was alive and it knew us. It seemed as though it communicated to our home camp that we were coming. I could sense our home's feeling of anticipation of our return.

Now, I felt it strongly. There is no other feeling like returning home to your own country, where you were born, where your ancestors were born, where the Kolunsuten originated your people.

In my mind, I soared like the family of hawks that followed us. I could see the hill before us, but in my mind I could see the next, and the next. I knew where every trail was, every stream, every meadow, every knoll and most every rock. The picture in my mind spread throughout our entire country. I knew I belonged. I was grounded here with deep roots that went way back to the first of my people, and even the ancient ones before them.

I breathed deeply the aromatic, natural incenses of nature. Sweetgrass growing down by the creek softened the air and left a peaceful, gentle feeling for all who would pass.

Children started to play and run around. The horses became fresh and energized. Some wanted to run, throwing their heads around and dancing as they were held back. The riders joked with each other saying "Hey-yah! Hey-yah!" as though they were riding a bucking unbroke horse.

With a deep sense of happiness and peace, we rode into our camp areas. Some bands headed straight for their own home camps, if they were nearby. Others would spend the night before going on again the next day.

It was truly a trip of destiny. We had defeated the enemy and acquired their horses. We had gathered our brother, the buffalo. We had witnessed the Kolunsuten's miracles and divine mystery through our great prophet Chief Circling Raven.

And, we had experienced heartache and loss. But everything is taken care of by the Kolunsuten's great plan and ways.

I felt blessed and fortunate as I thought about these things. These feelings made me go reverent and quiet.

We rode into to our home camp and the future.

CHAPTER 18
A Home Put Together

During the year of mourning, Rainbow Girl stayed mostly at home, quietly taking care of her own business and chores. The family of Deer Hooves had a memorial ceremony for him and released themselves from the mourning period. They were all free to go on with their lives, attend social gatherings and gather foods or hunt.

Rainbow attended the memorial service, but she said nothing to anyone. She only sat toward the back of the gathering of people. She was free to be courted by other men, but she said she would wait on that till she felt like it again. We respected her for it.

During the mourning period, to make it worse, Sila slipped into a prolonged illness that eventually claimed his life. Even though it was almost a relief to see his suffering end, still it hurt to know a loved one is gone from you, never to be seen again in this lifetime.

But the effect on Rainbow Girl was devastating. It was like pouring more hurt onto an open wound.

It made her know our Checheya's days also were numbered.

Rainbow Girl stayed busy taking care of Checheya and the herd of small children that were always around. But sometimes she wandered about the camp area, not aimlessly, but as though she had forgotten what she was going to do.

Even though she had been raised with a powerful religious experience, she was now shaken by what had happened to her. She wasn't willing or able to trust herself to love or hope to love again. It was neither a conscious decision nor a lack of faith. She just followed her heart, and her heart said, "Protect yourself."

More than a year had passed since her tragedy, and most of the time she did appear to be back to her old self. She laughed and visited with friends, she attended social dinners and gatherings, and she occasionally hollered and cheered at the horse races.

Still, to those of us who knew her, something was missing, as if a piece of the most tender place of her heart was being held back and protected, or just not there anymore. It made her seem more stern and serious, except during those rare times when she was amused or being friendly. Mostly she worked.

"I'll just pick up a little more firewood for Checheya," Rainbow said as she built a small bundle of sticks. She was returning with some of her nieces from gathering herbal medicines, mullan leaves, rosewood bark and the anti-infectant plant.

The girls were tired from working along the hillside and from the long walk back home. Still, Rainbow never rested, never went still, she always stayed busy. They were near camp so she told her nieces to go ahead and she would catch up later.

She gathered a few more sticks and wrapped a leather string around what had become a big bundle, and swung it on her back. It made her walk hunched over and strained because she had two sacks of herbs and roots that she carried too.

"Auntie Rainbow, Auntie Rainbow," all the little children yelled as she walked into camp.

"Oh, my babies," she said as she put down the bundles, and picked them up one by one until she held three or four of them in her arms while other children were entwined around each leg. They were beautiful children with shining eyes and a sparkling happiness.

Rainbow kept two of the smaller ones and started cleaning them up.

"We must go to the creek and bathe you. You're starting to smell like a wet coyote," she said teasingly, making all the children laugh and giggle. She was driven to keep moving. She couldn't relax and play anymore.

I couldn't help but think of the days when she, too, was a little bundle of joy in the huckleberry mountains and I swung her all around just to hear her contagious laugh. She'd lost that innocence and the exhilaration of just being alive. I suppose it takes a child's trust that everything will always be all right, no matter what, to really have that way down deep and innocent joy.

Rainbow just stayed busy occupying her time with work, chores and caring for other people.

"Big brother, Sun Bear, you must get my horse ready, please," she said to me. "I will go and get some more camas after I bathe the little ones."

As she cleaned the little children, she laughed and teased with them. Upon completion, she carried a bucket of water back with her.

As she led the children back, she checked on her earthen oven where the camas cakes were baking under the ground. She spread the wood around and quickly put more sticks on the fire. She set the wooden water pail inside a little tripod and placed some herbs in it and a hot rock from the fire to prepare a medicine for Checheya.

Rainbow went inside the teepee. "Oh, my Checheya," she said with pity and love in her voice. "Let me make you comfortable." She rushed around the teepee arranging things and digging out a pillow. She helped Checheya get the pillow under her head and straighten her blankets.

"I fixed some camas cakes Checheya," she told her. "They'll be ready this evening. Your medicine tea will be ready by bedtime."

"Granddaughter, you are my baby girl," Checheya reminded her, "but now I'm the one cared for like a helpless child. Please don't burden yourself too much for my sake."

Checeya was very elderly now. With Sila gone, passed away thirteen moons ago soon after Deer Hooves, she had aged very quickly, as did many of the elders who were married to one spouse for many years.

"I can't see good," Checeya said in a very old and strained voice. "Sometimes, I can't get around any more. I get dizzy and unsteady. I forget what I was going to do. I'm just no good for anything anymore. I am very thankful for a granddaughter like you." A tear ran down her cheek.

Rainbow wiped the tear and with her hand brushed Checeya's hair back and smooth. "There, there, Checeya. You're the best Checeya ever in the world. I just love being with you, talking to you and listening to you. I'm very lucky and privileged to take care of you."

Checeya seemed comforted and happy as Rainbow held her hand and smiled.

Sometimes, the very elderly can go way down in their life energy and feel like they do not want to go on. Our elders say, bring their grandchildren around them. Just to see them, they will be encouraged and they may be strengthened again to go on, even with better health.

Checeya seemed to be a little brighter and happier, now that Rainbow Girl was by her again.

Rainbow went out of the teepee, climbed on her horse and rode off to a nearby field of camas to begin digging and gathering. It was hard work using her peetsa, a stick with a single carved prong on the end to get under the root and lift it upward.

She worked and worked, thinking toward the sacred food plant in a thankful and prayerful manner. "Help us, sacred food. Make my Checeya strong and healthy, and all the little children, too." She silently meditated. "Thank you, Mother Earth, for caring for us and feeding us."

She rode back to camp carrying a sack of roots. Setting them by the teepee, she immediately started working on the camas oven. She uncovered the camas cakes by digging away the dirt and removing the big leaves that covered them. It was hot, sweaty and difficult work all by yourself. But this was a daily routine for Rainbow.

She would pound and grind the dried camas and mold it into round balls mixed with water, fat and dried berries. She would dig out the earthen ovens, place the big leaves at the bottom, arrange the camas, and place the other leaves on top. Then she would bury it and build a fire on the top, moving and spreading massive hot charcoals all around the top. She would keep the fire going, occasionally spreading more charcoal around. Each and every day, she repeated the hard work. Most of the time, she worked fresh camas this way. For three days, it baked. It melted together and was delicious

All the children ran up and gathered around. She gave them little pieces of camas cake to tide them over until dinnertime. This night everyone would eat in their own teepees so the children would have to wait for their parents, because they would have their own family dinners later.

Rainbow fixed a bowl with smoked meat, then, she whipped a bowl of foam berries, and brought the foods into Checheya. My Peepa and Noona came in carrying their bowls with some extra food. They sat down to join us for dinner.

Everyone visited and discussed the events of the day and the coming summer trip to the huckleberry mountains. During it all, Rainbow sat next to Checheya feeding her, and in between bites chewed the smoked meat for her. She rarely talked, but when she did, she was friendly and tried to seem happy.

As everyone finished eating, she gathered all the bowls and offered to take them to the creek and wash them out.

While she was gone, my Noona expressed her concern. "My daughter is still not herself, not entirely anyway. I'm worried she is getting in a rut she will never get out of." She looked to my Peepa for a response.

"A lot of young men ask me if they can talk to her, and even though I grant them permission, our daughter won't see them," Peepa added.

"We must do something," Noona said. "We tried talking to her, and encouraging her. Still, she holds herself back. Very young people don't always know what's best for them, or who is best for them. That's why the parents and grandparents sometimes must intervene."

My Peepa knew what she was talking about. "There is a young man, a son of my friend at the North Lake camp. His wife died of the fever a little over a year ago and left him with their two small children. My friend told me his son would be a good companion for our daughter."

"I met him and watched him. He is very kind, deliberate and steady with his emotions. He was born during the moon-the-deer-lose-their-antlers (February). He would balance well with our daughter who was born during the moon-the-huckleberries-ripen (August), Peepa explained.

"I must meet his parents and talk to him," Noona interjected.

Peepa knew to depend upon and respect his wife's judgment, especially when it came to family matters. So he agreed.

The young man's name was One Star. He was a quiet and easygoing person, easy to get along with. Rainbow was strong willed, but not mean-spirited whatsoever. Still, her opinions were strong, and she translated that to hard work, faith and commitment.

It could be a match in the making.

"Ah! Hee slaxt. Xaiheet chen limt ultsgwichstumen," my Peepa's friend, Old Horse, greeted him as he got off his horse at their camp by the North Lake. We had traveled all day to get there. "Ah. Sadumdumsen, it is good to see you too," Peepa said with obvious joy in his voice. They gave each other a hearty and happy handshake.

"I would have been here sooner but my brother-in-law was acting like coyote," Peepa said teasingly. It was our way to tease and make fun with your brother-in-law or sister-in-law, and they couldn't say anything back.

"He was bragging about being a great horseman," Peepa began.

"No, he was the one . . . ." my uncle, his brother-in-law, offered in futile defense. The teasing story was already on a roll, so all he could do was let it go.

Peepa continued, "My brother-in-law kept bragging. So, finally I challenged him — 'if you are such a great horseman, ride your horse backwards.' Just as he turned around on the horse, a bumble bee flew into the horse's tail. As the horse switched at the bee, it got tangled in the hair. Every time the horse switched his tail, he hit himself with the bee.

"The horse couldn't take it anymore. He started to dance around then buck. As the horse jumped high in the air and then kicked up his feet, my brother-in-law would fart. Every jump and kick he would fart, really hard, right on time. To make it worse, he was riding backwards flopping all over the place, looking ridiculous."

Everyone laughed loudly, enjoying the story. It was ridiculous, and hilarious.

"All our relatives traveling here today hollered and cheered, war whooped their praises to my brother-in-law. But he was losing his balance from riding backwards. Still, every time the horse would land and kick, he would fart.

"As he lost his balance he fell back over the horse's backside. His face was right over the horse's rump, dead center. Now every time the horse kicked the horse farted. The horse would jump up, my brother-in-law would struggle to sit up, but then the horse would land and my brother-in-law's face would be right back at the horse's rump, just in time for the fart. Hey-yah, Hey-yah."

Everyone laughed hysterically.

"I don't know why my brother-in-law didn't just bail out and jump off. Maybe he liked it too much." All the people laughed until they were coughing and wiping their eyes. All the children, the grown-ups, even all the elderly really enjoyed this ridiculous story.

What a picture he painted. It was the kind of story you could only tell about your brother-in-law.

"So, maybe he is a great horseman, in his own sort of way," Peepa concluded. "But the horses don't trust him anymore." Everyone started to laugh all over again.

It was the way of our people when friends, acquaintances or relatives hadn't seen each other in a while, they told funny stories first that made everyone laugh.

As the joking settled down, Old Horse said, "Come inside and eat with us. Under my teepee we are one people, brothers in spirit."

As they sat down, Peepa began the discussion. "So, tell me about your son One Star. We have come a long way to talk to you about him, and our daughter."

"Good!" Old Horse replied. "Young people don't know. They haven't lived enough yet to know what are the right choices and decisions for an entire lifetime. They might choose a companion because they like their eyes, or their laugh without considering deeper incompatibilities, or what is truly important."

"I agree," said Peepa. "My wife and I were arranged in marriage just for the reasons you expressed. We didn't know it at the time, but our parents were right. We have been true companions and best friends for a lifetime."

My Noona smiled at him and shyly put her head down.

"Let us talk of the attributes of our children so we can see where they are compatible and where they are not."

"Agreed."

They talked and talked, sometimes joking. They liked each other. That was important, because you wanted your children marrying into a family of good people.

As their comfort with each other and the notion of an arranged marriage grew, they called in their son to meet my Peepa and Noona. After introductions, Old Horse started to ask him questions. My Peepa could not do this, as it was not his son, or his place. But his friend knew the kinds of questions my Peepa and Noona would have asked, so he asked them.

"Son," Old Horse began, "tell us about the responsibilities of a man."

Clearing his throat, One Star answered nervously, "In the beginning, man was given the bow and the arrow to take care of the women and children, to protect them and to provide for them."

"And what about family and child raising?"

"It takes a man and a woman together to really contribute to the full needs of a child. The man and woman make the home, and the children make it a beautiful and happy place."

"Tell us your views on hunting, Son."

"The animals are our sacred brothers. We must take them only respectfully and only in need, and we must be generous to those in need like the elderly, the widowed and the orphaned."

He did not brag or mention his conquests. I knew Peepa would like that.

"What about taking care of a wife?"

"Treat them kind and good, take them visiting, and trust their intuitions."

He was shy and nervous, certainly not outstanding in any way, but he showed kindness and a good nature. Surely, he would understand devotion and commitment.

My Peepa looked to my Noona for approval. She nodded at him.

"Let us agree then," my Peepa offered. "Our children will be married."

"Agreed!" Old Horse said, getting up to shake hands. They would worry about a dowry later.

It was agreed although Rainbow didn't know about it yet. Nevertheless, she would surely respect her father and not question it.

As the plan was explained to Rainbow Girl, she just kept her head down. Every now and then, she looked surprised, and then worried. But she never complained or protested.

"What about Checheya?" she asked. "I cannot leave her, and she cannot leave our band."

"You will stay here, your future husband will make his home with you among us," my Noona assured her. "He is a nice young man, very easy to know and get along with. You can put your teepee up right where Checheya's is now, and still take care of her. It has all been arranged. Don't worry."

"When will I meet him?" Rainbow asked.

"In two days, he will be here to meet you," she explained. "You will talk and get to know each other before the wedding."

"You have one moon cycle to prepare. On the next new moon, the wedding will take place."

During this waiting period, they would have to fast, pray and go through ceremonies. They both had experienced broken hearts, and One Star was married before. This had to be addressed prayerfully in ceremony to make it all good going into a new home and marriage together. They had already mourned and cleansed themselves over the past year, but this was something new and special.

Home and marriage were sacred and powerful institutions, spiritually. You can't just break or end one, or walk away from one without consequences that may burden your mind or affect your physical living. Even separation by death had to be addressed through a careful and respectful mourning period, and ceremonial prayer. Otherwise, the new home may be unintentionally affected.

"What's the matter Baby Sister?" I asked her. She was fidgeting nervously, rearranging blankets, parfleches, the rawhide folded bags that served as storage and traveling cases.

"Nothing," she said. "I'm just, uh, looking for something. No, I'm straightening up things."

"It was already neat, Sister. Everything will be all right. Trust in our parents and the ways of our elders. I promise, I will not let any undue burden befall you."

She gave me a relieved and comforted smile, then took a deep breath and went back to her fidgeting. It had to be a very nerve-racking experience, committing to marrying someone you didn't even know.

"I wonder how my life will be," Rainbow thought. What if I don't like him? I've met many young men I just didn't like. And I don't feel like I want anyone touching me or interfering in how I live my life."

Nevertheless, she could only sigh and try her best to go along with her parents. In a way, she trusted them more than she trusted herself. So she arranged her belongings and prepared her best jewelry.

"What's wrong Baby Girl?" my Checheya asked in her loving, very elderly grandma voice.

I took my cue to leave.

"I'm all right, Checheya," Rainbow answered. She fidgeted, paused, thought about it and decided maybe Checheya was the only one she could talk to.

"Checheya, the women of our people are very strong, and quiet. We carry burdens and just remain silent. I have stood a quiet vigil and said nothing all this time," Rainbow began. "But, I don't know what to do."

"Help me up Granddaughter," Checheya said trying to move her arms and blankets as though she was getting up on her own.

Rainbow helped her up, then sat on her knees in front of her. She paused, played with her hands, and looked ahead at nothing.

"I know, Rainbow," Checheya said consolingly. "We all know. There is no shame in having feelings. When you are hurt way down deep, it is going to affect you."

Rainbow broke her silence. "I never knew such happiness and promise could be turned so quickly into hurt and doubt," she said, her voice cracking and tears welling up in her eyes. "I don't talk about it, ever, because I know that I cannot. I just can't."

"It happened, Baby Girl," Checheya counseled. "It hurt. He's gone. But you still have your life. Just one life. And it is precious. You can't spend it in mourning."

She pulled Rainbow's hand closer to her and she put her head on Checheya's shoulder.

"I don't know that I can be with a man, even out of respect for my parents," Rainbow explained. "I just don't feel it in my heart. He will want my time and attention and I don't have it to give. My heart is gone . . ." she started to cry again.

Checheya put her hand on her head and guided it down to her lap. Rainbow sobbed her feelings that were deeper than words. Checheya hummed her lullaby song one more time, comforting Rainbow.

As Rainbow thought about it, she remembered that day. "You are the one who comforted me, Checheya, just as you are doing now. I never thanked you. I am the luckiest girl in the world."

"All right, Granddaughter, you must get up now," Checheya said, with a firmness in her voice.

It surprised Rainbow, and she sat up alert and ready.

"That's enough now, Granddaughter. You know I have never told you wrong. I'm telling you now, get up strong and go on. Don't get carried away with yourself or self-pity. The Kolunsuten gave you five senses and a mind to comprehend and understand life by. Use them now, Granddaughter.

"Your parents understand more about life than you can know in your young years. Respect them and go along with them. It will all work out in the end."

Rainbow seemed stunned. Yet she knew it was all the truth, as the one person who could comfort her, the greatest person in all the world to her, told it to her.

"I'll try, Checheya," Rainbow promised.

"To our people, it is everything to us to mean what we say, and then do it," Checheya instructed. "Just know this is the way it is and go forward like you believe it."

"Yes, Checheya . . . . Yes, I will. You're right," Rainbow corrected herself.

"I'm tired. Could you make some tea? Help me to my bed." Checheya turned into a bedridden old grandma again; and Rainbow into the caregiver.

As One Star, his parents and family band rode into camp, we all came out and greeted them. We all wore some of our finest clothes, as did our visitors. It was beautiful.

Sitting in the big teepee, we visited over a small feast of our usual native foods. The respective parents discussed many things. But as the food was taken out, Peepa nodded his head toward my older sister, his sign to send for Rainbow Girl. My Noona went with her.

One Star now fidgeted nervously and kept pushing his long hair back over his shoulder. He looked really nice with a bone choker and breast-plate, blue colored deerskin leggings with white and yellow lines on them, and colorful moccasins with blue and white line pattern designs. He wore one feather in his hair, which was the appropriate style for this day as a single man.

First, my Noona entered, then older sister, then Rainbow Girl. She looked beautiful in her blue colored dress, dyed with the huckleberry, with the elk teeth sewn across the shoulders. She wore a soft, white eagle plume in her hair, contrasting perfectly with her dark hair. She kept her head and eyes down, only looking up when Peepa and Noona talked to her.

The parents talked and visited a little longer about different things while they let the nerves settle down in their children. Both of them looked uncomfortable, and everyone kept looking at them.

As the talk turned to the wedding, everything got quiet as people listened intently.

"My friend," Peepa started, "since our children will make their home here, the wedding should be here, also."

Both soon-to-be-weds turned, looked and listened how their lives would be unfolded.

"That is good and true, my friend," Old Horse responded.

"My son, One Star, this will be a good way to make our prayers and wishes right where you will make your new home."

One Star looked back realizing his father wanted him to respond. Surely, they were trying to get him to speak so Rainbow Girl could hear him and begin to know and trust him.

"Hey, it is good," he said nervously, clearing his throat several times, then looking toward Rainbow out of the corner of his eye.

He had no inclination to try and be impressive or talkative, and Rainbow studied him for the first time. Everyone waited for him to say more, but he didn't. He wasn't excessively attractive, but neither was he ugly. Maybe he didn't smile and joke all the time, but at least he wasn't a ridiculous windbag.

Maybe he's not so bad, she thought, but she didn't have anything to make her feel a deep familiarity either. He was actually handsome, but so reserved he was hard to notice.

She thought about the things her Checheya and Noona told her of what makes a man loveable over a whole lifetime. She told herself not to be afraid.

"Daughter," Peepa directed, "you will get a new teepee from your husband-to-be's family. Will you put it up exactly where Checheya and you stay now?"

"I don't know, Peepa. I hadn't thought about it," she said looking downward.

One Star heard his bride-to-be's voice for the first time and studied her. She was beautiful, shiny black hair with the eagle plume, her blue dress with the elk teeth, high cheekbones with an elegant look and her graceful demeanor.

More importantly, she came from a good family and she had a deep sense and appreciation for strict traditional values. In other words, she would know spiritually and physically how to make a home, family and marriage the very best way possible, with the right mix of kindness and respect.

"Son, what are your plans for right after the huckleberry season?" his father asked. He already knew the answer, but he was just trying to get him to talk.

"Well, uh, we will get our horses ready for the big hunt. Then we will leave for the buffalo country," he said rather sheepishly, but trying to appear more confident.

Rainbow didn't go on the last hunt so she could stay home and take care of Checheya. But, she probably had memories of the trip that still caused painful feelings. She looked the other way.

"Rainbow," my Peepa asked her, "what are the herbs you get to treat your Checheya, and where do you get them?"

"The blue flower root, and the miniature green fern," she answered. "They grow on the hills around here, about halfway up and higher on the north sides only. They help her with her breathing."

To the young couple, the feeling was tense and strained. To everyone else, it was festive. Despite their discomfort, everyone was sure enjoying their meeting, hanging on every word and expression.

The parents and others went on to more visiting and small talk, eventually deciding to leave the engaged couple to talk on their own. My older sister stayed with Rainbow Girl, and the little children just kept coming and going.

"Are you going to marry that man?" one of her little nieces asked her. Rainbow lowered her head, not knowing what to say.

"Are you going to marry my auntie?" the child then asked One Star.

"Yes, I am," he answered. It made Rainbow look at him and study him a little closer. He now had his two children by him, an infant boy about two years old and a four-year-old little girl.

Her heart went out to the little children who didn't have their mother anymore. They had a lonely look in their eyes, she noticed, even though they didn't behave any differently than the other kids. Still, they never went too far without double-checking to make sure their father was nearby. They know what hurt and loss are all about, she thought, and they didn't want their father to ever leave them.

"He must be good to his children," older sister, Berry Woman said to her quietly. "Notice how they are always around him. He must be a good and kind man."

Still, they said nothing to each other. They didn't know how.

Finally, at the point of being unbearably uncomfortable, One Star said, "I would like to meet your Checheya sometime soon. She sounds a lot like my own Checheya."

Rainbow took a deeper breath and replied, "I will take you to her when we are through here."

Then, it went quiet again. At least they had spoken to one another.

One Star started to help his daughter with her wing dress as it came untied over her shoulder. "It's too tight," she whined.

Then he started struggling with her hair. "Oww!" she protested. "That's not the way, not like that."

Still somewhat messed up, she walked over toward Rainbow. "Are you going to be my new mommy?" she asked her with the blunt innocence of a small child.

Rainbow studied her, and then smiled. "Yes, I am. Yes, I am," she said holding her hands out for the little girl to come to her.

As the little girl smiled and climbed into her lap, it seemed like the whole feeling of discomfort and uneasiness was lifted and gone.

"What's your name?" Rainbow quizzed her.

"Sunshine," she answered matter-of-factly.

Rainbow reached in and quickly reset her wing dress so it would fit comfortably, straightened it out, and sat Sunshine in front of her. She started to fix her hair.

"My mommy used to comb my hair just like hers. But she died," Sunshine said, sounding a little sad.

"I know, little girl Sunshine. But it's going to be all right now," Rainbow consoled her.

"I have something for you," Sunshine offered. She held up a small piece of jewelry. "My auntie helped me make it."

Rainbow took the gift. "Thank you Sunshine Girl. It is beautiful. I might wear it with my eagle plume when I dance," she said holding it up to her hair.

Her heart went out to the little girl, and the little boy. She always had her mother and didn't know what it would be like to be without Noona.

Your mother is the best friend you're ever going to have in this world, elders always said. When she's gone, no one will take her place and love you as freely and unconditionally as she did.

These poor children, she thought. Today, they are pitiful and don't even realize it yet.

"She's usually very shy," One Star said. "I don't know what brought that on. It was all her own thinking."

"What's your son's name?" Rainbow asked him. "His name is Little Star," he answered.

"Come here baby Little Star," she called to him, motioning with her hands and fingers.

"He won't go to anybody but his immediate family," One Star explained.

Maybe because his sister was enjoying the moment and trusting Rainbow, he toddled over to her and smiled really big. She embraced the child and held him, then sat him down in front of her.

She was in her element now. The care of his children became the first common thread between them.

They talked freely now about things, sometimes even making eye contact and smiling. They started to like each other.

Rainbow took One Star to meet and talk with Checheya briefly, then they parted company for the day. His family camped with us that night so the soon-to-be-weds could talk in the morning before Old Horse led the long journey back to their own home.

Rainbow went looking for our Noona, and found her in her teepee working on a buckskin shirt.

They looked at each other and paused. Noona could see apparently that Rainbow didn't bring in a pressing need or question, so she gave her the approving and loving smile of a mother.

"Noona," Rainbow started, "I just wanted to tell you how much I appreciate you, how much you've done, everything you are to me . . . and the whole family. You've always been there, no matter what. You brought us, me, in the world and have never stopped loving and nurturing."

"It's all right, daughter. You are my whole life. It's what I enjoy," Noona told her, holding her hand.

"I never realized how much you do and what you go through. It is so much." Rainbow had a tear in her eye and a quivering voice. She gave her Noona a hug and just held on and cried. Noona stroked her hair. "Shh, shh, now. It's all right my little girl."

During this moon cycle, the soon-to-be-weds fasted, prayed and entered the ceremonial sweat lodge to make ready for the wedding day. Every four or five days, One Star would come and visit Rainbow. They would walk and talk. His children started to really like her.

"What do you think of war and horse stealing parties?" Rainbow finally asked him. It had been on her mind and just under the surface of their discussions all this time.

"Sometimes there is no choice," he answered.

Rainbow didn't hide her displeasure. She sternly looked the other way and hesitated.

"Don't you want your men to be brave and strong?" he asked.

"I want them to be alive, well and loving," she snapped back.

"But no one will be killed if it's not their time to go," he said.

"If you put yourself in harm's way, harm may befall you. I don't want my husband or future sons foolishly testing danger or death for sake of some self-declared glory."

This was an important discussion. Parameters for their relationship were being defined right now. One Star knew he should think carefully.

"I cannot promise you I will never fight or war," he offered. "But I will promise you that I will never go along with other young men just for sake of glory. I will only fight to protect you, our home and children."

She felt comfortable with this commitment, but it would still be a worry to her.

She didn't want to be an overly bossy wife, but she knew that she wanted her husband to live a full lifetime with her.

One Star felt a slight concern. Maybe his new wife would browbeat him all the time. He tried not to worry about it. What she said did make sense in a way. It just wasn't what the warriors taught.

He knew what she had been through and gave some respect to her thinking. Maybe she knew things other people didn't. It was our way to trust the instincts and intuitions of the women regarding the home.

Also, he started to feel something for Rainbow. A new hope, a new spirit surged within him. If he ever had another chance, and he had learned the hard way, he would listen to his wife and stay right by her. You could never know when the Kolunsuten might take them back.

So they visited, got acquainted and prepared for the wedding.

In a way, it almost seemed as though they were prepared for each other and this time by destiny itself. No one could ever fully understand or appreciate them individually unless they experienced what they went through. They would know how to take care of each other.

The time to the wedding day flew by. It was already here. Rainbow could scarcely believe it.

People were gathered, food was prepared and the new white teepee stood clean and beautiful. It represented the new home, the new beginning of a life together.

Rainbow looked more than beautiful. Stunning described her more accurately. Over the years, so many men wanted to court her. Some even came with marriage proposals. She accepted none of them and ended up in an arranged marriage.

It was ironic, to be sure, but still proper and appropriate nonetheless.

As the wedding parties stood and waited, the bride and the groom fidgeted. Finally, a spokesman opened the ceremonies with an introduction of the purposes.

The family of the groom had arranged a spiritual leader to announce the wedding. They had chosen a man who was very brief because they wanted a short ceremony.

In this way, nothing would interfere in the beginning of their marriage and lives together. Everyone had their own individual thinking and opinions. Sila and Checheya always said it just depends on how you believe. Because if you really do believe, it will work for you. One Star's family wanted the marriage this way, brief and to the point.

The leader announced the wedding, prayed and fanned them off with incense and eagle feathers.

Rainbow looked nervous, but she was beaming too. I could feel her hoping and praying for the best. Maybe her hope was finally more powerful than her worry.

She studied her groom briefly, then thought about her life. Peepa and Sila had been the only men in her life up to now. Deer Hooves had been lost. I had been more like an equal or best friend. Now, she was a grown woman taking a man as husband, inheriting little children and making her own home.

What was it Checheya used to say? She thought to herself. It was something about knowing what makes a man loveable over an entire lifetime. Is he kind to animals and good to children? Is he prayerful and ceremonial? Is he respectful to the elderly and caring for the poor and needy? Does he really care to know how to take care of a wife?

She looked at One Star again. He was quiet, reserved, and now, nervous looking. But he was a good father to his children, and he was a fine man in all respects. She smiled way down deep.

The leader concluded, announced the wedding to everyone, nature and the Kolunsuten, and wrapped a wedding blanket around them. Everyone sang an honor song, and then a happy song for them.

Rainbow and One Star looked nervous and excited at the same time. People came up to shake their hands and congratulate them.

As the wedding ceremony started to conclude, Rainbow and One Star looked somewhat uncomfortable. They stood there together looking a little embarrassed and lost, like they wanted somebody to tell them what to do. I pointed at them with my chin to let Peepa know, and he recognized the discomfort. He quickly invited people to the placing of food set upon the ground.

As they sat and ate, a group of One Star's friends approached them. "Are you ready, friend?" one of them asked. "Or do you expect your friends and brothers to do all your hunting for you while you lay around a teepee?"

This was an insult in a friendly way. No man wanted to be accused of or known for laying around the teepee with his wife. Only good friends could even joke about it.

The usual answer to this kind of challenge was to deny the false accusation by doing whatever was challenged better and harder than the one who perpetrated it. One Star smiled, acknowledging his friends, but before he could say anything Rainbow spoke.

"We are only just wed. You know you should stay here."

One Star paused and seemed a little embarrassed. All his friends laughed and walked away.

"I know what to do," he told Rainbow. "I could have told them myself instead of being ordered by my new wife."

"I know. I'm sorry. I just don't want anything to happen to you," she said.

This show of concern and affection made him feel better about it. It was good to feel cared about again.

In the next few days, they tried to normalize their lives and find the routines that worked. With each new day, Rainbow seemed to be exerting more control and authority. In fact, it was down right bossiness that exceeded acceptable and traditional roles expected in a marriage.

One Star was a good man though. He took it without a word back. We all appreciated him deeply for it. Rainbow wasn't behaving this way for mere sake of control or meanness. She was trying to keep her husband and new family close and safe above all else.

Several days later, his friends rode in again. This time they wanted to ride into buffalo country to bring back maybe five or six buffalo.

"Surely, you want your wife and in-laws to know that you are a great hunter, and not afraid of any enemy," they challenged him.

Rainbow walked over to him. "Absolutely not!" she ordered. "A small little hunting party in the middle of enemy country, it's just foolish."

One Star looked downward.

"Well, what about it?" his friends taunted him.

A man has his own responsibilities and role. It was unheard of for a woman to tell him he could not hunt. That would be like telling a woman she could not gather berries or nurture her own children.

It was not that a woman was subservient, because it was more the opposite. The home actually belonged to the woman. But the roles of each were separate and distinct, and always respected in total.

My Peepa and Sila always gave the credit for any of their success to their wives, my Noona and Checheya. The women are closer to the Kolunsuten than the men, they always said. They were chosen to bring children into the world. Their feeling and intuition is stronger than a man's. So, listen to them if they are truly supportive and loyal.

One Star was caught between the respect he had for his wife and his manhood. He hesitated as his friends watched and waited. At last all his friends laughed loudly at him and rode away.

"Why did you do that?" he reprimanded Rainbow. "I should decide how I will take care of and provide for my family."

One Star's voice had a hint of hurt mixed in with the obvious annoyance. He felt his very manhood was being denied. It was impossible to choose between your wife and your responsibilities. For a man they should be the same thing.

"Together we will decide. I must know you and all my family are protected and safe. You must trust me on this," she ordered and walked away.

As family to Rainbow we all knew why she was this way. Even after a year of mourning, prayers and ceremonies to heal her broken heart and shattered spirit, she was still affected by what had happened to her before, when her fiancé was killed. Maybe One Star knew it too. He could have just ridden off with his friends, but he didn't.

I thought to myself, "Maybe I'll never get married."

CHAPTER 19
2 Years Later . . . .
The Spirit of the Home

"Congratulations, Sun Bear," people said as they walked by me.

"Two people will become one home, one life, this day," another chimed in.

"But, that is the magic of the generations," still another added, with chuckles coming from everyone.

I was walking with my family to the gathering place. Everything was ready. My brother, my Peepa and my Noona were leading me to the wedding . . . my wedding. Yes, I was more than old enough, but the elders always said to put it off for a while, do something great and powerful while you are young and free.

I followed this teaching like I did all the others. Now as a young but mature man with many horses, many buffalo robes, successful horse stealing missions and numerous kills in battle, my worthiness would never be questioned.

My bride and the new love of my life was Yellow Flower Girl. As a small child she would continually gather the little wild flowers for her

Noona and other family members. They started to call her Yellow Flower Girl and the name stuck.

We got acquainted at last year's big gathering and celebration while at the horse races. My brother and I, with two other friends, were running some of our horses. That time, I agreed to be a catcher. Usually I ride like the wind, and sometimes win. My younger brother wanted to ride and had asked me to catch for him.

I thought anybody could catch the racehorses as they came in. That's the least skilled job of all. Was I ever wrong.

The horses come in to the relay point where the riders get off one and get on the next horse held by a handler. Someone has to catch them as they come charging in, sometimes in groups, at break neck speed. That's when I learned the safest place at a relay race was on the back of a horse.

The fastest horses don't always win. It takes strategy and teamwork. Some contestants run their fastest horse first, others last or in a different order. Some with slower horses will try to choose a leg of the race when they can charge in with other riders and disrupt everyone else by running over all the catchers or handlers. The rider gallops in, the catcher catches and slows the horse, the rider dismounts and runs to the horse being held by the handler, mounts and rides off again.

We had our least swift horse running in the first leg, but he was still fast enough to stay with most of the pack, except for the extremely gifted horses that were in the lead. Some were warhorses. Some were buffalo hunting horses. They were the truly gifted and athletic horses with hearts to match their speed and power.

The horses running the course, the thunder of their hooves, and the power of their awesome strength was a breathtaking sight. The riders had the look of fierce determination, but were still no match for the thrilling power of a herd of horses running with all the energy they had.

The people gathered on the hillside to watch. Wagers were made. A lot was at stake on the outcome. Everyone's friends and relatives came to cheer for their favorite son. For our family this year it was Two Hawks, my little brother.

"Go, go, go, run faster!" everyone yelled, adding mock war whoops and victory cries. As they neared the transfer point people started to wave their arms in encouragement. Many jumped up and down.

I should have known I was in trouble when the horse in the lead came in. She was ahead by maybe ten lengths. Nearer and nearer she came. But there was no sign of any brakes. They didn't slow down at all.

Their catcher bravely stood his ground right in front of the horse. He waved his arms, but didn't move his feet at all. The ground was thick dirt, heavy due to races earlier in the day and rains that fell the day before.

The horse ran into the short relay area at full speed. She ran right over the catcher, but somehow he grabbed a hold of the reins. One moment he was standing there and the next he was being dragged way down the track. The rider wasn't able to dismount and they missed the exchange. I watched the catcher being dragged down the track and out into the field. I looked at where he had been standing and his moccasins were still in the dirt, side-by-side, right where he was lifted out of them! What an alarming yet telling image to portray the act of catching at a relay race.

"Oh, no." I groaned. "What have I gotten myself into?"

I turned and looked just as twelve to fifteen horses were charging down the homestretch right at the relay area as one monster pack. All the catchers started jockeying for position to be in the right place to catch their horse out of the jumbled pack. Pure pandemonium.

I traded places with other catchers three or four times trying to line up with my brother, the last time just as the horses charged into the line. "Hey-yah, hey-yah!" I heard several of them say. Some war whooped to focus their minds and call their bravery.

Boom, crash, yells, screams were heard as horses and riders ran head-long into the line of catchers.

I was run over, but grabbed a rein. My brother baled out at full speed to mount the new horse. But many of the waiting horses held by handlers were crashed into as well. They were all rearing and bucking, as the catchers were being dragged and stepped on. Some horses got away. Several catchers were just run over and trampled. Fortunately, miraculously, no one was hurt seriously.

The crowd roared their approval and encouragement. It was the best race they had seen in years.

My brother scurried to get in a position to mount the next pony while it reared and kicked. Whoever could get to their relay horse first would get a strong, perhaps unbeatable lead.

But all I could do was hang on and try to survive. That horse dragged me through puddles, into mud, over a log, and finally ditched me by a crowd of people. Right in front of me was Yellow Flower Girl with several of her friends and relatives. They were all laughing at me, especially Yellow Flower Girl.

As I got up, dirty and messy, I noticed something in my mouth and started to spit it out. It was little yellow flowers. That made all her group laugh all the harder.

There was nothing I could do or say. I was embarrassed, but I was old enough to know you only made it worse by acting angry or shamed. I pulled one flower from my mouth and handed it to her.

"Here, I went through all this trouble just to pick a flower for you," I told her, disarming the whole embarrassing situation.

She took it, smelled it and held it to her face. The color, shape and essence matched her and I realized how attractive she was with her soft black hair, perfect face and beautiful laughing eyes.

"I think you need it more than me," she answered, handing it back to me. "The horses are coming in again. Unless you want me to catch for you so you won't be dragged through the mud," she added with a smile.

If I would have tried to talk to her at almost any other time or place, I would have needed the permission of her Peepa, but this was an unusual and spontaneous moment.

I turned and looked. My brother was turning down the homestretch. I looked back at her and smiled way down deep. We exchanged a look

I had not experienced before, a knowing, very familiar, we're-so-happy-to-look-at-each-other look, a we-already-know-each-other-but-at-last-we-have-found-each-other look.

Without a word, I ran toward the relay area. I had to be at my best now. A beautiful girl was watching me.

I concentrated, stood in front of the horse, grabbing the reins and halter just as they got to me. I slowed and stopped the horse as Brother dismounted and jumped on the next horse.

"Go! Go! Go!" the people shouted. We were the crowd favorites now.

The last two horses were our fastest ones and we already had a big lead we easily won the races that day.

I looked back at Yellow Flower Girl and she gave me a smile back. Her sisters and friends pulled her to get her attention and probably help her mind her manners. We hadn't even been introduced, let alone authorized to talk or know each other.

But the rest was easy. We seemed to have known each other forever. Noona said it was fate that I was taken to her with yellow flowers in my mouth and then gave it to her without even knowing her name.

A mystery to me too, was that the horses were the ones who brought me to her. I'd always given them the best of care and respect, never beat them, never whipped them out of anger, but I prayed for them often. Maybe it shouldn't seem strange to me anymore, the mysterious ways they take care of me. Peepa and Sila always said if you take care of animals, they will take care of you, even in ways beyond the obvious. They will be a blessing to you, a protection and a provider. The horse will help you find food to eat, firewood to keep you warm and help you defend yourself and loved ones from the enemy. Give them good pastures, and feed them extra in the harsh weather of winter. Keep them a little fat.

I thought about all these things as I walked to the designated gathering place where I would be wed.

A man could simply take up with a woman, but that usually only happened with older people. Most families thought enough of their young grown sons and daughters to make everything right for them as they began their own homes.

After I arrived at the open ceremonial area, Yellow Flower and her family approached in a procession. She wore a beautiful white buckskin dress with colored quillwork designs, painted lines and shells. She wore an eagle plume feather in her hair. The long fringe on her dress swayed in perfect timing with her walk.

She looked like pure grace and beauty, but excited too. I felt anxious and nervous. But as she looked my way and smiled with those laughing eyes, I felt sure and confident.

I too wore white buckskin because our people considered this the best and finest of clothing. My shirt had long fringe down the sleeves and off the shoulders. My leggings were white with fringe and some painted designs, symbols of my family. I wore one eagle feather, which every man had a right to, representing his given name at a ceremony.

I had earned more feathers but there were other symbolisms and representations to be considered here. One feather may also mean you are a single man. Two feathers may mean you are married. Today I would receive the feather representing my marriage.

My sister, Rainbow Girl, joined the family with her own little family. It was only two years ago she was married and now she had a baby of her own, a little over one year old. Her life with One Star was good for the most part. However, she still browbeat him about doing things that might seem dangerous.

Life goes on, Kolunsuten's purposes are fulfilled and we accept it through prayer, ceremony and the paying of proper respects in mourning.

Rainbow Girl came to witness my wedding and offer her good wishes and support for Yellow Flower and me, as I had at her wedding two years ago.

We glanced at each other and she smiled at me, nodding her head. She carried her son, Sun Boy she called him using my boyhood name. She said she hoped he would turn out like Peepa and me. You could not use a name that was already being used, but this was a childhood name and I did not wear it any longer.

He wore little buckskin moccasins with a deer print inside an arrowhead, just like mine. He was a quiet and happy baby, not fussy or angry.

My Checheya was there, elderly and needing even more care now. Checheya still stayed with Rainbow Girl. She took care of her, got her medicines, nursed her when needed and even chewed all her food for her.

I turned to my bride's procession. As they approached, an honor song started and everyone joined in. Yellow Flower Girl started to bob with the beat of the music, which was the traditional way. Her family formed a line behind her. At the middle part of the song, they would raise their feather fans up toward Yellow Flower Girl, then toward the sky in honor of her.

It was a beautiful moment, all the people were happy, harmonious and dancing in honor and in time to the same beat of the drum, for the same purpose and with the same feeling. Without talking or telling, everyone knows what to do and what will happen next. It is uncanny and indescribable when you are all one people, one family and one thought. This is when our people have always been at their best.

As the song ended, Yellow Flower stepped forward towards a point halfway to me, and I stepped the remaining distance to her until we met in the middle. We turned to the leader our families picked to announce our marriage. Earth was his name.

"Relatives," Earth said loudly, trying to get everyone's attention. "This is a great day for this young couple and for all our people. Today, two lives will be brought together to make one life, one home.

"All of life has a male and a female part to it. So does the family home spirit. One half is man, the other half is woman. Through their love and devotion to each other and their home, children come forth and Kolunsuten's great miracle of life happens. The generations go on."

"For all that a man is, he can only go so far on his own. It will be the power of the woman that enables him to go further and to succeed.

Only where the woman is, can the spirit of the home be. A bachelor man living alone can never have that spirit in his dwelling."

"It is your wife who will bring your children into the world. She was chosen by the Kolunsuten to do this and therefore is closer to Him than man. A mother's love for her children is the most powerful force on earth, except for the Kolunsuten's power."

Then, he announced he would call on the family leaders to talk to the young couple.

Yellow Flower's Checheya came forward to express teachings and hopes for us.

"My granddaughter, Yellow Flower, be a good wife to your husband. Take care of him, encourage him and support him. Lend your strengths and your prayers to him."

"A man who is talented and capable, if he has a mean or self-centered wife, he may still amount to little or nothing. This man may get up to talk and no one will listen.

"But a good family man who is devotedly supported by his wife, even if he is limited in talent or ability, may achieve great things. When he gets up to talk, everyone listens carefully and agrees.

"The success he enjoys will bring you and your home prosperity, joy and happiness. Then, the success and blessing of it are truly yours together."

"So take care of your home, granddaughter. May the Kolunsuten bless you both with a lifetime together of happiness, children and protection," she concluded and turned to return to her seat.

Then, my Peepa came forward to express the thinking and feelings for our family.

"My Son, I am proud and honored to have you for my son, to be your Peepa. What you do now is very special and very honorable."

"A home and family will teach you about true love and responsibility. But the responsibility will look good on you because it is accepted easily when done out of genuine caring. One day, your children will teach you about love and it is one of the greatest blessings you will ever know.

They will teach you about how to be a man, how to be truly responsible, about the power of love and the special nature of your wife."

"All that a woman is, a man will complement her and make her life more complete."

"The Kolunsuten made man with a greater physical strength to be used to gain provisions and to protect his wife and family. That strength is never to be used against the woman, but only to help her. Then, your wife, children and home will be blessed with happiness and prosperity."

"In turn, she will get behind you to make you more than you are. It takes a man and a woman together to make the both of you achieve and be the most that you can be, to make a healthy and vibrant home spirit."

"Always remember, Son, your successes are because of your wife. Take care of her accordingly."

"The best man is not necessarily the best looking one, or the fastest talking one. What will hold a woman's love for a life time is the man who is kind to children and elders, good to animals and prayerfully ceremonial in his everyday life."

"May happiness be yours together. May you have strong and healthy children. May you grow old together and know the true and deepest meaning of companionship," he concluded with a hand gesture toward us, and walked away. Everyone said "Hey! Hey! Hey!" in agreement. His were powerful words, as always.

It was our way that you could not tell your son-in-law or daughter-in-law anything directly. So, it took someone from your own family to talk to you about marriage and life, and your new responsibilities. These were great words of encouragement.

As my Peepa moved back, the spiritual leader, Earth, began to speak again.

"Now we will announce the marriage."

He turned his attention toward the sky.

"Kolunsuten, hear us this day. We bring this young couple before you today as one. One family, one home they shall be. Bless them this day and recognize them."

"Let the Mother Earth and all that grows upon her and walks upon her know them as one family, one home. Let your divine spirits of nature and the four winds recognize them . . . ."

He had a big wedding blanket wrapped around us about the shoulders. It was beautiful doeskins sewed together and shaped, with quillwork designs in wide lines stretching across our shoulders and going down our arms. At the top of our backs, there were rounded designs within the quillwork, each depicting our family emblem or design. I noticed the deer hoof print inside the arrowhead by my elbow. Ermine skins hung down here and there. The back was dyed deep blue. The inside was white buckskin. It felt magical.

From a ceremonial fire, charcoals were brought.

"Kolunsuten," he continued, "bless them and their marriage this day. With this holy bird, the great eagle, I will fan them off with these sacred incenses of the cedar and blue spruce. This holy bird lives cleanly and purely, and lives a long life. They find one mate and stay with it for their entire life."

"If one of the eagle couple loses its life, the other one does not remarry, nor do they divorce. Some of our people follow this teaching of the holy bird, others do not."

"Bless this young couple by this holy bird's power that they will live a long time together. They will be companions, but also best friends. Recognize them as a home and a family in their own right this day."

An eagle feather was tied to my hair next to the one I was already wearing, representing marriage.

He put the incenses upon the charcoal and fanned us off individually, and then together. He announced, "You are married," and shook our hands.

An honor song started up again as all the people came by to shake our hands and wish us well. It was a beautiful sunny day in late spring. All the greenery and blossoming of new life was everywhere. My Noona said it was a fitting time to put a home together.

A teepee was erected for us, gifted by my Peepa and Noona. It was all new white buckskin. Even the poles were new and clean. They took charcoals from the ceremonial fire to start the fire in our new home.

My Noona and Peepa told me to always take my wife visiting wherever she wanted to go. That is one of the many things a husband should do for his wife, especially to her own family. Sometimes, however, take her to the dinners and gatherings to visit with many friends and acquaintances and even meet new people.

After all the festivities were over, the singing, some dancing and feasting, I asked her, "Yellow Flower, my wife, where would you like me to take you first?"

"To the horse races coming up," she answered. "I just have a great and special love of the horse races, especially the relay," she said with a knowing chuckle.

I just looked and smiled as we strolled to our new teepee, our home.

CHAPTER 20
The Family Circle

Each morning Yellow Flower would get up early, go outside with her buckskin tie, and gather firewood for the day, just as I had seen my Noona and Checheya do so many times over the years. My Checheya did this even at a very elderly age because she wanted to. "It felt right," she said. They tied a bunch and carried it on their backs.

My wife made good friends with Rainbow Girl, which I was very glad about. I got to see my sister often. We usually camped by each other, but sometimes we camped with my in-laws. I had my own things to do and responsibilities to fulfill, so I stayed busy with them. Yellow Flower would tell me though, about things that would happen during the day and what was talked about.

My baby sister worked very hard. With a husband, two little children and an infant of her own to care for, still she wanted our Checheya to always be absolutely comfortable. This was difficult because she made everyone's clothing, tanned the hides, did repair work, gathered wood, gutted and butchered, then cooked. She just worked and worked and worked, and overworked.

She chewed the meats and hard foods for Checheya, got her special medicines and prepared them for her. Sometimes Checheya would be very healthy, even youthful. Other times, she would be sickly and weak, even telling us to be prepared for her death.

Checheya had been making things for the giveaway at her own funeral, which was the custom of our people. She had accumulated many shawls, blankets and bags for this purpose.

I could see the concern upon my baby sister's face. Maybe if she tried and worked even harder, Checheya would be granted good health and live a while longer. So she endlessly hauled water, cooked, prepared and nurtured. Sometimes I would see her praying for her children, her husband, her Checheya and family loved ones.

Her children, my nephews and nieces, were beautiful children so precious and cute. The uncle on your mother's side has a special responsibility for the nephews. You are a teacher and a source for discipline. But for now, I just enjoyed them like they were my own children.

The boys and I played hunting, warrior and horsemanship games. They were getting pretty good. All a young boy's time was consumed in marksmanship, horsemanship and roughhouse games. My nephews were aching to play knock-each-other-off-your-horses with the older boys, but I didn't let them yet.

I fixed them toy bows and arrows, carved them images of deer and buffalo, and played with them.

Rainbow still bossed her husband though. We all knew why she did that, to protect him from danger, so that nothing would ever hurt or take him from her.

"I think I will go to the women's sweat lodge ceremony this evening," Yellow Flower told me. "I will bring my sister-in-law, Rainbow, and pray for her."

Yellow Flower couldn't go in the ceremony because of her condition, carrying our child. However, she could go over there, stay outside and perhaps find a blessing. A family sweat bath would be fine for her to attend, but this one would be conducted by the medicine women leader for the new moon. This meant she had to stay outside so neither the baby nor the mother would be overly affected by the power.

The men don't really know what goes on during these ceremonies for women. All prayers are for the good of our people and loved ones though. The women are very powerful in their own right. They did not attend ceremonies during their moon time because they might interfere with the ceremony. That's how great and powerful they and the miracle of life power they hold really are.

At the new moon sweat ceremony, the women gathered ready to go in. The lava rocks glowed with red on the fire. The dirt on the east side of the fire was shaped like the crescent of a new moon, which was the symbol of the generations. The rocks were moved into the lodge.

First, the medicine woman leader went in then everyone else followed in single file. The door closed behind them.

The leader poured water on the hot rocks as she prayed and called upon the Kolunsuten and nature. She was elderly but still strong enough to get around and work.

"Bless us and recognize us, O Kolunsuten," she started, pouring on more water. The hot rocks instantly turned it to hot steam.

"We are your people, and the daughters of our Mother Earth. We are womankind, mothers, grandmothers, sisters, daughters, granddaughters, aunties and nieces. We take care of the home, family, children, our elderly and our menfolk. We ask you to pity us this evening and see us gathered before you."

"We have ceremonial ways of our own to conduct. We pray you would bless us in them."

Rainbow couldn't help but think about her own life, the life of a girl growing up to be a woman. All the teaching and instruction, all the discipline and training, and all the ceremony and prayer.

"The men have their ways. We add ours that the good of the people will be fulfilled, that the prayers and ceremonies of the menfolk will be completed by our mutual support of them. We know the men can only go so far on their own. Yes, they have great physical strength. But the love and intuition of the woman is more powerful, and added to the efforts of menfolk, makes for a completed community."

Rainbow's mind flashed to images of the past, of childhood and of growing up under the careful and strict guidance of our Checheya, being pulled up out of bed at dawn to pray and greet the new day, bathing in the cold stream early in the morning. Eventually she ran with the older girls every day.

This was the teaching: discipline and strength were united together and inseparable. You could not have one without the other. She started to fade from her present surroundings in the dark of the sweat lodge.

"Rainbow, you do not hesitate. Never talk to yourself about not doing what you must. Just do it," she could hear the Whip Woman bark out.

Every village had a Whip Woman and a Whip Man whose job was to instruct and discipline the children. The children were not allowed to cry out or complain, neither could the parents.

These were honored, even spiritual positions of authority. It would be inconceivable for a Whip Man or Whip Woman to abuse their position, or to show favoritism. Even if they did favor a certain child, they would care enough to be even stricter that they would turn out to be stronger adults.

Rainbow remembered jumping in the cold river water and bathing with the other young girls.

"You girls pray and meditate while you are in the water. Talk to it in your mind. Ask it to make you strong, to give you a clear mind."

One of the younger girls hesitated to jump in and the Whip Woman switched her long stick toward her, not hitting her, but driving her ahead into the water.

"Blessing and prosperity of the home can only be yours because you are strong, and you can only be strong because you are disciplined," the Whip Woman repeated.

She remembered all the running and training and the words of the Whip Woman as they would all pass her.

"It is us, the women, who are the real power of our people. The home belongs to the woman, all the belongings and all the food, even all the meat the men might bring."

"We bring the children into the world. We nurture, care and comfort. Even the men, after concluding a day of all their glorious deeds, they seek their own comfort by the women."

Rainbow relived training on the hilltops and the instructions.

"Granddaughter," Checheya and Noona would tell her, "you must pray and meditate here in silence. You must seek your spirit helper that will give you strength and assistance. Without it, you might live in poverty, and everything you do will seem like it doesn't work out."

"You will need this helper to always find roots and berries and be good at preparing and drying them. Or, perhaps, it will give you the power and gift of hides and artwork, or song and comforting, maybe even interpreting what is wrong with people and doctoring."

So, she sat up and prayed diligently, looking for the Kolunsuten's designated spirit helper.

"It will come as a spirit, or maybe as a voice, a thought, or a feeling. Then you will look and see an animal or some aspect of nature. That will be your spirit helper."

She relived the hard work digging roots and helping the women with the hard chores, getting on her knees for hours at a time to work the hides.

"Finally, a woman will do what she does out of love, love for her husband, her home, her children and, someday, her grandchildren. It is her home and family, her life in all of them. So she must speak up from time to time and take care of them, or risk unnecessary hardships."

Rainbow regained her awareness. She was back in the sweat lodge. The prayer leader was still praying.

"So, guide and direct our Chiefs and men leaders. We support them and tell you they are good and right. It is good that you would bless them," the old woman offered.

"And, with this new moon, bless our families and homes again. The grandmother moon is directly tied to us women, all women. It's cycle matches ours. It affects the great waters, as the water is part of the miracle of life and so are we when we bring a new baby into the world."

"As this moon would grow stronger and brighter, make our children and families strong and protected. Bless all our people, from the very youngest to the very oldest."

"Bless all our women of the tribe. Teachers, mothers, caretakers, nurses, doctors, helpers, storytellers and healers that we are. Bless those who are expecting child. Let them have a healthful pregnancy and an easy childbirth."

"Bless our roots, berries, medicines and firewood we gather in nature, and purify us that we will be made ready to gather them."

Rainbow started, then stopped, and then began to talk quietly about her life.

"I would like to say . . . just to add . . . a little for my own family and home."

She sat up on her knees as the silence of the medicine leader meant approval for Rainbow to go ahead and speak.

"Kolunsuten, bless my own little home, too. Sometimes, we don't know how to take care of each other. I only mean the best for our protection, but it doesn't come out right. Then, my husband takes it wrong and we exchange words."

She started to cry.

Then two of the lava rocks on the top of the pile of hot rocks in the pit split apart! The inside halves glowed red with the heat. Incredibly, they were both split exactly evenly but a small piece fell out of the center of the one on the right.

The old woman quickly threw on some incense. "You must be careful granddaughter," she told Rainbow. "Don't you wait, or any of your family, to learn the hard way about appreciating life," she warned.

The leader continued her prayer with song and other incantations. Three times, they went in and out, three rounds they completed. This was our tradition. They made offering and talked to the earth and to the moon, because the land is our mother and the moon is our grand-mother. They are of the same nature as the women. Therefore, they had a special place to make offering to and communicate with them more one-on-one than the men.

The men don't know what these songs are, nor do they know the cer-emonies. They are sacred. Yellow Flower told me men live in their own world and choose never to fully understand the woman's world, that's why it's unknown to men. I accepted it.

It was all good. That is how we all supported one another.

Marriage was the institution by which the ultimate support, togeth-erness and devotion were exhibited. Parenthood was the next level, and a blessed home and children were the result.

I learned now, to never say you would never be married. It is inevitable.

But what about the sign in the sweat lodge ceremony? The two rocks split apart just as Rainbow prayed for the family. Therefore, it was clearly a sign for her, or her relatives. Why did two rocks split and not just one? What is the meaning? It worried the family and more ceremonial prayer would be required.

As days passed, I didn't worry too much any more. But I could see the concern in my parents, and sometimes my Checheya, too. They continually prayed for the family, unity and, of course, all their grandchildren.

Spiritual signs can be directly from the Kolunsuten himself and are not to be taken lightly. So, my Peepa had daily sweat lodge ceremonies every morning at dawn. Every evening, my Noona brought all the women of our family band to their sweat lodge.

Peepa said we should fast and pray on the mountaintops. I didn't see or feel the impending need or urgency, so I didn't go immediately. But I went with my Peepa one morning before daylight to help him sing and pray.

"Kolunsuten," he said, opening his prayer, "hear me again. I always talk to you in humble prayer, tell you what's going on in my life, sometimes ask you for certain help or blessings. You always do those things that I ask for my loved ones."

"Help my family now. Bless us. All the problems and discord my children are experiencing worries me. They are only young."

"Do not see this as a disrespect of your great gift of life, family and home. Do not let hardship be their teacher. Give me and the other elders of the family band a chance to teach and guide them. That's what we are here for."

"Bless my children and my sons-in-law and daughters-in-law."

"Thank you for the sign given to my daughter, Rainbow Girl, in the sweat ceremony. No doubt, this is you trying to take care of and provide for your people in a good way. And, we are trying to acknowledge you and interpret your signs in a good way, as we have been taught."

He concluded his prayer and we sang as we greeted the new day just as my grandparents had done before us, and their grandparents before them.

As we walked down the hillside, we talked.

"Peepa, I didn't realize what you were so worried about until now. Maybe I still don't, fully."

"Life is a sacred and special privilege, Son," he answered. "It has its beginning, its end and its purpose. Whether it is one hundred years or just a few days, everybody's life has a divine purpose to be fulfilled. If we're not careful enough in the way we live our daily life, the life of a loved one, a small child or our own life may be lost."

"Sometimes the Kolunsuten's purpose in one's life, maybe in a little newborn child, is to show and teach the people how precious life is. He may do this by taking that life back to Him. That way, the people will be mindful to be loving, kind and respectful enough to take proper care of their homes and each other."

"Now I'm worried," I said pondering the depth of his wisdom.

"No need to be worried, Son, live life in a good way that includes all the proper respects. Then, just be happy."

He put his hand on my shoulder as he did so often when I was growing up. I felt like a young boy for a moment.

Days and seasons passed. Things seemed normal enough. Contentment described my own feelings. A gentle and easy peace was mine. I prospered and felt rich in spirit just to be in the family band.

I spent a lot of time with the young boys of our family band. Whenever they saw me, the first thing they would do is get excited and want to show me at what new level of ability they could shoot, run or ride.

As I walked through the camp, today was no different than any other in this regard.

"Uncle, Uncle," my nephews called.

"Hey, boys," I greeted them with enthusiasm and put Beaver Skin in a mock headlock. I spun around with an imaginary war club and swung it at Little Wind. He pretended to block it, swing his own club, duck down and swing towards my knee, then he tackled me and laughed.

Buffalo Bull Boy jumped on too, joining in the fun as I rolled around with both of them. Other boys, my nephews from older sister, Berry Woman, and also from my younger brother started running over to join the great play battle.

I organized some foot races, roughly by age. Then, they wanted to show me they could ride. So, we went to the horses.

They were all getting good, especially the older boys. Trick riding and dismounting, leaning under the horses' neck at full gallop and shooting an arrow while leaning off the side of the horse. It looked easy and effortless the way they did it.

"Great riding!" I yelled at them. "You're about ready for the buffalo hunt!" My nephews war whooped their excitement and charged their horses ahead even faster.

I couldn't help but think about how good it was to be a young boy. The world was full of so much wonder and excitement.

True, little girls are precious beyond words. But, little boys have their own unique flavor of innocence. Their trust in their Noona brings them confidence and emotional strength. Then trust in their Peepa brings them good guidance. The grandparents and elders provide teaching and lessons. Their brothers, cousins and friends provide bonds that would last a lifetime.

And, me, well, I was an adult instructor-friend-parent-discipliner, all in one. That is what an uncle is.

I thought about my own unborn child. Maybe it's a boy, I pondered. I imagined all the coal black hair and tiny face on a body that could fit in my hands, then, growing up a little, playing hard and running fast, calling me Peepa and believing every word I had to say.

I couldn't wait.

"Uncle, uncle," several boys called to me at the same time. "Let's go hunt. Little brother said there were elk this morning just a little ways to the southeast."

"Well, we can go look for a short while. But if there's nothing there we must return home." Some of them were too little for a long strenuous, rough country lesson, but I did want to show them how to read sign.

We rode over to where the elk had been seen earlier and followed their trail to where it went into the thick forest. I dismounted and gathered my bow and arrows.

All the boys followed. I could feel their excitement. They wanted to hurry, yet tried to be quiet and patient. That is the internal conflict and challenge of hunting. They were all so special and innocent looking, trying to be determined and intent while moving fluidly and silent.

"Don't bounce or bob up and down," I advised them. "Don't turn your head quickly to look around, even your eyes should move slowly and fluidly. See your footsteps without looking down."

All the things my Peepa and Uncle Center Feather told me over and over again, I told them over and over again.

"Remember, the elk is our great and sacred brother. We can't just hunt him any old way. We must have respect. Talk to him. Talk to nature. Tell them what you want and why. Ask them to allow you to take one of our four-legged brothers for this necessary purpose only, and only with respect and prayer."

The littlest ones were a delight to watch walking like miniature warrior hunters, trying their best, dark hair braided or hanging down, breechcloths and moccasins. I was having the time of my life.

I showed them the hoof prints and told them what size they were, male or female and what direction they were going. I told them the legends of the elk and the spirit power they have today, which some of our people use ceremonially through the elk hide or horns.

This is what I expected. A quiet day teaching with my little boys. Suddenly I saw something move in the clearing in the forest up ahead. I went right into serious hunter mode. The boys saw me change my expression and demeanor. They all went still.

No more words. I talked only sign language now. I motioned for them to move around to the east. We would sneak up on the elk from down wind, where there would be a small hill to conceal us.

Slowly, deliberately, we made our way around. It was amazing to me the little ones were able to do this without a mistake that would send the herd running.

At the top, overlooking this herd of about twenty elk, I peered out so the boys could see how to do it. I selected a yearling bull, hoping its hide would not be too thick for their youth size bows to propel an arrow that would penetrate.

In sign language, I told them to shoot the spike as he walks near the little hill, on my signal. I readied my own arrow in case they missed.

I peered just over the knoll. Just as the spike was near and sideways to us, I pulled back my bow with the arrow ready. The boys did the same. I knew that four little boys all showing their heads and arms at the same time, no matter how slow and deliberate, would be noticed by the herd. We would get only one chance, maybe only one shot.

I rose up slowly with just enough room to shoot an arrow over the tops of the grass. The little boys did the same. The elk just looked at us. I moved my bow for the boys to shoot. Four arrows flew. Then, I let go my arrow.

The herd turned and ran in a direction away from us.

"What happened Uncle?" Little Beaver asked me innocently. "Did we all miss?"

"No. He's just going to run a little ways and lay down." I explained.

As we silently made our way, the boys saw the blood trail, but they knew not to say anything. They were so excited.

I had them stay back a little as I approached where I thought the elk would be laying. Sometimes, they are only wounded and can be very agitated, and even attack. So, hunters had to be ready.

The elk didn't move. He only laid there, no breath. I lowered my bow and motioned for the boys. Their excitement could not be contained. They were jumping around, squealing and talking loud.

"Quiet now, Boys! We must have respect first," I instructed.

I knelt down and they followed my lead. I prayed my thanksgiving and offering, as was our custom, mentioning in detail how we are related to the animals and how they sacrifice their lives for ours, so the young ones could hear it.

There were two arrows in the bull. One was mine, but the other was Buffalo Bull Boy's, Berry Woman's oldest boy. His first elk! I showed him the arrow with his personal design on it, and all the boys war whooped and slapped him on the back.

It was a good day, a good time. We rode back into camp victorious. All the family made a big deal about it, praising the boys. They all got credit. At the dinner, they got to tell their hunting story, one by one.

They were growing up perfectly.

As things settled down, I noticed my Peepa in deep thought with a look of concern and worry. I went to sit by him.

"What is it Peepa?" I asked.

"Ah, everything is good," he replied.

"I thought something was wrong," I explained. "I know you have been worried about the family."

He paused and looked like he strained for the next words to come out of him.

"We are supposed to believe everything is for the good, and that then it will be that way," he said. "I don't know how else to interpret the sign shown to Rainbow but as a danger. I fear life will be the ultimate, hard teacher for the family."

CHAPTER 21
Home Fire Spirit

I nervously watched my wife, Yellow Flower, as she performed several of the daily tasks, while I sat with my Peepa, younger brother and brother-in-law fixing arrows. I tried to pretend I wasn't watching her, but it must have been obvious.

"Don't worry, Son," my Peepa said almost impatiently. "We have done everything ceremonially we are supposed to. Your wife will bear you a healthy and beautiful child, and she will be all right too."

Yellow Flower was ready to give birth. She moved differently. Her body changed and transformed to that of a woman nine moons pregnant. She had that pregnant woman walk to her step.

But she was still beautiful, and I cared for her deeply. I had never realized how much you could care for another person until Yellow Flower. Her affection and devotion for me was complete.

"Uh, I forgot some of the materials I need in the teepee," I said getting up to head in that direction. The men of my band said nothing as I walked away keeping their eyes on their work.

Maybe I just wanted to talk to my wife because I didn't really need more feathers and sinew just at that moment.

"Husband, I think your son wants to come out and see you today," she said to me as I walked by. "He is really kicking and moving around like he's trying to tell us something."

"Maybe he just can't wait to get his chance," I answered with a smile.

It is our way to be very careful around a woman expecting child. You must not yell around her, argue or tell scary or frightening stories. Never say hurtful or critical things. All this will affect the baby.

Above all, never ever say anything that may indicate or reflect that you may not really want the child. Such talk could cause a multitude of health and emotional problems in the child, perhaps over the course of a whole lifetime or perhaps the Kolunsuten would take the child back. We have to be careful.

"Are you still going to take me to get some roots?" she reminded me.

"Yes, as soon as I am through fixing arrows for the buffalo hunt."

"Rainbow and One Star will join us," she said with joyful anticipation in her voice. "I have been stuck right here in camp so long now, I need just a short break."

"All right, Wife, all right," I assured her.

We smiled at each other with that knowing trusting and fully accepting look only happily married couples can give each other. I was going to ask her if she was okay, but clearly, she was strong enough to be bored around the camp.

Yellow Flower herself surely wouldn't dig due to her condition. She would only clean the ones Rainbow got. Still, she wanted to be out doing something to stay busy and be helpful. That was our way. There was no other thinking, no laziness, no over self-indulgence.

After we fixed about ten to twenty arrows each, we left on a very short root-digging trip. It was more a social outing.

I walked my horse from the ground. Brother-in-law, One Star rode his horse alongside at a walk. Yellow Flower and Rainbow walked side-by-side just a little behind us, carrying their root digging tools and sacks.

After a long silence, I asked One Star, "So, how are things going for you, my sister and children?"

"Good," he answered. That was it. But his face told a longer story implying perhaps that everything wasn't totally all right.

I hesitated, not knowing what to say, and One Star was silent.

"I don't know what to do, Brother-in-law," he finally said with a defeated sigh. "My wife is your sister, so I'm not trying to complain."

"I know. Go ahead. Say it," I coaxed.

"Well, I just don't know how to address and resolve some long standing problems in my home. I feel like I am being controlled by my wife."

"No," I consoled. "I'm sure . . . ." I went quiet, not wanting to say anything I knew to be untrue.

He continued, "I've never seen or heard of anything like it, to be wife bossed out of a deep and powerful love and concern. My wife cares for me so deeply, I am honored by it . . . . You know, I would never talk about this to anyone else all this time and . . . ."

"I know," I reassured him. "We are like brothers, one and the same. Do not worry. I will hold your confidence."

"Well, uh, . . . my confusion is that I am fortunate and honored to have and to hold the dedicated love and support of my wife. But at the same time, I can be humiliated by it. Sometimes, I don't feel humiliated, so I feel guilty that I ought to feel humiliated and say something. When I try to say something, Rainbow will just put it in her terms and walk away." He gestured with his hands as he spoke and his expression was more animated than I had ever seen him.

Clearly, he was troubled. I tried to think what I could possibly tell him that would be helpful, and peaceful. It sounded like a showdown was brewing. Maybe we should remember what the elders always teach," I consoled. One Star moved his head toward me, and his expression was one of intently listening. "Marriage is a true and complete partnership. One person cannot totally dictate. Concern and problems must be talked about and both sides addressed in the final decision."

"But every time I try to discuss it with her she will dominate the discussion then walk away like the subject is closed," he said.

"You have to find the way and the words, One Star. Don't give up on her, though. Tell her the teachings and have kindness in your voice. She will listen, eventually," I said.

One Star nodded his head and looked as though he was in deep intense thought. We walked off in temporary silence. I'm sure neither one of us imagined we would ever be in a conversation like this one.

Our wives followed a short distance behind. They were laughing and joking together.

"It's soooo good to get out and move around a little," Yellow Flower said. "Since this will be my first child I was a little worried about the labor early on. Now, I just want to get it over with," she sighed holding her hand to her belly.

"I wonder how many generations women have been saying that," Rainbow sympathized, then they both chuckled about it.

"I'm so happy for you," Rainbow said. "My son, and my husband, are the best blessings life has to offer. I don't know where I'd be, or how I'd be without them, and my adopted children. I never knew life could be so good."

Yellow Flower sighed in agreement. "Oh, my heart and my life are filled with love and happiness. I can't wait to be a mother. I'll be the best Noona ever, and my children will be so cute, well behaved, kind . . . and strong too." They continued to stroll along the trail. They both had a root sack over one shoulder and they carried a peetsa. The sun was warming, the sky was blue and the forest and meadows were alive with the life of early summer. Birds were singing and active, occasionally a butterfly would visit.

"I always loved the butterflies," Yellow Flower said coaxing one to land on her hand.

Rainbow saw the little girl innocence and joy in Yellow Flower, and maybe longed for that feeling. She went quiet for a short distance, while she contemplated it. Was it that long ago when she had a child's deep happiness and joy?

"Life works out, I suppose," Rainbow said. "I am thankful for all of it, every bit of it. It has led me to the many blessings I enjoy with my little family and home. Now I really, really know how to protect it and watch over it, so I do. But I fear my husband doesn't always appreciate it," she added with a slight smile masking a serious inquiry.

Now Yellow Flower went silent, wanting to be very careful how to tread in this subject. She nodded her head.

"Rainbow, we have been like sister-friends for over a year now, and . . . ."

"I know, Yellow Flower, don't worry. I boss him too much. I know it. I feel bad about it. I don't want to do it. I swear to myself I will stop. Then the next time a situation arises calling on him to leave for a hunt or whatever, then I am imposing myself again. I'm a woman of a home too," Rainbow continued. "I feel the problem is within the spirit of my home and it is festering. I am confused by it. My feelings are of complete love and devotion, but they come out in a bossy way." She shrugged her shoulders.

"Well, sister-in-law, maybe you just need to get back to the teachings of the elders."

Rainbow looked at her, waiting for her next words.

"Marriage is a partnership, Rainbow. You will have to talk about it fully and honestly to your husband. He will understand all right," Yellow Flower said.

Rainbow smiled with a slight tear. She grabbed Yellow Flowers arm and they walked together like little girls who were best friends.

"I've known for sometime my husband and I should talk about this. But, I'm afraid to. I'll have to get into things of the past, how I felt devastated and maybe why I am the way I am."

"One Star already knows, sister-in-law."

"I know. But that doesn't mean I can talk about it," Rainbow said.

"Well, we are women and mothers," Yellow Flower said putting her hand to her belly, then smiling. "We're the ones who know about the home, what's going on and how to take care of it, right?"

"Where would I be without you?" Rainbow said pulling her closer. "You're my best friend in the world."

They smiled and walked on enjoying the day, the moment, the closeness of family, and true, intimate friendship.

"What do you think the women are talking about?" I asked One Star.

"No telling," he said. "Probably about children or childbirth, or maybe root digging."

That night, One Star and Rainbow were getting ready for bed. She had thought about it all afternoon and evening. She knew what she had to say, but the words wouldn't come out.

One Star wanted to bring it up as the man of the family, but he just sat and occasionally fidgeted nervously. They sat on buffalo hides. The fire burned brightly but erratic in anticipation. It was like the home spirit itself knew it was time to clear the air.

"Um, my husband, the children are all sleeping and my Checheya is staying with my sister Berry Woman tonight. I wanted to talk to you."

"Yes, my wife, I want to discuss our home and life together, too . . . ."

Then, at the same time, they said, "Marriage is a partnership . . . ." They stopped and laughed at themselves.

She got up and moved across the teepee to sit by One Star.

"Go ahead, wife," he said.

"You are a good husband, and a wonderful man, the greatest father to our children imaginable."

"I just want you to know I appreciate you and support you with all my strength, all my spirit and all my love."

These were all words usually never spoken by our people. These were all sacred things better left to living them, rather than talking about them. However, this was Rainbow's way of getting to a problem, maybe the only way.

"I know that, wife. That's why it's so hard for me to understand sometimes, the bossing, and well, uh, well . . . the bossing. It isn't right, especially in front of other people. It's going to come between us," he said.

Rainbow felt the emotion and all the concern. But there was another feeling in her, a bigger and undefined feeling that blocked her words. She tried to choke out her expression.

"Husband, I don't know how to talk about this. There are experiences of life that forge you as a person, that are just there and beyond words. My life has been that way too."

One Star sat up, then got on his knee, a more serious and respectful posture. He gazed into the fire as he listened intently.

"Husband, like you, I know loss and mourning. I realize I don't handle it well, but I can't help it. I couldn't bear anything to happen to you. I just wouldn't bear it. My heart aches to think about it."

"I know loss, also mourning," he quickly interjected. "But it makes me appreciate you even more, so much that I want you to be happy. So, I go along with you as far as I can, even with the over protectiveness, and the bossing. But there is a point of mutual respect that must not be crossed."

"Husband, I can see this. But there is more. I'm trying to tell you, to help you to understand me. My losses and experiences make me appreciate you and to make you happy above all else." She stopped, choking on the words.

"I understand wife, it's all right." He did feel better. It was clearer to him now. That's why it was confusing to him before. He had felt loved and disrespected at the same time.

"Wife, I will never leave you in this life. I will always be there for you. I will never risk my life foolishly. Kolunsuten willing, we will grow old together like those couples who are always together, the best of friends right to the end."

She smiled and put her hand on his arm.

"I feel the power of your commitment and devotion to me and our children. Maybe this will be my healing," she said.

These were her words. She knew just like everyone else she would have to live them now.

"Wife, maybe it will take more than just words to help you. But my words are true and strong. The loved ones that have gone on to the other world are in a wonderful place. And they want us to live on to the fullest experience and benefit possible, because this is the one life we have. Once it is gone, we can never get it back."

"I will have a medicine man come here and conduct some ceremonial ways for you. We will sacrifice some food for your life, your good feeling and a strong mind. Maybe with all your family behind you and your husband, combined with ceremonial prayer, you will be healed again."

Rainbow put her head on his shoulder. One Star moved his head to hers. They sat there a while as a special feeling from each other's heart moved together through and around both of them.

The fire changed color an orange to amber, and burned down to a steady flame. The home spirit was at peace again, and Rainbow could sense it as the woman of the home.

"Bless my home, my husband and my marriage," she thought toward the Kolunsuten.

"Bless my wife and my little family," he silently prayed.

Understandings, even just simple ones, can go such a long way to heal, strengthen and build trust. It was all the teachings of our elders. Obviously, it was all true to anyone who had a mind to listen, and know the teachings.

As Yellow Flower reported to me the healing talk between Rainbow and One Star. She was glad for Rainbow, but I could tell she was deeply moved by it too.

She moved close to me and I put my forehead on hers. I thought about these words and all the teachings.

Even though you hear teachings your whole life, it seems as though you're never done learning or changing. Now, I could feel the presence of the spirit of my own home, for the first time. Togetherness and company were only a small part of what a marriage and home are all about.

The realizations of true adult manhood were coming over me, and it was another great wonder of life.

CHAPTER 22
First Step on the Road of Life

"Sun Bear, Sun Bear, you'd better come back." I heard someone calling. I'd gone hunting just a short distance away so I could be close, and I always told people where I'd be just in case.

"Over here." I yelled back.

It was One Star. He rode over toward me as I walked into a clearing.

"It's time, brother-in-law," he said. I knew what he was talking about. My wife was in labor, giving birth to my child.

He put out his hand and I grabbed it to swing myself over the horse's back behind him. I needed a ride over to my horse, and then I could go on to our camp.

I rode fast and hard. I felt nervous, excited, happy, scared, then anxious.

At the camp, I paced around outside the teepee. To hurry, hurry, hurry as fast as you can, just to wait, wait, wait, was something I hadn't prepared for or considered.

I tried not to worry, but sometimes I had to talk to myself. "It's okay," I thought. The teachings of our people cover all this. I didn't kill a mother deer while my wife was carrying child. I never put a lariat around a horse's neck, so that the cord would never wrap around my baby's neck. I watched what I said. We prayed regularly and we had prayer ceremonies done for my wife and the baby. I pictured him in my mind.

Yes, he's just waiting, no, now he's on his way to see me, I thought and smiled.

The door of the birthing teepee opened and one of the midwives came out. I took steps toward her with a look that pleaded for information. Did she give birth? Is she all right? Boy or girl?

The midwife just brushed by me, grabbed a bag, a couple of sticks from a small woodpile and went back in. I felt like a little child, over-anxious, frustrated and trying to stay out of the way.

It was our tradition that the birthing lodge would be erected a little distance removed from the rest of the teepees. This was a woman's time, a woman's power and the gift bestowed upon her by the Kolunsuten. It was not the place for a man to impose himself in the middle of it.

Besides, the power of the women was so strong it could actually interfere with the spirit power of the men, perhaps causing them bad luck in hunting, or even injury.

"Rainbow," I called out a little reserved. "Rainbow," I said a little louder . . . . No response.

As I walked away, the door opened and Rainbow came out. I walked toward her quickly without getting too close, with the same desperate look for information.

"Everything's all right," she said moving her hands slightly up and down in a "calm down" like gesture. "Sometimes these things take a little time. It shouldn't be much longer now. Auntie says the time is getting close, and she gave her some herbal tea to speed things along."

"It's evening, and the night is coming."

Rainbow just walked away like she didn't have time for me and entered the teepee. I knew I couldn't go in there. It was the woman's domain. Therefore, I waited.

Finally, my Peepa showed up.

"Hey Son," he greeted me. "The first one is always the toughest. After that, it gets a lot easier."

Just his presence consoled and steadied me. He put out an elk hide for us to sit on. "Might as well get comfortable," he instructed. I sat by him. He was dressed casually, breechcloth and moccasins, and he had his hair down but combed very handsomely.

I started to tell him I was worried, but before I could really explain it, he interrupted. "Don't think that way. Just know everything will be all right."

I nodded my head in agreement; I calmed myself by breathing deeply. Then, the thoughts came to me. What about the expectant mothers who lose their child, or they themselves die in giving birth? I sat up quickly and looked around in a panic.

"Don't worry, Son," Peepa said calmly, sounding almost bored. "Everything has been taken care of, it's all right."

We talked about other things, hunting, breaking horses, funny things that happened. Time went by, still, no baby. It was past dark and well into the night. Peepa went to bed. I was pacing again.

Inside the teepee, the midwife and family were helping Yellow Flower, wiping sweat from her forehead, holding her hand, occasionally rubbing her back and shoulders. She would contract in a labor pain, breath hard and eventually, contort her face, but she did not cry out.

Do not yell or scream, the elders taught, the child may have a hard time in life. So, she bore the pain, suffered and endured.

"I can see the head!" the midwife said. They moved to get Yellow Flower on her knees. She struggled in discomfort and weakness from the hours of labor.

On her knees, the baby would come out more naturally from the spirit world, from the mother, straight to the road of life and the Mother Earth. Rainbow and an auntie held her back and shoulders so she could lean back slightly without falling.

Another labor contraction came over her. She strained with all her might. Gradually at first, the head started to move out. "Here he comes," the midwife said. She continued to strain. Finally, the baby slid out into the waiting and guiding hands of the midwife.

Yellow Flower gasped and murmured faint noises of struggle and effort beyond exhaustion, past pain, as they laid her down.

Everyone hesitated and waited. The baby didn't cry, no sound. The midwife moved him around and cleaned out blockage from around his nose and mouth. She gently dried him off with a soft hide.

Finally, he breathed. He blinked his eyes slightly and gasped a little to get his breath, then he cried. "You have a baby boy," the midwife announced. Everyone showed relief and happiness. Rainbow clapped her hands together then squeezed Yellow Flower's arm gently.

"Your son wants his mother," the midwife said handing him to Yellow Flower. She held him and cuddled him. She talked to him with a smile. "I've been waiting for you, Son. Shh, shh, shh, everything's all right now."

"Sun Bear," Rainbow said. "I need to tell him."

I could hear the cry, so I went as near the door as I could. Rainbow tried to talk, but her hands only moved like she was talking while she smiled. "It's . . . He's . . . Your son . . . ." she said. "And, Yellow Flower's okay." She turned and walked all excited back into the birthing lodge.

I jumped and turned, swinging my hand through the air. I breathed a deep breath, holding my wide smile.

Then I went to my knees.

"Thank you, Kolunsuten," I prayed. "Just the way I asked you, you have fulfilled my prayers this night.

"Bless my wife and my new son. He has only just come into this world. Pure and innocent, he is. Watch over him, and his mother. Give them good health and strength.

"Let my wife heal and recover quickly.

"Let my son grow to be a strong, yet kind and gentle man one day."

I couldn't think of any more words. I just pictured them in my mind.

It was also our tradition that the new mother would stay in the birthing lodge maybe as long as seven or ten days. This would be an eternity for me.

I went to bed thinking about my wife and our family. Our teepee was lonely without her presence.

Now I understand it, I thought. Elders say the home spirit can only be where there is a woman taking care of her family.

I put wood on the fire and looked into it a while. The loneliness left me as I thought about her in our own home.

Finally it was the day Yellow Flower would come home. Rainbow came to tell me that she and Noona would bring Yellow Flower and our baby home today.

I couldn't wait.

I straightened a few things up. Rainbow made a bed. She set a baby board next to it, and a cedar cradle. These were her gifts to the baby and us.

"You are a good sister," I told her. "Thank you, Rainbow Girl."

She smiled as she worked.

I paced and waited and paced.

Finally, they showed up.

Yellow Flower carried the baby in and sat down as if she hadn't ever been weak or tired. She looked strong and healthy. Her hair was combed beautifully. She wore a buckskin dress, a blue colored one.

As I looked at my wife and my son, a new feeling came over me. It was magical, sacred and holy. I felt a tear in my eye. Among our people, there was no shame for a man to have deep feelings.

I went to her side and put my hand on her arm. "This is your son," she said introducing us. I gazed at him. He was perfect with lots of thick black hair, black eyes and beautiful skin. "Hey, Son," I told him. "We have a seat at our family setting reserved for you. As long as I'm alive, I will take care of you." My tone was soft and gentle. I held his hand and he grabbed one finger and held on.

My wife and I smiled at each other communicating in silence.

"You have a new boss in your life now," Noona joked, making everyone laugh.

My wife tried to rest a little during the short remainder of the day and night. I stayed up and kept the fire going. Sometimes, I prayed. I was a family man now. My life would be forever changed. My view and perspective, my thinking and feeling were now deeper and more sensitive. I speculated that maybe my prayers are even stronger now.

At the first sign of light, I woke Rainbow who had slept in our teepee. "We must get ready for Peepa," I told her.

We got ourselves ready. She wrapped our baby son up in a new soft doeskin hide, then in a deerskin that still had the hair on one side. Even though it was early summer, it was chilly in our country early in the morning.

"We will take our son to his grandfather, my Peepa," I told Yellow Flower. "There's some ceremonial things he will do."

"I will go too," she said.

It was her choice. The women were strong in their own right. She wanted to be present and standing in respectful reverence and support as her son was introduced to nature and blessed by the Kolunsuten and His Creations. Rainbow and I walked slowly to accommodate her.

As we scratched on the hide covering over the doorway of his teepee, my Peepa said, "Come in." He was already waiting. I entered first, followed by my wife and son, then Rainbow.

Peepa was sitting at the front of the teepee looking over the fire toward us at the doorway. Noona was seated to his right. He was dressed in his finest of regalia, beautifully beaded white buckskin shirt and leggings, matching moccasins and his grizzly bear claw necklace. He wore a multitude of eagle feathers in a circular fashion on the back of his head. He had earned every one of them.

My Noona was wearing her new blue colored dress with the dozens of elk teeth adorning the front, shoulders and upper back. It was a deep, true blue with a shine to it. It was hard to color buckskin with the fresh huckleberries and have it come out so uniform. But she looked perfect.

"Oh! My Grandson!" she said with quiet excitement.

They did this for every one of their grandchildren. The children were required to bring the grandbabies to them not vise versa. You should be adorned in your finest when you are first brought your grandchildren. That was the teaching.

I reached to take my son from his mother, held him close like he was something precious, and brought him toward Peepa. The others sat down. "Here is your grandson, Peepa," I said handing him the baby.

With a big smile and soft eyes, he took him and pulled him close. He just held him a while, gently murmuring and rocking him. He put his finger to baby's chin and mouth. He took hold of his hands, opened them and examined his fingers, and he gently rubbed his head and hair.

"My grandson, it is good to see you. I have thought about you a lot."

It was our tradition to talk to the babies like they were adults. If you were sincere, truthful and good-intending, they could understand you.

"Yes, these are some of your people here, but you have many relatives. Of course, you know your mother. You have already grown accustomed to her voice and her presence before you were born.

"You come from good people. We want you to grow to be a good person too, strong and kind in your own right. We want you to be recognized and protected always, each and every day on this road of life."

"So there are some things we will do for you," he explained to our baby in welcoming him to the family. Then he threw some incense on the charcoals of the fire, put his hand out to it, carrying some of the smoke to put on the baby. He wrapped him up again and got up to take him outside at dawn. We all followed.

Just as was done for me, and most all others of our people, our baby would be taken to the water where another prayer would be said and his feet would be dipped in the waters and his footprint placed upon the sandy shore. Others of our relatives had gathered outside waiting to be a respectful part of what would take place for baby.

Peepa faced the water and the east. A brilliant morning star was shining and an early morning fog was drifting about here and there. It seemed mystical.

He blew an eagle bone whistle to the four winds and called upon the divine natures to recognize him and his new grandson.

"From the other world and through the womb of his mother, he has come. Pure and innocent, he is just like this water. Let the Mother Earth, all the land, the hills and the mountains, and the forests and the prairies all recognize and know him. Let all the waters, the creeks, the rivers and the lakes recognize him and help him. Let the air, the wind and the sky know him and bless him. And, the great fire, our grandpa and the sun up above will see him this morning and accept him by imparting some part of their own spirit power to his good and protection."

He held him up above his head, and facing the east introduced him to that direction, then followed with the south, west and north.

"Kolunsuten and divine natures, I hold my grandson up before you. He is an Schi'tsu'umsh man, son of Sun Bear and Yellow Flower, grandson to me, Black Hawk, and my wife Basket Weaver, and to Drum and Shawl Woman.

"I put his feet upon the Mother Earth in ceremony and prayer that on this road of life he will be watched over, blessed and taken care of." He knelt down and put our baby's feet in the sand on the bank of the creek.

"These are his footprints. Let him make many more over many years down this good road.

"I dip him in the water that he will be recognized and fully accepted by you and your great Creation, that his mind and heart will be strong, and that he will live a full and beautiful life.

He leaned over and put the baby's feet in the water, then talked to the water and called upon its great powers to help and bless his grandson.

"You're all right, Grandson. You're all right," he gently consoled him and held him close.

We walked back to the teepee where Peepa had some herbs and things all prepared to use on our baby. He laid him on his back at the front of the teepee near the fire, but not where it would be uncomfortably warm and knelt down just behind him.

"My father-in-law used to have these ways," Peepa explained. "He left them with me to use. Maybe I could help his great grandchildren someday, was his hope in leaving them with me. Through him, Drum was his name, and by that authority I use them."

It was our way to explain where and how you got your ways. A person would never just copy or assume someone's spiritual ways, lest they would risk hardships, sickness and possibly even death. When Peepa mentioned my Sila, it made us all reverent and lonesome for him.

Ceremonial ways are sacred and powerful. Only those so authorized by the sacred beings of nature could conduct them, or pass them down to others whom they deemed worthy or qualified to conduct them.

Our ceremonial ways were protected from abuse or misuse. To mimic or just pick up someone's ways, without proper authorization, was more than just wrong or foolish it was dangerous. Spiritually, it would not work out for you, or the people you tried to help. Some great misfortunes may actually befall you, or your loved ones.

He asked all the non-family people, and the womenfolk, to excuse us for a short while in order to complete a ceremonial part reserved only for the men. Everyone understood perfectly. It was so sacred, it was secret. Just as the women had ways reserved only for them, this was one for the menfolk. This custom was not for the sake of a club or social symbolism, but it was because of the power of it, the very spirit of it that was related to the male side and the responsibilities of men and warrioring.

Only my Uncle Center Feather, One Star and my younger brother remained in the teepee with us. We sat on our knees, warrior style, straight and very still.

Peepa took out my Sila's hawk fan and other sacred objects and laid them out in a special order. He threw incenses on the charcoals and smoked everything off one at a time. As he arranged them, I felt things change in the teepee. A special, very ancient feeling moved over us. Even the light was changed. It seemed there were no shadows from the fire at all. True, it was getting daylight, but just a moment before, there had been shadows.

The fire went silent. The flame burnt steadily at one constant height and brightness. The wind and nature went still. Truly, this was a man, my Peepa, who had every right to do this ceremony by the proper authority and by how he lived his life.

In one hand he held a small buckskin bag and in the other, the hawk fan.

"Kolunsuten, sanction that which we do here in your name using some of your holy Creations in a good way."

"We have brought my grandson before you at this holy dawn of his new life. Now, we will call upon the warrior spirit, the great Thunderbird and the hawk to become a part of his own nature."

He uttered words that neither I nor anyone else must ever repeat, except in the same ceremony, for they are so sacred. He sang a special song of the hawk, and a prayer song for warriors. We all joined in. Sometimes, we war cried at the appropriate places and times.

Toward the end of the song, he stood up and held the bag and the fan out toward the east, then the south, then the west and then the north. He was turned toward the east as the song ended.

"Kolunsuten, bless my grandson. Make him strong. Let him grow up happy, healthy, kind, and good. Let him enjoy his childhood."

"One day he will be a young man. At that time, he will need your help again. He will have to know discipline, training, going without and enduring some suffering without crying out or showing self-pity. That's why we do this for him now, even though he has much time to just be a fun loving boy.

Peepa talked to the hawk and the holy Thunderbird in words I am not allowed to repeat. He called them by their true name and uttered incantations even I did not yet know or understand.

Then he took from the pouch he held, a little of the ground and dried heart of a special hawk and rubbed it on the baby's chest, exactly above his heart.

"You will be brave grandson," he announced. "You will be strong."

He moved his hands definitely as he did this, then threw some incenses on the fire and fanned him off with the hawk feathers. While he fanned, I could feel the precious feelings he held for the baby, and he did all this in the greatest degree of kindness, love and sincerity. To me, as always, he was the greatest man that ever lived.

"Okay, Son, let's take my grandson back to his mother. Maybe during the year, we will give him a formal name, at a memorial dinner. This is our custom," he concluded.

After everything was put away, we got up and headed back toward our teepee, and to my wife, Yellow Flower. Peepa talked and played with the baby all the way there. The baby never cried or fussed during any of the ceremonial doings. It was amazing.

As I took the baby and handed him to his mother, Peepa began to talk again.

"My grandson, is a great man, children," he said to us, but looking only at me as he could not talk directly to his daughter-in-law. "I do not say this for what he might achieve later, but for who and what he is right now."

"He will make many of your prayers fulfilled and your home a wonderful place. And, right now, he has brought to you the greatest blessing of all, love, hope and beauty of the mind and spirit."

"Treat him special. Talk to him special. He'll understand you. Teach him to pray. That very first cry he cried out as the Kolunsuten blew His breath of air into him, the Creator will never forget. Throughout his lifetime, when he is in need and comes before the Kolunsuten like a child and sheds tears in deep humility, He will recognize that cry and know it is one of His people."

"Your own lives are second now. Your baby's is first. So, do the best you can. I am very happy for you." "Hey!" I said in agreement with him.

Again, these were all the teachings of our elders from countless generations before us. It was all true to anyone who had a mind to listen and pay attention.

As we exited to return to our lodge, the small gathering of immediate family broke up and scattered toward their lodges. One lone figure remained. It was Rock.

"Good, brother-friend," he told me as I walked by. "You know you're getting old when your children start to grow up."

"Yes, brother-friend," I humored him.

He reached over to touch baby's cheek.

"Hey, little one," Rock said with the voice for talking to infants and small children. "Some day we will ride together on a great adventure."

I could feel his true feelings for baby. He was a good man.

"And, baby, when we find the enemy . . . ." he started to say.

"We know. We know, Rock," I interrupted.

Still, he made the motion of cutting off a tail.

CHAPTER 23

When the Home Spirit is Broken

The days were now filled with a new excitement and responsibility. Yellow Flower was consumed with full-time all day, and sometimes all night, caring for baby. On top of that, she had her other chores and responsibilities. But, she did it all with never a complaint.

She got up every morning and said her prayers with the holy dawn, then went and gathered a big bundle of sticks for firewood. She prepared a little breakfast for us and sometimes other family members before she went out to gather roots.

My wife worked hides to perfection: even my Noona admired them.

Every evening she worked on clothes for the baby, and a baby-board to use to carry the baby in. She carefully placed a rosewood branch around the face of the board while singing a lullaby protection song so that the baby would always be safe in it.

My days were now more colorful as well, but I always wanted to get home more quickly than before. If I were out on a hunting trip, I would want to take care of our business and get right back. I went out more often by myself. It was still always good to get out in nature, the forests, the prairies, the hills and the streams.

Just like someone else might be at home in their dwelling, I was at home outside. I knew where everything would be and how it should be. I believed in and trusted nature. It would always be true to you and you could trust it completely. Never would a wolf be a rabbit; never would a gentle mist be harmful; water would always be wet; and the fish would always swim. Sometimes a spirit might appear as an animal, but that was different.

Besides, it seemed like they all knew me, all nature, even all the animal brothers. Sometimes even the bushes and trees would slightly move and brighten, as I would pass. Maybe it was all just in my own thinking, but I believed it anyway. It made me feel good to be in my own country.

A person's or people's home country has a special meaning and feeling, its own spirit. When we traveled into a neighboring tribe's territory, we could all feel the change in nature. It was all Mother Earth; it was all beautiful in its own right. But there was a deep familiarity, based on a belonging, a spiritual tie, to a person's home country.

Today, I was out in nature taking all this in, seeing it, knowing it, feeling it, breathing it and living it.

I was hunting for my brother, the deer. I told him I was coming for him. I told nature, and the Kolunsuten. I asked them to allow me to take one deer for my family.

If a person is sincere, and his heart is good, they will listen. You will have to be worthy. You will have to work, and be patient and attentive. You will have to respect the deer enough to learn his ways and his nature. And, you must honor him by being truly thankful upon the taking of his life.

If you do these things, a deer will show himself and sacrifice himself. The people will live on.

To our people, it was the deer and the elk who would care for us, as well as our native roots and berries. To many of our neighbors, it was the salmon. To others, the buffalo. But one thing we held in common was the knowledge and understanding that our lives were tied to theirs. Our existence was tied to theirs.

Should they ever cease to be, the end of the world would occur. That is what our elders taught.

I hunted with a peaceful and happy feeling. I was on the trail of a big buck, and he was wily and cunning. He had led me in various circles and across a lot of land. At one point, he back tracked over his own hoof prints and jumped a great distance off to the side. I had to back up, find where he may have jumped, and begin following him again.

Finally, he deemed me worthy of a shot.

"Wssht!" Right on the mark!

"Thank you, Brother," I told him as I knelt alongside him. "You are a special and sacred brother. Because of you, my little family and people will live on.

"Thank you, Kolunsuten, and Mother Earth."

As I rode into camp with the deer on my packhorse, I noticed there was some commotion at my parents' teepee.

"What is it?" I asked my wife.

"It is some of your relatives from the camp where your sister, Berry Woman, stays with her husband and in-laws. They say she has been beaten again and thrown out."

I felt a deep protectiveness stir within me building to a slight fury. Our people had ways and laws to follow. You could not just ride into another's home and take over. You could not fight with others, unless you risked some judgment by the chiefs for damages and penalty.

Above all, you could not take another's life. You would be banished from all the people forever.

So what would we do? I needed to hear what my Peepa would say. He would be angry and hurt. But he would think of a solution, too.

"This has happened, again?" he said in disgust and protest. "I talked to them before. I made it clear this would not be tolerated. And, my grandchildren?" he asked in a demanding way.

"They wandered with their mother for two days before she was able to return home," the messenger said.

"That's enough, I don't need to hear anymore. Sons, get your horses ready. We will go to see about this."

My Noona was crying as she watched and listened. "Oh, my babies," she cried, "my little girl."

"Wait for me, husband," she commanded.

We silently rode into my brother-in-law's family's camp over by the waterfalls on the river. Immediately, there was a great tension in the air. My Peepa looked like he meant business and so did the rest of us. And, we didn't know what our brother-in-law or his family and friends would do.

We rode up to Berry Woman's teepee and stood there a long moment. "Daughter," Peepa called out. Surely, they all knew we were out there.

"Daughter," he said again.

Finally, she emerged out the door. She was embarrassed and ashamed about what had happened to her. She wouldn't look at us. Maybe she was marked or bruised.

We didn't know what Peepa would do. I imagined what I would do if anyone tried to hurt my new baby son. I would become the great grizzly and tear through them.

People always say that your children are always just your children, no matter how old or grown-up they get. If Peepa still felt the way I feel toward my baby, for his daughter Berry Woman, I understood and knew why he would be furious.

He looked at Berry Woman. "Are you all right, Daughter?" he asked her.

She looked at him for a moment. He could see the tear in her eye, the bruising and swelling on her face. She put her head down again, and said nothing.

Peepa moved his arms straight and quivered while he made a fist. Those of us closest to him knew he was in the battle mode.

Then, he covered his eyes with one hand, and cried. We didn't know what to do except wait for him.

"Where are my grandchildren?" he asked.

"Children!" Berry Woman called. "Come out here."

They all came out looking scared and unsure. You could tell they had been through an ordeal having witnessed the violence inflicted upon their mother and wandering with her for two days in the wilderness. Peepa looked at them for a while.

"Daughter, tell my son-in-law to come out here." Since he said it loud enough for him to hear, Berry Woman just waited for him to come out.

The door opened, my brother-in-law, Mountainside, came out looking defiant and angry. He looked at Berry Woman. "What is it?" he demanded.

She looked at my Peepa.

"Tell my son-in-law to get your mother-in-law and father-in-law," he directed.

Mountainside didn't wait to be told by Berry Woman. Peepa only talked to her because our culture prevented him from talking directly to his son-in-law in an aggressive manner. Mountainside would not be able to talk to my Peepa either, except through someone else.

As his parents nervously walked up to the teepee, Peepa stayed on his horse. My sister's father-in-law remembered his manners.

"Ahhh, my friend!" he said greeting my Peepa. "Get down from your horse and eat with us," he offered.

"We have no time today. We must ride all the way back to our camp before dark and the sun is high in the sky," Peepa announced. The mood seemed to be improving. Maybe there wouldn't be a conflict.

"I came here to get my daughter," Peepa explained in a firm tone. "I gave my permission for her to be wed to your son. Promises were made to me of good, devoted care. Time and again, these promises have been broken. I laid down conditions that made clear this would not be tolerated." Peepa took a deep breath.

"It is the right of a father, only when the pact is clearly broken, to take the daughter back. She is my girl, my baby."

The in-laws of my sister put their heads down. The truth was the undeniable power above all else.

"Further," he continued, "the grandparents are the ultimate authority over the children. A grandparent could take grandchildren even from their own parents, if they are not being taken care of properly."

"We are grandparents. This is our daughter. She is the mother of our grandchildren, and yours. Small children belong with their mother, if she is a fit mother and able, like our daughter." No one else spoke or moved.

"We are also taking our grandchildren to our camp. It is our right and our responsibility."

"Daughter, come over here with your mother. This is no longer your home. The home is cut into separate pieces today, from this time on. It is broken," Peepa said.

Berry Woman huddled her three children over toward our Noona, keeping her head down.

"That is all I have to say," Peepa concluded. "My word is my law."

We rode off at a walk.

The truth was his power, and it could not be denied. Berry Woman's in-laws looked stunned but said nothing.

Her mother-in-law started to cry, maybe for the grandchildren. She looked at her son with a displeasing look, like "now look what you've done."

I thought about all the teachings on the way back, the ones always spoken at weddings. Take care of each other. Never use the man's superior strength against the woman. The woman is closer to the Kolunsuten. The home spirit is alive and made up of the marriage between man and woman.

I wondered, what will happen to that home spirit? What will become of my sister? How will she get along? Who will take care of her?

I could tell she thought about these same things as she cried most of the way back. Noona talked to her off and on all the way home. Now and then they would both cry.

Peepa rode in the front, as always, I followed behind him. The other men of our family band took turns carrying some of the children. Sometimes, they walked. Mostly, we rode in silence.

When we returned to camp, Rainbow Girl came out and greeted the children. "My babies, my babies," she said, even though the older ones were getting too big to be babied.

They all gave her a big hug.

Berry Woman walked up to her, looked sadly into her eyes. "I have nowhere to go. I have nothing," she said breaking down into tears again.

Rainbow held her closely for a while. The rest of us went to put the horses away.

At the corral, I quickly put my horse in and must have looked troubled.

"What is it, Son?" Peepa said. "What do you think could have been done?"

"I feel I will not be all right until I can hurt someone responsible for harming my sister," I answered him.

"I know," he said solemnly, sighing and looking off into the distance. "But we did right, and now my daughter will surely be protected from this kind of danger."

I nodded my head in agreement.

In the teepee, my Noona, Rainbow and Berry Woman were talking.

"Marriage can be such a wonderful thing," Berry Woman said, "when everything's going good. But when it turns against you, it can be the most hurtful thing you will ever face."

They sat or knelt on buffalo rugs in the teepee. Noona stayed close by her.

"I know my girl, I know," she said. "It will be hard for you for a while. But if your husband doesn't take care of you, it is our responsibility again. Just stay close, rest and heal yourself."

"Noona," she said, in a childlike voice, "he hurt me. He was cruel to me, saying mean things. Then he kicked me out to walk and wander with nowhere to go. I loved him. I would have done anything for him," she sobbed, crying uncontrollably.

Noona held her closely and tried to comfort her.

"You're better off, Sister," Rainbow told her. "I would never let anybody hit me."

"That's what I always thought, too," Berry Woman replied. "Maybe that's what every woman who has been hit or abused thought, until it is them. None of us will take it. None of us should take it. Then you are stuck in a crazy situation."

"It's just the greatest confusion, to love your husband, but also despise him for what he has done to you. It tears your heart and soul in two," she cried, straining for words.

I walked back toward our teepee and my own little family with no knowledge of what they talked about in the teepee. Yellow Flower barely acknowledged me as she busily prepared various foods. Obviously, she had been cooking long hours for our return.

"How is my sister-in-law, Berry Woman?" she asked.

"She's all right," I shrugged. "She walked most of the way back. She seems strong and healthy."

"That's not what I mean," my wife snapped back at me. "Where is she now and what is she doing?"

"She's in the teepee with my Noona," I answered a little annoyed back at her, not understanding the tone she used at me. "They're probably doing some kind of woman talk about their problems," I said.

"You just don't even know what's going on, do you?" she said to me angrily and walked off toward my parents' teepee.

I stood there with a blank and confused look. What did I do?

Peepa called in spiritual leaders to pray and conduct ceremonies for Berry Woman. The home spirit had to be addressed ceremonially, or it would affect my sister with the way it was left broken.

She pushed herself during the following days, working and staying busy. Yellow Flower and Rainbow Girl stayed by her. They often talked for long periods of time. I didn't know what they talked about so long.

My wife was back to her old self again, after giving me the silent treatment for several days. One Star said Rainbow had been acting angry at him for something too, but he didn't know what. So we shrugged our shoulders and just kept going with whatever we had been doing. "Women," he said.

The days turned into weeks, then without notice or by advance runner, my brother-in-law, Mountainside, showed up. He was alone. He slowly walked his horse up to the center of camp.

He didn't look defiant anymore. He looked humble and seemed to be pleading. He wore some of his finest clothing and his hair was neatly combed.

As he stopped on his horse, he announced, "I would like to see my wife and children."

From around the edge of camp, Berry Woman heard him. She was working on a hide. She stopped and listened. Rainbow and Yellow Flower walked over to her to be with her.

All her children were running to their father. "My Peepa, my Peepa," they all shouted.

He jumped down and pulled them close, picking up the littlest one. They were glad to see him.

Berry Woman told Rainbow, "I don't know what to say to him. I don't know what to do." She looked at Rainbow for advice and direction.

"Maybe you can listen to him. Then, we can send him on his way," Rainbow said.

Nervously, they walked around the teepees toward the center of camp. Berry Woman looked afraid and confused.

I felt like showing him what it felt like to be beaten and abused so he would never do it again to my sister or anyone.

As she approached, they made eye contact. "I want to talk to you," he said, almost solemnly.

Before she could say anything back, my Peepa came out of the teepee.

"No, no, no," he said. "Daughter, tell my son-in-law I have already decided on this matter. I have taken my daughter back because she was not cared for properly, even beaten and abused."

"Berry Woman, tell my father-in-law I am very sorry for all that has happened," Mountainside replied, looking at my sister. She was the intermediary because they could not talk directly to each other, so she just stood there so they could communicate.

"That's not good enough," Peepa shot back. "Tell my son-in-law these kinds of words have been spoken before and they were empty lies that fell to the ground."

"These weeks by myself have taught me the greatest lesson of all. Tell my father-in-law there is nothing more important to me than my wife and children."

"Tell my son-in-law I have already spoken on this matter. It will take more than mere words to make things right," Peepa said.

"Tell my father-in-law to tell me what to do. What action beyond words must I do? Ceremony? Gifts? Brave deeds? What?"

"Tell my son-in-law to figure it out for himself. This matter is closed for now. Tell him to have a good trip back to his home camp."

Peepa turned and walked away. Noona collected the children and Berry Woman moved them into the teepee.

Mountainside looked deeply troubled and hurt as he walked his horse away.

A loud thud sounded and Mountainside almost fell from his horse. He had been hit by a rock right in the back. I turned and looked;

Rainbow had thrown the rock at him. She was picking up another one. So was Yellow Flower. They threw them, and one hit him again.

He ran his horse away. The women mimicked war cries like they had chased him away in battle. Then, they laughed and giggled at each other.

Later on, Berry Woman was very quiet. She stayed with the other women. Finally, she spoke.

"He looked very sorry, didn't you think?" she offered.

The others looked at each other like it was the one thing they didn't want to hear her say. No one responded.

"Well, the children were sure glad to see him. I hadn't seen him so puppy-dog eyed and pleading since he wanted to marry me," she continued.

"Let it be for a while daughter," Noona said in her soothing voice. "Your mind and heart need to heal before you will be thinking clearly again."

Days went by. Just as Yellow Flower and Rainbow told me he would, Mountainside returned.

This time people were doing chores and my Peepa was out looking for game.

As he rode into camp, he announced, "I want to see my wife and children. I have some things for them."

The children all ran up excited and jumping all around him. He had a packhorse, too, with bundles tied upon its back. While he unloaded, Berry Woman walked over in his direction. She didn't look nervous or afraid anymore, only confident and willing to listen. But, she didn't smile or show him any positive sign.

"Wife, tell my father-in-law I have some things here for you, things you will need, baskets, root digging tool, bags, and hides, and serving equipment."

"My father is not here right now," she said. "I must not talk to you until he has returned." She turned and walked away.

It would not be in our thinking, even as adults, to disobey our father or disrespect him in any way. Nor, did we talk about him behind his back about what he knows or doesn't know; neither did we debate our views with him, or our Noona. We would be their boys and their girls as long as they lived.

Mountainside waited and waited for my Peepa to return. Toward evening time, Peepa rode into camp with two deer. He saw his son-in-law at the center of camp with his goods laid out.

Berry Woman came out to hear what he would say.

"What does my son-in-law want?" he said. "I have already spoken on this matter."

"Tell my father-in-law," he said looking again at Berry Woman, "I have thought long and hard about what he has said, about it taking more than mere words to fix things and make them right. So, I have brought things that a woman needs to take care of herself and her family. A man should get these for his wife. I have done it," he announced proudly.

"Tell my son-in-law it will take more than mere gifts, in a token way, to heal a home and set things right.

"Ask my father-in-law what it is I can do. I have prayed and fasted. I put up a dinner and a giveaway. I would give up everything I have to get my family back," he said begging for mercy, pleading for a solution.

"A man will have to get back to the very beginning . . . ." Peepa said.

"The very beginning of what? I already am at the very beginning of our marriage. I feel just like I did then, more so. I would do anything, anything to get my wife back."

"That's not the beginning. In the very beginning, the Kolunsuten himself made man and woman. He made man strong and fast, and he put a bow in his hand, that he care for, protect and provide. He did not give us men these qualities to use them against women and children or any helpless people."

Mountainside paused and listened. He thought and thought about what Peepa said to him.

"I don't understand. Ask my father-in-law, what does this mean, what kind of action must I take?"

"My son-in-law's peace is not to be made with me, but with the Maker who gave him the strength and physical powers he has."

"I still do not understand. How do I do this? What action must I take? When? For how long?"

"My son-in-law will have to find out all this on his own, Daughter," Peepa turned and walked away.

Mountainside sat there looking puzzled. Rainbow and Yellow Flower gathered the gifts he had brought for Berry Woman and took them into the teepee. He just sat there looking hurt and frustrated.

As night fell, we all went to bed. I don't know what happened to my brother-in-law.

As the weeks passed, Berry Woman was doing much better. She laughed and joked now. Sometimes she made fun of her husband with my wife and Rainbow.

Then sometimes, she talked like she missed him. "Did you see how pitiful he is without me?" she liked to say.

"Yes, but he had to get shaken out of his tree to realize things," Rainbow would tell her. "He thought he was a power all to himself. He was too dumb to see his wife was the one at the center making everything work well for him."

"No man realizes that," Berry Woman quipped. They all chuckled their agreement.

Over the days, Mountainside thought about what Peepa had said. He concluded that what was meant was that he had to be a good traditional man all the time, not just show up once or twice and expect everything to be all right again.

So, he started showing up everyday with provisions. He camped out near our camp and stood guard over his wife, children and all of us. Peepa started letting him talk to Berry Woman again, but stopped short of letting them get back together.

"When will you come home with me?" Mountainside asked her.

"We said we wouldn't talk about it anymore. It's up to my Peepa," she reminded him.

"It seems he will never give in. It's already been too long. I will never let any harm ever come to you from anything or anyone," he whined.

Berry Woman said nothing back. She just ignored the subject. She missed him too though. We all knew it. It was only a matter of time.

In my parents' teepee they talked often about things, the family, children and grandchildren, where they would go, what they would do next. They always did. They were like a team, a pair working in unison on the problems of life.

"Husband," my Noona called to him as they got ready for bed, "when will you let our son-in-law back in the family? He has done so much to prove himself. Everyone forgives him."

"I know," Peepa answered. "But I need to know that it will never, ever happen again. And that he will be the most dedicated and devoted husband a woman could ever have."

"Do you know that yet, husband?"

"I want to be sure. The only way I can be sure is if he lives here among us with our daughter and grandchildren."

"Husband, can I tell our daughter this news?"

"Yes, but our son-in-law will have to commit to this, and his word must be his law. After they are married again, he will have the right to take his family away. There will be no protection except for the promise he makes to me. So, his word must be honorable."

My Noona squealed with joy, putting her hands together. "You know, you turned out to be a great husband, father and grandfather! Your plan worked perfectly."

"In the beginning, I hoped that it wouldn't work and he would never be back. I'm only thinking of our daughter's happiness."

The next day, Noona told Berry Woman and she quickly told Mountainside. He war whooped and danced around. He picked up Berry Woman and spun her around. She squealed and held him, their first open display of affection in months.

Their children saw them and ran to join in the fun. They were all dancing, hugging and wrestling. It was a happy day.

That evening, Berry Woman had her teepee up and all her belongings in it. We had a big dinner. Her in-laws prepared it. Most of it was furnished by Mountainside himself.

Peepa sat quietly never dictating or orchestrating what would occur or how. This troubled Mountainside, for he thought his father-in-law might announce his blessing, re-authorize, and re-dedicate their marriage.

Finally, he got up, cleared his throat and went over to my Peepa. He knelt near where Peepa sat stoically and silent.

"Father-in-law," he said. "I'm not supposed to talk to you harshly, but this is a different time and situation."

Peepa just looked out in the distance like he might be listening, or he might not.

"I promise you I will take care of your daughter. I will devote myself to our home together, to her and to our children.

"I will defend and protect her from all threats, from all dangers. I know now more than ever, beyond what most other men can know, she is precious, she is the great value in my world.

"With my own life, I will take care of her, even before myself," he concluded.

Peepa looked at him. This also was rarely done, certainly not to communicate something directly.

"Your little children that you love so much," Peepa said, looking sternly and deeply into him, "what would you do if an enemy came here and attacked them?"

"I would ride over and kill the enemy, protect my babies with my own life if need be," he quickly answered.

"And what if the one harming your baby is your son-in-law, then what will you do?" Peepa said to him.

He put his head down and paused. "I would want to kill him too, but I wouldn't know what to do."

"Then, now you know how I feel," Peepa told him.

"Do you really love my daughter?" Peepa pushed. "Do you really care for her, not in words but in life and in action?"

"Yes, father-in-law, I do."

"Then live it son-in-law. If we go through this again, it will not be so simple. Take your wife, make your home here. There is nothing for me to say or to announce."

That was it. They were back together again.

CHAPTER 24

Sacrifice of Love
For the Home and the Family

In late autumn, the land is beautiful, the days are warm and the nights are cold. The earth is alive with the fruits and wellness of life. My home really was a blessing and I cared deeply for my wife.

The daily routines were simple and easy. We were at peace and harmony. The young children were playing while their older sisters were working on hides, repairing clothing, gathering wood or visiting. Just like the days before.

Men were casually making ready to go to the great river to trade for salmon, and the time was soon. Various relatives had gone to our neighbor tribes to check on availability of salmon. We would leave in five to seven days in order to time our arrival with the availability of some roots to gather that were only available in the late fall.

We had various fall camps to choose from and this one was upstream a little farther and near some of the other family bands at the fork and by the mouth of the creek.

Suddenly, we heard loud noises, war whoops, screams of terror and other sounds of battle from our neighbors. The sound of charging horses was thundering toward us. It was the enemy.

"The Chop Faces are coming! The Chop Faces are upon us!" people screamed and scurried in panic.

The enemy was dressed for war, faces painted, horses painted, war clubs, and bows and arrows, about twenty-five of them.

We were of no mind for trouble or fighting. We were at peace, quiet and enjoying family. No warning was given. They were not detected.

Still, in a way, it didn't really matter that we were surprised. Most of the men were prepared for this moment since birth. All the running at dawn, training with the warriors on horseback, fasting and praying, it all was for this.

I yelled my war cry from way down deep. The warrior within me was awakened. My blood boiled with anger. My wife brought me my weapons. I carried my war club and strapped my bow and arrows over my back. We only had about eight men at the camp, so we were seriously outnumbered.

Some of the women and children were still scurrying to find each other and find a safe place to hide as the enemies rode into the camp. The men on that side were already engaging the fight, but they were on foot against enemies mounted on war horses.

The enemy drove their horses into them with shields up and war clubs ready. Some of our warriors shot arrows at them, but they ricocheted off their shields. Others stood ready with war clubs, but they were run over by the charging horses.

One of my cousins ducked under the swing of an enemy club, turned and swung at another, but was hit in the head by a third enemy running by. Down he went.

Rock ran to help and quickly engaged the enemy fighting from the ground. He dove into one on horseback knocking him to the ground. They struggled in a life and death battle. Rock killed him with his knife.

The enemy charged into the teepee area and our families. Several ran around each side of the teepee with a rope and pulled it over. Children were running and crying, women were carrying toddlers and babies. One of the young boys was struck down.

I was almost there. The cowards would all die if I would have my way.

Suddenly, my Peepa rode into the battle on his best war horse. My nephews showed up with some horses. I got on one of them and charged.

Now things were different. They would have to deal with pure bravery and courage, and extremely motivated Schi'tsu'umsh warriors!

Some enemies were afoot reigning terror on our loved ones. I rode up and killed one not paying attention. I just rode up and hit him on the back of the neck or head. I slowed and turned while also grabbing my bow and arrow.

"Wssst!" I hit another right in the upper stomach. Down he went.

My Peepa rode into several enemy horses like a flurry, flailing his club. One of them fell, others rode off and circled.

Some of my other cousins, uncles and brothers had joined the battle. We fought them hard for a long while in vicious combat. We killed five or six of them, and several of our warriors were down.

The enemy would want several things to take back: scalps, horses and maybe women. We had to stop them.

While we were engaged, several enemy attacked the teepees. Some teepees went down. The children and women were running for cover. My older sister was tackled by an enemy. Rainbow Girl jumped on his back and cut his throat.

She helped older sister up toward safety. She set her toddler, Sun Boy, down by his sister and brothers to help our older sister, but they ran off toward the bushes.

Suddenly, Peepa was surrounded and blocked by as many as six enemies. His horse couldn't move. He fought without any hesitation or doubt. But he took a vicious blow to the shoulder, and then, to the back. But he cried a different war cry, higher pitched and eerie.

The enemy closest to him looked startled and hesitant. Peepa whirled his horse around and got on his feet on the horse's back. Standing, he faced the rear of an enemy who briefly lined up with other enemies.

He jumped on the back of the enemy horse landing on his feet striking the enemy on the back of the head. In the same stride, he did the same to another, and to a third. Finally, he dove from this third horse tackling a fourth enemy knocking him from his horse. He quickly overpowered this enemy and killed him with his club.

Others were starting to ride down on him when I broke away from the enemy I was fighting and charged in that direction to help my Peepa. I let go an arrow while charging full speed. "Wssst!" Right in the back. One of them fell!

I charged forward. Peepa had tripped one of the enemy horses and he was fighting on the ground. Several other enemies were riding up to kill my Peepa while he was engaged on the ground.

My horse was swift and fresh. I had to go right by the first enemy to get to the front rider who would have the first chance at striking my Peepa. Right as he cocked his war club back ready to strike, I leaped and knocked him from his horse. We fought on the ground. He was the strongest enemy I had ever encountered, and he was fierce. But I refused to let it change my thinking.

I faked a down strike with my club and spun around with a back blow just as he moved to counter the fake. His club went by my head as I ducked and turned driving my club into his ribs. He hunched over. He was broken and wounded.

I spun again, striking him in the temple with a powerful swing. He was dead.

The women were still fighting off some of the enemy. They weren't at all helpless. Some of them were nearly as strong as a man and had worked hard every day since early childhood.

I guess the warrior I killed was one of their leaders because when they saw him go down, some of them started to ride off.

I looked to the edge of the camp. One of their war chiefs was there — the one who rode parallel to our people talking to my Peepa in sign language, the one who led the party to kill Deer Hooves and the others. He still painted his face black, and looked pure hatred and evil.

He could see his warriors riding off with no scalp, no horses and no women. He called to them to come back and fight, but to no avail.

They were pulling back. We had killed at least ten of them, and some of our people from downstream were on the way to help us. We had made it. We knew our neighbor family bands were fighting too. But we didn't know how badly it was for them or if there were more enemy ready to attack.

As people pulled back, Baby Sun Boy appeared in the middle of the field where Rainbow Girl put him down to fight the enemy. The evil war chief of the enemy rode his horse right toward him.

Peepa and I weren't mounted. We ran to catch a horse, but they were in panic and flight mode and were hard to catch. I turned and ran on foot to try to head off the enemy. Every ounce of strength I had, I put it into my running.

"No, Kolunsuten. Don't let this happen to my nephew, to my baby sister." I thought in my mind. "All the foot races I had won, all the early morning running and training, help me now."

I ran harder and faster than I ever have. I felt like I was flying across the ground. I noticed Rainbow Girl was racing toward her baby too. This was very dangerous because she was what the enemy really wanted. But, a mother's love is a very powerful force indeed.

It would be close who got to the baby first. Sun Boy cried in confusion and fear, but headed toward his mother, Rainbow Girl.

The enemy in an instant rode down and snatched the baby just as he went by me. I couldn't get a swing at him. As he turned, Rainbow Girl latched on to his leg and saddle and pulled. The enemy had his other hand holding the baby. He tried to pull Rainbow Girl up, but she came up swinging. She was a terror and a whirlwind herself.

The enemy threw an elbow at her smashing her behind him and across the back of the horse. I thought he might ride off with both of them. She saw his knife, grabbed it and stabbed him in the back. He swung his arm around behind him, knocking Rainbow Girl to the ground.

But he rode off with the knife in his back, and with her baby, Sun Boy. They disappeared over the first set of hills.

I slowed my run as I gave up the chase on foot. Rainbow Girl didn't get up. As I approached her, I could see she was crying out of loss and defeat, not injury.

I helped her up. "How can this be?" she cried with a puzzled and hurt expression on her face. "My baby, my baby," she moaned and cried.

I turned and surveyed the field of battle. Several teepees were down, children were crying, relatives of those killed-in-action were wailing. Adults scurried looking for children. It was a horror.

I looked back at my sister. She was sitting up now, but rocking back and forth. "What will we do? What will we do?" she asked with an innocent pleading look, almost like a small child. "What about my baby?"

"I'm going to get him back," I told her with confidence. I felt it and meant it. She knew I always did what I said I would.

She looked at me. There was no room in our culture for mixing words, or talking out of turn. Your word was your law, period. I said it, now that's the way it was.

I looked for Peepa. He was sending one of my young nephews with a horse up to me. I helped Rainbow up and started to walk her down the hill. As my nephew approached and dismounted, I gave him Rainbow to lead to her children and husband.

As I rode up to Peepa, he said, "Two of your cousins, one of your uncles, and two of your in-laws are dead, and two other men who were visiting. Fifteen of the enemy are killed. Several of our people are injured."

My Peepa himself was bleeding from the side of his head, his shoulder and his thigh. He didn't show any affect from it.

I thought about myself and mentally looked for any injury. I was untouched. It was no time to think about it any further.

"We must get as many people together as we can, and go after my nephew," I advised. I couldn't tell him, not even in an emergency situation. He was my father, but I could respectfully advise him.

"I have talked to my brothers-in-law, as you rode up, but they went to look for their wives and children. Maybe they are hurt or injured, or maybe stolen, too. We must wait for some help," he said.

I rode over to my cousin-brothers and talked to them, but they were both injured. "Riders left to the big lake village to get help. They will be here by night fall. Wait for them to return. They will be here by nightfall," they advised.

Nightfall would be too late. The enemy could disappear into their own country if we didn't stay right behind them. We had to leave soon to catch them. But we needed help or it would be certain suicide.

I noticed Peepa was talking to Uncle Center Feather, who had been away visiting. I was never, ever so glad to see him.

I rode around him and war whooped. "The enemy came. We killed many of them. But they took our baby." I yelled. "We must go and kill some more to get Baby Sun Boy back!"

My brother-in-law, One Star, and Rock would go, and my younger brother. That made six of us. Six against many.

Still, we knew what we had to do. We didn't know how we would do it, but we knew we had to try something.

I looked at Rainbow Girl as she cried and couldn't help but think of when she lost her young fiancé. How could someone who is all good, does everything right, does nothing but help so many people, deserve or be made to suffer this way? When did fairness and justice balance out?

I tried to quit thinking that way. We needed the Kolunsuten's help now, not doubt and confusion.

I grabbed a few more things, more arrows, a blanket, and my knife. I put on my hunting and warrior-road moccasins. My wife burst into the teepee.

"What will we do?" she cried.

"I will go after him and bring him back," I told her without hesitation. Her look changed from sorrow to concern.

"My husband, we have been married such a short time. I couldn't bear anything happening to you."

"I believe I will return to you," I reassured her. "We will have many children and grandchildren. We will grow old together, we will be lovers, companions and the best of friends over a lifetime."

She leaned toward me and I leaned my forehead toward hers. We held each other briefly. I could feel her love for me deep in my heart and I tried to love her back in a way that she might feel it in her heart too.

As we pulled apart, I looked at her and walked out.

I could hear my Checheya's voice, "What's happening? Where is Rainbow Girl? My granddaughter takes care of me? Where is she? What has happened?" she asked in confusion. My heart hurt, and my blood boiled again. I only wanted one thing: my chance to kill the enemy.

"It's all right Tupiya (great grandmother)," one of the children told her. The Chop Faces stole Sun Boy but they're going to go after him."

"Oh, my!" she cried with the dismay and concern of a loving old grandmother and great grandmother.

"My Son," Peepa called to me. "Come over here. It's time to make final preparations and depart."

He prayed briefly and lit a sweetgrass braid. We all used the smoke incense by putting our hands to the smoke and then touching our hands to our heads, chest, shoulders, arms and down our bodies.

It was an emergency. Every minute counted. But, if at all possible, some preparation was necessary. We had to tell the Kolunsuten what we were going to do and why, and invoke his great sanction and protection. It was a sacred mission upon which we were about to embark, with near impossible odds.

There were six of us. At least ten of the enemy tribe rode out from our camp, and our neighbors said at least thirty of them rode away. That made six against forty. Impossible odds in a head-on confrontation. It would take something beyond our mere human power to make it come out right.

We could only apply every measure of strength, courage and faith that we had. The rest would be up to the Kolunsuten. We had to believe without doubt.

The laws of nature were simple and unchanging. Fire would always be hot, water would always be wet, a fish would always swim and a bird would always fly. Never would you see a bear that was really a deer, or a wind that was really a mountain. Nature did not lie to you or deceive.

So, it could be said that six against forty could never win as a fact of nature. But, we could be like the flowing waters that can never be stopped, like the hail in the wind that can overpower and like the badger that can fight ferociously when challenged no matter the odds or foe.

Peepa painted his face, then turned to me and my younger brother with the paints.

"Kolunsuten, Mother Earth, and all of nature, bless my sons. Give them courage. They are your warriors this day. Let them be recognized and granted the warrior power," he said as he applied the paint.

As my brother-in-law, One Star, showed up, Rainbow Girl was with him talking loudly and defiantly.

"I want to go," she said. "I know how to ride hard. I know how to use a bow and arrow. I grew up with my brother doing these things every day. He is my son."

She was right about that. She could ride and shoot as well as many men. I know because I'm the one who taught her. But we had no time to consider or argue.

"No," our Peepa said overruling her and her husband. "It cannot be. The enemy may take you or kill you. It is not the time." She put her head down not to disagree with her father.

My Noona came over and put her hand out to him and he touched it affectionately. I leaned down and put my forehead to my wife's. One Star looked at Rainbow Girl and said, "I will be back with our son."

Rainbow didn't browbeat him now, or protest his participation. She knew this was the day and time for which the Kolunsuten made men warriors, not the petty glory some men seek to feed their own sense of self-pride.

We rode off after the enemy. We knew they would ride all day all night, and the next day. So we would have to do the same. They would try to get over the mountains and into the buffalo prairies as quickly as possible because they knew we would be close behind. They didn't know how many or when, only that we would come. We headed in the direction the enemy left away from our camp and loved ones, and disappeared over the same hill.

The rest of the day we rode, and rode hard. The trail was obvious during the day. We knew shortcuts here and there. But we had to make sure we didn't pass by the enemy either.

After dark, it was up to Uncle Center Feather. It must have been the Kolunsuten who inspired him to come home when he did. Without him we wouldn't have been able to track them as perfectly in the night, perhaps riding blindly into a trap.

I was able to ride in the middle of the pack and follow Uncle Center Feather. He had the great tracking power. He lived out in nature and with the horses. He could disappear into it if he wanted to. It gave me time to think, and conduct a meditative prayer. I know my Peepa did the same.

We were riding into a situation that many others, if caught in it, would be looking for a way to sneak out. It would take all the courage, all the strength, all the faith, all the ferocity of the warrior way and all the invoking of the great mystery power. The Kolunsuten would have to pity us and bless us with a special strength. We would have to be prayerful and attentive, or risk losing the opportunity to gain a spirit helper. It was our only chance for success. Otherwise, we would lose our baby and our own lives. It was the test of a lifetime.

I thought about the prayers and preparation, the fasting and running, and the horses and spiritual power.

"O, Kolunsuten," I prayed, "you have helped us much over the days of this road of life. But I ask you, help us this much more. Do not let my nephew be kept by the enemy. Let us return him to his mother, my baby sister."

A little after nightfall, about fifty Schi'tsu'umsh warriors left our home camp on the trail of the enemy, but they were more than half a days' ride behind us, and they wouldn't run hard all night long as we would have to.

Circling Raven, himself, came to the camp to witness what had happened, comfort the mourners and authorize the warriors. He would go to see each family one at a time. First, though, he had to pray.

The great chief had a teepee erected for him where he conducted his ceremonial prayer. Some of the families joined him. My Noona, Yellow Flower my wife, and others were included. During the whole ceremony they prayed with all their strength and all their hearts for their husbands, brothers, sons, fathers and uncle, and baby, Sun Boy.

As Circling Raven addressed what had befallen our people, the enemy attack, the fighting and the deaths, he came to the situation most on the minds on the women of my family. He prayed for the men who departed first, only a handful against many.

"Bless them, Kolunsuten, my nephews and my grandsons who left on the warrior trail," he said, calling us by the nearest relative term he could.

"You are the Kolunsuten, the Creator of all things. You made the four elements, the earth, the fire, the water and the air, our grandfathers, and the great sky above and our Mother Earth below."

"With these, you made the day, the night, the winds, the seasons and the time of the road of life. All your great Creation moves together to make your miracle of life happen, and they move the way you told them to with the properties and power you gave them."

"First there was vegetation upon the land, the greenery of new life. Much of it became a preparation for the people, the foods, the medicines, the prayer tobaccos and incenses. Recognize us this day by your great Creation and what grows from the land." He put on cedar, blue spruce and sweetgrass upon the fire in offering to and calling upon the vegetations.

"Then the animal realm was created by you and they took their place within all that you had made. They are our brothers and they made a preparation for the coming of the people agreeing to feed, clothe and shelter us. Our animal brothers have great spiritual power too. If we take proper care of them, like brothers, then they will in return take care of us beyond the mere physical ways."

"Finally, the people were created with the power to think, choose and communicate with words. And, by your great Creations, we live."

"We need your Great Spirit power now for our relatives who have traveled on a sacred mission of right and good. They have intended no harm to anyone, neither have they neglected the responsibilities you have placed upon them as men. They go to help and defend their loved ones."

"Anoint them with your holy spirit power. Let them be recognized by your divine natures, and strengthened and protected. Give them the power of the animals to blend and hide in nature that they would be unseen and unheard. Grant to them the presence of your hail and wind to be the fury with which they will ride into battle."

"The sacred hawk, our great brother, is the warrior bird of bravery, strength and tenacity. By our great brother, move to impart this awesome power to them."

"My brother, Drum, he had knowledge of the hawk power and he used it to help people and pass on the strength of the warrior way." Circling Raven spoke words and incantations of the hawk way. He briefly sang a short song that was the spirit song of the hawk. The holy hawk was called upon.

"We know the warrior road is dangerous, but we must ask you to bring our loved ones back safely. Bring our little infant child, Sun Boy, back to us."

He put incenses upon the fire and fanned to the four directions, then fanned to the direction we were traveling and envisioned us.

I knew beyond all doubt I could feel the prayers of our relatives at home. I knew my wife was behind me, as was my Noona and everyone else.

Inside the great teepee, people gathered quietly around Circling Raven.

"Where is Rainbow Girl?" my Noona asked my older sister.

"I don't know. I thought she was with you. Maybe she is with Checheya," Berry Woman answered.

They continued to sit in front of the fire and meditate, hope and pray.

My Checheya came in to join them and help support the great cause and purpose for which we fought. She took a seat with great effort and help from some of her great granddaughters. Still, Rainbow Girl wasn't there.

Circling Raven had been singing and meditating, calling upon his spirit power for guidance and interpretation. Finally, he started to speak again.

"My relatives, we are charged as a people and as warriors to be ready to protect ourselves and our people. The foundation upon which we stand as a nation has been paid for and preserved by the blood of our warriors. There is no guarantee of safety on the warrior road, but we must pray for it with everything we have and all that we are."

"We want peace. We want the goodness of life. That is why we are blessed by the Kolunsuten. We never kill or take life indiscriminately, nor do we take slaves. All people are equal."

"War at just any cost is insanity; but peace at all costs is slavery! We will not be slaves to anyone. We will not sit by and have our loved ones killed, injured or captured! With every measure of life and strength we have, we will never allow this!"

"We will do all we can in battle, in loving support and in prayer. If we are strong enough, we will prevail. If we are weak, we will not."

"This is the guidance I am shown."

The warriors had to be strong. There was no guarantee of their safety. They were in danger. It was a disturbing picture to all. But what was there to do but go at it with every measure of strength and faith possible.

Circling Raven left to see and be with some of the other families who had loved ones killed.

"Where is Rainbow Girl?" my Noona asked. "Everyone is here now; my daughters-in-law, my older daughter and my Checheya."

"She left the children with their older cousins, and they said she rode off behind her brothers, husband, and Peepa." Checheya explained.

"Oh my babies, my children," Noona cried. "All my sons, my husband, my baby grandson and now my baby girl, Rainbow, are gone and in harm's way. My whole family, my whole life is confronting the spirit of death. What will I do?" she moaned, fighting the panic.

Checheya turned to her and took her hand. "Maybe it will be all right if we are strong enough, pray enough and believe enough, my baby girl. It will be all right, daughter," she consoled her with a mother's soothing voice. My Noona was her daughter, her little girl no matter how old she ever got.

Checheya told everyone to listen to her. She had them go to different places to fast and pray. She sent my Noona to the south to a small hill to pray to the Kolunsuten while telling the Moon of our plight and asking for help. Noona was a grandmother, and the moon controls the cycles of motherhood and the waters of life, so she had more right to do this than the younger women.

Checheya directed my older sister to go to the west by the riverbank to address the great waters and the Thunderbird. She sent my wife, Yellow Flower Girl to the east, toward the morning star and the holy dawn.

To the north, she sent my sister-in-law, my younger brother's wife, the ancient ways and teachings of our people would help us.

She told everyone "Do not to move around, do not talk to anyone and let nothing interfere with your concentration and meditative prayer. Continue this until we have word of the safe return of our loved ones."

Checheya stayed in the teepee. From there she would pray and give her support near the fire and the Mother Earth.

Alone, up on the hill, Noona fought the panic that gripped her mind and spirit. What about Rainbow Girl? Is she all right? The men could stand equal in battle with anyone, but what would her baby girl do? Would she be all right?

On horseback, Rainbow rode hard into the night down the trail behind the men. She had a bow and quiver of arrows slung over her head and one shoulder.

When we were growing up she played with me much of the time, riding horses, shooting arrows, fishing, traveling to a neighbor camp, and even hunting.

She was as good as most men and better than many with a horse and with a bow. She was never helpless and she knew it. But, this was different. Could she manage being on the warrior trail against mighty enemy warriors?

"I must use my mind to counter their superior strength," she planned. The love of a mother for her child in danger made her forget fear.

"I will hide and shoot arrows from a safe distance to help the men. When the time is right, I will take my son." On she rode down the trail and over the pass toward the buffalo country. She was behind the men somewhere but there was only one way through the pass and down the other side, and daylight was not too far off. If she could stay close enough to pick up the trail, she could follow them through the day.

There were fifty enemy and five of her men all going the same direction in a hurry so it was not difficult to follow the trail.

Rainbow rode hard. "O, Kolunsuten, please help me," she prayed. "I have never questioned your ways even when overcome with tragedy. I never questioned why or said it was wrong. Help me now.

"All that I am, for all that I am worth, I am still just a humble and loving mother. I am a daughter, a granddaughter, wife, sister and auntie. I'm not a great leader or medicine power person.

"Let my love be great enough before you with this humble prayer. Hear me and help us to return my baby," she shed tears with her prayer.

She thought about her husband, One Star. She had grown to love him. The parents were right in putting them together. She realized it now.

"I could not bear anything happening to my husband. Please, Kolunsuten, protect and guide him, and my brothers, my Peepa, and my Uncle," she pleaded silently.

She wondered if she'd been a fool to go on this warrior trail. She thought about the closest moments nurturing her baby. Her resolve strengthened and deepened.

"How can you measure the depth and power of a mother's love? What it could really do was perhaps limited only by people's faith or lack of it," she thought.

"If I must die to gain the life of my child, so be it but let not my sacrifice be in vain."

In a neighboring camp, where the great Medicine Woman lived, the women entered a sacred lodge to conduct ceremonial prayer in support of the effort. They addressed nature, life and the deep feelings a woman has. If she lives and abides by these deep feelings, she will be grounded in culture and teaching, and she will be a rock in the foundation of her family.

The women of the tribe were the real power of the people. If they did not agree or support what the men were doing, it could not continue.

They prayed, chanted and sang. They called upon the Kolunsuten and the holy beings of nature. Medicine Woman's power was the turtle. The turtle was very deliberate and knowing. It's power was wisdom and knowledge. She shook a turtle shell rattle and called upon the Kolunsuten to bless and protect the warriors, and to give them guidance.

In the great teepee Checheya continued her meditative prayer and fasting at the center of the four directions to which she sent her daughter and granddaughters to pray. She remembered her husband and all the trials and tribulations she had faced in her lifetime. In the end, it all worked out with faith and some hard work.

She was troubled by the words of Chief Circling Raven. Sacrifice is what he said. Safety is not promised on the warrior road. The foundation of our nation is the blood of our warriors spilled upon the ground to defend it and the people.

It worried her deeply. "Don't take any of my boys, my grandsons or son-in-law," she called to the Kolunsuten. This is the one life you have given us and the one family we have. You didn't give it to us for nothing, and neither do we live it without order. Bless us." She put incenses upon the fire.

Chief Circling Raven made his way to a hilltop with his ceremonial peace pipe. He wanted to be praying before first light and then during the sunrise.

CHAPTER 25

Bravery Means Disregard for Your Own Life for a Higher Purpose

All our riders rode with a prayer and a focused determination. Rainbow Girl never let go of her prayer and a mother's hope. All the women of the family band prayed and fasted toward the four directions, the Sky, the Moon, the Earth and the Water. The medicine women conducted ceremony. The holy men prayed in support. Circling Raven prayed from the hilltop.

All the thinking and all the prayers were the same. The same humility came over everyone. Everyone shed a tear, moved by the feeling of the spirit. The spirit drew near for sake of sincerity, humility and love.

Everyone thought at the same time, bless our little baby. He is innocent and pure. He deserves the rights of living with his father and mother. He has never done wrong. His feelings are precious and his life is sacred. Help us to bring him back safely to our people.

As our small group of warriors rode down the mountain, a small flash in the sky caught my attention. We all turned to look. It happened again. It was a red flash, like the flat, sheet lightning that happens in the scattered clouds around the mountains: but this one was red.

Peepa slowed the horses to a walk and we turned and looked. Again, a third small, low flash, all red like the other two. It was as if some low lying, thin clouds had lightning in them. We looked across the sky. There were no clouds anywhere.

It was mysterious and sacred. It was a sign. We paused for a moment to contemplate and interpret it.

"It is what our old people call the 'red thunder'," Peepa explained. "It is rare, few have seen it. We have the blessing of the Kolunsuten, but remember, we must do our own fighting. So, fight bravely."

We raised our hands to the sky in recognition and to receive the blessing. We didn't war cry or yell. We were reverent in the presence of the holy spirit.

The sky and the night were beautiful, and alive. Stars were brighter, the moon was closer. We turned and rode off to continue our mission.

Rainbow stopped her horse. She turned and looked upon the phenomena in the sky. She gasped and covered her mouth.

"You helped me before as a young girl, holy thunder. Please, let me help my own baby now," she pleaded.

The thunder seemed to gently roll around a distant mountaintop.

At dawn, we walked the horses to let them catch their breath, and then drink some water.

The enemy was easy to track now, fifty or more horses all running at a reckless speed. The ground was torn with their tracks, obvious in the morning light.

As we let the horses walk, we had our first chance to talk.

"We will encounter the enemy this night," Peepa said. "They will be expecting us, but they won't know how many of us are coming."

"Some of their scouts will hold back when we near their camp. We must be careful not to ride into a trap."

Uncle Center Feather said they were only two fingers of the sun ahead of us and we should keep our distance. We knew he would find them in the night.

"What about our brothers, the Salish?" I asked. "Maybe they know what has happened because the enemy passed through their country and they will be waiting to attack them," I said.

"No, Son," Peepa explained, "They are good brothers and relatives. But they want no trouble with the enemy. They are afraid. We must do this alone, and use our wits."

"This night, I will do whatever it takes for my grandson and my baby girl Rainbow. If it takes a major sacrifice to make it happen then so be it. Let that sacrifice be me. I accept death, but I choose life."

"When I engage the enemy, go get my grandson and bring him back to his mother. All our lives are in the hands of the Kolunsuten, including mine."

I felt a deep panic and worry. This could not be. There could be no trading of lives, a loved one for a different loved one. This was impossible.

"We will make a plan on the way and work it out when we see the their camp," Center Feather said.

Peepa agreed and motioned to keep going like everything was all right. But I knew him. His words were never just to be talking. He said it, and he meant it.

As warriors we all have to acknowledge our own death. I had made peace with it. But, I could not conceive of a world without my Peepa.

I tried not to think about the terrible odds we faced. I started again trying to believe, have faith and be strong. We rode on.

A family of hawks flew along with us for a while. They were a good sign. The hawk is the warrior bird, and there were a family of them, just like us.

Also, I thought about the ceremony my Sila did for me at my birth with the heart of the hawk mixed with the powder of white clay. I felt strong and confident again. We must go ahead with all the blind faith and confidence we could.

One of the young hawks flew back in the direction we came from and then followed from there. I wondered what that could mean.

Meanwhile Rainbow traveled behind us, although we didn't know.

"I hope my baby is all right. He has specific needs and habits, how he likes his food, how to make him comfortable when he wakes at night, and how to reassure him. What if they have abused him or killed him?" Tears swelled up in her eyes.

She searched her feeling for a tie to him. Yes, she could feel he was still alive, but she had to get to him soon. He had been brought horse-back, half-a-day, all night, and then probably all day again. Her poor baby. She cried, a worried mother's cry.

She knew the men would be focused on where they were going, not on what was behind them while they were in such a hurry. So she pushed on, not worrying about getting too close.

Besides what could anyone do now? She was already here, and no one could send her back. She must do something to save her baby.

She remembered all the times she spent with her brother shooting a bow and arrow. She had even killed her own deer, several of them.

She thought toward the Kolunsuten. Even in my darkest hours, I never questioned you. I never quit praying to you. Please don't let this ordeal turn into tragedy, she begged. Our elders taught that, sometimes the hardships of life may befall you. Someday you may be praying for the very life of your loved ones, your children or even yourself. At that time, the help you need will be hard to get. You must be deeply sincere and humble. It will move you to shed tears.

Rainbow knew the depth of this sincerity and the true meaning of this teaching as she rode on through the buffalo country.

As the sun prepared to go down in the west, Center Feather said to hold up. The enemy would send back, in small and larger circles, scouts to detect any presence by us. So we rode into a secluded thicket and waited for dark.

Uncle Center Feather left on his own, on foot, to scout the situation. I wanted to go but he said he could be more effective and quicker on his own.

He was amazing at stealth and camouflage, and imitation of animals of the night if detected. He walked into the night and disappeared.

It was a clear night. In the direction he went, there were no bushes or trees. Yet, he was gone!

Center Feather first would use the deer power. He kept a strip of hide that included the nose, a thin strip all along the back, and the tail of the buck deer. It was only several inches wide, but long. He kept it in a pouch on his belt with other medicine bundles.

He rubbed the pouch and talked to deer, "I need you now. Help me now in the time of our greatest need."

The deer can turn invisible just by going totally still. Uncle would use this power to conceal himself. He would use a special bow medicine to track in the dark along with the wolf power. The wolf is nocturnal and can hunt quietly and perfectly without mistake. With the incisor fangs of the wolf tied to his tiny power bow, he would get insights as to which direction to go.

Uncle got his night eyesight from the morning star. He heightened all his senses by staying out in nature, eating only fresh food, disciplining himself physically and spiritually, and always remaining very, very quiet.

He needed all his tools and powers this night. He would walk or crawl only a step or two at a time, watching carefully for enemy scouts. Here and there, he would detect a presence, not a noise or a figure, just a possible presence. He would avoid those areas, move ever so quietly, and smooth.

Finally, he had a view of their camp. Then three of the enemy suddenly walked right toward him. He gently crouched in the grass, shutting down all his energy.

The enemy stopped right by him and began to look around like they suspected someone was near.

Center Feather thought about the deer, the fawn. They have special camouflage power and a natural stillness to make them seem invisible. He touched his pouch and meditated. He became the deer.

One enemy walked right over to where Uncle laid on the ground. He could have reached out and touched him. Should the enemy turn toward Uncle, he would trip over him.

Uncle waited. No panic. No presence.

The enemy all looked at each other and walked away.

With the same stealth, Uncle headed back toward us.

When he returned, he told us:

"They have no teepees, as they are camped light and ready to travel again at a moment's notice. There are six campfires almost in a row. Our baby is near the third fire from this side. No one is taking care of him. He is crying."

Then he said quietly:

"I think the enemy may kill him if he does not quit crying. The evil one who took him lunged at our baby like he would strike him, but he only hollered at him."

We felt the powerful need to act, and act now.

Peepa said he would charge in to them and kill as many as possible. Uncle Center Feather said we needed a plan. I suggested some things that as soon as I said them, knew they wouldn't work.

My younger brother, Snow on the Mountain, is a very quiet man. He rarely speaks, and when he does, he is shy about it. But, tonight he said he would go down to the far end of this camp where their horses were, stampede them and make a commotion. Then, he would run out like he was stealing horses. He would try to only take about ten or fifteen, to leave the enemy enough horses to follow.

The rest of us could attack and engage whatever enemy was left behind, drawing them away from the third campfire. One of us would be designated to run right up, get baby Sun Boy and take him out and away to the meeting point. After which, we would all withdraw and make our getaway.

It was a good plan. Even Peepa added nothing but a sound of agreement, "hmmm!" he said, "Hey! Hey!"

Quiet people are respected by my people, for quietness is strength. My brother showed it tonight.

Peepa sent his son-in-law, One Star, Rainbow Girl's husband, to help my younger brother. Center Feather and Peepa would attack with fury. Whatever enemy ran to the far end of the camp to fight would have no horses to follow. I would be at the nearest point to Sun Boy waiting for the best chance to get him and I would act quickly to get him as far away as possible as soon as I could. Rock would wait with my horse, and should anything go wrong, he would ride up and try to take back the baby himself.

With prayerful concentration we moved into position. My heart was pounding, my palms sweated, my legs ached with anticipation. I was chosen for this job because I was the fastest foot racer. I needed more than all my speed this night.

In the home camp, all the women of the family held their positions for the second night. All this time they had not eaten, nor had they drank. They pushed with a deep inner strength to continue and focus their prayer without letting their minds wander.

Checheya prayed in the teepee, sometimes she sang, sometimes she meditated.

An owl hooted just to the east of her. The owl is a messenger. He can tell you what's going to happen. Some of the people could talk to him one on one. But he also comes often to tell about danger or death.

Checheya listened, trying to interpret, "What is it, our brother?" she said to the owl. But she could not understand the owl's reply.

"Help me Kolunsuten. I do not understand." She threw some incense upon the fire. She gazed into the flame and glowing charcoals and strained her mind and senses to understand what the messenger had said.

Suddenly, one of the charcoals moved and split apart, taking the shape of a man. As she looked closer it started to resemble her son-in-law, my Peepa! The image had black and red paint from the eyes up over the forehead, and feathers worn around his head, just like Peepa.

"My son-in-law!" she exclaimed.

The image then fell, tipping over and broke apart.

"My son-in-law might fall in battle," she cried. She prayed and prayed with all her heart. Sometimes, we are shown things so we can do something about it so that it won't happen. Checheya hoped and begged.

She rocked back and forth, hummed, and moaned her concern. She couldn't help but shed some tears, but without sobbing so it wouldn't be bad luck.

The other women heard it too. They tried to be thankful for the sign and the messenger. They prayed all the harder.

Preparing for battle, everyone was in position. Center Feather gave them the call of a night bird.

Younger brother and brother-in-law, One Star, moved toward the horses just away from the far side of their camp. Stampeding horses and commotion would be the first action. Shortly after, Peepa and Center Feather would strike.

This night, they moved with deadly silence, concealed by the night and nature. Wherever the enemy scouts were, we picked our way right up to the designated positions. It had to be the prayers and the help of Kolunsuten, but also the great powers of Uncle Center Feather.

Brother moved into the middle of the horses catching the lead rope of one.

"Wait," brother-in-law, One Star whispered. "Hold a horse for me."

He crept toward the nearest fire. Quickly, he charged toward the fire and the eight or ten enemy seated and laying near it. He grabbed one of the flaming sticks and threw it to the dry grass and brush, starting a small fire. He jumped over the fire and in stride he clubbed an enemy in the head who was sitting near by and struggling to gather his weapons. Through all this, they made a lot of noise, then he ran toward the horses.

Brother was already mounted and holding a horse for brother-in-law. He did a running mount. They had untied and cut the hobbles on ten horses, which they quickly stampeded out and away from the camp.

The enemy scurried to gather themselves and find a mount. In a short while, groups of five and ten left to make chase after the stolen horses. But there were still at least fifteen enemy remaining in camp.

Peepa waited several minutes, then Center Feather and he attacked the camp at the point of the brush fire.

"Oww! Oww! Hey-yah, Hey-yah!" they yelled and charged, painted up for battle, war horses breathing fire, nostrils flared and ears down.

The enemy was on foot so we had a temporary advantage. But some were already trying to get their horses and others might return who had left chasing the stolen horses.

The evil one who stole Sun Boy fell for our trick and ran toward the action. I saw my chance.

I ran across the meadow toward the baby. Horses were returning, not many but at least five or six. They engaged my Peepa and Center Feather. The enemy on foot without horses readied their arrows.

I picked up baby Sun Boy and turned to run. It worked. All I had to do was run to my horse at the meeting point.

I looked at Peepa and Center Feather. They were surrounded and fighting furiously. They were slowing the movement of the horses giving the archers a clear shot at Peepa.

I paused. I couldn't leave Peepa to die. I couldn't trade one loved one for another. I needed for everyone to come home.

I ran toward the battle. The first enemy I saw taking aim and ready to fire an arrow, I shot him in the back with an arrow. Down he went.

I took aim at the next one ready to fire. "Wsssht," right in the back. Down he went. The enemies in front of the ones I shot still hadn't detected me.

Whenever I moved, I kept baby Sun Boy right by me.

Peepa fought bravely, as usual. He always told me to fight with courage but know what the enemy is doing. One mistake, one opening, and you are dead.

He fought recklessly. He had total disregard for position and mistakes. He was trying to win the battle with pure ferocity and power.

There were still at least ten of the enemy on foot running about for position. If they turned on me, I would be in trouble to fight that many hand-to-hand while holding a baby.

Peepa was surrounded again, and so was Center Feather. A handful of enemy were all in position to shoot arrows into them. Peepa couldn't pay the archers any attention or he would be killed by the enemy on horses.

With no choice, I shot into the group. Several now noticed me and turned to confront me. Just as they would have let go their arrows, younger brother and brother-in-law ran their horses into the group of archers clubbing two of them and scattering the rest. It was strange. It was like we all knew where the others were, what would happen next and what we needed to do.

We had to finish here and find a point to break away. I had no horse. Now, I was the problem. They couldn't leave baby Sun Boy and me.

The enemy who saw me shoot arrows earlier were charging toward me, yelling their war cry! "Owww! Owww! Oww! Oww!" Others started to follow them.

I set baby Sun Boy in some taller grass and moved forward to meet them. "Hey-yah! Hey-yah!" My blood boiled, my warrior power surged, I could feel it. I charged into the first one hard, knocking him over and smashing him in the side of the head.

The next one stopped and circled to fight a tactical fight, or wait for help. I charged at him and made him fight. He was strong and we ended up wrestling to the ground struggling with our knives.

In trying to cut my neck, he sliced me in the chest. It was the first wound I had ever had. It just made me more ferocious. I rolled over, pushed his knife upward and drove my knife into his stomach and twisted it, and then drove it again!

As I got up, two more were running toward me, and the evil one discovered the baby. He could hear him crying. He picked up Sun Boy just as the two enemy got to me.

I never fought so hard. I had to get baby back again. I screamed my war cry from way down deep in my soul. It sounded shrill and mysterious. I thought about the attacking hawk. One of the enemy was startled by the strange sound, and hesitated, backing up a step.

I ducked down low and spun swinging my club right across an enemy warrrior's knee. Down he went. His leg dangled, bleeding profusely. I turned just in time to block another's club with my war shield. We fought as the evil one ran off with Sun Boy.

"Nooo!!!" I yelled fighting with a fury I had only seen in my Peepa. With disregard for my own life, I fought. The enemy started to back up and cover up with his shield. I dropped my shield and swung my club, beating him down to a knee. I kicked him over and then killed him with my knife while he covered his head with his shield.

I turned to find Sun Boy. The evil one was putting him down over by the campfire. He took his bow and placed an arrow in it. He took aim at my Peepa. Peepa was engaged by three enemy fighting furiously for his life.

The evil one was too far away for me to shoot an arrow. Peepa was stalled in one place, an easy target, and the evil one was only a short distance.

"Nooo! Nooo! Not my Peepa!" I hollered and ran toward the enemy.

Checheya prayed and meditated, and she worried. She knew this was the night of the battle. She kept praying for protection and success, especially for her son-in-law, my Peepa.

"He is like a son to me now," she said. "I couldn't take care of my daughter and grand children forever. I knew someday I would be unable, like now. He's the one who has come to take care of them for my husband and me after we are gone. Bless him and protect him.

"If someone must die, let it be me. If a sacrifice is required, let it be I. I know I'm old, and I don't get around well anymore. But I have a will to live and my life is precious and wonderful to me.

"Maybe in death, in spirit, I can help my son-in-law, and in this way help my daughter, grandchildren, and the baby. My baby girl, Rainbow, could not endure another loss, nor could it possibly be right for her to have to.

"Bless my family, my loved ones . . . ." She slumped over and leaned to the side, at first looking like she was only pausing. She was gone.

The evil one drew back his arrow with an easy shot at Peepa. I was running, but I was helpless to stop it. Just as he was going to release it, a stiff wind blew up dirt just to his side and tossed his hair around, blowing dust in his eyes. On the wind, you could hear a woman's voice holler, then laugh. It scared some of the enemy and they ran off.

It sounded like Checheya's voice.

The evil one paused, moved to different ground and took aim again.

I became aware of a horse running toward me from behind. I turned and looked. It was Rainbow Girl. She had the reins dropped on the horse's neck. She had a bow, and an arrow loaded and pulled back.

She was riding hard and furious, like the strongest of warriors. Her horse looked fierce and determined, strong in every stride.

Her arrow was the sacred thunder arrow, the red and black one with the yellow stripes given to her as a child.

"Holy Thunder, help me now as you did when I was just a small girl. Help me save my baby," she thought as she took aim.

A thunder cracked and rolled across the sky. The evil one paused and looked around. Quickly, he took aim again at my Peepa.

Just as he was going to release it, "Wsssht!" A red and black with yellow stripes arrow struck him right through the neck from the left side below the ear, partially exiting through the right side below the ear.

A thunder mysteriously rolled again across the cloudless sky.

The evil one choked and gasped, turning to look. It was Rainbow Girl.

He looked at her in disbelief.

Suddenly she recognized him: the evil one who captured her sister when they were girls, and the one leading the party who killed Deer Hooves; the one who rode parallel to her Peepa at the buffalo hunt battle.

"Wshtt!" She let go another arrow at full gallop. Right below the heart, she hit her mark. Down he fell.

The evil one went down to a knee, then fell over, dead.

It was as though time momentarily paused. Some of the enemy warriors stopped to watch. It was unbelievable! Of all the miracles in battle I could have ever imagined, this was beyond them all!

I was never so glad to see her. It was like she was riding out of a holy mist, like she had appeared out of the Mother Earth to rescue us.

I had been running up to where the evil one put Sun Boy. I picked up the baby and held him high for Rainbow Girl. She rode up and gathered him up to her.

"Oh, my baby, my baby!!" she cried, cuddling him.

"We must go now baby sister," I told her. "Ride to the edge of the meadow where Rock is waiting and we will meet you there."

The fighting was subsiding and the enemy were breaking away one by one. The last one to leave, as usual, was my Peepa. But he knew right where I was; he rode by and picked me up behind him almost in stride, like we had done so many times when I was a child.

We rode off, joined Rainbow, went to the meeting point and got my horse. We rode off hard and fast. The enemy would be following. They wouldn't need daylight because it was simple logic that we would head straight for the pass back to our country. Our only chance was to stay ahead of them.

If we killed about ten of them, there were still about forty of them left. They would be angry, and confident in numbers. When they heard there was only six of us, they would be even more determined.

So we rode through the night making our getaway. Over hills, crossing streams, we raced. Rainbow wondered, "Is this what Deer Hooves went through when he went to steal horses?"

At dawn, you could see them several hills behind us. The horses were tired, but they gave us everything they had. We couldn't stop now. It would mean certain death. As they closed on us, we approached an open meadow with a river down toward the other side. We ran, but our horses slowed, their muscles quivering and shaking.

As we neared the river, some of the enemy were riding right behind us and alongside us.

Maybe this is the best that we ever could have done, I wondered. I will take as many of them with me as I can, I decided.

The meadow dropped sharply and went down to the river at a natural crossing. We sped right across.

The enemy alongside us had to slow and turn to come to the place where we crossed, dropping behind us again.

"Don't let it end this way!" Rainbow Girl cried out in prayer. She wondered, "Is this what my dream about the two eagles has foretold? Is this what the sign in the sweat lodge with the two rocks splitting apart meant? My baby would be taken and my husband and I killed?"

She tried to think determined again. No one . . . NO ONE, would take baby Sun Boy as long as she had a breath, even just one breath left in her.

"Hyah! Hyah!" she kicked the horse forward and faster.

Suddenly, a small group of five or six of our Schi'tsu'umsh showed up on the trail and started riding with us. Not enough to turn and fight, but it was encouraging. My friend riding alongside me told me there were more of our people coming too.

I had new hope. We just might make it.

More of the people began to show up and meet us. Even some of the women and children joined us, and thought about celebrating, until they realized we were in danger.

As we rode toward the pass, yet another small group of our people were riding toward us. It was Circling Raven himself and his helpers. Now we had enough warriors to turn and finish the fight.

We rode up anxiously to meet him and shout our victories, but Circling Raven was moving his hands downward at us, signaling us to quit.

We quietly gathered around.

"You are not through yet, my children," he cautioned. "We are not out of danger. I have been told a bigger force of enemy has joined with the war party you have fought and they are riding hard this way!"

"We must not engage them. We must not kill any more of them. If we ride straight ahead with faith, we will suffer no more losses. There will be no more widows, no more orphans, no more crying mothers and fathers!"

Likewise, all the people must be one with nature by the way we live each and every day, by the way we think and by the way we believe, pray and communicate with it. There really is no difference between our everyday life and religion; and no difference between religion and ceremony. So we pray to the Kolunsuten to sanction all that we do religiously and ceremonially first, bringing ourselves near to nature that He would move to bless us and fulfill our prayers through nature.

I felt strengthened and encouraged, and deeply fulfilled in my own thinking. The teachings of our elders really do come to life in our living if we try to uphold them by our own conduct.

We moved with nature, the land, the seasons, the animals and the weather. The earth is our Mother, the sun is our Father, the mountains are our grandfathers, as are the four directions; not in symbolism, but in fact of spirit. They all care deeply for us, their children and grandchildren, and we felt a deep and abiding love for them in return just as we would for our physical mother, father or grandparents.

I could feel our oneness with all the divine Creation.

The enemy who was right on our heels peeled back a little and joined a larger group of their warriors. They moved again as a much bigger force.

As we approached the valley before the pass, the enemy was right upon us. I looked back and was amazed at their sheer numbers. Circling Raven was right, as usual. His prophecies were divinely inspired.

The back of our line was nearly caught by the front of the enemy warriors. War cries began to fill the air. We tried to hold strictly to Circling Raven's instructions and keep riding.

I wanted to turn and ride into the enemy. I worried for our people close to the attacking warriors.

CHAPTER 26
Where Life Comes From

We rode straight for the pass. It was unusually cold, bitter cold. We started up hill in the rain. It was so cold, even the horses put their ears and heads down low feeling the bite. It wasn't middle of the winter cold, but it was late autumn and we weren't used to it, nor were we ready for it.

Clouds were thick and rolling actively like they were angry. A cold, heavy rain poured from the sky.

"My poor sister," I thought. She was trying to ride hard, hold baby and keep him covered from the cold. I moved right behind her to guard them from the enemy.

"What is the weather doing?" I wondered looking around, trying to read it.

War cries coming from behind us refocused my attention.

"We must keep moving," was the word from Circling Raven. I turned and looked behind us. The enemy horses slowed to a trot, some to a walk.

We got about halfway up the last hillside to the summit, and the rain had snow in it. Almost that quickly, it turned into snow. It flurried and blew with a biting wind. Giant snow flakes so thick you could not see at all filled the air around us. The enemy disappeared in it.

The horses slowed to a crawl. All anybody could do was let the horses go. They always knew the way even if a person was lost.

The snow quickly piled up. We knew we had to get over the pass, or wait till spring. There were stories of families who tried to cross the pass too late in the year and perished here, unable to go either direction. They froze, or starved.

The horses were belly deep in snow already, and we still couldn't see. People were driving their horses hard to encourage them to go forward, but they were stopping.

A winter spirit and feeling came over the land, just like the one in the middle of winter. It was the Old Man in the North, our grandpa. He brought the snows when he knew it was time in order to take care of nature. He covered the Mother Earth in a white blanket while she, the vegetation and many of her creatures slept. Under this white blanket, however, the sacred nature was preparing and making everything ready to greet us again in the spring with an abundance of life, blessing and caring.

Winter and the snow were a major part of the great circle of life. If you go along with it, be prepared, then there is nothing to fear. It will take care of us, too, and bring ceremonies that are only for the winter.

I never thought to be afraid. But, the snows kept falling. We stopped and huddled together. "We should put up shelter," someone hollered.

"No," Peepa answered, "we must stay ready to move across the top and down the other side when we get our chance."

So, we waited, and waited. The snow was deeper than a tall man when it started to let up. We could see a long way now, and the whole tribal band was in a line of huddled little groups down alongside the mountain pass. The snow was wet and heavy. Thick gray clouds were all around us and took the whole sky.

"These are snow clouds," someone else exclaimed. "We must make a plan to escape this place now, or we will be trapped here."

Now I felt worry and fear, and not for the enemy. I looked downhill. They were gone. They must have tried for a getaway downhill back toward their country.

The air grew cold and the snow on top began to freeze, becoming icy and crusty to the touch. We were in trouble. It would be cold after dark, freezing cold. All the firewood was covered with deep snow.

Small hunting parties were often caught in the harsh weather and they could get by foraging for themselves. But this was maybe fifty people all in one place. Where would they all get wood? What if it didn't melt and just got deeper and deeper every day until we were buried? What a dilemma.

Everyone wanted to know what Circling Raven would do, but it was too deep to drive the horses up the hill to get to him.

"What shall we do?" others called out.

"Wait. Wait." Peepa answered.

We sat, huddled together and waited. It was so cold.

We were all right for the time being. It was what was going to happen next that was uncertain. Something had to be done quickly though.

Circling Raven prayed and meditated. "What can we do?" he pondered strenuously. "How can this be reasonably addressed to the Kolunsuten and the great spirits of nature?"

"We are told that when that old man of winter blows in you cannot stop it, no matter how many peace pipes you line up, and no matter how many ceremonies you do. We are suppose to be ready for him ahead of time with winter camps, firewood, dried foods, everything. How are we to explain this in a true way that is acceptable and proper?" He pondered in meditation.

He quietly sang a prayer song, reaching out to the Kolunsuten. He sent his mind to the four directions and asked them to help him as he pushed his thinking for a solution. He held his ceremonial pipe, the one with the long stem, carving, beadwork and buckskin fringe. This one was only used in emergencies. He prayed:

"Grandfather, Kolunsuten, help me. Help my people. This is your world, your Creation, and it moves and works the way in which you instructed it. These are the laws of nature, primeval and ancient, pre-dating the coming of man and coinciding with the dawning of time. By them, we have physical life and life goes on one day to the next."

"Our living is at stake, our people, our children, our loved ones. Hear me, my Great Creator, Kolunsuten. Let us live. Send your great power in nature to help us."

He turned and offered the pipe to the four directions, the east, the south, the west and the north. But he stopped in the north and talked:

"Grandfather in the North, thank you for all you do, all you are, and all you watch over in the north. We must always, always, go along with nature, including you. But we are suffering. Help us and recognize us in just this way. We only had to take care of our loved ones and inno-cent baby child.

"It is in the north that all the teachings of our elders are kept with our elderly Grandfather with white hair. And these teachings are what we were left, by which to live. By these teachings, we took care of our loved one and have rescued him.

"I offer this tobacco and pipe to you. Pity us, help us, your grand-children."

He turned to the east and began to sing an unfamiliar song. It was beautiful.

"Help us Kolunsuten," he meditated as he sang. He sang with a deep feeling and a sincere prayer for his people. He thought about the smil-ing and innocent children, about the elderly, and the young mothers. He sang with a powerful love for them.

With that force of love, he sent his mind to the Creator even as he sang.

"These are my people, my loved ones. This is the one life you gave us. Accept the humble offering of tobacco, holy pipe, sacred song and our devoted love to one another."

He continued to sing. Others joined in on the song. Others prayed and cried. Even some very young men who joined us, really just boys, prayed and helped the best they could.

Circling Raven thought about the sun. He envisioned it, full, hot, like a summer day. He went toward it in his mind.

"Kolunsuten, send your warm winds to melt this snow and clear this trail."

In his mind he envisioned in the sun a strong fire. As he held the image, the picture moved and took life. He was inside a sacred teepee and this fire was at the center with strong flames and long even sticks. There was an invisible and powerful presence in the teepee. "I beg you. Pity us. Send your warm winds to help us."

Like a breath of air, a wind blew over the spirit fire he envisioned.

As he continued to sing, the clouds moved strangely up above us, as if something was coming. A warmer wind blew in the air about us.

Circling Raven held onto the pipe, but he began to dance and motion with his arms like they were wings. The wind picked up even stronger, a bright light flashed, and a warmth came over everyone from the inside out.

Warm winds rushed all about us. Our hair blew in the wind. The horses went calm and docile, yet attentive. Time stood still, and this moment seemed delayed and long.

The clouds were trembling and rolling with a bright light among them. A red light flashed among the clouds and a strong thunder slowly rolled across the sky from the west, to the east then to the south. As it faded off into the southern sky, the clouds parted and small beams of bright sunlight appeared, shining down all about us and ahead of us.

The feeling in the air was spiritual, and miraculous. A numbing but joyful warmth came over me. I knew beyond any doubt, it was the Kolunsuten himself. I turned my heart and my mind toward him as I got on my knees.

My heart, my feeling, was overcome with his presence. A sacred and powerful love is what it felt like. Way beyond words.

"Thank you, my Creator, Kolunsuten," Circling Raven said, tearfully.

Some of the people became afraid, some fell to the ground, some just shook and could say nothing. There were gasps of amazement echoing about the mountainside.

"It's the Kolunsuten! It's the Kolunsuten!" I heard various voices and choruses exclaim.

"Hey-yah! Hey-yah! Help us my Creator!" my Peepa uttered between singing along with Circling Raven. The song continued as people prayed and sang.

Rainbow thought about her own life too. She couldn't help it after all she'd been through.

She sang along with the song, meditated with all the concentrated effort she had, and asked for the life of her child first. But, also, "bless me," she thought. Without knowing any words or language to express how she felt, she turned her feelings into the song. She looked up toward and reached for the clouds and the sky, one arm holding baby.

Many of our songs have no words. They are meant for the expression of feeling that is beyond words. Rainbow used the song this way, too.

Suddenly, a small beam of light came through the clouds and she reached for it.

In the beam of light, she could see into the sky world. There was the eagle she had seen in her dreams, flying alone. She sang and prayed, overcome by the spirit.

As she gazed at the vision of this great bird, suddenly another eagle joined it and they flew together. She could feel their happiness. They flew, dove and darted in the winds of the highest sky.

Suddenly, as they flew near where the sun appeared behind them, they flew right into the bright light of the sun and disappeared.

Now she knew everything would be all right. The Kolunsuten had a plan and, in the end, everything would be set right. She heard, or rather, she felt someone say, "You'll be all right, my child. Take your baby home. Always do what is best for him, and that will be what is the best for you."

It was a miracle. This was truly a miracle. The snow melted from the warm winds, but only on the trail, nowhere else. Rainbow Girl appeared as though she had been touched by the spirit. Although she said nothing, her face beamed, and tears streamed down her face. She held her baby close and tight.

People raised their arms and hands toward the sky and the Kolunsuten. Many gave praise and thanks.

Circling Raven motioned with his hands in sign language to "go."

"Move forward and over the mountain," his helpers signaled.

We all went up and over the top, and then down over the other side. Not even halfway down, it began to rain ever so gently. I turned and looked up the hill and it was snowing heavily again at the summit.

It was a miracle. Kolunsuten himself acted directly in our behalf. We were all numb, not with cold, but with amazement and thanksgiving. A softer, rolling thunder moved across the sky. This one was called "white lightning" by our people, thunder during a snow storm.

We rode all day to the base camp at the foot of the mountain. The rain stopped and it turned into a sunny, warm day. Teepees were erected and many of the women were gathering firewood. No one spoke as we rode at a walk. I think everyone was at their best, prayerful, thankful and trusting in the Kolunsuten.

I was never so happy to see our people. Even my horse was happy and started to run around. I war whooped my joy with my people. Others among us did the same.

All the warriors ran their horses around us, war whooping and holding their weapons in the air toward us to honor us. Some of them shouted "Six against fifty, Owww! Owww!" Then, I realized what an impossible feat we had achieved.

I breathed again. A deep happiness came over me. I cried and walked my horse over to Rainbow.

"I told you. I told you we would get him back."

She smiled and cried. I held her hand for a moment, and put my hands on Sun Boy's head as he nursed from his mother.

Peepa and I were wounded, so was Center Feather, and my brother-in-law was smashed in the thigh. He walked his horse over by his wife and me. She looked so happy.

Rainbow would look at her baby, then to her husband, Peepa and me. She was joyful and thankful beyond words, yet she communicated it in her face. She shed tears of joy, thanksgiving, and love. She hugged her baby, held him up to the sky, then hugged him again.

As we rode into our home camp, all the people were there. They traveled from far and near to our camp when they heard the news. Many had relatives that went in the war party. Riders had come ahead to tell them the outcome.

Everybody was there, all dressed in their finest. It was so beautiful, a truly great day! The riders rode in, still in their war regalia, and painted up. They made a grand entry, circling, war crying, mock counting coup. All the people yelled their approval and the children ran with excitement.

Over the mountain, my Peepa could barely ride, barely stay on his horse, but he sprinted around the camp and people now, stopping hard and whirling his horse around.

"My daughter killed the evil one and took back her baby! My daughter killed the evil one! Owwwww! Owwww!"

"My sons killed the enemy and saved our baby! My daughter saved her Peepa! Owww! Owww!" he shouted.

He was beyond proud. Peepa was in a spiritual zone, a special frame of mind and being brought on by the deepest of emotion and experience. It was like he was riding on air and his horse glided slightly above the top of the ground.

My Noona ran up to him and she could see he wasn't all right. She called others over to help her get him down and into the teepee.

"I'm all right," he assured everyone and waved as he limped away with help.

What an amazing man he is, I thought, pure warrior, all bravery and total family man all in one. With the power of the Kolunsuten, it all made him powerful, unbeatable.

My wife, Yellow Flower, was standing with my older sister and sister-in-law. They had kept vigil with us through all the ordeal, until they received word from runners who brought word of the outcome. I was overcome with emotion to see her.

I rode through and around the camp shouting my victory cry, "Owww! Owww! Owww!" I shouted.

I whirled my horse around just like my Peepa. All the people shouted in return and held their hands up toward me.

I rode over to my wife and family. She put her hand on my thigh. I covered her hand with mine. We looked at each other in a way I never knew before. Our expressions and feelings were way beyond words.

Singers and drummers started to sing welcome and victory songs. Some blew whistles toward the sky.

I looked across the village and saw an entire people cheering and celebrating, not for a horse race, or a contest; but for life, for family, for the tribe. It was beautiful, the most incredible scene ever beheld.

I took it in. A tear rolled down my cheek.

Suddenly, I noticed Rock jumping and cheering, war crying his deepest victory and thanksgiving feelings. He looked back at me.

With a definite and quick move he held up a tail. It was black and wiry, and rather wooly and wild on the tip. It was crazy looking, like no animal tail I have ever seen or heard of.

Rock took his knife and made the cutting motion sound he had been doing so much of his life. He held up the tail and danced. "Owww! Owww! Hey-yah, Hey Yah!" he yelled.

"Now the enemy will never be back! Owww! Owww!" he celebrated.

My Peepa, Noona and I all looked at each other questioningly and amazed, and back at Rock. Then, Noona smiled, and we all smiled and shrugged. Peepa shook his head in disbelief.

I got off my horse. I was weak and dizzy, but overjoyed too. My wife put her arms around me. I put my forehead to hers. My Noona came and put her arms around both of us.

Rainbow Girl and her husband rode over. Their other children ran over excitedly jumping on them and talking all at once.

My Peepa limped over to us, smiling at my Noona, and nodded his head. She looked at him and cried, but smiled at the same time.

We all stood together and looked at baby Sun Boy and Rainbow Girl and each other. Circling Raven joined our little circle of joy, celebration and thanksgiving. He held Sun Boy up in the air, and turned to the four directions with him. He held him to the ground and put his footprints in the dirt.

Then, he held his hand to the sky, the Mother Earth and the nature all around and put his hand upon baby Sun Boy's head and body. He repeated this three times.

I knew this is what my Sila would do if he were here. I felt his presence. I wondered if I would hear his voice in the singing or perhaps the war cry and victory yells. I realized a deep and fulfilling satisfaction knowing my Checheya was with him again finally.

Tears again rolled down my cheeks; not of mourning, but tears of joy, love and thanksgiving.

Circling Raven then smiled joyfully and handed the baby back to his mother, Rainbow.

My Noona held Rainbow close to her and told her, "Your Checheya didn't make it."

Rainbow cried, held her baby close, and then smiled even in her tears. "Thank you Checheya," she whispered. "Thank you for everything, for being the best Checheya in all the world."

The word was passed that Circling Raven wanted all chiefs and family leaders to attend a ceremonial dinner in his lodge to recognize and respect what our Creator had done this day.

There were now several hundred of us so we couldn't all fit in the ceremonial lodge. I would get an early seat just outside so I could listen. My Peepa would be inside as a war chief and a band leader.

People were all settled in, gathered about the lodge in order. The war chiefs all sat together, as did the hunting chiefs, the Council leaders and the band leaders.

Everyone wanted to hear the words of our great chief on this occasion.

> *"My relatives and friends," he began. "There is nothing any man can say in mere words to describe fully what has taken place this day. The Kolunsuten is a great and wonderful being, perfect and true to His words. His promises are kept, His love and power are without limits, and His pact with men is a sacred bond, never broken or forgotten by Him.*

> *"Not only us, but even our descendants in future generations will be heartened by what we have witnessed and experienced this day. And they will have the great teachings and traditions of our elders to live by, forever.*

> *"Maybe only once every hundred, or even thousands of years, the Kolunsuten will show Himself in a way that will last over the generations of time.*

> *"This miracle occurred to save our people as they struggled in a life and death conflict against seemingly impossible odds. Their quest was one of goodness and right, but also of love, faith and courage. This was the foundation for the Kolunsuten's miracle.*

> *"A mother's unconditional love for her child really is the most powerful force on this earth, second only to the Kolunsuten's infinite love and power. As the depths of a mother's love were challenged, perhaps all mothers' love was challenged.*

> *"The earth really is our mother. The spirit loon really is our grandmother. Where there is disrespect for woman, these holy beings of nature know it. That is why they moved through Rainbow*

when she was a mere toddler years ago the only way they could to fight back. It is so sacred, it would take the purity and innocence and bravery of a mere child, a little woman to work.

"Acts of cowardice and malice against women are an abomination to nature. This is what the Mother Earth and the Grandmother Loon told the Great Thunders as the spirit thunder arrow was given to Rainbow Girl. And, the Thunders did as he asked out of respect. He made the thunder and the lightning when he saw the arrow fired for a great purpose.

"These are the reasons Rainbow Girl was the one to stop the evil enemy. The Kolunsuten made men more powerful physically than the woman. This strength was to be used to care and provide for the woman, the children and the elderly of the people.

"The men of this family went out to defend and protect the women and a child of theirs, perhaps against impossible odds. To combat these great odds, it took the great power of womanhood, motherhood, the Mother Earth and the Grandmother Loon to call upon the great miracle. And, it took Rainbow to save those who came to save her."

It all made sense to me. It was clear the way our great Chief interpreted it.

Some of the womenfolk gathered around started to cry, touched by some spirit of the words our prophet Chief expressed, or a spirit connection only they could understand or know about.

I saw my Noona look toward my Peepa through the open doorway. At first, I thought she looked sad, perhaps for my Checheya, her mother. But in her eyes, there was another look of utter thanksgiving and joy. Not simple joy, but the kind that is way beyond smiles, laughing and joking.

I looked for my wife, Yellow Flower. She moved her head to catch my attention. We gave each other that knowing look of tenderness and affection that close married couples know.

Circling Raven continued:

"And it was the Mother Earth who called upon the mountains to ask for snow. The Thunderbird provided the moisture. The Old Man in the North turned it to snow.

"The Kolunsuten made a miracle through His holy nature. That is why when we pray; we bring ourselves near to nature. His blessings will come to us back again through nature.

"And it is true that we can never go against nature; only go along with it. No matter how many sacred pipes you line up, no matter how many prayer ceremonies you do, you cannot stop the snow and the cold winds of winter.

"The snows were melted by the Great Kolunsuten himself, not by anything we did!" he said, his voice crackling with emotion.

He paused to compose himself. All the people were silent and reverent.

"It is a great miracle. We have seen a divine intervention by the Creator in our lives. We must work, we must live to make ourselves worthy, more worthy, each and every day."

The chief sat down.

He called on other chiefs to talk and express what this great and spiritual miracle meant. It seemed various individuals were affected in different ways, some were healed, some felt they were spoken to.

"Hey! Hey! Hey!" everyone said in agreement.

"My son had fallen off his horse four days ago and injured his head," another offered up. "He was dizzy, faint and sick ever since. When the Kolunsuten appeared, he was instantly well."

"My parents said they were talked to," another tried to explain.

"Mine too," still another quickly interjected.

"It is holy. It is truly sacred," Circling Raven offered in explanation. "Whatever anyone is told by the Kolunsuten, it is for them alone, unless He instructs that others be told. So we must not ask what they heard."

"Let us pray, sing and dance our praises this night. We have been blessed in protection from enemies, our baby has been returned and we have been given our very lives again."

They prayed and concluded with an eagle ceremony and chief dance.

There was a big feast, and dancing that night with storytelling. Feathers were given out, honors were bestowed and appreciations were communicated to the Kolunsuten. It was true celebration, not celebration for sake of celebrating.

I knew now that I would always pray and be true to the Kolunsuten all the days of my life. Even as an old man someday, I would still be talking of this day, this trip, and the meanings interpreted by our prophet chief.

People went to bed late that night. Sometimes, I would awake and get on my knees in silent prayer and meditation. My Noona stayed up all night praying. I heard some young men stayed up on the hilltops all through the night to sacrifice and fast to represent their offering of thanksgiving.

Rainbow stayed up with our Noona. Her voice was somehow different now, stronger, and calmer.

It was a blessed time. We were blessed, a chosen generation to have witnessed what we did. We were still speechless, but happy, so happy.

When Rainbow Girl and One Star's baby was older, they named him Red Thunder, for the events surrounding his miraculous return to our people.

It was a great day!

The enemy never came back to our country again in my lifetime.

Epilogue

Now, even as an old man, I tell these histories of our family and people and I feel like I am living them again. I feel the joy, the fear and the exuberance all over again.

I remember the aftermath of those great days, and the deep spirituality it instilled in me and all of us, which we try ever so intensly to pass on to our children and grandchildren, and they to their children and grandchildren.

I remember the burial services for my Checheya. It almost seemed a happy occasion in a religious sort of way. She offered up her life that her family would live, and the Kolunsuten heard her.

Even Rainbow Girl seemed to understand life in a new way. She was changed forever, healed from all her hurts and emotional scars.

Rainbow and One Star, my sister and brother-in-law lived a happy and long life together. They had three more children, two girls and another boy. They were the truest of companions and the best of friends over a lifetime.

Even though many years have passed since the glory days of my youth, I still pray with the morning dawn, sometimes at the hilltop. Now, I understand why I always saw the elders shed tears when they prayed. It was the great feelings stirred by the realizations of living life, and understanding that this life is a precious, truly special and sacred privilege extended by the Kolunsuten.

When you really know way down deep that the Kolunsuten promised no one a tomorrow or an easy time, then you know how to be thankful in a spiritually joyous way. And, you can make sense of life while truly making the most of it and yourself.

Red Thunder

David Matheson

READING GROUP GUIDE

Matheson has beautifully rendered the essence of long-standing customs and teachings in his moving memoir of the Schi'tsu'umsh Indians, now called the Coeur d'Alene Tribe. Until now, these stories have been guarded secrets among his tribe, partly from fear and partly from a need to protect what they have left. Matheson feels the time is now right to share his people's history because it is a story so much of the world yearns for; it is a story of faith, courage, and togetherness.

This guide is intended to enhance your group's reading of this inspiring and enlightening story of harmony — man's harmony with the natural world, as well as his quest for peace and unity of purpose with a Higher Power.

DAVID MATHESON

David Matheson was born into the Coeur d'Alene Indian Reservation in 1951.

Ben Marra Studios, Seattle, Wash.

Matheson has spent a lifetime learning and living the teachings of the Coeur d'Alene. Hunting, root digging, berry picking, and camping are a major part of his family's regular routine, as are observing the Tribe's traditions and ceremonial dances and events. He has worked and lived most of his adult life on the reservation, where he has served as a Council leader, the Tribal Chairman, and manager of various tribal operations.

David Matheson is currently the CEO of the Coeur d'Alene Casino & Resort Hotel in Worley, Idaho. Matheson holds an M.B.A. from the University of Washington. Over the past twenty years, Matheson has held many esteemed positions and has received many honors for his work in preserving cultural traditions, the native language, and ceremonial practices. He has served as the Deputy Commissioner for Indian Affairs for the U.S. Department of the Interior; the CEO for Coeur d'Alene Development Enterprises; an advisor for the President's Commission on Reservation Economies; a delegate to the People's

Ben Marra Studios, Seattle, Wash.

Republic of China's Native American Trade Mission; and a recipient of Commendation from the Secretary of the Interior for Outstanding Service.

In his spare time, Matheson enjoys training and riding horses, competing in cutting and reining, as well as participating in Native American traditional dances and pow wows.

He resides in Northern Idaho with his wife, Jenny. They have six full-grown children.

THE COEUR D'ALENE TRIBE

The original Coeur d'Alene homeland spans almost five million acres, stretching from Montana in the east to the Spokane River Valley in present day Washington State, from near the Canadian border in the north to near the confluence of the Snake and Clearwater Rivers in north Idaho.

Coeur d' Alene Indian villages were established along the Coeur d' Alene, St. Joe, Clark Fork and Spokane Rivers. The homeland included numerous and permanent sites on the shores of Lake Coeur d'Alene, Lake Pend Oreille and Hayden Lake.

This tribe traded among themselves and with dozens of tribes far away on the Pacific coast. Ancient trade routes connected the Coeur d'Alenes with the Nez Perce, the Shoshones and the Bannocks to the south and southeast. To the east were the tribes of the Great Plains and the vast herds of buffalo. With the coming of horses, young Coeur d' Alene men journeyed east to hunt buffalo. These journeys, however, were not necessary for survival. They were viewed as adventures, and even rites of passage, for youth who would emerge into manhood and into leadership roles.

All ancient tribal trade routes and paths remain today. In fact, those very same routes are still used all across the country. Today, however, we call those tribal routes "Interstate highways."

The first white people to encounter the Coeur d'Alenes were French trappers and traders. It was one of these Frenchmen who found the tribe to be vastly experienced and skilled at trading, thus the name "Coeur d'Alene," meaning "heart of the awl." The nickname stuck. One Frenchman described the tribe as "the greatest traders in the world."

FOR DISCUSSION

1. Red Thunder takes place in the early 1700s, before the Schi'tsu'umsh Tribe's widespread contact with European settlers. In what ways is Sun Boy's story a product of the time in which he lives? In what ways are his experiences timeless?

2. In many ways, **Red Thunder** is a spiritual journey. What are the forces that guide Sun Boy and his tribe? How does he see his place in the world?

3. Discuss the Schi'tsu'umsh's relationship to nature.

4. "They were our elders. They sacrificed so very much for us." Throughout the novel, Sun Boy shows great respect for his elders. What are some of the ways in which his family shapes his character? What lessons did you learn from Sun Boy's relationship with his elders?

5. Matheson's writing style is deceptively simple and direct and mirrors the classic form of storytelling told through oral tradition. Why do you think Matheson may have chosen to use this timeless technique to tell his story?

6. Sun Boy explains the many traditions of his people and their different purposes. In what ways could these traditions help us in today's world?

7. Matheson says, "The backdrop to the story is part of our genuine oral history." Why do you think he chose to write this history in novel form? In what way is fiction more effective than nonfiction in telling this story?

8. Red Thunder follows several generations of a family from birth to adulthood, old age, and death. How are these four cycles of life depicted in this story?

9. Discuss the numerous ways in which animals inform the telling of this novel.

10. Sun Boy yearns to become a respected warrior. Why is the warrior such an honored position in Schi'tsu'umsh society? What characteristics define the warrior role in this novel?

11. "The beauty of nature was more than something good to look at; more than something to get food or shelter from." What are some of the other benefits of nature that this book brings to light?

12. What role do the women play in **Red Thunder**? How do they shape Sun Boy's character?

13. In what ways does Matheson challenge the traditional depictions of Native Americans? Which characters do you find especially surprising?

14. The Schi'tsu'umsh tread very carefully around a woman expecting a child. "You must not yell around them, argue or tell scary or frightening stories. Never say hurtful or critical things. All this will affect the baby." Do you think this is mere superstition, or is there merit to their concerns? How so?

15. When Berry Woman is beaten by her husband, Peepa takes her back home. Do you think this is an affective method for dealing with spousal abuse? How affective would this method prove to be in today's world?

LIFE LESSONS

When war is necessary: "We want peace. We want the goodness of life. That is why we are blessed by the Kolunsuten (God). We never kill or take life indiscriminately, nor do we take slaves. All people are equal. War at just any cost seems insanity; but peace at all costs is slavery!" p. 282.

Our animal protectors: "A low flying eagle passed overhead looking intently back and forth through the forest. He was the guardian of the land, the protector against evil. Should he ever disappear or cease to exist, the land and all upon it would perish." p. 78.

The healing power of nature: "Nature has a medicinal power just to be in it, by opening your heart and your mind to it. As you turn your mind to it, the soul is refreshed. When the soul is renewed, the heart and mind are joyous, and the body is healed. It makes you turn to the Higher Power in thankfulness. And, in your spiritual thanksgiving, the soul rejoices. The healing power of the natural world is truly incredible." p. 86.

Respect for ceremony: "Ceremonial ways are sacred and powerful. Only those so authorized by the sacred beings of nature can conduct them, or pass them down to others whom they deem worthy or qualified to conduct them. Our ceremonial ways are protected from abuse or misuse. To mimic or just pick up someone's ways without proper authorization is more than just wrong or foolish, it is dangerous. Spiritually, it would not work out for you, or the people you tried to help. Some great misfortune may actually befall you, or your loved ones." p. 249.

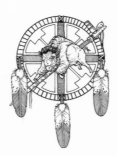

To order additional copies or send a gift
of

RED THUNDER

ORDER INFORMATION

NAME _____

ADDRESS _____

_____
CITY   STATE   ZIP

TELEPHONE _____

EMAIL ADDRESS _____

☐ Please notify me about upcoming books.

NUMBER OF COPIES _____ @ [PRICE OF BOOK] = $_____

Shipping and handling $3.00 per book $_____
(3 books or more, just add 15% of book total)

                    TOTAL AMOUNT ENCLOSED $_____

Please send check or money order to:

    Red Thunder
    P.O. Box 308
    Worley, ID 83876

Please allow 3-4 weeks for delivery.

www.redthunders.com